DEMONS Prefer Blondes

SIDNEY AYERS

Copyright © 2011 by Sidney Ayers
Cover and internal design © 2011 by Sourcebooks, Inc.
Cover design by Jamie Warren/Loose Change Studio
Cover images © Comstock; Stephen Youll

Sourcebooks and the colophon are registered trademarks of Sourcebooks, Inc.

All rights reserved. No part of this book may be reproduced in any form or by any electronic or mechanical means including information storage and retrieval systems—except in the case of brief quotations embodied in critical articles or reviews—without permission in writing from its publisher, Sourcebooks, Inc.

The characters and events portrayed in this book are fictitious or are used fictitiously. Any similarity to real persons, living or dead, is purely coincidental and not intended by the author.

Published by Sourcebooks Casablanca, an imprint of Sourcebooks, Inc.
P.O. Box 4410, Naperville, Illinois 60567-4410
(630) 961-3900
FAX: (630) 961-2168
www.sourcebooks.com

Printed and bound in Canada
WC 10 9 8 7 6 5 4 3 2 1

*To my mom and sisters,
whom I strong-armed into reading
my very rough first draft.
Brenda, I'm sorry my sex demons kept you up
past your bedtime.*

Prologue

"What do you mean the chest is missing?" Rafael Deleon managed through gritted teeth.

Even though the clacking of boots on the polished black marble grated his nerves, he continued to pace the expansive room. Candlelight flickered and flitted, sending silhouettes darting against the ivory walls.

What about his sister? Jacoba had all but begged to join the guard, even though he'd pleaded with her not to. Unfortunately, Jacoba didn't need his approval. She won the Fore-Demon Council over, instead.

Dominic Duvane, shrouded in darkness, stood solitary in the corner of the High Council chamber. A forlorn expression was etched across his face, adding to the already foreboding mood. The news was worse than Rafael had imagined. *Utterly horrible*.

Dominic drew in a ragged gulp of air. "The guards were ambushed."

"Who?" He shook his head. He didn't even need to ask the question. Belial, the bastard prince of northern regions of Hell.

Blasted Fore-Demons!

"Belial's Infernati warriors. Have a seat, my friend." Dominic motioned to the burgundy jacquard and gilt divan in the far recess of the room.

Rafael's heart sank. Dominic meant to talk to him as a comrade and not a colleague. This didn't bode well. He clenched his fists. He couldn't panic. To do so would show weakness. He needed to be strong—or at least appear so.

"What... happened?"

"The Infernati swooped in and torched the encampment." His friend's gaze grew somber. "I suggest sitting, Rafe."

Rafael folded his arms and raised his chin. "I'll stand." He'd receive the news like a man, not a coward. "Say whatever you need to say, my liege."

Dominic growled. "I might outrank you, but I'll be damned if I let you call me *my liege*."

Rafael shrugged. "Too bad we're already damned, Nic."

"The chest was to be our salvation." Dominic blew out an exasperated breath. "Bloody hell, Rafe. Why must you be so stubborn?"

"It runs in the family."

Dominic grabbed him by the arms, his eyes blazing. "Your sister was captured."

"She isn't dead. Our connection isn't severed."

Dominic nodded. "Yes, but who knows what tortures Belial has bestowed upon her." His gaze hardened and he clenched his fists. Jaw ticking, he paced. "I begged her not to join. I stood by you."

Rafael shook his head. "Coby wouldn't take no for an answer. Even if the council forbade her, she would've found a way."

Fighting the thought of his beautiful sister, with her magnificent flowing silver hair and enchanting silver eyes at Belial's mercy, Rafael crossed his arms in front of his chest. "What happened to her?"

"Coby's a hero." Dominic's jaw twitched, the demon

blood tears rimming his eyes. "She managed to send the chest away before the guards could take it."

A soft smile curved his lips. Leave it to Coby to save the chest instead of saving herself. Despite his despair, he was still proud of his twin sister. However, he wasn't in the mood for Dominic to divert his questions. His gaze grew stern. "Where is she?"

"I guess I shouldn't hide the truth..."

Rafael arched a brow and leaned against the wall. "Well?"

Dominic sucked in a ragged breath, sending candles flickering. "This hurts me as much as you, you know."

"I do."

His friend nodded. "My sources report she's in Belial's dungeon."

Rafael clenched his fists as he held his anguish inside. Grinding his teeth, he paced. Bloody hell. Only a few of the strongest Paladin warriors had escaped that hellhole, but they were never quite the same after.

"Where did she send the chest?" he managed.

"Earth." Dominic flashed a halfhearted smile, his eyes wide and alert. "Your favorite place."

He didn't even want to think about the chest being opened on Earth. Belial already controlled half the underworld—what would happen if he took over Earth too? But Rafael had to save Coby first. The Paladin needed her. She'd been the one the Fore-Demons had prophesied.

"Too bad I'll be busy vanquishing Belial's buffoons." Rafael stood firm, holding his chin proud. "My sister needs me."

Dominic shook his head. "No, I'm afraid not. You've

been ordered to retrieve the chest." His black eyes grew stony serious. "I'll save Coby."

"Ridiculous!" Rafael stormed. He gritted his teeth and clenched his fists. "She's my sister. I need to rescue her. Why should you go?"

Dominic drew his lips into a straight line, his nostrils flaring. "Because I..." He wrenched himself around. "I ordered her to attend to the chest, so the Fore-Demons assigned me to her rescue. It's *my* duty."

"She's my blood. That should trump duty." Rafael steepled his fingers. Why must the Fore-Demons do this? They knew how much he cared for his twin.

"They make their decisions for a reason, Rafe." Dominic turned to face him, blood tears threatening to spill. "In the end, everything will fall into place. I'll see to it."

"Where on Earth is the chest?"

Rafael grimaced. He remembered the last time he'd traveled to Earth for such a large mission. He'd been sent to quell an outbreak of Infernati possessions during the early eighteen hundreds. And those clergymen thought they'd done all the work. Earth wasn't all bad, if you could ignore the mortals and their easily tempted ways.

Not that temptation didn't serve a purpose. As a Paladin Demon, he was taught only to tempt when times were dire. The Infernati, however, chose to be a bit more overzealous with the skill. Money, sex, drugs, and alcohol, to name a few. He'd learned his lesson with temptation—a skill he wanted to live without.

"You know what happened the last time I was sent to Earth for such a large mission."

Dominic shrugged. "I'm sure you'll remind me. You always do."

"Miss Amanda Newell."

The other demon rolled his eyes. "So you slept with a human. Demons do that all the time."

No matter how hard he tried to forget the past, it always came back to haunt him. The time he used temptation for his own good. "She died because I tempted her. I killed her."

"That was two hundred years ago. Times have changed on Earth. Why, they even have horseless carriages now."

Rafael rolled his eyes this time. "I know what the world is like. I haven't completely closed myself off. Even with all their technology and fancy cars and airplanes, one thing remains the same."

"Which is?"

"Humans are still human."

Chapter 1

WHEN LUCIA GREGORY BECAME A COSMETOLOGIST, she never expected this. Here she was, sitting over a bubbling footbath, scraping the calluses off Mrs. Gunderson's bunion-ridden feet and sandblasting her thick, yellow toenails.

Got Lamisil?

Thank goodness for the soothing scent of lavender foot scrub and the protection of latex gloves. This wasn't what she had in mind, at all. But when your nail tech calls in sick again, what can you do? Grin and bear it. Bearing it was easy. The grinning part she still needed to work on.

"There you go, Mrs. Gunderson," she said, a wide smile pasted on her face. "You're all set." With a quick pat of the towel, Lucia—Lucy to her friends—dried the woman's feet. Feet that shouldn't be seen in public.

"Oh dear, you've got it all wrong." Her voice, high and whiny, would make fingernails on a chalkboard sound like a symphony.

"Standard pedicure, Mrs. G." Lucy ripped off the rubber gloves, powder flying, and threw them into the wastebasket.

Mrs. Gunderson huffed and crossed her arms. "Suzie always gives me a paraffin bath."

"That's a deluxe pedicure," she replied, pointing up to the pricing chart that hung on the wall.

"Suzie ain't ever charged me extra."

Suzie ain't here, damn it!

"Okay, Mrs. G."

The door jingled open. Lucy turned her head. In sauntered her 1:30 customer. Then again, was she really even a customer? In some circles, she'd be called a best friend.

"Hey Lucy, I'm home!" Serah said in her worst Ricky Ricardo accent.

Lucy stifled the urge to roll her eyes. Yeah, Serah's jokes were lame, but she still loved her. "What up, Serah Bear?"

"I need a wax." She paused. "Oh, I also came across the coolest chest at the antique store."

Mrs. Gunderson shook her foot and huffed. "Where's my paraffin?"

She wasn't ready to have a full-blown argument with a woman who could use her feet as weapons of mass destruction, so Lucy called over to her second-in-command, who lounged in a dryer seat reading the latest in celebrity dirt. "Frankie, hook Mrs. Gunderson up with a paraffin bath, please. My appointment just came in."

Tossing his magazine, Frankie huffed. "Appointment, my flaming ass. She visits us more than a government official visits a high-priced harlot." The mixture of effeminacy and southern flair rolled from his mouth like honey.

With a dramatic flip of her brunette curls, Serah put her hands on her hips and whipped off her Dolce frames, her sapphire eyes sparkling. "Do not!"

Frankie mimicked Serah and sashayed back and forth. "Do too, hon."

"Yeah, whatever, Frank." Serah gave Frankie an

over-dramatic glare. "You know you want me. When you gonna get back in the closet, big boy?"

"The apocalypse could come, and I'd still wave my rainbow flag. Sorry, toots," Frankie smirked.

Mrs. Gunderson shook her edema-swollen cankle in front of Lucy's face. "Can someone just dip my feet, please?"

Frankie sighed. "Right away, Mrs. Gunderson." Glaring, he swiveled to face Lucy. With a point of his always manicured finger, he mouthed, "You owe me—big time."

He assisted Mrs. Gunderson from the foot spa and led her to the private room where the paraffin bath was located. Poor Frankie. She did owe him. He could have tomorrow off. That always worked.

Serah shook her head. "Why are all the cool ones either gay or already married?"

"Because that's life, *toots*." Lucy ambled toward the shampoo bowls and reached up to the shelf where they kept the wax. "So do you want me to tame those wild bushes or what?"

Serah ran her fingers against her eyebrows. "Are they that bad?"

"Whoever said the Amazon was the biggest rainforest in the world hasn't had the opportunity to explore the wild recesses of your brows."

"Whatever!" With a roll of her eyes, Serah whacked Lucy's arm. She plopped into the chair and leaned back. "Work your magic, girl."

"Sit back," Lucy said as she swirled the wooden spatula in the gooey mass of wax.

Taking the spatula, she spread a layer of wax in

between Serah's eyes. Those eyes always made her jealous, all sapphire and sparkling. Lucy's hazels did nothing special at all. Smacking the wax strip down, Lucy smirked. With a firm grip, she ripped the strip off.

"Ouch!"

"Sorry." Gazing down at the strip, she inspected her handiwork. Success!

Serah chuckled. "No, you're not."

"Got me there." Lucy lined her brow with another thin layer of wax. "So you got another dusty old antique for your collection, eh?" With the same gusto as before, she yanked the strip off.

Lucy's friend yelped. "I should've had Frankie wax me."

"Too bad he's already got his hands dipped in wax elsewhere."

Serah drew in a deep breath. "I swear you enjoy torturing him." She leaned back more as Lucy prepared to deforest the other eyebrow. "As for the chest, it has an inscription carved in old Latin."

Latin—Lucy's least favorite subject in high school. Not because she failed, but because she was able to pronounce and read the language better than any of the nuns in Catholic school. And she wasn't afraid to correct them either. *Talk about getting your habit caught in a knot.*

"So you want me to read it?"

"Yeah, remember how bad I was at Latin?"

How could she forget? Imagine that, someone of Italian descent who wasn't able to decipher a lick of Latin. Lucy pulled off the strip, a little gentler this time. "It probably says, 'When in Rome, get the hell out.'"

"Ha-ha! Funny." Serah's gaze searched hers. "Something about that chest draws me to it." She heaved a sigh. "If only I could open it. It's locked."

Grabbing a pair of tweezers from the shelf, Lucy shook her head. "You got ripped off. A locked box with no key?"

"I bought it as a conversation piece, but when I got home I just had to look inside." Serah winced as Lucy plucked the remaining hairs. "Are you almost done?"

"Yeah." Lucy shoved a mirror at her. "How's that?"

"Perfect. So you'll look at it?"

Lucy arched a brow. Serah's odd interest in this chest piqued hers. "Umm… if it's locked, how will we open it?"

"I meant the inscription, you dork." Serah thrust the mirror at her and bounced from the chair. "I think it will tell us how to open the chest."

Taking a deep breath, Lucy nodded. "Yeah, okay. Meet me here at nine."

"Thanks girl. I owe you one."

"Yeah, sure." She'd just add another item to the long list of things Serah still owed her for.

After two hours of sweeping the floors and cleaning the stations, Lucy flopped down into the dryer seat. Taking a swig of warm Coke, she grimaced. Where was the Captain Morgan when she really needed it? She picked up the tabloid Frankie had been reading earlier and thumbed through the pages. So-and-so's hidden baby bump, someone caught at the beach with someone else, the drunken socialite who went commando and bared all to the paparazzi, the professional bowler who had fifteen mistresses. Each week, everything was the same. Only the names had changed.

The soft rap on the back door broke Lucy's thoughts. Glancing at the clock, she sighed. Punctual as always. Serah was never late. Throwing the tabloid trash on the stand next to the dryer, Lucy bounded from the seat and walked toward the door.

There stood Serah, her arms wrapped around a huge chest. It had to be at least three feet wide and just as tall. How she managed to lug the thing would remain a mystery to Lucy. She looked like she would tip over at any minute. She unlocked the door and let her friend in.

"Whoa! You carried that all the way from your car?"

Nodding, Serah toddled into the shop. "The chest isn't as heavy as it seems. I think it's empty. Where can I put it?"

"I suppose here," Lucy said, pointing to the reception desk. "Let me clear it off." She picked up the display of hair products and set everything on the floor next to the desk.

Serah took in a deep breath and grunted as she tried to set the old chest on the desk.

Lucy rushed over and grabbed the other end.

"Let me help." Tingles of electricity traveled from her fingers through her arms and chest down to her legs and feet. Her toes twitched. Her hand fell away, and the chest landed on the desk with a deafening thud.

Serah's mouth fell open. "Hey, that cost me a lot of money!"

"Your box just electrocuted me!" Lucy retorted, her fingers still tingling.

"It did not." Serah crossed her arms in front of her.

She gazed down at her fingers and gasped. *What the freaking hell?*

"I see, so I am supposed to be gentle with your box, while it's allowed to send jolts of electricity through my body. Look!" Lucy thrust her hands toward her, showing Serah her singed fingertips. "Well?"

"Maybe it's hair dye from earlier." Serah threw her head back in laughter. "And stop calling it *my box*. It weirds me out."

"Whatever. Let me see this *chest* so I can set sail with Captain Morgan. It's been a long day."

Serah shrugged. "Fine by me, if I can stow away."

"The captain says, 'Aye aye. The more the merrier.'" Lucy hunched over the chest and rubbed her fingers across the lid. Tingly, but not as tingly as before. Wiping two hundred years of dirt and dust from the chest, she had her first look. Along with the fading inscription, weird symbols dotted the lid. Then she discovered a title etched deep into the sturdy oaken chest. A box with a title? Strange, indeed. Almost as strange as the hieroglyphics decorated all over the lid.

"*Arca Inferorum*." Lucy said. Now if that wasn't a title to try and scare someone away, she didn't know what was.

"Arca what?" Serah's blank expression filled her face. "What's that mean?"

"It means Chest of the..." Lucy thought long and hard about the last word, and then Dante's *Inferno* came blazing back at her. "Damned."

"Damned?"

Lucy nodded. "Yes, damned. It was probably

designed by some over-devout monk wanting to scare mankind into repenting for their sins. I wouldn't be surprised if there's a 'Made in Rome' stamp on the bottom."

Serah wasn't amused. "Whatever. Just read the inscription."

Lucy wiped away more grime and traced her fingertip over the words. Stronger tingles zipped through her body. "It must be equipped with a security system. Every time I touch it, I get zapped."

"Doesn't happen to me," Serah replied nonchalantly.

"Guess it's my electric personality." She leaned over the chest and began translating the inscription.

"At the beginning of the total eclipse of the winter moon, shall this chest be opened only by one of demon blood. They shall call forth the legions of the underworld. By the power of this one demon will Earth be theirs."

Lucy shook her head. "Yep, it's a hoax. I hope you get your money back."

"Oh my God!" Serah exclaimed, oblivious to Lucy's words.

Bemusement filled Lucy. Her gaze narrowed. "Oh my God, what?"

"There's supposed to be a total lunar eclipse tomorrow night!" Giddy laughter burst from her lips. "This will be so cool!"

It was as if they were kids again and this was their first sleepover. Only they weren't kids. Lucy was pushing thirty and Serah wasn't far behind.

Rolling her eyes, Lucy shook her head. *Here comes another one of Serah's harebrained ideas.*

"Even if what the inscription says is real, what part of 'Only by one of demon blood' do you not understand?"

"There's a demon inside me," Serah replied.

Oh brother, Serah and her demons. "But you usually shut the bitch up with chocolate."

"Even so, wouldn't it be fun to at least try and open it?"

"Whatever," Lucy replied with a shrug. "If you want to wait until tomorrow for me to translate the inscription better, that's fine."

"Demons in a box, how cool."

"Yeah, cool. Too bad demons don't exist."

Chapter 2

"YOUR FATHER WOULD BE DISAPPOINTED IN YOU." HER mother's admonishing voice echoed on her eardrum. "Richard Fenton is a nice young man. Why won't you go out with him?" Her loud huff boomed in Lucy's ear. "It's bad enough you dropped out of med school. For what? Doing hair?"

Adjusting the cordless phone, Lucy sucked in a deep breath. This wasn't the time or the place. "We'll talk later. I'm working on Mrs. Carlson's perm." The noxious odor of chemicals wafted to her nose, sending her head spinning. Permanents weren't her favorite treatment, with all their disgusting odors. They did pay the bills, though.

"Fine, darling." There was no tone of affection in the endearment. "I'll see you for dinner."

Was that tonight? Too late to cancel now.

"Bye." She hung up the phone and slammed it on the counter with a little more force than intended.

"Such anger!" Mrs. Carlson clucked her tongue and shook her head. "My Josh is lucky you left him."

Lucy turned her attention back to Mrs. Carlson. She sat high and mighty in the chair, staring down her long aquiline nose at her. Clearly, she'd allowed being the mayor's wife to go to her head. Either that or she still hadn't forgiven her for "breaking her baby's heart."

Then again, neither had Mom.

So what that Joshua Carlson attended an Ivy League med school. So what that he was gorgeous. So he had brains and a body. But he was boring as *hell*. Every time he opened his mouth, Lucy wanted to fall asleep. As for breaking Josh's heart, the breakup was mutual. Too bad Mrs. Carlson and her meddlesome mother couldn't seem to realize it.

She'd chalk up Josh Carlson—and Rich Fenton, for that matter—to the never-ending list of her failures that her mother would never let her live down.

"I'm sure he is, Mrs. Carlson. Isn't he engaged to Larissa Harding?" Lucy flashed her favorite pasted-on smile. "She's so lovely." She was smart, pretty, and just as boring as Josh. They were perfect for each other and the mundane life of matrimony. Squirting more solution on each wound-up rod, she gritted her teeth. Lucy loved her job, but with people like Mrs. Gunderson with her fucked-up phalanges and Mrs. Carlson and her holier-than-thou attitude, her patience was fleeting.

"Maybe Larissa will come here for her updo. Imagine that! It could've been you." The snide remark, meant to cut, had the opposite effect, but Lucy managed to control her laughter, anyway.

"Who'd style my hair then?"

Mrs. Carlson rolled her eyes. "One of these days, you're going to have what you did to my son happen to you. When it does, don't come back crying."

Lucy could only smile and nod in agreement. After all, she was always right. Even after her son's numerous pleadings to leave Lucy alone, she wouldn't let things go. After five years, she still hadn't given up.

"I probably will."

Mrs. Carlson narrowed her gaze. "Are you patronizing me?"

"Me? Never!" She squeezed the last bit of solution on her tightly wound rods. If only she'd rolled them tighter. She grabbed some cotton and wrapped it around Mrs. Carlson's wound-up hair and affixed a plastic cap over her head. "Time to let the perm set."

Turning the minute minder to twenty minutes, Lucy breathed a sigh of relief. She was free! Well, almost.

The door swung open. "Hey, *chica*!" Gerardo Martinez flounced into the shop, his pink feathered shirt blowing with the breeze. Bright magenta leather clung tightly to his legs. It always amazed Lucy how he could walk in those things. The camera around his neck swung with each sway of his hips.

Yep! Lucy liked surrounding herself with gay men. They had a lot in common. And it wasn't an extreme attraction to Gerard Butler, either. But boy, could they do hair!

"I got the photos developed." He held up a black leather portfolio in triumph.

"Do you really think you have a shot at *Model America*?"

"Hell yeah." He sashayed and placed a hand on his hip. "I know how to work it. Naomi Campbell ain't got *nada* on me."

"Better not let Naomi hear that, or you may end up in the hospital with a case of cell phone abuse."

"Puh-lease! She only does that to her assistants." Gerardo took off his camera, sat it on the counter, and ran his fingers through his dark slicked-back hair. "Do you want to see the money shot, or what?"

Lucy fought the chuckle that formed deep in her

chest. "Money shot? I don't want to go there. But if you want my honest opinion, I'll have a peek."

"You have to try out!" Gerardo sauntered around the counter and plopped the portfolio down. Kicking Serah's chest with his dainty boot, he yelped. "What the hell?"

Lucy picked up the heavy box and lugged it to the chair. Her fingers tingled again and she dropped it.

Arrgh! Serah and her security-enabled chest. If she had a choice, she would've shoved it up her skinny little ass.

Despite the film of dust and dirt, it was one of Serah's more unusual finds. Along with the strange inscription and title, the symbols on its surface were expertly carved. Barbed vines and ivy wrapped their way around the edges of the entire box. On the center of the box sat a solitary outline of a handprint with a pentagram carved inside it.

"This box is creepy," Gerardo said, gazing down at Serah's box. "My *mamá* showed me something similar when we still lived in Mexico. '*Muy malvado*,' she would say. Very evil."

She rolled her eyes. Yep, definitely designed to get everyone to church. "It's a bunch of crap. I already told Serah to get her money back."

"It isn't crap," Gerardo said, his Latino accent getting thicker. "*Mamá*'s told me stories you wouldn't believe. She never lied."

"Whatever, Gerardo." Brushing a strand of dishwater blonde hair from her forehead, Lucy took a quick glance in the mirror. Dark circles lined her eyes and her cheeks were sunken. She needed a nap. But for some reason, she couldn't sleep. "Let's check out your headshot."

"You're gonna love it!" He clapped his hands with giddy excitement. Ripping open the portfolio, he pulled out his photo and held it up with pride.

Lucy's eyes boggled. Gerardo lay across a lavender-and-green speckled tarp with his violet pleather clad legs kicked high in the air. His tight green-and-purple striped chest jutted out like a peacock, feathers included. What was the deal with feathers? And here Frankie had called himself the flamer.

"Nice," she managed through a chuckle. "But I think *GQ* wants something a little less showy."

Gerardo shrugged. "I can do dull and boring, too." Pulling out some more photos, he thrust them at her. Gerardo had each pose mastered. Wearing a black Armani suit, with his arms crossed, he lounged against a silver Maserati.

"Where'd you find the fancy ride?"

He held his head high, a wide smile spread across his face. "Photoshop, baby. Here's yours." He pulled out another 8x10 and slid it across the desk.

Lucy glanced down at the picture. She stared back from the photo, her eyes vacant and mouth wide in with surprise. Her dirty blonde hair hung limp around her head. It looked like she'd been picked up after a hard night of hitting the bottle. "What the hell?"

"Watch your language!" Mrs. Carlson admonished from beneath the dryer.

Ignoring the old bat, Lucy tossed the picture back at Gerardo. "Are you trying to blackmail me?" She grabbed up a bottle of water and took a swig.

"You're beautiful. It shows your natural element! You should send it to the TV show."

She choked and snorted, water flying out her nose. Clearing her throat, she shook her head. "So I'm supposed to send this photo in and say, 'Hey, I want to be a model. Here's my Nick Nolte?' I don't think so."

Gerardo picked up the photo and shoved it back into the portfolio. "Whatever. I'll just take another picture."

"Let's not and say we did, okay?" Modeling wasn't her thing, anyway. "Enough with the pictures, Ger. Your haircut will be here any minute."

Gerardo nodded and sauntered toward his station. "Where's Frankie? He owes me fifty."

"I gave him the day off."

Gerardo rolled his eyes. "That's *nice* of you."

"It's the least I could do, after Mrs. Gunderson's paraffin foot bath."

Gerardo's eyes widened as he scanned the shop. "What happened to Suzie?"

"She called in again." Lucy snorted. "Then Frankie called to say he ran into her at the tanner. So Suzie is no more." Didn't anyone ever warn her about the dangers of UV rays? Oh well, it wasn't her skin Suzie pumped full of carcinogens. *Got melanoma?*

"Sucks to be Suzie," Gerardo murmured. "You gonna hire someone to replace her?"

"We haven't been that busy lately." Then again, losing Suzie was probably a blessing. One less person to pay.

"What? Who's going to take care of the pedicures?"

Lucy flashed a devious smile. "Why, you and Frankie, of course."

He huffed. "Gee, thanks." Pouting, he crossed his arms and turned his back. *Can't please them all.*

Sucking in a deep breath, she turned her attention

back to the chest. Although Gerardo said it was evil, even with its strange electromagnetic shield and bizarre etchings and carvings, Lucy didn't get that vibe at all. Weird? Yeah. Mysterious? You bet. Evil? Nah. She usually had a good sixth sense about those things. She looked forward to Serah's little escapade tonight—lunar eclipse and all.

Filled with an odd curiosity, Lucy wandered over to the chest. Running her fingers across the engravings and inscription, she allowed the tingles to travel up her fingers and into her body. She moved to the handprint in the center of the chest. Amazed at the perfect fit, she closed her eyes. It was as if the imprint molded to her hand. Warmth spread throughout her entire body, right to the pit of her stomach, then moving lower.

Oh dear.

The doorbells chimed, ending her semi-orgasmic encounter with Serah's... erm... chest. Ripping her hand from the box, she turned toward the door.

Speak of the devil. In pranced Serah, holding two department store bags in each hand, while two others were stuffed under her arms. "Hey! Check out my new shoes!" She wiggled her red polka dot patent leather kitten-heeled slide as if she were Cinderella admiring her new glass slippers. *How the hell could she wear shoes like that in the dead of winter?*

Lucy raised her eyebrow in bemused wonder. Here, just the night before, she'd complained about destroying her most recent antique store purchase. Wasn't there anything thing else she did besides shop? Not a discriminatory shopper either. Lucy turned a covert eye to her chest and back to the gaudy designer shoes. Old, new, weird, ugly. Serah would buy anything.

Red wasn't her color, but it went well with Serah's bouncy brunette curls. "Cute, if you like fire engine red polka dots."

"Cool, because I bought you a pair... in purple." She dropped all her bags, except the one in her left hand, on the floor. Rummaging inside the bag, she pulled out a shoebox and ripped it open. "Look!"

"You shouldn't have," Lucy said, taking the box from her. She really shouldn't have. They'd come in handy, along with the other two hundred or so other pairs of shoes she'd bought Lucy over the years.

Gerardo attacked her other bags, oohing and ahhing at their contents. Some might think it odd, but Lucy wasn't into the fashion and style thing. She'd much rather be stuck in a pair of jeans, T-shirt, and sneakers than some of those torture devices those divas try to pass off as shoes. For someone who was on her feet all day, some of those shoes made no sense. She didn't want to end up with feet like Mrs. Gunderson, anyway.

Lucy turned a surreptitious gaze back to the chest. What was the deal with it? She grumbled beneath her breath. She was almost as excited as Serah—if not more. Maybe it was contagious? Whatever it was or whatever it held, it was now a distraction. And Serah had to take it with her.

"Hey, Serah. Gerardo's scared of your box." Lucy just couldn't resist. "You need to take it with you when you leave."

Serah rolled her eyes. "Whatever. Are we still on for tonight?" Her eyes twinkled with childish delight.

"Yeah, sure." Lucy wouldn't let her know she was excited to open the box. Perhaps it was excitement about holding the episode over Serah's head after nothing happened. Yes, that was it. It had to be. Hell in a box? How absurd!

"I should sue you!" Mrs. Carlson shrieked. "My hair is ruined!" Fuming, she glared at the mirror. "I look like a giant mushroom!"

Lucy had nothing to say. She truly did look like a giant mushroom. Like she'd just stepped from the 1970s where the people wore their afros with pride. A big puff of gray frizzy hair burst from her head. If this had been a comedy, Lucy would've been rolling on the floor laughing. But it wasn't a comedy. It was her life.

"It's not so bad, Mrs. Carlson," she lied. This was the worst hair disaster ever. Even worse than giving the sheriff's wife pink highlights. And it couldn't have happened to a worse person.

Mrs. Carlson spun around and glared at her, her gray eyes blazing. "You did this on purpose! I'm ruined."

Lucy sighed as she remembered those people who say, "Cheer up. It's only hair. It'll grow back." Maybe if it was a bad cut or something minor. The fact that it involved Mrs. Carlson meant they were on the verge of World War Three.

"I'm sorry, Mrs. C. No charge. I'll fix it, I promise."

Gerardo glanced up from his twelve-year-old's haircut. "Holy shi… shiitake!" The kid's mother looked up from her magazine in the waiting area and scowled.

There went his raise. She turned her attention back to Mrs. Carlson. "How about we wash it and go from there. In a few days, if the curl doesn't loosen, I'll straighten it."

"I have a charity auction tonight, you witch." She snarled like a pit bull ready to attack a jogger's leg. Spittle formed at the sides of her mouth.

Lucy cringed.

She offered her everything under the sun, from pedicures, to facials, to a body wrap. The woman wouldn't budge. What a huge stick in the mud. Then again, she refused the mud bath too. Lucy turned to Gerardo who just sat in his chair in bemusement. Fat lot of help he was.

She tempted pulling her hair as she racked her brain for answers. *On purpose?* Lucy couldn't believe it! She who came in every other week for some silly reason? She who harped nonstop about breaking her soon-to-be married son's heart? Lucy wasn't even as fine of a catch as the richer-than-sin Larissa Harding. Why did she hold such a grudge? And here Lucy thought Larissa was a blessing in disguise and would get Mrs. Carlson off her ass. But she never counted on the mother of her ex-boyfriend having the memory of an elephant.

"Help me out here, Mrs. C. What can I do to make it better?" If that wasn't a loaded question, she didn't know what was.

"Make it better?" she shrieked. "You can't do anything to make it up, Lucia Anne Gregory."

Oh no! She used her full name. She was pissed.

Dump the mayor's wife's son, fry her hair? What was next? Spontaneous combustion? With all the chemicals the woman has put on her head over the years, it wouldn't surprise her. "Umm, Mrs. Carlson—"

"Mrs. Carlson," came a deep husky voice that sent

shivers down her spine and into her... ahh... special area. British, yet with a hint of something else. "She's apologized enough."

Lucy snapped her head up. No chimes rang, announcing a new arrival. Sure, she and Mrs. Carlson were in a heated discussion, but she still would've heard the door open. Turning, Lucy came face-to-face with a god. Well, what she would have assumed was a god, if she were a practicing polytheist. He stood about six foot four with at least two hundred and thirty pounds of solid muscle. Her body did a shwing to the left, then to the right. At least that's what it felt like.

Wearing a tight black T-shirt and equally tight black leather jeans, he cocked his head to the side. And where was his coat? He must be freezing!

Was that really his hair, all shiny, dark, and long? Gorgeous. She turned to see Gerardo. His mouth gaped open and his eyes widened in awe. He was just as affected.

"Frankie's gonna be pissed he took the day off," he managed to squeak out before he grabbed his cell phone and started clicking away. What was the deal with Gerardo and his obsession with photos?

Thank goodness, the mother and her twelve-year-old had since vacated. The heat must've risen at least ten degrees since the stranger had arrived. Either that, or it was a hot flash. Then again, she was a little too young for menopause.

"Who turned up the heat?" Gerardo asked, fanning himself. So she wasn't the only one?

Hormones, hot and heavy, hung in the air like a thick morning fog. A mist of sweet spices wafted through the air. Even Mrs. Carlson seemed to be in lighter spirits.

"Can I help you?" she squeaked out. *Gee, way to go, Lucy.* Squeaking at the sex-god. Not good at all. Please don't say haircut, her inner naughty girl whispered. His gaze burned, sending waves of heated desire racing through her. A man hadn't looked at her like that in... forever.

"I thought you could use some help." He smiled, taking long strides toward Mrs. Carlson and her. "I'm a very good negotiator." He turned to Mrs. Carlson and gave her a mind-melting smile. Hell, the smile wasn't even for Lucy and her mind melted. "Lucia gave you some very generous offers. Why not take one of them?"

Mrs. Carlson blushed—something Lucy had never seen her do—*ever*. This man was a god. "I suppose a pedicure would be nice. I haven't had one in a while." She giggled like a young schoolgirl and turned to Lucy. "I'm sorry I yelled at you, Lucy."

Lucy? The old withered witch never called her Lucy. Amazing. She tossed a sidelong glance at Gerardo, who stood with mouth wide open.

"It's okay, Mrs. Carlson. I got sidetracked and didn't mean to leave the solution on so long. If you want me to flat iron it, I will. Then you can come back in a few days for a relaxer. No charge."

Mrs. Carlson nodded and smiled. "Okay, Lucy. Thank you."

Hot-Bod grinned, took a seat, and waited while Lucy and Gerardo worked on Mrs. Carlson, who chose the deluxe pedicure instead. Lucy wasn't one to argue. Strangely enough, neither was Gerardo. Luckily for Gerardo, her feet weren't near as bad as Mrs. Gunderson's.

When they were finished, Lucy and Gerardo turned Mrs. Carlson around for her approval, which, ever since Mr. Universe appeared, seemed to happen more often than not. "I love it," she exclaimed with glee. "I'll send Larissa down to make arrangements for the wedding."

Wow! She'd almost fried her head and Mrs. Carlson still wanted her to do her prospective daughter-in-law's hair? Bonus! She should bring him home to mom and let him work his magic. Then she'd know for a fact if he was a god or just lucky.

"Sounds great, Mrs. C. See you on Saturday?"

Smiling, Mrs. Carlson nodded and slipped something into Lucy's hand. "A little tip for your trouble, dear."

Lucy glanced down at the money. A hundred-dollar bill? She must've been transported to an alternate universe where things were the opposite. Then again, she didn't feel any different.

"Sorry, Mrs. C. I can't take this." Lucy handed the money back to her. "Not until you're completely satisfied."

She pouted but took back the money. "Oh, all right, sweetie. I'll tell Joshua you said hello?"

"Please do." Lucy smiled back, despite the weirdness. "And Larissa, too?"

"Sure." Mrs. Carlson raised her hand into a friendly wave. With a spring in her step, she left the salon.

With a wide grin, Hot-Bod rose from his chair and approached the desk. "I hope you don't mind my interfering?"

Hell no, she didn't mind him interfering. He could interfere anytime he wanted. "Not at all. Like you said, you're a very good negotiator." Lucy smiled and her cheeks warmed. "Although, I admit, 'very good' is an understatement, Mr...."

"Deleon. Rafael Deleon." The man smiled, deep dimples forming in each of his cheeks. His silver eyes swirled like two giant pools. Beautiful in a completely masculine way. "You can call me Rafe."

So, Rafe, do you want a job? She wouldn't mind having some smooth negotiating for those *hairy* situations. "Thank you, Rafe. I don't know how to repay you. I haven't seen Mrs. Carlson that happy in a long time." More like forever. "Right, Gerardo?"

She turned to Gerardo. If this were a cartoon, he would've had those animated hearts in his eyes. He batted his eyelashes and a giddy smile curved his lips. She'd never seen Gerardo this excited over a little eye candy. Maybe she was lucky Frankie had the day off. Then she'd have two enraptured gay men on her hands.

"Gerardo!"

He jumped about a foot in the air. "What?" He glanced around, a sheepish smile on his face. "Oh, my bad. Can I help you?"

Lucy shook her head. "Sorry, Gerardo's a tad occupied with his new toy. So how can we help you?"

Rafe crossed his gloriously ripped arms. Fabio had nothing on this guy. His muscles bulged in places she didn't know muscles existed. Yummy with a capital Y. "I came to search for something."

"Something?" Lucy snickered. "What sort of something? We've got a lot of things here. How about a pedicure?" If his feet looked as good as the rest of his body, he didn't need one. "Or some shampoo and conditioner. You seem like a guy who knows how to take care of his hair."

"That's for sure," Gerardo chimed in. "I've never seen hair so shiny. Not a split end in sight. What brand do you use?"

Rafe arched a brow. "Brand?"

"Conditioner." Gerardo leapt over the desk and reached for a strand of Rafe's hair.

In a blink of an eye, Rafe spun around, grabbed Gerardo's arm and pinned him against the desk. Elbow at Ger's neck, he held firm, his gaze stony. "I did not give you permission to touch me."

Great! Her fantasy come to life was a homophobe. Not that she had a chance in hell with such a fine specimen of man. Even if his gaze looked like he wanted to eat her up. And he was manhandling her employees anyway. "Let him go! He didn't mean any harm. He just wanted to check your hair out."

Loosening his hold on Gerardo's feathers, Rafe lowered his elbow. Several crumpled feathers floated to the ground. Poor Gerardo. That was his favorite shirt.

He raked his fingers through his hair and backed away. "Next time, ask."

Rubbing his neck, Gerardo nodded. He slumped against the desk. "*¡Ay Dios mío!*" he murmured as he crumbled to a little ball on the floor.

"I'm not sure how things are done where you're from, mister, but here we frown at violence." Lucy raised her chin. Call it her defiant nature.

Rafe crossed his arm. With stony intensity, he returned her defiant gaze with one of his own. Despite the furor, crackling heat raced through her body. What was happening? "Yet people seem to thrive upon it. Since the dawn of time. TV, cinema, fisticuffs."

"Fisticuffs? What in the hell is that?"

Rafe growled a sound that, despite its gruffness, caused her gut to flutter. "I suppose it's called boxing, now."

"I hate boxing." Lucy stood proud. "As well as professional wrestling and that ultimate fighting shit. I hate watching people getting the crap kicked out of them." Then again, the sight of blood—period—made her cringe. She crossed her arms. And this guy had her rambling like a buffoon, too. Now she needed to put her foot down. "So tell me what you want so you can get the hell out of my shop."

Rafe groaned in obvious frustration. "It's not here anymore. I would have felt it." His gaze still burned. "Don't you know what you are?"

Any attraction she felt for this man faded as anger took over. "Sure I do. I'm the owner of this establishment, and you've overstayed your welcome."

"You need protection." He stalked toward Lucy, his gaze steady, yet still wounded. "But I cannot stay where I am not welcome. If you need me, call my name."

What a god complex! "I can take care of myself, Mr. Deleon. I've been doing it for almost thirty years."

"Very well, Miss Gregory. Have a good day." His silver eyes sparked as he bowed. In one swift turn, he spun around and stalked toward the exit. With a loud whoosh, as if a hurricane force wind swept through the building, the door swung open. Rafe, unaffected by the gust, stepped out onto the sidewalk and proceeded down the street.

As if on similar wavelengths, Lucy and Gerardo sprinted toward the window. They trained their gazes toward the direction in which Rafe had walked off. Not a person stood in sight.

Chapter 3

THERE WAS SOMETHING ABOUT LUCIA GREGORY. While the other two people in the shop were easily enthralled, she seemed unaffected. There was only one explanation—she was of demon blood. Strong demon blood, at that. She weaved a spell of seduction with her every move. And the worst part of all was he'd been affected. The moment he saw her, heard her, smelled her, all he wanted to do was take her, in more ways than one. It amazed him he was able to hide the desire that reared itself against those blasted tight pants Nic insisted he wear.

"This isn't good," he muttered, pacing his personal chambers. He'd been drawn to her building from the beginning, but then he'd lost contact. What sort of spell had she woven to hide the chest?

She wasn't all human, that much he knew. From her shaggy, shoulder-length dark blonde hair to her mesmerizing brownish gold eyes, she radiated untapped energy. She said she was nearly thirty years old. Thirty years of latent energy? What would happen if that energy were released on Earth? He needed to speak to the Paladin council, before it was too late.

"Dominic Duvane!" he called to his friend. Stalking to the emerald velvet settee, he flung himself into its plush splendor.

Dominic, wearing a suit of polished black armor,

appeared before him. Scowling, he gripped his large broadsword, ready to slice.

Blowing out a deep breath, he ripped the helmet from his head. "You have the worst timing." He wiped a tinge of blood from his cheek, the wound instantly healing. "I do hope it's important."

Rafael nodded. "The chest has moved again."

"From the antique store?"

"Yes." He crossed his arms. "To a place women—and some men—go to make themselves presentable."

Dominic arched a brow. "A beauty salon? Why?"

"If I knew, I doubt I'd be sitting here having this conversation with you." He paused, the words forming in his mind. "We have a serious problem."

"Problem? A hair salon, although bizarre, is the perfect place for the chest to hide. Especially in a small town." Dominic stripped himself of his armor, letting the metal clank to the ground. He took a seat next to Rafael. "What else is there, my friend?"

"There's to be a total lunar eclipse and tonight is the eve of the Winter Solstice. Connolly Park, Michigan, isn't as isolated as we thought."

Dominic drew his mouth into a straight line as he steepled and unsteepled his fingers. "What are the chances of the chest ending up in another demon's hands?"

"Greater than you realize, Nic." He had no choice. He needed to return to the salon. He had to get the chest. Most importantly, he needed to protect Lucia. From what he could see, her aura was clean. However, if the Infernati got a hold of her, who knew what would happen.

Dominic brushed a strand of sandy-brown hair from his brow. "What do you mean?"

"The woman at the shop. She has latent powers." Rafael clenched his fists. "She's not all human."

Scratching his goatee, Dominic narrowed his eyes. "Are you sure?"

"As sure as her immunity to my enrapture. Everyone else in the shop was affected, except her."

Dominic shook his head. "This isn't good. Does she know?"

"No." Rafael blew out a deep breath. This mission became more urgent as the minutes ticked by. "She has no idea, but I had to restrain her friend. Before I could explain myself, she ordered me out."

"Back up a second. What do you mean restrain her friend?"

Rafael tugged at his hair. "Her friend tried to touch me."

"Oh, that's not good." Dominic leaned back against the settee. "A mortal touching a demon without permission?"

Rafael nodded. If only he could explain. "I didn't want to risk it. The last time it happened…" Miss Amanda Newell's face, her long golden hair, and her bright blue eyes flashed before him. He refused to cry. It had been over two hundred years anyway. "I won't hurt another innocent mortal again."

"But didn't you just say Lucia Gregory wasn't completely mortal?" Dominic crossed his legs and stretched his arms behind his neck. "Impossible."

Rafael shrugged. "She may be a descendent of Lilu. Her energy is more sexual."

"Interesting theory." Dominic took a deep breath. "No one has been able to prove that an incubus has ever procreated with a mortal, even though mortal folklore says otherwise."

"There's something about her that doesn't add up." Rafael gritted his teeth as he remembered her intense glare, full of untapped energy. That energy threatened to consume him and drive him mad with desire. He couldn't tell Dominic though. If his friend heard that his powers were diminishing, he'd be removed as a Paladin. And that wasn't going to happen. He would fight Lucia Gregory's power. He would not submit. But with that much power, she was a target for the Infernati. They would use her for evil. And from what he saw, she was far from evil.

"I need to protect her." And by protecting her, he could also retrieve the chest.

Dominic's gaze grew serious. "I've known you for over four hundred years. If you feel strongly about this, then you need to do it. We need the chest, regardless."

"What should I do with Lucia?"

Dominic's voice remained firm and full of resolve. "Keep her from opening the chest, of course. Then bring her here. If she's of demon blood, as you suspect, she should have no problem crossing through."

"How goes the search for my sister?" Rafael asked, turning to his friend. "I need to know she's safe."

Dominic's gaze grew somber. "We're still searching for her," he replied with a determined tilt of his chin. "I won't stop until I find her."

"I don't think I could find a better demon for the job." Rafael, despite the despair clutching at his soulless heart, managed a wan smile. "Thank you, Nic."

Dominic nodded. "It's the least I can do. You and your sister mean everything to me. You're like a brother to me."

But Coby was more. Everyone knew, even though Nic adamantly denied it, his affections for Coby were more than brotherly.

"The feeling's mutual." Rafael extended his arm, allowing his friend his elbow. Once Dominic grasped it, Rafael returned the favor. "I appreciate the update, my friend, but I must return." And, despite his earlier objections, he wanted to go back. It had nothing to do with the chest, either. Much to his chagrin.

Why in the hell did she agree to dinner with her mother? Then again, it was too late ask that question. Lucy loved her mom, but there was only so much nagging one could take.

"Are you sure this is what you want in life?" Victoria Gregory asked in between sips of white zinfandel. Lucy never cared for wine. She liked her alcohol a bit harder.

Contemplating a clever reply, Lucy took a sip of her own drink, a Captain and Diet Coke, of course. "The shop's doing well."

It wasn't a complete lie. In the six months Luscious Locks had been open, a steady stream of customers had passed through the door. "I couldn't be happier," she added with a confident smile.

"Your father wanted you to follow in his footsteps." Her mother dusted off her fingernails. Fingernails she traveled across town to have manicured. Talk about twisting the knife in someone's back. "You would have made an excellent surgeon."

Lucy coughed on her drink. Did the woman not remember what the sight of blood did to her? "Maybe I would have. But would I have been happy? I don't know about you, but I'd rather have a happy hair stylist working on me than an unhappy surgeon."

"Are you sure you're all right?" her mom asked, oblivious to the banter. She reached across the table and brushed a strand of hair from Lucy's face. "You look horrible. No amount of makeup will cover those dark circles."

Lucy rolled her eyes. "Yes, Mom," she said in the firmest voice she could muster. "I'm just peachy keen. I just stayed up a wee bit late last night." More like the entire night, but she wasn't ready to divulge that information.

"You know, your father didn't save all his hard-earned money for you to slave over a shampoo bowl."

Truth be told, her dad would have supported her in whatever career she chose. Unfortunately, he'd passed away before he got the chance to see her succeed. "Dad knew I wanted to be a cosmetologist. He respected me for making my own decision. You're the only one who wanted me to go to med school."

Once Victoria Gregory got started, there was no stopping her. "But you could've done so much more with your life."

"For the five-millionth time, I enjoy it." Lucy annunciated the sentence with slow deliberateness, making sure she caught every last word.

"You know," she continued, now that she had her mother's attention. "I'd rather butcher someone's bangs than butcher their insides. 'Oh dear, Mr. Johnson,'" she said in a mock-concerned voice. "'I'm sorry, but I cut a little too deep. Don't worry. It's only your liver; it'll grow back.'"

Then again there were women like her mother, who'd rather get their liver cut out than live with a hack-job haircut.

"Lucia Anne Gregory!" Her mom chided. "That wasn't funny at all."

Lucy shrugged, pushing the empty glass to the side. Too bad it was a work night. She wouldn't have minded slamming a few more of them down. "I wasn't trying to be funny. I was making a point. The point went sailing over your head."

Her mom opened her mouth to speak, but at that precise time the waitress appeared with their order. Thank goodness for talented waiters and waitresses. The young woman pulled out a stand and set the tray down. An array of different concoctions, from entrees to desserts to a rainbow of beverages, blanketed it. It always amazed her how they could balance such a large tray with a single hand. Lucy wouldn't have survived the first day on the job. She would have been feeding the floor more than the customers.

"Who ordered the tequila-lime roasted chicken?" the young girl asked with a cheery smile, her light blonde ponytail bouncing behind her.

She held the plate out and Lucy's mouth watered. A huge golden brown chicken breast surrounded by myriad gold, blue, and red tortilla strips. If arranging a plate were an art form, the chef would have given da Vinci a run for his money. If she wasn't hungry earlier, she was now.

"Me!" Lucy said with eager excitement. She drooled. Steam rose from the succulent chicken as the waitress placed the order in front of Lucy. "Here you are." Then she placed Mrs. Gregory's grilled dijon-crusted salmon in front of her. Picking up the empty glass, she asked, "Would you like another?"

"No, but I wouldn't mind just a straight Diet Coke this time. The captain tells me I need to drink responsibly."

The waitress giggled and nodded. "Sure thing." After seeing to Mrs. Gregory's coffee, she scurried off.

This was the time Lucy most enjoyed with Mom. Stuffing food in their mouths, so they didn't have to talk much, and limiting that bit of conversation to the food on the plates. "How's the salmon?" Lucy asked as she cut into her succulent chicken.

Pulling a tiny piece of bone from her mouth, her mom shrugged. "Dry and bony. And this rice pilaf needs some more flavor." Maybe she should be happy she wasn't the only thing her mom disapproved of.

"That's too bad," Lucy said, picking a piece of chicken with her fork. With as much gusto as she could muster, she took a bite. *Mmm*. Her favorite. Tangy bursts of tequila, lime, cilantro, and spices exploded in her mouth. Closing her eyes, Lucy savored each bite.

"If chicken is sex, then this is the best orgasm ever." *Dang. Did I just say that out loud?* Hearing her mom's soft gasp, she held back the urge to chuckle. *Yep, I did.*

What was the deal with the sudden hormone rush? First Serah's *chest*? Now the chicken at McIntosh's? She wasn't even a food-and-sex kind of gal. With a sheepish blush, Lucy set down her fork. "Sorry. It's really good."

"Hush. We're in public," her mom huffed, then plucked a steamed carrot from her plate. "At least the carrots are palatable."

Bet you wished you ordered the chicken. Chuckling, Lucy dipped her fork into some pico de gallo.

Mom threw her napkin down on the table. "What's so funny?"

"Nothing. Let's just eat." Sighing, Lucy picked at the festive display of tortilla strips and dipped them into a side of spicy black bean dip. This was the life. With a sigh of deep contentment, she sat back and enjoyed the meal. If this is what dinner did to her, she didn't want to know what dessert would do.

Heck, she'd have that dessert. Besides, it would be fun to give Meg Ryan in *When Harry Met Sally* a run for her money and freak the crap out of her mom. Lucy turned to scan the restaurant for the waitress when something caught the corner of her eye. What the heck?

Across the restaurant stood a solitary figure draped in a long billowing black robe, with a hood covering most its face. The hairs rose on the back of her neck and her pulse raced. Stomach clenching in knots, she continued to stare. People bustled about, chatting, drinking, and eating while this thing just stood there in the shadows. Didn't anyone see him? Blinking, she rubbed her eyes and turned to her mom. "Whoa! Look at that."

Her mom arched a brow and set down her coffee cup. "At what?"

"That!" She pointed and turned back to the shadowy figure. But, lo and behold, it was gone. Mom was right about one thing. She needed rest.

The blonde bouncy waitress appeared with dessert menus. Instantly, Lucy's salivary glands—along with her stupid hormones—kicked into overdrive.

She would rest after a huge helping of chocolate lava cake.

Revitalized by a sudden burst of sugar and espresso, Lucy fumbled with the keys to the shop. Cold gusts of December air flicked her face, sending shivers through her body. Serah would be meeting her later and she needed to catch up on some paperwork anyway. Hopefully, Serah would arrive sooner rather than later, so they could open the box and be done with it. She cracked her knuckles as an odd sense of excitement coursed through her body.

Taking confident strides into the building, she held her head high and allowed the tingles to tease her skin, oblivious to the swirling snow around her. She ran her fingers through her hair and stretched.

Heading to the back office, she recalled the strange events of the day. From Gerardo's photography, to the almost-orgasm from touching the chest, to Mrs. Carlson's mushroom perm, to Rafe... especially Rafe.

Never had she seen eyes so silver and vibrant, even more so than the costume jewelry she sold. His glistening dark hair that danced across his shoulders, beckoning her to reach out and touch. Would he have reacted the same way he had to Gerardo? Then again having a dowdy hairstylist touching his gorgeous locks was probably the last thing Rafe wanted.

And how could she forget that body? Thick muscles straining against his T-shirt and leather pants that molded to each ripple and bulge. He radiated power, and not just the physical kind. But then he'd put Gerardo in a choke hold. Why did the drop dead sexy ones always have to be homophobes?

Settling into her office chair, she fired up her computer.

The only thing she hated about running a business. Balancing the budget. Maybe someday she could hire an accountant. After a few hours of boring bookkeeping, she wanted to pound her head on the keyboard.

The sound of Justin Timberlake's latest hit broke her thoughts. Rifling through her striped Dolce and Gabbana purse, she searched for her cell phone. Curse Serah for buying her such a gi-normous purse. It was so huge; she could've stuffed the Statue of Liberty in it and still had room for the Eiffel Tower.

Flipping up the receiver, she answered the phone. "Hello?"

"Open up. I'm waiting in the back." Serah's voice, full of urgency, echoed in her ear. "I think someone's following me and it's freezing out here."

Lucy chuckled. "Please! You think everyone's following you. It's just some weird chest, not the Arc of the Covenant, for God's sake."

Something deep inside nagged at her, but Lucy ignored it. She wanted to open this box. At first it was to prove Serah wrong, but now something else drove her. Something dark and dangerous. Maybe opening this chest wasn't such a good idea after all.

"So are you going to let me in or what?" Serah huffed with obvious irritation. "It's kind of hard standing here with a huge chest in my arms. Thank God for Bluetooth." A loud clunk soon followed. "Just let me in." The phone went dead.

Flinging her phone back into the purse, Lucy trekked toward the back door. The sooner she let Serah in, the sooner they could open the chest. Then her stupid curiosity would be sated.

Serah's pounding, followed by a groan, came muffled through the door. "Stupid box. Ugh."

"I'm coming!" Lucy said in the most annoying singsong voice she could muster. From the sounds of Serah's grunts and grumbles, she was none too pleased. With a wide smile, Lucy threw open the door. Serah stood there glowering, the chest propped atop her pink Jimmy Choo-clad foot.

"It's about time," Serah grumbled, pulling her foot from under the chest. With another loud grumble, she kicked it. "Ouch."

Lucy shook her head and chuckled. "Then don't kick it."

With an irritated huff, Serah hobbled into the shop. "Seriously. This thing isn't worth the trouble. I'd return it if I could."

"Why can't you?" She reached down to collect Serah's forgotten chest and followed her inside.

Serah plopped down into one of the dryer seats and pulled her shoes off. "The guy said, 'No returns.' He seemed pretty eager to part with it."

"So you don't want to open it anymore?" Leave it to Serah to deflate her eager curiosity. "This was supposed to be the highlight of my evening."

Serah chuckled. "Yeah, I know you want to burst the bubble in my overly active imagination."

"Something like that," Lucy fibbed. Her reasons now went deeper than that. Something about the chest had put her curiosity into overdrive. "To be honest, I thought it'd be kind of fun, like we were in grade school again."

Flailing her mangled Jimmy Choo in the air, Serah

sucked in a deep breath. "Do you know how much these cost me?"

"More than your *über-expensive* box?" Lucy asked, arching a brow.

Serah took an exhausted breath. "Okay, fine. You got me there. I exaggerated on the box. I got a deal. The guy couldn't wait to get rid of it."

"Yeah, a pentagram on the top of a box tends to do that to people," Lucy added matter-of-factly.

Serah shrugged. "I didn't see the pentagram until you pointed it out. The only visible thing was the inscription." Her gaze grew serious. "I know you think I'm a loon, but maybe we should just forget it. I can put it on eBay."

"Yeah, you do that. I'd hate to see the freaks who'd bid on that thing." Then again, *she* was the freak who itched to open it. "Well, it's here now, so why don't we just have some fun?"

Serah shifted in the chair and blew out a deep breath. "Fine. I Googled the eclipse. It's supposed to happen just around two-thirty."

"In the morning?" Lucy craned her head toward the clock on the wall. One a.m.? "Time flies when you're not having fun."

"Yeah?" Her friend arched a brow. "That's why I have an accountant to handle my books. I hate math."

"You and me both." Lucy plopped into a chair next to her and stretched her legs. "I don't have enough business to hire one yet."

Serah grinned. "Soon, girl. Trust me. I'm sending a few of my best clients your way."

"That's awesome." Knowing the type of clients

Serah's catering business had, Lucy could make a killing. Then again Mrs. Carlson was one of her clients. *Yippee!* "Just make sure they aren't Mrs. Carlson's cronies."

Serah shook her head and snorted. "That old bat? I dropped her as a client. Way too demanding. You'd think it was her wedding. I swear she sprouted horns when I walked in earlier. You're so lucky you dumped him."

Why did everyone think she broke it off? "It was mutual. We dumped each other." Raking fingers through her hair, Lucy looked out the front window. Her loud gasp echoed through the empty shop. The faint light of the moon trickled in. An eerie blood red hue surrounded the slowly eclipsing moon. If only she had a camera. Where was Gerardo when you needed him?

"Check that out!" Lucy pointed at the creepy moon.

Serah stared, transfixed, at the reddish orb. "Amazing! Are you ready to do this or what?"

"I thought you didn't want to do it anymore?"

Lips curved into a wide grin, Serah shrugged. "Like you said. It'll be a big sleepover, like in junior high."

"Okay!" Lucy leapt from the chair and skipped toward the box. Maybe she was taking this junior high thing way too seriously. Lugging the chest to the center of the room, she allowed the tingles, no longer painful, to fill her body. She threw her head back and allowed the current to race through her veins. It felt so good.

"Lucy!" Serah's shout broke her daydream. "What the heck?"

With heavy reluctance, Lucy pulled her hands from the box. Wiping her damp brow, she turned to face her friend. "I told you it shocks me whenever I touch it."

"Shock?" Serah chuckled. "You looked like you were enjoying it. If that's electrocution, sign me up."

Now Serah thought she was into that kinky shit. Then again, Josh did say she was "too wild." How much fun was the missionary position all the time? Sex should be fun and adventurous, not the same ole, same ole. What would've happened if she'd pulled out the *Kama Sutra*? A coronary, probably. Quite a feat for a thirty-something cardiologist.

His idea of fun was jogging five miles a day, and the most excitement she got from him was necking in a movie theater. Call security! Then again, maybe that's how he kept his ticker healthy. Recalling the many times she'd tried to spice up Josh's dull life over the years, she allowed a devious smile to curve her lips.

Serah cleared her throat. "What's on your mind?"

"Nothing. Just recalling my life with Josh."

She threw her head back in laughter. "You mean lack of life." She smiled, her gaze warm. "Trust me, Lucy. He gets it from his mom. Be very happy."

"Hello! It's been five years. I'm over him." Enough was enough. "I'm happier than ever."

"It's just that you haven't dated since him." Serah squatted down next to her. "People talk, you know."

None of the men in this suburban hellhole held that spark of life Lucy needed, and it irritated her beyond reason. And, to her utter chagrin, the first spark ever had to come from a homophobic ass-crack. *Lucky me!*

Lucy put on a mask of indifference. She ground her teeth and her heart thudded. Gripping her fists tightly, she turned to her friend, her gaze ready to burn. "Let them talk." Her voice came out deep and gravelly, almost inhuman.

Serah jumped back, her eyes filled with alarm. "You know, maybe we should call it a night. You're obviously stressed or in need of something else."

"Let's not talk about my love life, all right?" Lucy slammed her fist into her palm. What in the heck had come over her? "We came here to have fun, not argue," she added, her voice softening.

"Deal," Serah said offering her hand. "On one condition."

Lucy narrowed her gaze. "Your condition?"

Serah's mouth spread into a wide smile. "We can't talk about mine, either."

"Deal." She took Serah's hand and shook. She turned her attention back to the chest. "So let me look at that inscription again."

After spending a half hour translating the words, they needed to choose the victim. They solved it in the easiest of ways.

"Rock. Paper. Scissors!" Serah danced around the box like a giddy schoolgirl. Then again, that was the purpose of this experiment, to relive their pre-teen years. To be honest, there wasn't much reliving for Lucy. Her mother had kept her on lockdown for most of her junior-high years. But, much to her mom's chagrin, Lucy finally rose up and put her foot down.

"Fine." After all, it did beat a thumb war. Lucy held out her fist, waiting for her friend to return the favor. Smiling, she nudged Serah's with her own.

"Rock, paper, scissors," they both chanted. Lucy held her hand in perfect scissor position.

Serah, unfortunate gal, held out her paper hand. A large pout quivered on her lips as a loud whoosh of air came from her nose. "I knew I should have called rock."

"Oh well," Lucy said with a smirk. Glancing at the dim, reddening moon, she narrowed her eyes. "You know, the moon is getting creepier."

"I looked up some websites earlier. That's just the Earth's reflection." Serah craned her head to look. "But you're right. It is creepy."

"Tell me about it," Lucy said. "So how much longer?" She snuck a glance at the chest, her gut clenching. Not in fear but something more carnal. Like it contained a treasure trove of toys, and not the kind that you give a kid. Had it been that long that she now craved inanimate objects? She needed help.

"Like now," her friend replied. "It's two-twenty-five, according to my watch." Serah held up her hand and twisted her wrist, sparkles glistening against the dimmed lights of the salon. Oh brother, yet another crazy purchase. But if you have the money, you might as well spend it.

"New watch?"

Serah shrugged. "It belonged to my granny. Just wanted to wear it for some reason."

Lucy smiled and hugged her friend, allowing her comfort. Even though her grandmother had died almost a year ago, Serah still mourned from time to time. It wasn't her business to pry, but Serah dealt with her grief the only way she could. And truth be told, Lucy wasn't a psychologist anyway. Much to Mom's chagrin, of course.

"Let's do this," Lucy said, pulling from their friendly

embrace. With a quick lick of her lips, she focused her attention back to the chest.

As if a golden orb had surrounded it, the chest glowed. Her body ignored her conscience, disregarding what she knew to be wrong or right. Lucy took slow, almost sensual, steps toward the box. Her lips spread into a devious smile as warmth enveloped her. Never had she felt so alive. Her stomach twisted in knots and her insides throbbed. She had to touch it, and no one would stop her.

Serah's concerned voice faintly echoed in her mind. "Lucy, are you okay? You're acting strange." She reached out to grab her hand.

"I am fine," Lucy gritted out, digging her nails into Serah's palm. "I know what I'm doing." The bad thing was she actually did, but she had no idea how she knew.

"Ouch, that hurts," Serah yelped and pulled her hand from her superhuman grip. "We should forget this, Lucy. Something isn't right."

Lucy turned to face her friend and narrowed her eyes, her glare challenging. With a wide, calculated grin, she reached up to brush a stray hair from Serah's brow. "No, Serah. Everything is just right."

With that, she slammed her palm into the handprint and closed her eyes.

Chapter 4

RAFAEL PUSHED INTO THE MORTAL REALM, PULLING himself from the shadows. He dusted off his black leather trousers and cursed Dominic for dressing him like a bloody biker. Taking in the scene before him, his stomach lurched. The moon hung low in the sky, full and taunting, as if it knew the direness of the situation and welcomed it.

Blasted moon.

Pulling the antique watch from the inner pocket of his black leather pea coat, he flipped it open. He needed to act, and fast. He took long, purposeful strides toward Lucia's shop. Peering into the window, he groaned. She wasn't alone.

With a low growl, he clenched his fists. He was no longer welcome in her shop, and she had yet to call for him. He needed in—*now*. Before it was too late. He raised his fist to rap on the front door.

"Rafe," came the haunting voice, floating in the air. "Save me... please."

Coby. His only weakness. His only reason for living the life of the damned. He gulped down the lump in his throat. Curse the angels for giving them each a weakness. It was inevitable that his twin sister would be his. Clenching his fists, he turned toward the sound of her heavenly voice. Yes, she may have been a demon, but her voice belied her species.

"Over here, Rafe," her voice drifted in the air, luring

him across the street. "I need you. Please! Before Belial returns."

The thought of his sister at Belial's mercy—even though the fiend more than likely didn't possess any—spurred him onward. He jogged across the street, following the sound of his sister's voice.

"Coby?" he called, keeping steady with each movement. "Where are you?"

Her laughter filled the air.

Laughter? She was being held by Belial and she was laughing? The hair at the back of his neck pricked. He clenched his teeth and dug his fingers into his palms. Something wasn't right.

"Behind you, brother."

Spinning on his heels, he did what they called a *complete one-eighty* in this time. Her silver hair whipped around her head as she floated above the ground, her silver gossamer gown fluttering at her feet. A dress? Coby never wore dresses, even though she looked stunning in them. Her eyes, usually silver sparks with life, reminded him of dull pewter.

"Took you long enough, brother." Her voice, no longer wispy, grated in his ears. Curse his hide, he'd been duped. Before he could reply, Coby lunged at him, her features molding into something more primal.

Lamia.

Her legs wrapped around each other, green scales replacing her porcelain skin. Her silvery waves of hair twisted into a torrent of blood red corkscrews. She smiled, then bared her serpent teeth, an eerie hiss escaping her lips. Allowing her long barbed tongue to loose itself from its cavern, she traced it along his neck.

"Always the fool for your sister, Rafael. It will be your undoing." She lashed her tongue out, the forks catching his cheek. "Tasty as ever."

Smashing his fist into his palm, Rafael sneered. "And here I thought you'd never submit yourself to Belial's will. What a disappointment."

Lamia sucked in her tongue and threw her head back in laughter. Her obsidian eyes, rimmed with red, sparked. "When I heard the mission involved you, I couldn't refuse." Her snakelike body slithered back and forth, spiraling along his leg.

She craned her head toward Luscious Locks and a devious smile curved her lips. "One of my sisters, it appears, with a silly mortal. Belial is right. She's strong. I'll enjoy vanquishing her and devouring her friend."

Not on his watch. Yes, she may have been assigned to him, but something else drew him to her. Something he didn't understand.

"Moved on from children, I see?" His stomach roiled as he remembered the last time he and Lamia clashed. Recalling her penchant for innocent blood, he gritted his teeth. He'd caught her on a small island just off the Virginia coastline. By the time he and Nic had arrived, it was too late. The children were dead and the parents, torn up with grief, had taken their own lives. His first assignment as a Paladin and he'd failed. Roanoke remained in the history books a mystery, but Rafael knew the truth. And sometimes fiction was better than the truth. Humans weren't ready for it. Which is why he needed to get inside that shop.

Reaching inside his pea coat, he extracted the silver

dagger. It wasn't enough to vanquish the bitch, but at least he could slow her down.

"When times are dire, I do not discriminate. Adult blood, although diluted, can be very satisfying."

She tightened her hold around his body, her dark eyes flickering. "What's happened to you, Rafael? I remember a time when we got along so well." Her tail slithered up his leg and between his thighs.

The silver blade glinted in the streetlight as he arced it down toward her scaly green tail.

Her face curved into a frown. "You wouldn't dare hurt a lady, would you?"

"No, I would never hurt a lady." His grip on the dagger remained firm as he sliced her tail clean through. "But you, Lamia, are no lady."

Lamia screeched in anger, her severed tail vanishing into a cloud of dust. Reaching down to grab what remained of her severed appendage, her eyes flashed. Dark crimson blood, almost black, dripped from her. "Bastard," she seethed. Craning her neck toward the shop, she threw back her head and cackled. "Look at that, Paladin."

Rafael turned to the shop, his breath catching. "Fuck," he grumbled, opting for a more modern curse. There was no mistaking the glow that emanated from inside. Diamond sparks spewed in the air as Lucia Gregory stood over the chest, her hand firmly planted on the lid. An aura of bright light surrounded her as she absorbed the energy from the chest. She may have been a latent succubus earlier, but she wasn't now. He could feel it.

Lamia lashed out with her regenerated tail, wrapping it around his wrist. "Looks as if you're too late… Again."

Rafael spun around, sending Lamia flying. Thank the demons her newly grown tail hadn't fully absorbed her power. "Better late than never you bloodsucking bitch." With that, he sent the dagger flying. It connected with her chest, sending her into a giant puff of dust.

Lucia and her friend would be safe—for now.

Heat shot into her palm, up her arm and into her chest. She threw her head back as wave after wave of energy, growing stronger by the second, coursed through her body. The intense heat radiated through her entire being, edging her on.

"What the hell?" Serah's voice, distant yet close, came out like a squeak. She reached out to shake Lucy, her hands clasping her friend's shoulders. Crackles filled the air and she went flying against the wall. "Oh my God," she wailed as she crashed against the shampoo bowls.

Lucy opened her eyes and turned her gaze to the chest, her hand glowing against it. Alertness raced through her body. Wrenching her hand free of the chest, she spun around. Panting unevenly, Serah clutched the foot of the shampoo bowl chair.

What have I done?

With a loud whoosh, geysers of water erupted around them. Spray hoses flung themselves around as jets of cold water gushed through the air. Mirrors one by one, cracked, sending bursts of shards flying across the salon. Lucy stood tall and confident, as if she'd taken a huge dose of liquid adrenaline. Oblivious to the glass slicing at her face, she took smooth confident strides toward her friend.

"Serah?" she asked, hovering over her.

Serah glanced up from where she crouched and brushed needles of glass from her face and hair. "Oh my God!" she screeched, scurrying away. Cowering in her corner, she held up her fingers in the sign of the cross. "You're a demon!"

A what? "Just because some silly box electrocuted me and blew the crap out of my shop doesn't mean I'm a demon."

Thanks, Serah. My shop's just been destroyed and you're accusing me of being one of Satan's minions?

Lucy sucked in a deep breath and ran trembling fingers through her hair, dislodging a few stray shards of glass. "I'm not a demon."

Serah reached out and pointed. With a shaky breath, she said, "Look."

"Fine," she replied with an exasperated huff. Jerking herself around, Lucy took in the scene. The box sat in the middle of the room, open, with glowing amber light emanating from inside. Showers of vibrant sparks shot up in a small yet beautiful fireworks display. *Great! Now the place would catch fire.*

Her insurance company wouldn't believe this. Heck, she still didn't believe it.

"Close the chest!" she heard echoed in the air. Her breath caught and her pulse raced. Heat crackled inside her in sizzling waves. On its own accord, her tongue traced along her lips.

Rafe! Mmm...

Spinning around the room, she scanned every recess. More fountains of water erupted as more and more amber energy escaped the chest. Her gaze trained on the front door. There stood Rafe, taking up most of the entrance, his dark hair whipping around his face. His eyes flashed like two giant diamonds and glinted in the midst of the eerie light and sparks.

"Close it. Now," he urged. "Before more escape." The intensity in his glare showed he was serious.

As if a fire had been lit beneath her ass, Lucy sprang into action. Like she'd just stepped into a kung fu movie, she leapt over a dryer chair and tumbled into a somersault. *Whoa! Where'd that come from?* With as much strength as she could muster, Lucy pushed the lid closed.

"Say this: 'By the power of the Paladins, I command thee closed.'"

"By the power of the Paladins, I command thee closed," she repeated. All of a sudden, with a forceful whoosh, what remained of the amber glow shot back into the chest and the lid slammed shut.

Rafe stood tall, his hands on his waist, the muscles bulging in his biceps. "Do you know what you just did?" His jaw twitched as his gaze bore into her. That intensity made her melt. And she absolutely loved it.

It scared the shit out of her. Where did all these hormones come from? She'd gone five years without sex, with only a slight urge every so often. The minute this man walked into her life, she became a walking orgasm.

She raised her chin as defiantly as possible. What was it about this man that drove her bonkers? "No, but I'm sure you'll enlighten me." She looked back at Serah, who struggled to right herself.

"I told you to call if you needed me." He crossed his arms in front of the rocks that were his pecs. "Why didn't you?"

Raking her fingers through her hair, Lucy chuckled. "Sorry, but you didn't leave a number. How do you expect me to call?"

Rafe growled, a deep sound that left her senses reeling. What kind of cologne was he wearing? "You know what I meant, Lucia."

"Well, Mr. Deleon, I'm sorry, but I had other things on my mind." Lucy crossed her arms and raised her chin. "If you look around, you'll see."

Rafe stood ramrod still, his shoulders almost touching each side of the doorway. His gaze smoldered. The intensity morphed from anger and frustration to something more dangerous. Something naughty. She shivered at the images of that gaze in the midst of some hot, sweaty, monkey sex. Something she hadn't had the pleasure of doing in... a long-ass time. In a flash, it was gone. Frustration creased his brow.

A loud clanging in the corner caught her attention. Serah ambled toward her as she plucked glass from her corkscrew curls.

"I can't believe it! You *are* a demon." She craned her head toward the door, her breath catching. "Have I died and gone to heaven?"

Here we go again, she thought as she recalled Gerardo's enamored reaction to Rafe earlier. "No, Serah. We're still in Connolly Park, Michigan." Leaning in, she whispered. "The man's a homophobe, by the way."

"So what, he could be an ax murderer for all I care. He's got major drool factor." She smiled up at Rafe. "I'm sorry my friend's being rude. Why not come in and help us tidy up?"

Rafe shrugged and skimmed his fingers through his

silky mane. "Your friend hasn't invited me in. I can't enter until welcome."

"You came into my shop earlier." Lucy arched a brow. "How do you explain that?"

Rafe threw back his head in a throaty roar of laughter that sent her heart fluttering. *That homophobic, pheromone-inducing bastard.* "Your sign said, 'Open. Come on in.'" His eyes flickered. "Then you ordered me to leave."

"What are you? A vampire?" Lucy asked as she pulled a broom from the closet. Then again, with the amount of glass on the floor, she doubted ten brooms would help. At Rafe's lack of answer, she sucked in a deep breath. "Fine, come on in. How's that, big guy?"

Serah paced the shop, mumbling beneath her breath. "This is terrible. What are you going to do?"

Truth be told, she had no idea. And even scarier, she didn't care. Her dream lay in front of her, in a pile of glass and a giant ocean upon the floor. "Yeah, sucks, doesn't it?"

Serah grabbed her by the shoulders. "Don't you care?"

"Do not touch her," Rafe ordered. He leapt in the air and pulled Serah away. "You need to ask her permission."

What was the deal with asking permission? "She's my friend, that's permission enough."

"Very well," Rafe said. "But heed my warning for future reference. A mortal may never touch a demon without permission."

Not this again. "Not you too! How in the hell can I be a demon? I have two very *mortal* parents."

"Succubus," Rafe mumbled with a shake of his head.

"Suck a what?" Serah asked, interrupting the not-so-private conversation.

Rafe grabbed Lucy and turned her head to face him. "You're a succubus. A sex demon."

Yeah right! Because she was just screaming sex. "And I bet you're the pope come to save me from eternal damnation?"

Rafe pulled her closer, their lips inches apart. His breath danced along her lips and she ached to kiss him. *Absolutely nuts!*

His eyes glowed hot and angry, leaving her hungry. "We have serious problems, succubus, so I wouldn't joke." He took her chin between his thumb and forefinger and inched her head up. The action, even though forceful, held gentle care. His gaze smoldered like hot embers. Lucy's body quivered with need.

"I am not a succubus, demon, or whatever. Do I look like I'm seeping sexual energy?" But he certainly seeped plenty of it.

Rafe's breath teased her cheek. "Your energy was latent. Opening the chest has changed that." His lips remained centimeters from hers. *Kiss me,* her mind urged. *What the heck?*

"I know what you're trying to do, my dear Lucia. It won't work. It only works on humans." He ripped himself away and turned his back to her.

Lucy exhaled a deep breath. "Oh, so you're a demon, too?" She turned to her friend who stood still, broom in hand. "Hey, Serah, do you believe this?"

"I don't know," she replied as she swept up the shards of glass with her own broom. "You obviously have some powers. How do you explain what happened?" She gave Rafe a once-over. "So are you going to introduce me or what?"

Lucy sighed. "My bad. Mr. Rafael Deleon, meet my friend Serah SanGermano."

The wannabe demon bowed. "Call me Rafe."

Serah nodded and extended her hand in greeting. "Nice to meet you."

He took her hand in a hearty shake. "I wish your friend here were more accepting of her condition, as you are."

"So say I am in fact a demon," Lucy countered. "What'll happen to me?"

Rafe crossed his arms. "You'll need to feed… soon."

"I suppose since I am a suck-you-whatever, I need to suck someone's blood?" She turned to Serah and smiled. "Give me your wrist, baby."

Rafe rolled his eyes. "Your humor does little to help the situation. A succubus feeds on the sexual energy of men."

"Sounds fun," she replied with a wink. "Let's get it on then." Bonus if he accepts. The way her body acted, she hoped to hell he would. But sensing the hot and cold vibe this man gave off, she doubted he would. One could hope, right?

"I'm not a mortal. I will be of little use to you." Rafe blew out an exasperated breath. "Perhaps it would be better if we discuss this in the morning."

Lucy nodded. "Sounds good. I'll meet you at eight a.m. at the Starbucks on A-Line Road."

"I can't leave you alone. You and your friend are in danger. Belial will come for you and the chest."

"Oh please!" As much as she fought the truth, she

knew something was happening. It was in her blood. It kept her alert... *wanting*. "Fine. We'll go to my house. What about Serah?"

"She'll have to come with us for the time being." Rafe roved around the salon, gathering their coats. "I need something to cover the chest. When the handprint is exposed to the moonlight, it becomes a beacon. Every demon on Earth will know where we are."

Lucy grabbed a styling cape from the back of her chair, brandishing the purple nylon as if she were a matador tempting a bull. "Voila!"

She threw the cape down, letting it drape across the chest, and turned to Serah. "Are you okay? You took quite a hit."

Serah nodded. "Yeah, I'm fine. Just a little frazzled."

"You really think I'm a demon?"

Serah shrugged. "Something's going on. Look at your shop."

She did have a point. How many boxes came with a free fireworks display and light show—and a hunk with glowing silver eyes, of course?

But Lucy Gregory? A demon? What would her mom say about that? She didn't even want to dwell on that reaction. Another thing her mom could add to her long list of disappointments.

Throwing on a coat, she heaved a sigh. "I know. I'm just trying to understand this all. Imagine if it were you?"

"I get your point, Lucy." Serah brushed her fingers through brunette curls. "Yeah, I'd do the same. I'm such an angel, you know."

What a bunch of bull. "Yeah, you go on and think that."

Rafe cleared his throat. "We don't have time for idle

chitchat, women." He scooped the chest beneath his arm as if it were a weightless feather. *Amazing*. "The longer you dawdle, the quicker Belial's guards will find us."

Belial? He'd mentioned that name earlier. "Who?" she asked, grabbing her friend and pulling her toward the door.

"One of the kings of Hell. There is only one higher than he," Rafe explained as he ushered them toward the door. His hand on her back sent jolts of excitement ripping through her veins. You'd think he was the sex demon.

"Let me guess?" Lucy flashed a wry smile. "Lucifer, himself?"

She wrinkled her nose. *Hell no!* Their names sounded way too similar. *Hi! My name is Lucia. My daddy's the Prince of Darkness.*

"*He's* not my father, is he?"

Rafe, sensing her displeasure, traced his fingers lightly across her shoulder. *Wow!* He was gentle when he wanted to be. "An unfortunate coincidence, I assure you."

It would have been a relief if what this man said were true. She bit her tongue. *Relief? Yeah right*. "So what's not to say this isn't just some weird dream?"

"If it's a dream, then how do you explain this?" Serah grabbed her arm and pinched.

Snapping her arm back, Lucy yelped. "Ouch!" Her brow furrowed, and she flashed a warning glare. "Whatever, Serah. Do that again and I'll kick you to the underworld and back."

"Let's go. Now." Rafe crossed his arms across his chest. He stood tall and formidable, his midnight hair whipping around his shoulders.

Talk about domineering. He certainly didn't beat

around the bush. In any normal circumstances, she'd buck it up and stand tall. Truth be told, it was almost three in the morning, and she was tired as hell. "Fine. Serah," she said, turning to her friend and grabbing her arm. "Let's go." After all, she had a futon. After an hour on that uncomfortable contraption, Rafe would be begging to leave.

Then again, did she really want him to?

Chapter 5

HE DIDN'T SLEEP.

He sat ramrod straight in her dilapidated La-Z-Boy. It was a hand-me-down and her favorite chair. Lucy couldn't believe her mom wanted to toss it. So what if it only opened halfway and the maroon upholstery was way beyond repairable. Leave it to an arrogant wannabe demon to steal it.

"Aren't you going to sleep?" she asked as she plopped onto the wrought iron futon. The chest beckoned her from the middle of the living room. Her fingers itched to touch it—open it.

Rafe scraped his fingers through his gorgeous locks. *Need help?* she asked to herself.

"I don't need to sleep." He reached down to the lever and pulled.

Impressive! A demon who knew how to operate an easy chair. "It only opens halfway."

Halfway between open and closed, Rafe shrugged and pulled back the lever. "These chairs are supposed to be comfortable."

"It is to me. Wanna trade?"

Rafe narrowed his gaze. "No, thank you."

"That's too bad. You can do some great tricks on this futon." She leaned against the back, pressing her chest forward. Her toes traced along the seat cushion. Was she coming on to him? It sure felt like it. Running her fingers through her hair, she threw back her head and sighed contentedly.

Rafe's eyes sparked. "You're coming into your time. You have to feed."

"Can't you feed me?" Her body throbbed and her heart thudded. Thank goodness Serah was conked out in the bedroom. This whole thing, despite the surrealism, scared Lucy. Heat seared through her as she gritted her teeth. She was alive, hungry, and needy. What was going on? "Please?"

Licking her lips, she crawled along the rose-hued, pancake-thin cushion and leaned over the futon to lock gazes. Rafe returned the gaze, his silver eyes glowing like the moon on a clear night. She smiled and batted her eyelashes like a little puppy begging for food. But she didn't want food. She wanted something else. She reached out her hand, her fingers longing to run through his hair. "So do I need permission? Since I'm a sex demon and all?"

"Depends on the reason for the touch."

Rafe reached out and, without a blink of an eye, grabbed her wrist and held firm. His eyes flickered like giant diamonds. Never had she seen eyes so silvery and bright. Heat crackled through her body, radiating from where he held her. If demon energy didn't affect her, she'd be a monkey's uncle. If they really were demons, that is. After all, didn't demons have horns and tails? She scrunched her brow in frustration.

"Lucia," Rafe said, his voice soft and soothing. "I know this is all foreign to you, but you need to cooperate." His gaze remained fixed and intense, showing not even a drop of warmth. He might be certifiable, but he was a serious, brooding, drop dead sexy nutcase. Just her luck!

She extracted her wrist from Rafe's loosening grip. "Yeah, just a little foreign," she replied with a snide grin. "So you just expect me to accept this? Sorry, Charlie. Things don't work that way for me." She turned her head toward the closed bedroom door down the hallway. "If you're trying to take advantage of someone, you're talking to the wrong girl." Not that Serah was naïve, but she was more accepting of the occult and that voodoo hoodoo. Lucy grinned, recalling the one time Serah convinced her to use a Ouija board. The only words that came from the *great beyond* were the words "Happy Birthday, bitch." *Ha!*

"Serah isn't the demon. You are." Rafe rubbed his chin and attempted to change his position in the chair. "In time, you'll see."

Lucy leaned against the rigid cushion of the futon. "Sure I will." Tucking her legs beneath her, she sighed. Yeah, she knew something weird was happening. What's not to say it wasn't her hormones finally come to haunt her. It had been over five years since she'd had sex, and an even longer time since she'd had good sex. "So, umm, Rafie-poo, if I'm a succubus, why have I been able to survive without doing the nasty?"

"You're only *part* succubus. There's mortal—and immortal—energy within you." At her blank stare, Rafe growled, deep, gravelly, and oh so sexy. "This is worse than I thought."

"What's so bad? I shut the box. I didn't see any of your demon buddies come flying out."

Rising from the chair, Rafe stalked toward her, his

eyes blazing. He grabbed her shoulders and brought her eye-to-eye, his smoldering glare melting her to mush. "They don't show themselves until the moon has completely left the Earth's shadow. We have approximately..." He reached into the pocket of his black leather coat and pulled out an old antique watch. Thank goodness Serah was in bed. She'd be drooling all over the timepiece—if she already wasn't drooling from Rafe's superhuman sexiness. "Two hours."

"Huh?"

Rafe took a deep exasperated breath. "Six in the morning. That's when the eclipse is over. Once the Moon leaves the Earth's reflection, they'll have enough energy to make their presence known." Tossing his hair to the side, he sucked in a deep breath. "I don't know which is worse. Having the chest opened up by a legion of Infernati or having it opened by a clueless succubus."

Oh, hell no! He didn't just call her clueless! Time to put her foot down! "Look here demon boy. I might be new to this whole succubus thing, but that doesn't mean I'm clueless."

Lucy's gaze burned as heat filled her body. This man irritated her more than her mom! But why in the hell did she like him so much, and how come she was beginning to buy his whole sex demon story? This, of course, irritated her even more. The hairs at the back of her neck crackled and sparks formed in her eyes. Clenching her fists into tight balls, she inhaled and exhaled deep hot breaths. Like a raging bull, she supposed. Sans the nose ring, of course. She'd save that for some other demon. One who sported cloven hooves. *Try wearing a pair of Serah's pointy toe pumps with those!* She shivered. Then again, the devil did wear Prada, right?

There she went, rambling in her own turbulent mind again. Curse Rafael Deleon. Then again, if he *truly* was a demon, wasn't he already cursed? And if she was a demon, did that mean she was cursed, too?

As if sensing the inner turmoil, Rafe vacated the recliner and took a seat next to her on the futon. Lifting her chin between his thumb and forefinger, he locked gazes with her. His silver eyes glowed in the soft light of the floor lamp poised tall in the corner behind the futon.

"I sense your unease, Lucia. I vow to protect you. You've nothing to fear. Fear only makes the dark stronger." The gentle caress of his fingertips, meant to comfort, sent bolts of every emotion she'd ever known racing through her body. Anger, joy, pain, sorrow, and lust. Especially lust. It electrified her. Made her heart burst into overdrive. Any faster and they'd need a defibrillator to bring her back.

"Rafe," she said. She wrapped her arms around his neck and did what she'd been longing to do all night. Her fingers danced along his skin and inched closer to the prize. What was the deal with this man's hair? Fingertips laced into sleek silky strands. With a soft whimper, she allowed his hair to cascade against her skin. She nibbled her lip and lowered her head to his shoulder, brushing her cheek against his. His stubbly chin rubbing against the softness of hers sent crackles of heated energy coursing through her. She had to kiss him. She'd be damned if she didn't. Then again, wasn't she already damned? Might as well go down happy.

"This shouldn't be happening," Rafe whispered, his

breath hot against her ear. His heartbeat echoed her own as he pulled her closer to his rock-hard chest. It felt so good.

"What?" she asked, with a daring flick of her tongue along his neck. Sizzling heat raced through her, exploding in her toes. "This?" With more courage than she knew she possessed, she pulled his face to hers.

It was now or never. She straddled his hips and ground her body against his. With a devilish grin, she lowered her lips to his, reveling in the warm breath dancing along her aching skin. Breathing in the scent of exotic spice and male sexiness, she moaned. Usually Lucy would be embarrassed about acting all hot and horny for someone she just met. Right now, she didn't care.

"Lucia…"

"Lucy. Only my mother and her cronies call me Lucia, and I'll be damned if I let any of them ruin the mood." She brushed her lips against his, taking in the sizzles that erupted between them.

Sucking in a deep breath, Rafe growled against her lips, the vibrations rippling through her entire body. "This is impossible," he murmured, crushing her against him.

Her nipples tightened against her bra and T-shirt as they brushed against the hardness of his chest. Running her hands up, under his tight T-shirt, she let the electricity crackle within. She threw her head back in pleasure as she felt her arousal. Then she felt his, straining against that tight leather. Thank goodness she wasn't the only one who was turned on. With a wide smile, she traced her finger against the firmness of his lips. Perhaps she could soften them some. "Kiss me, Rafe. You know you want to."

"You know not what you do," he whispered, lacing his fingers through her choppy hair. His breath teased her lips.

"Enlighten me, then." Her hands moved down his shoulders to splay against his back. "I need an instructor to teach me the ins and outs of becoming a sex demon." And as far as she could tell, the bulge in his pants said he'd be a very willing one, too. With a small sigh, she pressed her overheated core against his erection.

"Your need for sexual energy has clouded your judgment, Lucy. You'll find no nourishment in lying with another demon." Despite his stony words, he traced a long finger down her cheek.

"I just want to kiss," she whispered. But if he wanted to do more, she wouldn't object. She turned her head and swirled her tongue around the tip of his finger. "Please?"

Rafe groaned from deep inside his chest as he crushed her against him. She enveloped herself in the warmth of his steely chest and brought her lips to his. She wouldn't be denied. With as much confidence as she could muster, she pressed her lips closer to his and traced her tongue along the crease. Red hot heat raced from her tongue through her entire body. What a rush!

To her utter delight, Rafe returned the kiss. Rough, yet gentle, his tongue pushed its way against her lips and swept inside her mouth. Electricity crackled in the air and rippled through their bodies. Her mouth, in total acquiescence, parted, allowing him even further access. Then again, it didn't need that much prodding. Despite being a demon, he tasted delicious, like exotic spices and peppermint. How odd. Not wanting to dwell on demon dental hygiene, she intensified the kiss.

Her tongue snaked along his and instant friction sizzled inside their mouths. If touching the chest was the best thing ever, then this was the absolute best-est. It was like their mouths were made for each other, swirling in a delicious tango of tongues.

Screw the tango. She wanted a full-out Lambada. Rafe obviously did too—he grew harder against her. Poor pants, if he got any bigger, they would certainly split. Try to explain that to a tailor!

Taking Rafe's lower lip into her mouth, she nibbled and sucked with more hunger than she knew she possessed. To her surprise, he wrapped his arms around her and eased her onto the futon. *Yum! A take charge kind of guy.* She wouldn't complain.

He moved from her lips down to her neck and swirled his tongue along her ear. She shivered in intense pleasure as he nibbled and sucked. *Oh boy!* He'd found her sweet spot.

Holy hotcakes!

"If you keep doing that," she breathed out. "I'll need more than just a kiss."

She allowed her hand to run down his granite-like pecs to the eight-pack that were his abs, and lower to the muscles just above his waistline. Locating the buttons on his fly, she fumbled with them. Just her luck! He wasn't making this easy for her at all.

"Lucy," he murmured in her ear. With dexterity, he inched his hands up under her T-shirt and swirled his fingers against her skin. *Oh dear!* Cupping her breasts through her cotton bra, he traced her nipples lightly through the fabric.

Moving back to her mouth, he devoured them with as much hunger as she felt. Her lips were a feast for his taking, and she didn't care. He lashed his tongue within her mouth as his hips undulated against hers.

This would be more than a kiss.

Her body zinged with that knowledge. With a savagery she didn't know she possessed, she ripped open Rafe's fly, sending the buttons shooting in every direction. Definitely gave new meaning to button-fly. Metal buttons, to boot! Yep, she was clearly worked up.

Rafe grabbed her arms and pulled them away. "No." His voice, despite his desire, came out firm. "We cannot." Grasping her hands over her head, he continued the kiss. She couldn't fault him, and this commanding role really turned her on. He lowered his mouth to hers, gently swirling his tongue against her lips. She arched her hips into his, rubbing them against his erection. He certainly knew how to prolong the effect. This was definitely what she'd been missing the last ten years of her life. She'd never felt so empowered, ever. Wrapping her legs like a giant vice around Rafe's waist, she thrust upward. "Please."

Whoa! She was horny to the infinite power.

"Holy shit!"

The sound of Serah's voice filling the room sent the heat right from her body. Lucy glanced down at Rafe's package. It went from his big friend to his little friend in a flash. She attempted an icy glare at her friend. "Do you mind?"

Serah simply rolled her eyes. "Get a room already."

"Kind of hard when someone's already crashed it."

With a reluctant sigh, she pulled herself from Rafe's embrace and sat against the hard cushion of the futon. Was this thing made in the Middle Ages? It would've made an excellent rack.

"So much for your demon story," Serah said, flashing Rafe a wink. "Didn't you say demons weren't affected by the succubus charm?" She threw her head back in laughter. "Man, you two were stuck together like Super Glue."

Lucy glared at her friend. "Don't make me put that glue on your lips." And, being an owner of a hair and nail spa, she had plenty of it.

Rafe grunted, fumbled with his fly, then grunted some more. Grunting men weren't supposed to be attractive. She remembered Tim the Tool Man and his buddy Al and cringed. But there was something sexy about Rafe's grunt that caused warmth to spread throughout her body. And she enjoyed every minute of it.

Rising from his perch on the futon, Rafe glanced over to the floor lamp, bemusement filling his face. He reached up and grabbed a stray button from the top of its flat glassy surface.

Lucy covered her mouth and hid her smirk. "Those could be dangerous weapons."

"We need to move." He glanced up at the wall clock. *Whew, thank goodness*. She didn't want to see Serah go all orgasmic over his fancy pocket watch. "It's almost six a.m."

After all his buttons had been retrieved from various corners of the room, Rafe pocketed them. So much for sewing being one of his demonic powers. Cool! Male demons were just as inept as the human kind.

"So what's on tap today?" Serah asked, sounding a bit more chipper than Lucy would've liked. Lucky girl. At least someone got some sleep.

Lucy glanced at Serah and back to Rafe then, looked down at her pink painted toenails. "I don't know about you guys, but I have to go to the shop and survey the damage."

"There's no damage."

Lucy quirked a brow. "No damage? I saw the insides of the salon."

Rafe crossed his arms in front of him. "I sent for some help. Your shop is spotless. No one but us know about the legion of demons you let escape."

Wow, demons had their own crime scene cleanup unit. "How very helpful of you."

"It's the least I could do." Rafe lounged against the edge of the futon and crossed his legs. He looked so sexy standing there with that gorgeous hair flowing around his face. "After all, we can't have our secrets revealed."

She shrugged and heaved a sigh. It wasn't like she knew demons actually existed. Fancy that. Guess she wasn't agnostic anymore. "Yeah, I suppose that would suck." She took a breath as she tried to find the right words to say.

In the blink of an eye, a bright flash of lightning streaked through the sky reflecting against the flecks of snow dancing in the air. Where the hell was the thunder?

"What the hell?" Serah squeaked. Then more flashes lit the sky right over the vicinity of the shop.

"So much for the demonic cleanup crew," Lucy muttered, slumping onto the futon. So what if it was as comfortable as a torture rack. Any remaining heat left her body, cold radiating in its place. From the look of the lightning in the distance, her shop was screwed. Probably because *she* was too busy trying to get screwed.

Chapter 6

RAFAEL TRIED TO DIGEST THE ENTIRE EVENING, FROM Lamia's inopportune attack to the sight of Lucy standing over the chest, the golden aura surrounding her to... No, he wouldn't remember that, no matter how much he might have enjoyed it. What happened was impossible. A demon was supposed to be immune to the succubus's seduction. Yet in a matter of a few minutes she had him caving. Then again, the minute he spotted her that afternoon in the salon, he knew he'd been ensnared. And the minx didn't even know what she'd done.

Maybe he was losing his demonic powers. Bloody hell, he was being demoted. His third strike. It didn't surprise him one bit if the Fore-Demons diminished him to impish duties.

Glancing over at Lucia, heat swelled within him. She sat on the hard settee she'd called a futon, her head in her hands. Her friend sat next to her, wrapping her arm around Lucy's shoulder. Suddenly he felt like an intruder. With long strides, he walked to the window and took in the sight. Lightning zinged across the sky, relentless, as the loosed Infernati warriors searched for the chest. If only she unleashed some Paladin Demons too. Not that he wanted a war on Earth, but his options were dwindling.

An incessant noise echoed through the room, coming from his leather jacket. Blasted contraption, but Nic insisted he bring it along. He hated modern technology, but it was the most convenient way to keep in touch on Earth. Glancing over at Lucy and her friend, who both stared with bemusement, he fumbled inside his pocket and pulled out the mobile phone. He flipped it up and put it to his ear. "Speak."

"The salon is clean, milord." The familiar feminine voice rankled his nerves. Leave it to the Fore-Demons to send her. "I just love cleaning up your messes."

"Stubble it."

Kalli chuckled, a deep vibration that echoed in his ear. "Please, Rafe. That expression died out at least two hundred years ago."

Rafael contemplated throwing the phone into the wall. Struggling to maintain his anger, he gripped the phone tightly. "Whatever. Is there danger? The succubus wants to get a few things."

"The succubus?" he heard Lucy say, her voice indignant. "My name's Lucy, you jerk."

Rafael craned his head and narrowed his eyes into a scowl, yet on the inside he cringed. But he needed to stay as distant as possible, lest he fall under the spell she didn't know she'd spun.

Lucy stood there, her eyes blazing, hands on her hips. Her glare burned deep. Even when angry, she was beautiful. The way her lower lip jutted out, the intense spark in her hazel eyes. He needed to find a way to steel himself, or he was doomed. Never had a demon been ensnared by a succubus—or an incubus for that matter. Leave it to him to be the first.

"Demons have cell phones?" Lucy asked, her voice laced with sarcasm. Her eyes narrowed into a searing glare. "I suppose you've got an iPod too?"

Lucy's friend smacked her arm. Luckily it was only a small slap, or she might not have blown it off. "Shh. Can't you see he's on the phone?"

"I'm worried about my shop."

Rafe pulled the phone away from his ear. "Your shop is fine." Reluctantly, he put the phone back to his ear.

"Is it safe?" he asked Kalli.

"What's going on? It sounds like there's more than a succubus there."

"Her friend," he replied tersely. "The chest belongs to her."

"What?" Kalli's question boomed in his ear. "You're just telling me now?"

Rafael adjusted the phone and stole a glance at Lucy. She paced back and forth, clenching and unclenching her fists. He didn't blame her one bit. He'd act the same way. "I only just found out myself."

"I'll bring it up to the Fore-Demons and see what they recommend." There was a brief pause. "The sun is out. I believe our loosed friends have realized the chest is no longer here."

"So they can come back?"

Kalli huffed. "For now. Shit!" There was an annoying scratching sound followed by some muffled arguments. "...I'm the cleaning lady. Here's my card."

"Kalli, is everything all right?" He couldn't hide the concern in his voice.

Lucia stopped mid-stride and turned to face him, her eyes filled with horror. "What is it?" she asked, her breath catching.

"Kalli?"

Kalli continued her discussion. "Lucia Gregory hired

me. Feel free to call her." She blew out a deep breath that rumbled in his ear. "Some of her employees have arrived and they aren't pleased." Kalli chuckled. "Can't blame them."

Rafael could only imagine. The last time he'd seen Kalli, in the eighties, she'd worn pink-and-white striped hose and a magenta skirt. Her hair had stood tall, teased to high hell. She'd looked ridiculous, but apparently that's how they dressed back then. Another reason he'd chosen to stay in the underworld. Humans and their strange fashion habits. At least fashion had improved slightly in the last twenty-five years. He looked down at his clingy leather breeches. Well, almost. "We're on our way."

"Good. See you." The call ended.

Lucy clenched her fists. From the tone of the conversation, it was urgent. There was no way in hell—she needed to stop using that word—she'd let anything happen to her shop.

Shutting his cell phone, Rafe turned to face her. *A cell phone for a demon? Yeah Right! How good was Hell's wireless signal?*

"You're right, we will." She didn't spend the last five years to see her dream erupt in a fountain of exploding shampoo bowls. "We shouldn't have left."

Throwing on his coat, Rafe glowered. He stuffed his phone in the pocket and stormed to the closet. With more force than she liked, he ripped open the door. "I wasn't about to risk your or your friend's lives."

"I didn't seem to be in danger. There was tons of

glass flying, and not one scratch on my body. How do you explain that?" *Take that you sexy knave!*

Rafe yanked her coat off the hanger and threw it at her. "It takes a lot to injure a demon."

Of course he'd come back with an answer like that. How predictable. Then again, she wasn't the only one in the shop with barely a scratch. "I understand that. But what about Serah? If she's not a demon, why wasn't she hurt?"

"Luck, I guess," he muttered.

What was the deal with this man? He hadn't said much since they met. It was as if he distanced himself. But there was that part of him—she stifled a grin—that had no qualms about being up-close and personal. He wasn't a complete jerk, and his gentle caress showed he cared. Men! Even ones of the demon variety would remain a mystery.

"I suppose." But she still wasn't convinced. The glint in his silvery eyes showed he hid something.

She glanced over to Serah who stared out the window. The lightning bolts had since faded as sunlight danced with the fluffy snow.

She played with one of the ornaments on the artificial Christmas tree. If Lucy had any choice, she'd throw it in the trash, but her mom insisted she *get into the spirit*. So she got a small tree from the local Goodwill and *borrowed* some of her mom's lights and ornaments.

Lucy wasn't a real spiritual person. And now she knew why. Church probably wasn't a popular hangout for demons. She stifled a chuckle remembering the many times her mom tried to get her to church. She'd laugh and say, "If I walked into a church, I'd probably burst into flames."

Who knew? Maybe she would have. How ironic!

Now she had more important things to think about, like her shop. With a quick toss, she threw her coat on. "We better get going." Rafe still acted pretty hush-hush about everything, and she was sick of being kept in the dark. "Since you're not that forthcoming with information."

Rafe grabbed her shoulders and gazed down at her, the silver in his eyes burning her, filling her with need. "In time, Lucy." Despite the intensity of his gaze, his voice calmed her nerves but stirred something else deep inside. *Call the fire department!*

Pushing her hormones to the side, Lucy clenched her fists. "I've spent the last five years pouring my blood and sweat into that salon." She took long even breaths as she fought for the words to say.

Two could play this game. She'd show this hunk of a man she wasn't one of the weak-minded females he was used to. *I'm a businesswoman, damn it!*

"Your answer is unacceptable. Tell me what's going on—now."

"The shop is fine." Rafe's grip on her shoulders loosened. "Your co-workers—not so much. They want to string our cleaner from the rafters."

A wide grin spread across her face. "Thank the... whatever for Frankie and Gerardo."

At that precise moment, her own cell phone rang. The familiar sounds of Justin Timberlake filled the room. Rafe arched a brow. Serah giggled, and Lucy simply shrugged as she pulled the phone off the coffee table and flipped it open.

"Hello?"

Frankie's frazzled voice greeted her. "Lucy, some lady is here claiming she's been hired to clean the shop." He rambled on about purple-and-red dreadlocks, tattoos, and body piercings. "What should I do?"

"Uhh, let her clean?"

"You sure?" he asked, clearly shocked. Silence followed. "But I am amazed. I've never seen the shop so clean."

"Cool. Where's Gerardo?" she asked nonchalantly.

Frankie giggled. "He's busy interrogating the cleaning lady."

Lucy chuckled. "We'll get there before he resorts to any finger-breaking. I need to freshen up." She took a glance into the mirror hanging on the far wall. Or maybe not.

Her face took on a glow she'd never noticed before. Her eyes were different too, like two giant topazes set in gold. The hair she expected to hang limp around her face now flipped up all on its own. And her lips! Plumper and rosier than ever! She could only gape in shock. If being a succubus meant she never had to do her own hair, sign her up! She loved doing other people's hair, but her own was another matter.

"Lucy, hon? Are you there?" Frankie's concerned voice brought her back to the world.

"Do you believe you're a demon now?" Serah quipped. "If only I could look that good." She bit her lip. "Not that you weren't already pretty, but—"

Lucy threw Serah a warning gaze and went back to talking to Frankie.

"Tell Gerardo to stop with the CSI routine, and I'll

be right there." Modeling, photography, all sixteen million *CSI* spin-offs—to name a few of Gerardo's guilty pleasures.

"Sure thing, hot stuff. Smoochies."

Hot stuff? What the hell? Frankie was calling her names he usually reserved for men he found attractive? Would he call Rafe *hot stuff*? He certainly was hot in her book.

"Smoochies?" Lucy arched a brow, even though her friend couldn't see it. "Frankie, are you okay?"

"Just fine, baby. Can't wait to see you." He kissed her through the phone. *Eww!* Some people would think her rude, but the way Frankie talked was like she was his newest fling.

"Uh, okay. See you in a few." Before Frankie could whisper any more sweet nothings in her ear, she folded the phone shut.

She smiled at Serah who stood ready, wearing her puffy Juicy Couture coat, looking like an Aspen snow bunny. "That's weird."

"It's Frankie," Serah replied. "Were you expecting normal?"

Lucy chuckled. "Okay, let me rephrase. That was weird—for Frankie."

Rafe crossed his arms, his ripped arms bulging against the leather of his coat. God, he was sexy. Was her tongue wagging? It sure felt like it. She stole another glance at Serah. Hers certainly was. An intense shock of jealousy streaked through Lucy. *Whoa! What was going on?*

"Is everything handled?"

"Frankie's handled, but your friend is about to experience *CSI: Gerardo*."

Serah cringed. "Ouch."

Rafe arched a brow. "*CSI*? Isn't that a TV show?"

"Which one?" Serah chuckled.

"There's more than one?" Rafe's brow furrowed in consternation. Despite his severe façade, it was cute.

"There's like two or three set in different cities across the U.S." She shook her head. She had more important things to do than stand here talking about television shows and their many spin-offs. "Okay, let's go. I have a salon to inspect."

Serah snapped to attention and saluted her. "Sir! Yes, Sir!"

She narrowed her eyes into an intense glare and contemplated giving Serah her own special salute—the one-fingered kind.

"How on Earth do you drive this sardine can?" Serah's knee jabbed her through the back of her seat. "Oops. Sorry." With an exhausted sigh, she wriggled her legs over to the side.

"Easy," Lucy replied, glancing at her through the rearview mirror. "I drive alone."

Serah squirmed as she turned to sit sideways in the seat. "Remind me to drive next time."

Taking a left onto A-Line Road, Lucy shivered. "I prefer to arrive in one piece, thank you very much."

Serah rolled her eyes. Didn't she realize Lucy could see her in the mirror? Then again, it was Serah. She probably did. "I'm a good driver. You just bring me bad luck."

"How do you explain that time in Chicago when I

was three hours away scrubbing shampoo out of someone's hair?"

Serah huffed. "I was thinking about you."

"Yeah, whatever." The light ahead of them turned yellow and Lucy slowed to a stop. Didn't these lights know they were in a hurry? It was as if the traffic light gods had it out for her, giving them every red light on the street. Both of them.

"How much further?" Rafe asked, bashing his knee into the dashboard. "I despise modern transportation."

"Me too, especially when I have to fill the tank." She often wondered what riding in a carriage or stage coach would've been like. She remembered the time she drove through northern Indiana and passed a bevy of Amish wagons. She shook her head. Way too slow. "It's faster, you know."

"True, but I prefer my comfort, Lucy."

She loved it when he said her name. The way it rolled off his tongue with his sexy English accent. She leaned back and exhaled deeply. "Sorry, but a Kia Rio was all I could afford. Maybe when I hit the big time, I'll get you that Mercedes."

"What the hell?"

Lucy looked in the rear view mirror at Serah, who nibbled her lip. "What?"

"I think we're being followed."

She rolled her eyes and opened her mouth to speak. "Oh—"

"Don't even say it!" Serah exclaimed with a huff.

She loved having a friend who could read her mind. Then again, that's why they were best friends. They had a bond. That bond had never faded since second grade, even when Serah had stolen her "I love NKOTB" shirt in junior high. She smiled. She wasn't ashamed of her childhood infatuations. Jordan had always been her favorite.

Rafe turned his head, his hair flying around his face. His eyes narrowed into a thoughtful gaze. "Damn, we are." His tone, however lacked urgency.

"You don't seem worried," Lucy mused out loud.

She stole another glance behind her. Men of all shapes, sizes, and ages ran down the road, snow pelting their faces. They waved their hands to and fro waving someone down.

Me?

Cars honked their horns. At first, she thought they honked at the marathon of men—until the guy next to her rolled down his window and blew her a kiss. He held up a piece of paper with his phone number scrawled across it, flailing it in his hand and shouting like he was having a grand mal seizure.

With both brows quirked up, she nodded at him. She just didn't have the heart to say, "Go away, you freak."

He held his pinkie and thumb to his ear and mouthed the words, "Call me." With a wink, he rolled his window back up and drove down the road.

Her eyes just about popped out of her head. "What the heck?"

"Your sexual energy is off the chart," Rafe said. "This is worse than I thought."

"So you're saying these men only want me for my new superpowered hormones?" How utterly ironic. When you wanted a guy, they were never around. She stole another glance at Rafe. Or throwing off mixed signals. Then—when you didn't need them, they wouldn't leave you alone.

"Do you know what this means?" Rafe's gaze drilled holes into her.

"I'm the newest demonic It-girl?" she asked with a hit of sarcasm. "I don't know—what?"

Rafe growled. *Yum!* "It means you're no ordinary succubus."

"Of course, you said I was only half-sexy, remember?"

Rafe shook his head, his eyes scanning her from head to toe. Tingles raced through her body. "You shouldn't have this much power."

"Maybe I'm special?" she quipped. Then her mind spun with questions. "Maybe some of the chest's energy is inside me."

Rafe shook his head again. "That's a good explanation, Lucy. But the chest has no energy. The energy now in it is yours. It is your energy that opened it and it's your energy that is keeping it shut."

So now she was a walking sexpot and couldn't do anything about it? Life couldn't get any more fucked up. For five years she'd been content being alone, but now it seemed she was heading toward a stampede—literally—of rampaging testosterone.

"Unbelievable," she muttered. What on Earth—or more appropriately, hell—did she do to deserve this?

With a quick right, she turned into Green's Corner shopping center. Thank God they were almost there.

Who's my maker now?

All of a sudden, a man dropped down in front of the car, his gaze challenging and his stance ready to fight. "Something tells me that he's not one of the good guys."

"You would be correct." Rafe snorted. "Belial hasn't changed. Sending his goons to do his dirty work."

Serah squeaked in the back seat. "Demons can come out in the daylight?"

"Helio-demons. They pull their energy from the sun."

A sarcastic chuckle escaped her mouth. "Great! A walking solar panel. Lucky for us, it's cloudy right now."

They had two options. Either A—run into the mob of crazy obsessive fans, or B—fight a sun demon on a cloudy day. Did Britney Spears have such monumental decisions? Then again, she *did* run over a photographer's foot to escape the paparazzi. If this was what celebrities went through on a daily basis, she didn't envy them one bit.

She settled for option C—putting the pedal to the metal and running over the evil demon. With a wicked grin, she ground her foot on the gas. The car sputtered and shook as it accelerated. Stupid little four-banger. Then again, how would she know she would have to go zero to sixty in five seconds when she bought it. At least it got good gas mileage. If the thing in front of her was a demon, would it have blood and guts? Hopefully not. However, she'd rather take chances with one demon than five hundred pheromone-intoxicated men.

"What in Hades are you doing?" Rafe ground out. He gripped the *oh-shit* handle tight in his hand and braced himself in his seat.

Puhlease! This guy was sexy and could kiss with the best of them, but he needed to lighten up. All her jokes went straight over his head. "I'm taking matters into my own hands," she said, shifting into fourth gear. She made a mental note: *Next time buy an automatic*.

"I forbid it."

Forbid this, asshole.

"Look," she said, pointing behind her. Two Santa Clauses—sounded like a grammar lesson gone bad—tore at each other's suits, throwing lefts and rights. One hiked up his knee and kicked the other in his gigantic gut. The man gripped his stomach in pain and doubled over. Guess it wasn't padding, after all. The other smiled triumphantly and raised his hands over his head in victory. The other Santa reached up and grabbed his belt, pulling his red velvet pants down. His victorious smile turned into a shocked *Oh*. Reaching down, he covered his Christmas *package*—thank goodness. Why this Santa chose to go commando would remain a mystery to her, and she was quite happy keeping it that way. With a quick turn, he ran back down the street, tripping on his pants, two giant cheeks jiggling like bowls full of jelly. Lucy shook her head, struggling to block the image that played like a low-rate B movie out of her mind.

Serah threw her hands over her eyes. "I'm mentally scarred."

"Trust me, you aren't the only one." Lucy shivered in revulsion.

Rafe simply shrugged. "Demon it is."

Chapter 7

"I FIGURED YOU'D COME AROUND TO MY WAY OF thinking." Lucy slammed her foot on the gas and the car lunged forward. Rafe's grip tightened on the handle and his face scrunched.

The *thing* stood foreboding with yellow glowing eyes, fangs glinting in the sunlight that peeked through puffy clouds. Menacing evil flashed across its face as clumps of matted hair tufted its cheeks. Cold and lifeless apathy shone in its expression. Soulless—if there truly was such a thing. Evil radiated from the being like a case of bad BO. From the glare in its eyes, this would not be easy.

All of a sudden another being fell from the sky. A cute little ball of fur that stood about three feet tall, it spread its elongated arms wide, sending a huge ball of energy at the other demon. The monkey-like being jumped high into the air and did a back flip, landing right on top of his shoulders.

Lucy spun the steering wheel and veered to the right, tires squealing in protest. Thank goodness the parking lot was empty. "What the hell was that?"

"An imp," Rafe said, loosening his grip on the handle. "Just what we need." He shook his head.

She arched an eyebrow. "An imp? It looked more like a monkey on speed." She pulled into a parking spot and put the car in park. Looking into her rearview mirror, she blinked. The imp had the demon pinned and jumped up and down on him. "Are you sure I'm not dreaming? 'Cause this is fucked-up."

Rafe shook his head. "I wish I could tell you something different."

Maybe someone had laced her vanilla latte with acid. Why else would she be having such crazy hallucinations? Then again, experts did say no two people ever share the same hallucination. Damn the experts. Why did they always have to be—well—experts?

"Fucked-up is an understatement, girl." Serah shuddered. "Let's hurry before your group of fawning admirers finds you."

Lucy slid her keys into her pocket and, with caution, swung the door open. The stampeding men had since stopped to help the imp take care of the evil demon.

"Wow," was all she could mutter. A few straggling men jogged toward her. Would they ever give up? In normal circumstances, she'd be all for a little attention from the opposite sex. But this much attention wasn't what she had in mind.

"Hey baby!" a bespectacled, pocket protector–sporting guy shouted. His pants came well above his waist, giving her a glimpse of white socks and just-as-white ankles. *Hell no!*

"Hot damn! You're one sexy broad," an overly muscled, steroid-popping body builder said. Maybe their brains shrunk when their muscles inflated. He flexed his muscles, his pecs bobbing against the tight wife-beater shirt. How long would it take for those nipples to shrink in the cold?

Someone grabbed her hand. Shocks of energy raced

through her. *Rafe*. He looked at her, his gaze urgent. "Let's move!"

Not one to object, she put her feet to icy asphalt and allowed Rafe to pull her across the street to her shop. Why on Earth did she choose this building? Oh, that's right. It was all she could afford. Then again, she loved it. It was her baby, after all.

They dodged cars, ice slicks, and men, of course. There wasn't any way to avoid them. Catcalls, horns, and men shouting the worst-ever pickup lines echoed in her ears.

"This sucks." She shook her head in frustration, petulance lacing her voice. "Make it stop."

Only six hours into her stint as a succubus and she was already overwhelmed. Just what everyone needed—a sex demon near mental breakdown! With a deep sigh, she pulled her coat tightly against her body.

"Kalli will help you," Rafe whispered in her ear as he pulled her closer to him. Shivers of excitement ripped down her spine. She might be a succubus, but she hungered for one six-foot-four of pure demon muscle. None of these puny men following her had anything on him.

As if sensing her excitement, Rafe pulled away. What the hell? She knew he enjoyed that kiss. Mr. Happy Pants had shown her that earlier. Now he was cold, distant, and utterly aloof. Maybe it was because she forgot to shower and put on deodorant before they left.

Stupid, stupid, arrogant man.

She shifted her gaze to her shop. The early morning sun reflected against the windows. Her eyes burned. She tried shielding them with her arm, but nothing helped.

"That's bright." Add the white fluffy snow to the mix, and it was a migraine waiting to happen.

"Your new eyes need to adjust." Rafe, ever the gentleman, thrust a pair of sunglasses in her hand. "You'll need to wear these most of the day."

With a huff, she pushed the glasses on. "How do I explain the shades, smarty-pants?"

Serah trudged up from behind. "You got shit-faced and your eyes are all red."

"If only that were the truth." She turned to face Serah. Despite the beating she almost gave her last night, not a hair on her pretty little head was injured.

Serah's mouth gaped open. "Prada! He got you to wear Prada? Dang, Rafe. You're good."

Lucy narrowed a glare at her friend. "I can be a fashionista—when I want to."

"You look stylin'." Serah smiled. "You should do it more often."

"Sit and spin," Lucy said, flipping the bird.

Serah grinned. "You'll hate yourself in fifty years when arthritis sets in."

"Cool, then my finger will be ready to salute you when we're old and in our rocking chairs."

Rafe shook his head as he pulled the door open to the shop. "I have business on the other side. I trust Kalli to keep you safe."

Peering into the shop, Lucy's breath caught. The shampoo bowls shined brighter than they ever had since she bought them. The floor sparkled. The tiles were so clean she could've eaten off them if she wanted. Every fixture in the shop seemed to glow.

"Rafe? Is that you?" The voice, low and sultry, sent

a bolt of jealousy streaking through her. Dang, she had it bad for this man.

Emerging from the back office, she smiled. Her dreadlocks hung around her face in myriad reds, purples, and blues. A silver ring jutted from her lower lip and more dotted her eyebrows. Her ears were concealed by the mop that topped her head, but it was safe to assume they were equally decorated. She flung her rainbow hair to the side, revealing a tight purple and black lace bodice.

Her cups ran over—big time. Her black leather miniskirt gave way to ripped fishnets and huge honking-heel buckled combat boots. Not to be outdone, beautiful vines of ivy and flowers snaked up her arm and down her chest to hide beneath her bodice. Lucy wasn't one to get ink, but she did admire the art. This was some of the most beautiful inkwork she'd ever seen. No wonder Frankie and Gerardo flipped a lid.

"Enjoying the view?" Kalli asked with a cute chuckle. For all her dark facade, her smile radiated friendliness. She took Lucy's hand in hers and shook. "You must be Lucia. Nice to meet you."

"Thanks," was all she could mutter. "My shop looks great. Where are Frankie and Gerardo?"

Goth girl beamed. "It was nothing. A lot easier to fix than most Rafe's other messes." She flashed him a wicked smile.

Rafe crossed his arms and snorted. "I didn't do this."

"True, but why did I find demon blood out there on the street? Old blood too." Kalli wrinkled her nose and clucked her tongue. "I could smell it for miles."

Rafe's jaw tightened, clearly irritated by her

interrogation. "Lamia ambushed me before I could intercept the chest."

"Lamia? What's she doing here?" Kalli muttered something in a language Lucy didn't recognize. Greek maybe? "For God's sake, why didn't you say anything?"

Rafe clenched his fists into tight balls, his jaw throbbing harder. "It was late and my only concern was…" His voice drifted as his gaze drew Lucy in. "…the chest."

The chest? What about this "I'm here to protect you" baloney he rattled off earlier? She should've known. He was a man after all.

Lucy's heart sunk and a lump formed in her throat. "Your precious chest is fine, Rafe. You can go back to Hell now."

"Smooth move, ex-lax." Kalli shook her head. "Still the same. You've got a real way with words, Rafe."

Rafe narrowed his eyes and crossed his arms. "I can't bring the chest back until the loosed demons are rounded up, and we can't do that without Lucy."

Hello! She was standing right there. Was she supposed to wave her hands to get attention while they verbally sparred? From their intense glares and gazes, that answer would be yes. No way would she let this be an A and B conversation, so she would C her way in—one way or the other. "So how do I get the demons back in?" Obviously not with chocolate, that would be too easy. If only she had an easy button. Damn those TV commercials for making things look so simple.

"I need to guard the chest."

The door swung open. The ape-faced imp from earlier waddled in. "Nope. Rafael Deleon, you've been summoned," it said, sounding like Joe Pesci on helium.

"The Fore-Demons request your presence. I've been ordered to watch the chest."

No one would believe this crap. "A talking monkey? I've officially seen it all."

"What? An imp guarding the chest?" Rage boiled in Rafe's eyes. He clenched and unclenched his fists.

Grinning, the imp handed Rafe a piece of parchment. "Not just any imp. Your imp."

"Bloody hell," Rafe muttered. He crunched the fancy paper and threw it against the wall. "Can things get any more complicated?"

"Complicated?" The imp scratched its head then moved to its under-pit. How like a monkey! At least it didn't smell its finger. "I'm a blessing. I saved your asses back there."

It walked around the shop, eying everyone suspiciously. "Whoa! We gots lots of demons here." Scratching its butt, it approached Serah with cautious steps. "What in Tartarus?" Its eyes bugged out and it cringed as a squeak erupted from its mouth. What looked like fear sparked in its eyes as it scuttled back behind Rafe and attached itself to a leather-clad leg. Lucky SOB!

Now she was jealous of a wannabe monkey?

Rafe growled and shook his leg, sending the poor imp flying against the wall. "Enough!"

"Owwie!" the imp cried, rubbing its head. "That hurt. Not a good way to start our relationship."

Lucy arched a brow—a talent she was getting more proficient at. "What's the deal? It's kind of cute in a weird sort of way."

Serah shrugged. "Yeah, even though it doesn't like me."

Rafe crossed his arms across his chest and stood stony still. "I'm not at all amused with this."

"There isn't much that amuses you. Lighten up some." This coming from Kalli. She turned and shook her head at the imp. "Squeaky, I told you to wait until Rafe met with the council."

Squeaky? How appropriate. Lucy tried to stifle her snicker but failed miserably. Squeaky's fur-covered brow scrunched into a scowl, his hairy hands clenching into balls. "Sorry, I'm trying to get over the fact that you're an imp that looks like a monkey that sounds like a chipmunk."

Squeaky huffed, a sound like an annoying whistle. "I'm not a monkey. I'm a freakin' chimpanzee. I'm pretty suave, though. Right?"

Oh brother! Did this thing think he was an extra from *The Sopranos*?

"Uh, sure." She extended her hand to Squeaky, who had since given up Rafe's leg. "My name's Lucy. Thanks for saving our butts back there."

He smiled, revealing giant yellow teeth. "It's not my fault I got saddled with this body. I was busy teaching a lesson to some punks at the zoo and hopped into the first form I could find. Why in the hell couldn't I have been near the Antarctica exhibit? I've always wanted to be a penguin." Squeaky sighed. "Now I'm here, picking fleas from my stinky ass."

An imp who was a chimp that wanted to be a penguin. *Priceless*. "Well, chimps are cute, and an impish chimp is even cuter."

"What a woman! If I could take a human form, I'd give you a call."

"You can't take a human form?"

Squeaky shook his head. "Being an imp, I'm forced to take on the form of those less intelligent beasts. But I'm strong. I took your cousin's form, y'know?"

"Why is Rafe so ticked?" Lucy turned her head to glance over at the enigma of a man. He stood in the corner glowering as he punched a number into his cell phone.

Kalli snorted a chuckle. "Because instead of a tiger or a lion, or some other beast for a familiar, the Fore-Demons sent Squeaky the Wonder Chimp instead."

Talk about a blow to the male ego. "Chimps are intelligent, though."

"It's his familiar, an extension of his inner self. Seeing a part of you as a lower class primate isn't that great."

"Well, he *is* a man."

"More than you realize," Kalli said with a wink.

Rafe cleared his throat. "I am still here, Kalli. I'd appreciate it if you'd stop humoring yourselves at my expense."

"But it's so easy to ruffle your feathers." Kalli grinned, giving Rafe a playful punch to his shoulder.

Lucy's eyebrows arched. "Speaking of feathers, where are Gerardo and Frankie?"

"They are checking inventory in the back." Kalli grinned, clasping her hands in front of her. "What a great crew you have."

Lucy beamed. She couldn't get any better than Frankie and Gerardo. They were dedicated, had great personalities, and most importantly, they were awesome stylists.

"What can I say? They rock."

"Kalli, Lucy, and I need to talk." Rafe motioned to Serah and Squeaky. "Privately."

Serah took the hint. "I can go check on the guys." She looked over at Squeaky, who cowered in the corner.

"Do I have to?" Squeaky eyed Serah as if she were a lion ready to pounce. "With her?"

"Yes." Rafe's answer was firm, leaving no room for refusal. He pushed the reluctant chimp toward Serah. "Go."

Lucy wagged a finger at Squeaky. "And no *monkey business*. Gerardo and Frankie aren't to know a thing. Got it?"

"Yes," Squeaky said with a little mope.

Serah grabbed his hand. "Don't worry. I don't bite, unless you piss me off."

He squeaked with a visible gulp as Serah led it down the back hallway.

"Is this some sort of mockery?" Rafe paced the expanse of the shop. "A chimpanzee? What are the Fore-Demons up to?"

Kalli plopped down into a dryer seat and flipped open a magazine. Wrinkling her nose, she set it back down. "You know Squeaky was chosen long before he took on the body of a chimp."

"Even his name leaves something to be desired." Rafe raised his chin in an arrogant display. "I'm insulted."

Talk about proud. Poor Squeaky to get saddled with him. "I think it's a cute name." She had only just met the little guy, but even with his high-pitched voice, she liked the chimp.

Kalli nodded. "It's a lot easier to say than Quetzalcoatl, don't you think?"

An Aztec god? No way. "You're shittin' me."

Rafe's eyes widened in equal surprise. "Preposterous."

"I shit you not." Kalli extended her legs and crossed them at the ankles. "Didn't anyone ever tell you not to judge a book by its cover?"

Rafe pursed his lips and scratched the growth of hair on his chin. "Why is a powerful demon-god acting as a lowly imp?"

Kalli smiled. "That, my friend, is a question for your familiar."

"Always a well of information, aren't you?" Rafe rolled his eyes.

Kalli ignored Rafe and turned to Lucy. "Where'd you find this guy?"

Lucy shrugged. Rafe might've had the social skills of a toad, but he still had a gentle side. She caught a glimpse of it earlier. "Discount Demon Mart."

Kalli threw her long multi-colored dreads over her shoulder. "A little rough around the edges, but he means well." She turned to Rafe. "So what else is on your mind? You've been sporting that scowl long before Squeaky arrived."

"He's mad because I forced him to sit in a cramped car seat." It was more than that. He'd been acting like an ass since that sizzling and oh-so-delicious kiss. She licked her lips, wishing they were his instead. She should've smacked Serah for interrupting their tongue-wrestling match. Now she'd never experience such ecstasy again.

The demoness arched a brow. "Your succubus is in need."

"That's why I need your help, Kalli." Rafe crossed his arms and took a seat in one of the seats. "Look outside."

Scads of men waited patiently—and some not so patiently—outside the windows and doors for the salon to open. From the looks of it they weren't all here for haircuts.

Her eyes widened. "Are you sure she's only half succubus?" Raking a hand through her rough locks, she shook her head. "We need to contact Lilu. She may be bred of one of his higher court. What of her mother?"

Oh! There was no way she would introduce these demons to her mom. She'd have her committed in a heartbeat. Heck, she was ready to commit herself. If it weren't the fact that she and Serah were seeing the same things, she would've already done it. Delusions of grandeur, indeed.

"You don't need to meet my mom. She's a devout Catholic. Goes to church every Sunday. Wouldn't she spontaneously combust upon entry?"

Rafe scowled, but Kalli broke out into giggles.

"I take that as a no?"

"Humans and their silly superstitions." Kalli motioned Lucy to sit next to her. "The Infernati, yes, but demons such as us are blessed by angels. If anything, it would strengthen us."

A supposedly evil being had an angel's blessing? It was surreal. A trip to make a hippie jealous—if it really was a trip.

"Sorry, I'm not into that religious stuff."

Kalli grasped Lucy's hand, her amethyst eyes flashing with intensity. "That's too bad."

"No, not at all. I call it not getting my hopes up." That way, when she faded into nothingness, she wouldn't be disappointed. It had worked for the past fifteen years— that's when she'd grown a backbone.

"Don't let *him* hear you." Kalli smiled.

"Rafe? I could care less what he thinks."

Kalli rolled her eyes. "Me neither, but I wasn't referring to *that* him, although he's arrogant enough."

Rafe glared from across the waiting area. "We have important things to discuss. Like helping Lucy control her powers. Don't you see the eager crowd gathering outside?"

Lucy and Kalli shot their gazes back toward the large window. Men pushed and pounded against each other. Noses pressed against glass. Some waved their hands like little kids and even more blew kisses. One guy brushed the back of his hand across his forehead and fainted, slumping against the man ahead of him. *Yay! I'm a rock star!*

Kalli and Lucy groaned. Thank goodness the shop didn't open for another hour. From the look of it outside, it would take longer than an hour to get things under control. Just her luck!

"Perhaps you should call in sick today," Kalli suggested. She twirled a purple dread in her finger. "I can help your guys. I have experience with hair."

Lucy could feel the enamel rubbing from her teeth as she ground them. "I have clients to take care of."

Kalli's eyes brightened like two giant amethysts. "I have styled many famous people's hair. I can handle a few haircuts and perms."

"What sort of experience?"

Kalli's eyes glazed narrowed in thought. "Back in 1788, I styled Marie Antoinette's wig."

"Before or after they chopped off her head?"

Kalli rolled her eyes. "Before, of course." She continued her résumé. "In 1534, I served Anne Boleyn."

Interesting trend. Lucy snickered. "I suppose you styled Mary, Queen of Scotland's hair, too?"

She crossed her arms. "I assure you, it was completely coincidental."

"Darn. Because I would gladly let you style Mrs. Carlson's hair." Then again, that wasn't very nice. No one deserved their head on a chopping block, even that old bat.

Kalli turned her glance to Rafe. "You can take Lucy home and teach her what you know. I'll stop by after the shop's closed to continue." She turned to Lucy and flashed a wide smile. "And before you worry about sleep, demons don't sleep, so we can train all night long."

"No sleep?" Hell no! That was her favorite part of the day. Her lips curved downward even farther. "That sucks!"

Kalli shrugged. "If it's something you wish for yourself, then it can be done. But why you'd want to do that is beyond me."

"There's nothing I'd rather do than sleep." At least that's how it used to be. Ever since she laid eyes on that crazy chest, sleep was the last thing on her mind. "I consider it a hobby. I enjoy it."

"It's time to find a new hobby," Kalli said with a quirk of her pierced brow.

Lucy put her arms behind her head and stretched out her legs. "I'd like to stay here for a few hours. I need to take care of a couple of things."

Kalli bounded from the chair. "Fair enough. I can show you your new equipment."

"Equipment?" she asked, her eyes bugging out.

Kalli jogged to one of the stations. "Yep. You've been upgraded."

Chapter 8

KALLI PULLED OUT A CURLING IRON FROM THE holder attached to the front of the counter. "Check this baby out."

She held the curling iron out to Lucy, its shiny rod glinting against the bright fluorescent lights. "Notice anything about the barrel?"

She took the instrument and ran her fingertips across it. Besides the top, which had been carved into a sharp point, it resembled an everyday curling iron. She was supposed to stake demons with a curling iron?

"It's silver!" Kalli, apparently thrilled by her ingenious invention, beamed. Then she whipped out a pair of shears. "But these may work better."

Lucy arched an eyebrow. The idea of using scissors that she'd used to hack up a demon on a client left little to be desired. "I don't have to cut hair with them, do I?"

"No, the silver is in case of an emergency, when an unwelcome demon attacks." Kalli handed them to her.

"I take it silver and demons don't mix?" Why couldn't they have intolerance to some other heavy metal—like lead? It would be so much easier if she could just load a couple slugs into those pesky demons. Alas, life is never that simple.

Kalli nodded. "Fortunate for us less voracious fiends, we can take silver in small doses." She twirled her labret piercing with her tongue—which, of course, had even more silver. *Small doses?*

Kalli handed her more items, all as silver as the ones before. A comb, a pick, even a bobby pin. "Even a touch of silver can cause the Infernati pain." She placed the silver bobby pin in Lucy's hand.

Maybe she could *do* them in by giving them a new hairdo. "Won't it hurt me? I don't think any angels have blessed me lately."

"Good point." Kalli glanced down at the fingers still gripping the pin. "Guess not," she said with a pat to her back.

"Odd." Rafe's voice, even just that one word, teased Lucy's ears, sending her into fits of excitement. He stood behind her, looking over her shoulder. "There could be a logical explanation. It's best we exercise caution. She may be descended of the sect of Sexubis that severed."

"How many sects do demons have?" *Sect this, sect that. Here a sect, there a sect…*

"Two," Rafe replied, examining Kalli's handiwork. He drew his fingertips against the shiny blade of the scissors and took the weapon in his hand. How Lucy wished it were her he stroked. Ugh! This sex demon stuff had to go. "The Infernati and the Paladins. Those who chose the dark path are Infernati, and those who strive for redemption choose the latter."

Kalli nodded. "Lilu, the Sexubi king, chose the Paladins, but there were several who weren't happy with that decision. They chose to join Belial, instead."

Sexubi? Why were they worried? Obviously she was one of the good guys, right? Taking in both Kalli's and

Rafe's serious expressions, there had to be more. "Okay, spill it."

Rafe blew out a long breath of air. "You have yet to choose your side, and Belial can be very persuasive." His warm gaze swept over her, calming one side, yet driving her naughty side bonkers. "You need our protection."

"You've said that—numerous times." She extended her legs and stretched. "But now it's time to open my shop. I have customers to serve."

Rafe scrubbed his fingers through his hair. "I understand. Kalli and I can attempt an enrapture similar to yesterday afternoon."

She knew it! "Ha! I knew you had us under some sort of spell." Not that she was complaining. After all, he had taken care of Mrs. Carlson. "Next time warn me when you do something like that."

Rafe arched a brow. "You, my dear Lucy, were unaffected."

Unaffected? Yeah right. That man had her wanting to swoon on sight. No way in hell had she not been affected. She still was affected almost twenty-four hours later. "Bullshit. I was just as enthralled as Gerardo and Mrs. Carlson." *If not more.*

"Maybe," Rafe said, rising from his perch. The muscles in his arms and legs flexed with each step toward her. His silvery gaze burned into her, causing her body to shiver in delightful excitement. "But the fact that you were aware of the situation proves everything."

The heat radiated from his body, inches from her, and flooded her. Her pulse raced and goose bumps sprouted all over her body. God, he was good.

"Okay, enough already, Rafe." Lucy crossed her arms across her chest and stiffened her lip. "I get your point."

He narrowed his gaze. "Enough of what? I wasn't doing anything—yet."

"Really?" She shook away the tingles of excitement that kept barraging her body. *Yeah right!* Like her body always did that when a hot guy gave her a searing gaze. "I felt something."

"He's telling the truth. The effect of an enrapture is more like this…" Kalli turned to face her, her eyes sparkling like two giant amethysts. Tiny pricks of electricity tickled her brain. "The effects on humans aren't quite so dull."

Dull wasn't quite how she would've described it. Maybe because she was only half succubus? Well, *if* she was a succubus. She was falling into this story a little too easily.

"Fine. Do what you gotta do," she said, turning toward the back hallway. "I need to talk to Gerardo and Frankie." She flashed a bright smile Kalli's way. "New employee and all."

Kalli nodded. "Fair enough. Rafe and I will manage." She turned back to gaze out the window and shuddered. Men pressed and pushed against the door.

Blinking, Lucy shook her head. She couldn't believe her eyes. Pressed against the plate glass window was none other than Josh Carlson. His blond hair hadn't changed one bit since college. Same style and all. Heaven forbid a strand fall out of place or he'd probably have a heart attack. Predictability had been his forte—until now. Now he stood there acting like a fool with the other one hundred or so male admirers.

This wouldn't be pretty. Josh fawning over her would be just what her mother ordered. Not what she had in mind as a way to win her mother over, either. Hopefully, Rafe and Kalli could truly handle the situation—for her already-dwindling sanity's sake.

Kalli popped to attention, her eyes wide and alert. "What is it?"

"Ex-boyfriend, ten o'clock."

Rafe exhaled long and deep. His jaw tightened. "Bloody hell. How long has he been your ex?"

"Five years, but he's engaged to someone else now." She'd be damned if she break up Josh and Larissa and leave his meddlesome mommy with something more to harp on about. "I'm supposed to style the hair for their wedding," she added lamely.

Kalli's brow shot up in an ever-permanent arch. "You must be strong if you can overtake the power of love."

Rafe groaned. "This isn't good, and I don't like leaving the chest unattended." His silver glare seared. "Go talk to your employees. As soon as the crowd is controlled, I'm going back to check in with the council. Do what you need to do here, Lucia."

The formal use of her name sent her heart plummeting for some unknown reason. With a curt nod, she spun on her heels and stalked toward the storage room.

Wasting no time, she threw open the door.

"Hon, that chimp ain't talking." Frankie grabbed a bottle of developer and sat it up on one of the shelves. He breathed a sigh of relief and stretched his arms. "Hey Lucy, honey." He sauntered over to her and wrapped an arm around her shoulders. His other hand snaked down and massaged her ass.

Not Frankie too!

"Get your *manos* off *mi mujer*. I saw her first." Gerardo, holding two gigantic bottles of Ultra Shine Spray, came into focus. "I am her photographer."

"Hell no, she's mine."

She flashed a glance at Serah. "How long has this been going on?"

Serah's lips tightened. "Too long. Gerardo pulled out your *mug shot* and it's been on since."

Ha! At least someone agreed with her. "I told you to get rid of that photo, Ger."

Gerardo sighed and batted his lashes. "Oh, my dear, I had every intention of tossing it, but your beauty called out to me." He dropped the hair spray and threw himself into her arms. "Take me, *mi amor*."

"Oh, hell to the double no!" Frankie grabbed Gerardo by the feathers of his shirt and ripped him from Lucy's arms. He took his fist and gave Gerardo a girlish punch to the shoulder.

"Ouch," Gerardo cried out. "That hurt. You brute." He slapped Frankie's face. With an irritated huff he turned to her. "Such a Neanderthal."

"Me, a Neanderthal? That's the pot calling the kettle black." Frankie huffed dramatically, placing his hands on his waist and sashaying to and fro. "And before you say anything else…" He arched his chin. "Lucy's mine!"

"Boys!" Lucy shouted, sounding like a mother. "I'm not anyone's. Not ever." *Aha!* She turned to Serah. "Bring these *cavemen* outside and see if Rafe and Kalli can work their magic on them too."

"Sure thing, Lucy. What about Squeaky?"

"What about me?" he mimicked, flailing his super long arms. He added a few chimp squeaks for good measure.

Lucy covered her ears. "Okay, Squeaky, go with Serah."

Squeaky flipped her off. "I take back what I said earlier. You are mean."

"Ooh wee, maybe he can talk," Frankie chimed in as he bounded out the door. "With his fingers."

"Yeah, it's CSL for 'have a nice day.'" Lucy narrowed a glare at Squeaky.

Gerardo scratched the new growth of a goatee. "CSL?"

"Chimpanzee Sign Language."

Squeaky flashed a toothy grin, turned around and wiggled his butt. "I can talk with more than my fingers."

"I don't want to know."

"Whatever," the chimp muttered. "Your friends are kind of cool. Even if they don't understand anything I say."

"The chimp is cute and all," Gerardo said, sidling up to Lucy and brushing his hips against hers. "But an animal like that violates every health code here." He drew out his Latino accent and breathed in her ear. "What would Tabitha say?"

Bravo Network, yet another of Gerardo's guilty pleasures.

"She wouldn't say anything, because she won't be taking over this salon—ever. Spank you very much."

He batted his eyelashes. "Please?"

"Let's not and say we didn't." She gave Gerardo a gentle nudge out the door toward the shop. "Now go open the salon. We've got a lot of customers."

Lucy managed to control her snicker. That was an

understatement. Hopefully, once Kalli and Rafe finished with their mumbo-jumbo, most of them would be on their merry way. "I'll be out in a minute. I've got to… ahh… check our towel inventory."

"Yes, my love." Gerardo blew her a kiss and a flourish, à la Don Juan, and followed the others.

She waved. No way would she blow kisses. "This sucks," she whispered beneath her breath.

Frankie's screech echoed throughout the shop. "It ain't free haircut day, is it?"

"*¡Ay Dios mío!*" came Gerardo's frazzled voice. "Who let *him* in here?"

Guess they saw Josh. For some reason, they—along with Serah from time to time—liked to blame Josh for the "breakup." And to make matters worse, they were her newest admirers. She wasn't looking forward to the cat-and-dog fight that was sure to follow.

Time to make her presence known.

She took a peek in the mirror and scraped her fingers through her hair—even though she didn't need to. How great it was to have hair with a mind of its own when it did exactly what you wanted. Bad hair days were obviously a thing of the past. Throwing open the supply room door, Lucy took determined steps toward the vicinity of the commotion.

"Where's Lucia?" Josh asked. Same ol'… same ol'. In the five years they dated, he always called her by her given name. Then there was the coronary he had every time she dared called him Josh. Then again, that was his boring nature. He always said Joshua sounded more professional. Lucy thought it sounded like he just stepped out of the Old Testament. "I've missed her so much."

Yeah right, like a heart attack (unless the heart attack belonged to a patient, of course). It was only his pheromone-induced hormones talking, not his mind.

"Five years, Josh." Serah said amongst the clamor of voices. "You think she hasn't moved on?"

Josh sighed. "It's Joshua... only Lucy can call me Josh. And I certainly haven't moved on. Last I checked, she was still single, so I know the feeling has to be mutual."

Oh, this became even more interesting. Her own private soap opera in her little salon. And did she notice a hint of arrogance? Josh was bolder than she last remembered him. She loved a good soap opera every so often. But not now!

"What about the lovely Miss Harding?" asked Gerardo, his Mexican accent carrying across the room. "Your—*madre*—was here yesterday and gave Lucy the honor of styling your bride's hair." When Gerardo slipped into Spanish, all hell would soon break loose.

Bemusement filled Josh's face. "I want to marry Lucy."

Squeaky let out a high pitched chuckle. "Damn, Lucia. You have your own posse. Need some more bodyguards? I got some underground connections, y'know." Squeaky had apparently watched one too many episodes of *The Sopranos*.

Ignoring Squeaky, she gazed directly into Josh's eyes. "No you don't, Josh," she said, striding into the sitting area. "You love Larissa. I'm way below your mother's standards. Especially since I dropped out of med school."

Josh's lip jutted out in a big pout. "I just had this epiphany today, Lucy. I love you! I don't care if you don't want to be a doctor." Throwing himself at her, he wrapped his arms around her and slapped wet kisses all over her lips and cheeks. "I saw you driving by as I finished my morning run and I knew what I was missing. *You!*"

Anger and jealousy flashed in Gerardo's and Frankie's eyes. Scanning the salon, Lucy breathed a sigh of relief. The other men had since been cured and sent on their way.

She craned her neck toward Rafe, whose gaze bore into her. What was he thinking? She still hadn't figured the man out. She needed to... had to. He turned his gaze from hers. "The men who know you best are more affected."

"Even ones that don't swing that way?" she asked, pushing Josh away. "Sorry Josh, but you're marrying Larissa. She's so sweet, and I won't let you break her heart."

"Larissa who?"

Lucy swiveled her body and flashed Kalli a concerned gaze. "Do something!"

Kalli nodded, closed her eyes and spoke in her Greek language. She lifted her arms and threw a bolt of energy at Josh, then two more at Frankie and Gerardo. Josh let out a loud gasp and slumped against a counter. He rubbed his head. "Wh... Where am I?" He looked around. "Lucia? What's going on?"

Kalli snapped her fingers.

"I came to say thank you for the offer to assist Larissa and her bridesmaids." He rubbed his head some more. "What a horrible headache."

Lucy arched a brow at Kalli, whose lips spread into a wide grin. *Thanks, I owe you*, she mouthed to her and turned back to Josh. "Would you like some ibuprofen?"

Josh nodded. "Yes, please."

"Kalli will go get you some. Right, Kalli?"

Kalli shrugged. "If you say so."

Gerardo and Frankie slumped down on the waiting room seats too, their heads in their hands. Frankie moaned softly.

Gerardo groaned. "Something's in the air."

Serah sidled up next to Lucy. "Something in the air alright," she whispered. "Pheromone freak."

Rafe shrugged. "Perhaps."

Kalli arched a brow. "Glad I brought the entire bottle," she said, shaking the Advil.

She padded around the seating area, handing out pills and little paper cups filled with water. All that was missing was her nurse hat. Naughty nurse, maybe. Lucy stifled a chuckle.

She stopped in front of Josh, a spark of amethyst in her gaze. She scrunched her brow in consternation and her lip straightened. "Here you go, *Joshua*." She thrust the Advil and a cup of water into his hands.

"Thank you, Kalliope." He placed the pills in his mouth and tipped his cup before downing the contents. Just like Josh to insist on calling someone by their given name. He still insisted on calling Frankie Francis, much to Frankie's chagrin. Judging from Kalli's faraway expression, however, she seemed to enjoy it. Now that was odd.

"I hate to stop in and go, but I need to get to work." Standing, Josh turned to Kalli. "Nice meeting you, Kalli and Rafael." He nodded at Gerardo and Frankie and flashed Lucy a smile. "Larissa will be stopping by later to make arrangements." His gaze grew warm. "I appreciate it. My mother was so pleased with her hair the other day."

Lucy stifled the chuckle. After all, it was Rafe he should thank. Not her. "Sure thing, Joshua. Come by some time for a trim."

He turned to flash Kalli a surreptitious gaze. As if they all wouldn't notice. "I certainly will." With that, he left, the door jangling with his wake.

Scratching her head, Kalli turned to face Lucy. "We need to talk… Your *boyfriend* has the scent of succubus on him."

Rafe lifted his head from his magazine, instantly attuned to the conversation. He threw down the magazine and rose, taking quick steps toward them. "This private conversation of yours involves me too."

"Whatever," Lucy said. "Knock yourself out, buddy."

"Is he truly your ex?" Kalli's expression remained deathly serious.

A flash of something lit in Rafe's eyes. He clenched his jaw. You'd almost think he was jealous.

"Yes, I haven't slept with him—or anyone else—in over five years."

So don't get your boxers in a knot, Rafe. Oh that's right, he went commando. She did her best to hide the blush as she remembered the flying buttons and the glimpse of his excitement beneath the black leather.

"Maybe it's left-over energy?"

"Perhaps," Kalli said. "From the way he attached himself to you, I see no reason to doubt that assumption."

"Which means you're strong, Lucy. Stronger than we realized." Rafe's intense gaze left her stunned, as if she'd been slammed against the wall. "We need to take care of the chest, so we can get you to Lilu."

What? She crossed her arms and raised her chin.

There was no way she'd let them take her away from the shop, especially when the place they wanted to take her to was Hell. "I don't think so. I'm not leaving. Send the king of kink here."

Kalli shook her head. "Lilu will not walk Earth. As if things could just be this simple. We wouldn't be here otherwise."

"Doesn't he need to feed?" Serah asked, plopping into a pedicure massage chair. She picked up the controller, pushed some buttons, and relaxed. "Mmm."

"No," Rafe paced back and forth. "He absorbs the energy from his subjects. When the Sexubi split, it weakened him. He has not stepped on Earth since."

So a long distance orgy, Lucy guessed. Kinky. But then again, not being able to walk the Earth must've sucked. After all, Hell was... umm... hell? She really felt for this Lilu dude.

"Poor guy, not being able to visit Earth and all."

Kalli shrugged. "He made the decision on his own."

"What a king, to forgo his pleasure for his kingdom." If only some of the world's leaders would do the same.

"What are you all going on about over there?" Gerardo demanded, stomping over to them.

Crap! In her excitement, she forgot her employees were in the same room. She had to be honest with them. They were loyal and she could trust them with her life. They deserved the truth—as fucked-up as it sounded.

She turned around and motioned Frankie to join them. Always the dutiful employee, he bounded from his chair and loped across the salon to stand next to Gerardo. "What's going on, Lucy?"

"Frankie... Gerardo..." With a sigh, she sought out

the right words. "Ahh… you better sit down." Jeez, she sounded like she was about to close the shop. Not on her life!

Guessing from their stricken expressions, that was what they thought she was about to do. "Oh, don't worry. The salon's fine. It's about me."

"Oh no!" Frankie clutched his chest. Melodrama was his forte. "Tell me you ain't dying!"

Lucy snorted out a laugh. "No." She bit back more giggles. Immortality more than likely was included with her succubus powers. "Umm… I'm healthier than ever. Check out the new makeover."

"I was going to say," Gerardo replied. "You're smokin' hot. So can I take your picture now?"

"No." It was bad enough dealing with a small crowd of men. Imagine what would happen if she went international. She cringed.

Serah cleared her throat and took the blunt approach. "Lucy's a succubus."

Thanks, Serah. Now all hell would break loose.

Chapter 9

"A WHAT?" GASPING FOR BREATH, GERARDO THREW HIS head back. Laughter rose from his throat and filled the salon. With a feminine fanning of his hand, he succumbed to a fit of giggles.

Frankie rolled his eyes. "Very funny, Lucy, but we…" He prodded his friend. "…we aren't buying it."

Rafe crossed his arms and strode to the sofa where they sat. His silvery gaze intense, he leaned down to face the two. "She speaks the truth."

Gerardo's dark eyes flashed and he raised his chin. "Why should I believe you? You waltz into the shop and act like you own us." He blew out a breath of air. "I recognize you from yesterday. Love your hair."

"Thanks, I think," Rafe mumbled.

Lucy rose from the sofa and pulled Rafe to the side. "Does he remember you trying to kill him?"

"I did not try to kill your friend," he said through gritted teeth. "And, no, he doesn't remember. The only thing he recalls is to ask for permission."

"Mind control. Cool."

Rafe's eyes flashed. "We do not control thoughts. We alter perception. Infernati are the ones who misuse mortal minds."

"Oh sorry, I didn't mean to offend. I'm a newbie, you know."

Rafe's expression softened. "No offense taken."

Smiling, she glanced up at him. Beautiful dark hair danced around his face and silver eyes sparked at her perusal. She laid a gentle hand on his gloriously ripped chest, reveling in the feel of hard muscle pressed against the tight cotton T-shirt he wore. If only they were alone and… ahh… naked. Perhaps she should close shop and send everyone home. Everyone except Rafe.

The thudding of his heart increased, yet his gaze remained steady. Talk about control. Could she ever break through? From the way his heart raced, he had to feel something.

The door chimes jingled, announcing the arrival of their first customer. Alas, alone time with Rafe wasn't meant to be—for now.

"Lucia!" Her mom's frantic voice grated in her ears. "Please help me."

Not now! She wasn't ready to foist this woman onto some poor unsuspecting demons. She couldn't spring the news of her demonic destiny to her either. If her shop was bad after she opened the chest, she didn't want to see the fury of mommy dearest.

Her mother scanned the shop. "I love what you've done here. Business must be doing well."

Props to Kalli for that. The only time her mom had been impressed by anything regarding her job, and it wasn't she who'd done it. At least she'd gotten somewhat of a compliment.

"Uhh… thanks Mom." She replied lamely. "What do you need help with?"

Her mother's eyes widened with panic. "Tammy overbooked. I need my hair done for the Christmas party tonight."

Not the family Christmas party. It would take a small miracle to get out of this one. "Oh."

"Don't tell me you forgot!"

Lucy cleared her throat. "Not exactly, but we're busy tonight. Holidays and all."

Her mom huffed. "You have four employees. Surely you can take off early."

"I'm not an employee," Rafe stated firmly. "I'm a customer."

Thank you Rafe!

"I've come to get my hair cut." He scrubbed his silky locks. "It's getting too long."

Never mind. She took back that thank-you. No way in whatever they called the underworld would she cut those gorgeous locks. "Gerardo, take care of Mom." She flashed Kalli an apologetic smile. *Sorry, Kalli*. She preferred to keep her mother's head intact—for now. She turned to Rafe and flashed him a smile. "To the shampoo bowl, sir."

"Lucia!" her mom demanded. "I want *you* to do it."

What the hell? Why all of a sudden did she want her to do her hair? She'd never shown an interest in her job in the past five years. Lucy wasn't ready to hear her fuss when she wasn't satisfied. "Sorry, Mr. Deleon has an appointment. Gerardo is one of the best stylists in the River City region. You're in excellent hands."

"I need you."

She leaned into Rafe. "Now would be a good time to do your rapture thing."

Kalli arched a brow and joined the little powwow. "It's not working."

Rafe squeezed his eyes shut and clenched his fists.

"Bloody hell. Your mother has a demon's protection. And since I can't break through the barrier, it's a strong demon."

"Maybe that's why the thing didn't work on me the other day."

Rafe shook his head. "If that was the case, you wouldn't have been able to open the chest."

"Oh." Leave it to Rafe to deflate her hopes of getting out of this succubus thing. The idea of screwing the life out of a guy wasn't how she planned on spending the rest of her days.

"Lucia, please, I'm begging you." Her mom's pleading voice, although five years too late, tugged at her heart. Whatever inspired her was big, and she wouldn't stop until Lucy agreed.

"Fine," Lucy said with an exasperated sigh. Not because she had to bond with her mom, but because she was losing the chance to run her hands through Rafe's water-soaked hair. Ah, hell, it was probably a good thing. Going orgasmic in front of her mom wasn't something she wanted. She turned to the walking art display. "Kalli, please give Rafe a trim." Emphasis on the word *trim*.

Gerardo sighed. "I wanted to cut his hair."

"What can we do?" Frankie asked, coming to stand next to his partner in crime.

"Clean the foot spa." Lucy replied with a wink. "Just kidding." With Kalli's fine detail, there wasn't any need. "Watch the phones."

"Aye, aye, captain." Gerardo replied with a salute. Gerardo marched to the reception desk and stood poised and confident, Frankie following with equally confident strides.

Kalli grinned and tossed the same rag she was reading earlier onto the table. "Interesting title, crappy literature. A haircut would be a welcome change. Like I care about Jessica Simpson's new rack."

"Inquiring minds want to know," Frankie said, his hands defensively on his hips.

"Wrong tabloid, Frank," Serah replied. She let out an exhausted sigh. "I suppose I'm on chimp duty?"

"Nope." Squeaky popped out from underneath the desk. "I'm on Rafe duty. You're dismissed. *Arrivederci*."

Her mom gasped, eyes wide with amazement. "Is that a chimpanzee?"

"No, it's a kid dressed as a chimp," Lucy quipped. *Wow! Mom knew her primates!*

Lucy snuck a glance at Squeaky who was equally impressed.

Her mom nodded. "Ahh... That explains the talking. I thought I'd have to call my therapist there for a second." She smiled at Squeaky. "Great costume."

"Umm..." Was there something her mother wasn't telling her? "Yeah, well..." she turned to glance at Rafe, whose eyes had narrowed into silver slits.

"This is impossible. I need to talk to the council."

Kalli nodded. "Maybe it's the solstice?"

Not this again. Eclipses, solstices. What's next? Halley's Comet? "Don't ask me. I failed geography and astronomy." She contemplated a smartass comment, like she mistook it for astrology, but, taking in their dire expressions, refrained.

"No." Rafe shook his head. "I don't think so. This is strange. Two mortals who can communicate with lower imps?"

Kalli shrugged. "It's obvious her mother had a connection with a strong Sexubi." She turned to Serah who sat on the sofa, scratching Squeaky's head. Lucky—or unlucky—for Serah, Squeaky warmed up to her and murmured contentedly.

"Hello, Lucia dear. Hair?" Her mom tapped her toe.

"Yes, Mom, be right there." It amazed her how calm she remained. Perhaps it was her mother's new enthusiasm. This situation, despite the bizarreness, was real.

Direness clouded Rafe's expression. "Don't feel obligated to stay here and protect me. I've got Kalli and my new tools at my defense."

"You're only part demon, Lucy." He said it like she was a freak of nature. Then again, she probably was. She wasn't quite human, and not quite demon. She was... Well, she didn't know what she was. She didn't like it one bit.

"Thanks for the vote of confidence, Rafe." With a turn of her heels, she stalked to her mother. Her graying dark blonde hair hung limp around her head, her ocean blue eyes wide and pleading. If there was one thing her mom was good at, it was the puppy-dog look.

"Quit the dramatic, Mom. I'll do your hair."

She crossed her arms and pouted. "Lucia..."

"Fine. I'll do your makeup too." She pointed a finger. "But that's it." Why did her mother have to care so much about her appearance? She didn't need any help. She was fifty and didn't look a day over forty. Lucy could only hope to be so lucky. She snuck a gaze to Rafe and Kalli, who whispered in the corner. Never mind that, she was that lucky... or maybe unlucky. She had yet to find out.

Rafael sat in the chair next to Lucy's mother, amazed at the resemblance. Both women had beautiful dark blonde hair, delicate cheekbones and delightful clefts in their chins. The only thing besides age that set them apart was their eyes, each woman's beautiful in its own unique way. Where Mrs. Gregory's were the color of a placid ocean, Lucy's were a mixture of lush greens and exotic amber—breathtaking. Her enchantment became too much. Even the presence of her mother did little to slake his desire. He needed to speak to the council, and he needed to speak to them soon—before winter officially rolled in. Kalli had mentioned the solstice. How could he have forgotten? Keeping himself isolated in Limbo had faded his knowledge of the Earth and its cosmic proportions. When the Earth ceased to revolve, the underworld would still exist. It was immortal, after all.

"Stop staring at them, Rafe," Kalli said as she leaned in and snipped a few hairs. "You're making her mother uncomfortable."

Rafael grumbled. "I understand, but something's amiss. Two Pure-Bloods within the same city limits?" He shook his head. "Not bloody likely."

"What makes you think they're Pure-Bloods?" Kalli ran a comb through his hair and snipped.

Not that he worried about how much she'd cut, it'd grow back in a matter of an hour, regardless. Such the luck for an immortal. Only the strongest of demons could change their appearances. Not that he wasn't strong, he just happened to like his hair. And Lucy liked it too. What in the deities? Where had that come from? Stupid enchantment. He had to speak to the council. He'd waited too long.

"Do you have any other brilliant suggestions?"

"There haven't been any Pure-Bloods in twenty-five years. The Infernati wiped them out." She set the scissors down. "The last one was burned alive in her home."

"Where?"

Kalli scratched beneath one of her rough locks. "Chicago."

"That's not far from here." Rafael knew he grasped at straws, but his options dwindled.

"True, but Lucy's mom had carnal relations with an incubus. What's not to say that that incubus simply gave her his protection?"

Chuckling, he leaned back in his chair. "An incubus protecting his victim? You're losing your touch."

"It's time you realized I had a touch to begin with." She thrust him the mirror and turned him around to examine his back. "You like?"

With a quick nod, he swiveled the chair back to stare his friend in the eye. "Good job." Sure, he and Kalli didn't agree on things, but he still admired her. She was the best damned cleaner the Paladins had, and she was the best stylist they had too. There wasn't anything the demoness couldn't do. "I can't take any more chances. I need to speak to the council." Something didn't add up.

"There is more than the possibility of the Pure-Bloods that concerns you," Kalli leaned in to whisper. "I sense it." Kalli's lips spread into a devious grin. "You're attracted to her, aren't you?"

Was it that obvious? With that information, Kalli could bring him down. Not that she would. But— "Don't be ridiculous. I'm a Paladin. We're immune to succubi."

"All right then. Sorry I suggested it." Kalli snickered.

"Demons have needs too, you know." She twirled a purple dreadlock in her finger. "Even me."

Yes, he may have needs, but he wouldn't let his needs fail the Paladins. Too much was at stake. "I don't want to discuss your needs, Kalli." Brushing snips of hair from his shoulders and chest, he rose from the chair and turned to lock gazes with Lucy.

Her hazel eyes glinted in disappointment and a small frown curved her lips. Perhaps Kalli hadn't done that great of a job. "Wow," she muttered. There was no masking the disappointment that cracked in her voice.

Kalli scrubbed her fingers through her thick mane. "I didn't think it was that bad." She snorted in laughter. "Never mind. I did *too* good of a job." She knelt to the floor and scooped up some of his discarded hair. Swinging a dark lock in her fingers, she shook her head. "I forgot she said *trim*. She'll be pleasantly surprised in a few hours when you have a full head of hair again." She flung the hair to the floor.

"*¡Ay caray!* You chopped it off." Gerardo pranced their way. Reaching down, he snagged a piece of snipped hair.

"*¡Madre de Dios!*" Gerardo waved his reddened hand frantically. What used to be Rafael's hair crumbled in the effeminate man's hand and blew away in a cloud of dust.

Rafael drew in a long breath of air. "See why you must ask for permission first, Gerardo?"

With a downturned gaze, Gerardo nodded. "Talk about 'killer hair.'"

Apparently, Lucy's smartass sense of humor was contagious. Didn't surprise him one bloody bit. Tossing him a stern glare, Kalli reached down and grabbed Gerardo's hand, drawing her fingertips over his singed palm. "Any better?"

"Wow, that's awesome! What you got in those hands? Aloe vera?"

"Something like that," Kalli muttered. "I'll take care of the hair. Go handle the client who just walked in."

He clapped his hands with excitement. "You're a regular Florence Nightingale." Gerardo turned and flashed a friendly smile and swished toward the desk to greet the customer. Rafael shuddered. Never in his four hundred and fifty-five years had he seen a man move his hips in such a way.

With a quick scrub of his recently shorn hair, Rafael shook his head. Humans were bizarre. Then again, here he was saddled with an *imp*anzee. He sidled a gaze toward Squeaky, who sat snuggled in Serah's arms. How bloody strange.

Squeaky, sensing the perusal, looked up. "Stop staring, buffoon, and get going."

"I plan on it," he grumbled. And the next business after the chest would be the assignment of a new familiar—preferably one whose voice didn't grate on his eardrums.

"Plan on what?" Frankie asked, eyes glued to the tabloid in front of him. Flipping the page, he let out a loud chuckle. "Lucy, listen to this… 'Child Compelled by Demon Eats Family Pet.'" More laughter erupted. "'A ten-year-old boy from Jackson, Mississippi, grabbed Nibbles, the family guinea pig, and bit its head off.'" Frankie wrinkled his nose and cringed. "'When questioned why he killed the pet, the little boy said, "The Golden Guy made me do it."' That's crazy."

"What's the kid's name? Ozzy Osbourne?" Gerardo asked, his head thrown back in laughter.

Rafael's jaw twitched. They had no idea of the evil surrounding them... infecting them. The fact that they acted so glib regarding such a terrible incident irked him. "Human suffering is no laughing matter."

"Human suffering?" Frankie asked, eyes wide in shock. "It's entertainment. Most of it isn't true." He shook his head, mirth rolling from his smile. "I'm sure the kid didn't really bite off a guinea pig's head."

Rafael narrowed his eyes into a scowl. "How do you know it isn't?"

Frankie opened his mouth to speak, his eyes sparking.

"Frankie..." Lucy warned.

Frankie lowered his lids. "Fine, Lucy."

Rafael shook his head. Impressive. Her commanding presence left him awed—again.

As she brushed a light-brown gooey substance onto her mother's hair, Lucy flashed Rafael a gaze with just as much warning. It chilled him to the core. He didn't like his reaction. He was through hemming and hawing. He'd go to the council now. Kalli was capable of protecting Lucy. She'd be in good hands.

"I have to leave for a few hours. I need to speak to the Fore—" He darted a gaze toward Lucy's mother. Despite the bizarre ooze on her head, she sat tall and proud. He allowed his gaze to examine the younger woman. Like mother, like daughter. The only thing different besides their eyes was the effect Lucy had on him. Energy pulsed through him at the devious thought. He throbbed in a place he didn't want to. His body tingled.

"Uhh… what I meant to say was I need to meet with my… ahh… boss."

"Boss?" Lucy, although she tried—rather admirably—to control herself, snorted in laughter. She had a cute laugh, Rafael noted. And her voice, it melted him. More tempting than that of a siren who caused sailors trouble. Demons, every last one of them. Now he was affected all over again.

"Yes," Kalli chimed in. "He has to present his report." She pushed him toward the door. "Poor guy's nervous as a cat in a rocking chair factory. Right?"

Rafael slanted his eyes into a penetrating glare. "Not on my life. I look forward to it."

"I'm sure you do." Lucy rolled her eyes. "Good luck, Mr. Deleon."

His heart plummeted. What had he done now? Women! He stopped trying to understand them. He had a hard enough time with demonesses and an even harder time with mortal women. Throw in a half mortal/half sex demon and he was even more clueless. "Thank you, Miss Gregory." He turned to Lucy's mother. "Mrs. Gregory, it was lovely to meet you."

"Thank you, Mr. Deleon. I apologize that I confused you with the help. You're a true gentleman." She smiled. "We need more people like you in Connolly Park."

"You're welcome." With that, he threw open the door and turned to Squeaky, motioning to him with his finger. "You. Come. Now."

He would get this whole imp fiasco settled while he was at it, too.

Squeaky rolled his eyes as he pulled himself from Serah's arms. "Someone needs a lesson in politeness."

"Or humility," Kalli said, sweeping up ashes that were once his hair. Thank goodness Lucy's mother was too busy enjoying her daughter's spa treatment to notice.

Rafael stood tall and flexed his arms. "Whatever. There's too much at stake to be humble." However, the more time he spent around Lucy, the more humble he became. And it scared the demon out of him—if that was possible.

"Such a party pooper," Serah sighed out. With a quick pat she prodded the reluctant imp his way. "Go, Squeaky. You're our only hope."

Everyone—except him—broke out into laughter. What was wrong with them? Didn't they realize the urgency of the situation?

"I've yet to understand this humor, but now isn't the time." Rafael grabbed the imp's arm and led him to the door. "We'll be back soon."

Lucy's eyes sparked as she set down the brush she'd been using to color her mother's hair. "Is that a threat or a promise?"

"It's whatever you want it to be."

He pushed open the door, the jangling of bells vibrating in his ear. With a quick yank, he pulled Squeaky out the door and walked out into the cold blowing snow. Rafael willed the mists to envelop them and carry them through the portals of Limbo back to the chest.

Chapter 10

THE DOOR SLAMMED SHUT. WHAT WAS HIS DEAL? SHE needed to get Rafe out of her system fast. She hadn't been so turned on by a guy in… forever. Even as she stood over her mom and concentrated—scratch that—*tried* to concentrate on dying her hair, desire rippled its way through her body. She yearned and burned for him to touch her. Not good! Especially when her mother was sitting right in front of her.

"You're our only hope?" Gerardo rolled his eyes. "Where are your Princess braids?"

Serah twirled a bouncy brunette curl in her finger. "I left them at home. Halloween was two months ago." She blew out an exasperated breath. "And besides, Princess Leia wore buns in that movie."

"Oh that's right." Gerardo grinned. "I still think she looked the best in that metal bikini. I might be gay, but I still appreciate the feminine form from time to time."

That's for certain. After all, hadn't he and Frankie nearly gone at it with drawn claws for her in the catfight of the century? Where was that camera when they really needed it? She turned her attention back to her mother. She couldn't believe how encouraging she'd become about her salon. It was like the flame of support had just been lit under her ass. Lucy had yearned for this for so long. Now that she had it, she was completely weirded out.

"Time to tune in to Timbuktu," she said as she led her to the dryer area. Maybe making lame jokes would change her recent interest in her profession. Hah! This was her mother. Some people—*cough*—Rafe—thought she was a determined person. Well, they hadn't met her mother.

It didn't work. "I'm sorry I wasn't so supportive, Lucy."

Whoa! She called her Lucy. This was a leaf she didn't want to turn. Maybe some other day, but not the day after she found out she was born to suck the life out of unsuspecting men.

"Thanks, Mom," she said, frustration lacing her voice. Did this woman know when to stop?

Nope. She didn't.

"I thought you'd be better off doing what your father loved." She nibbled her lip. "But now I know. You should do what *you* love." She traced her fingers over Lucy's brand-new sterling silver dryer. "In a way it's like surgery. You do have to cut things, after all."

"Less blood, too," Lucy added lamely. Awkward was the understatement of the century. What in the hell was going on?

Serah, attentive friend that she was, stepped in to help with her budding apprehension. "How's the museum, Mrs. Gregory?"

Mom smiled and provided them with a long dissertation of all the renovations they planned for the Connolly Park Historical Museum. Not that there was much history to be found in the quaint little town, but the women of the historical society were dedicated to preserving Connolly Park's not-so-vivid beginnings.

"Sounds fascinating," Lucy mumbled. "I can't wait

to see that Red Brick of A-Line Road exhibit." Lucy stifled her yawn.

Her mom huffed. "I absolutely *hated* that idea, but Mrs. Carlson insisted. I'd rather watch paint dry." Her eyes brightened. "Mine will be much more interesting."

Probably not by much, if she knew her Mom. "What's yours?"

"Connolly Park's bootlegging history."

Wow! Her mom was becoming creative. The apocalypse must be near. Shock left Lucy speechless. Boggled, baffled, and bewildered. "Did we really have issues with Prohibition?" After all, it was Connolly Park, not Chicago.

"Capone did have a summer home on Lake Michigan," Serah said with a grin. "At least that's what I heard."

Lucy laughed. "I'm sure he had a home for every season, if not more."

"Makes me wish I lived back then. Good times. Flapper dresses, speakeasies, and gangsters." Serah's eyes twinkled in excitement.

"Capone died of syphilis. Good times, indeed." Lucy patted Serah on the back.

Serah shook her head with exasperation. "Now look who's party-pooping now." She looked down at her watch. The same watch she had worn the night before. "Oh! I have to go. I have a client coming in at noon."

Lucy caught a glimpse of her friend's hand and cringed. Serah had been hurt! Lucy's gut clenched. A long scar stretched horizontally across her hand. On each side of the scar, two perfect puncture wounds marred her porcelain skin.

Ouch! Scar? That meant the injury happened a long time ago.

"What happened to your hand?"

Serah looked down and shrugged. "Oh, that." She waved her hand dismissively, pulling her sweater sleeves over her hands. "It happened before I moved here."

Noticing Serah's lack of forthcoming information, Lucy prodded some more. "How come I've never seen it before?"

"I don't know." Serah bit her lip and wrung her hands. "Sorry, I don't have time to discuss my childhood injuries. But, if you're interested, we can compare scars later. I have an awesome one shaped like Djibouti on my ass. Bet you're wondering why you never saw that one either." A weak smile peeked from her lips. "Never sit on a rat trap."

Lucy's eyebrow jutted up. Regardless of her flippant dismissal, Serah was hiding something. They'd been friends since Serah moved to Connolly Park twenty years ago. But she'd give her friend the benefit of the doubt—*for now*. "I'll heed your advice." Lucy gave her friend a quick hug. "Be careful. If anything strange happens, call me ASAP."

"Sure thing." With a quick wave, she threw her coat on. "See you in a few. I'd stay if I could, but this client is huge."

"No problema," Lucy said in a pathetic attempt at a New Jersey accent. "See youse later."

Too bad Squeaky, the Godfather of all chimps, wasn't there to appreciate her mobster-speak. Not that she'd be winning any Oscars. Her performance was lacking. Then again, so was Squeaky's.

Serah smiled and nodded as she pulled the door open, then stopped dead in her tracks. "My car! Duh!" She smacked her forehead. "It's still at your place."

Brilliant move, Sherlock. Taking the Rio sounded like such a great idea earlier. After all, Rafe said he couldn't just *poof* them there because of the human cargo. Like they were illegal immigrants, or something. Lucy grabbed her purse from beneath the counter and pulled out the keys. "Here you go," she said, throwing the keys to her friend. "If you crash it, I'll kick your ass."

"I'll be gentle." A deceptively sweet smile swept across her face. Gentle? Hah. Lucy had seen this woman drive. "You have my word."

Then again, her word was as good as gold. Serah knew she was a woman of her word, too. "One dent, and I'll flog you with a wet noodle."

"Ooh! Sounds fun! You know I like my spaghetti kinky." With that, she waved and scuttled out the door.

Lucy's mom shook her head. What looked like a genuine smile graced her face. "She's an odd one, but she's good for you."

"Eh?" Her mother *never* approved of any of her friends, including Frankie and Gerardo. Apparently, Lucy was supposed to schmooze with her doctors, dentists, and gynecologists. Yep! She actually tried to set Lucy up with an OB-GYN. A truly clinical experience. Fortunately, Lucy managed to send him away before the pelvic exam.

Her mom raised a brow. "What? Is trying to be a better mother so wrong?"

"Sorry," Lucy muttered. "I'm just stressed and all your newfound interest creeps me out."

Her mom blew out a breath laced with dejection. "I... I... just..." Her lip quivered and jutted out into a pout.

A pout? She'd never seen her mom do that before. She gnawed her lip. Now she felt like a complete bitch.

"Lucy's had a hard day, Mrs. Gregory." Frankie swizzled his way over and wrapped his arm around Lucy's shoulders. Frankie to the rescue. What a guy! "She didn't get any sleep last night. Bookkeeping, you know." Frankie turned his head to glance at the clock. "Oh no! I've got a highlight coming in. I need some foils."

With a sneaky little whistle, Frankie bustled to the back room. Hmm. Didn't he know alone time with Mom wasn't what she needed?

Thanks a bunch Frankie!

"I knew this wouldn't work." With another sigh, she clasped her hands in her lap. "But I just wanted to make up for lost time."

Lucy shrugged. "I'm still not going to your family's Christmas party." Lucy clenched her fists. They never approved of her father, and that disapproval had since passed on to her. In fact, part of her mother's constant pushing stemmed from them. Always the one to please her family... that was Victoria Gregory.

"This has nothing to do with the party tonight, dear." Her mom's lips spread into a wan smile. "I'm talking about the big picture. As for Aunt Sally, I think I'm taking a pass, too."

Did she hear her correctly? Standing up Aunt Sally and the whole Jennings gang? "But didn't you just say this was an emergency? That the party was tonight?"

Her mom just offered a cryptic shrug. "I changed my mind."

"Somebody pinch me. I think I'm dreaming." She had to be.

Gerardo sauntered over to the crowd, a devious smile wide upon his lips. "Okay, *chica*. You got it." With a loud giggle, he clinched his fingers on her shoulder.

"Ouch!" Then just as instantly, the pain faded. Presuccubus, she would have had a bruise the size of a chicken egg. She pulled up the arm of her sweatshirt and caught glimpse of a just-slightly reddened circle that already faded.

Lucy gave the Latino a playful smack and sent him on his way.

"How much longer, Lucy?" Her mom's whine pulled her from their friendly repartee. She scratched her plastic-capped head. "It's itchy."

Lucy checked the timer then leaned down to inspect her mom's hair. "Five more minutes."

Her mom let out a deep sigh. "Oh, all right."

"Ah, hell nah!" Frankie's voice echoed from the back. "Where the hell are the foils?"

Kalli, whose nose had been glued to the *Daily Executioner*, lifted her head. "Foils? This is a hair salon, not a fencing studio."

At the lack of laughter, she shook her head. "I'd never make it as a comedienne." With a deep sigh, she flung the tabloid back on the table and jumped up. "Kalli to the rescue." With the grace of a gazelle, she bounded down the hallway to help Frankie with his quest for foils.

Shaking her head, Lucy returned to inspect her mom's hair. Thankfully for her and her itchy head, the color had completely processed. "All set, Mom. Let's get you rinsed."

"Thank goodness, I thought my scalp was burning off."

Lucy's face fell, horror replacing mirth. The only time her mom set foot in the salon and she'd fried her head. This was worse than Mrs. Carlson's seventies-reject perm. She clenched her teeth and bit her tongue.

"Get that look off your face, Lucy," her mom demanded. "I have a sensitive scalp. I forgot to tell you." She flashed an apologetic smile. "I'm sorry."

Lucy's horror only slightly waned. This whole situation was surreal at best. Mom and her bonding at the last place possible—Luscious Locks.

"Your father would be proud of you." She grinned as she slid into the shampoo chair.

Her mom's words sent Lucy's expression over the edge as a wide smile spread across her face.

"I took his advice, you know."

"I know," she said, leaning her head back in the bowl. Glancing up at the fixtures, she blinked. "Is that silver?"

"Yes," Lucy said. "All the fixtures are silver."

Her mom glanced up at her as she turned the faucet on. "I didn't know they made silver faucets! You *are* doing well. I'm glad you took his advice."

Shock prevented her from replying. Never in her twenty-nine years had she expected her mom to share in her happiness. Why couldn't it have happened sooner?

How did that phrase go? Better late than never? Whoever coined that phrase didn't know her or her mom. The fact was Lucy loved her, despite their differences of opinion. But now wasn't the time to bond, with evil demons lurking. The last thing Lucy wanted was her mother's soul on her conscience. She couldn't—wouldn't—do that to her. It was bad enough she had dragged Gerardo, Frankie, and Serah into this mess. Then again, wasn't it Serah who had dragged her into it in the first place? Nah, Serah didn't want to open the chest that night. Lucy did that all by her lonesome, despite Serah's pleadings not to.

Lucy scrubbed and sprayed the dye from her mom's hair. Deep inside, her sudden interest filled Lucy with peace. But turmoil outweighed the peace. Her mother wouldn't understand. Yesterday, Lucy would've welcomed her with open arms. Today, however, she couldn't handle it. Isn't it funny how things can change in just one day?

Then an idea hit her. Perhaps she couldn't bond with her mom because she wasn't the same person she gave birth to. Yeah, that had to be it. She was now a closet nymphomaniac, and her mom was as conservative as... never mind.

The truth was simple. Lucy was scared as *heck*.

"I look magnificent!" Gripping the mirror, her mom beamed. "I'm so sorry I ever doubted you." She thrust the mirror back into Lucy's hands and squealed with glee. "Even Tammy doesn't do as good a job."

Lucy couldn't help but smile. Her mom's epiphany, or whatever it was, began to grow on her. *Wonderful*. And for the first time in like forever, she wasn't being facetious. Nothing could ruin this moment.

"What the hell!" Frankie's voice carried throughout the salon. "This is so not happening."

Lucy's breath caught. This did not sound good at all. Frankie stalked in from the back hallway, his breath ragged. Then again, Frankie was known as quite the drama *queen*. But with everything going on, she wouldn't take any chances.

"What is it?" she asked, concern lacing her voice.

Frankie sucked in a long breath of air. "All of our foils are ruined." He threw out his hand and held out a charbroiled foil. "What the hell were you doing last night? Kalli won't tell me anything!"

Lucy rolled her tongue along gritted teeth. "Not now... not in front of my mom," she ground out.

"We'll figure something out," Kalli said. She turned and flashed an apologetic smile. "I'm sorry, Lucy. I must have missed those. It's been a while since I've been in the business."

She wouldn't complain. Without this woman, there wouldn't even be a salon to stand in. "It's okay. You've done so much as it is. My mom's just about done. I can go to the supply store and pick some up."

Kalli shook her head. "I'm afraid you can't leave the salon, at least not until Rafe gets here. I promised him." She paced back and forth, scratching her dreadlocks. "We've surrounded the building with an enchantment that reduces your... ahh... condition." Thank goodness Kalli chose to speak in a hushed tone. Despite her mom bonding with her, Lucy wasn't quite ready to drop the bomb on her just yet.

"Who's going?" Frankie asked, flinging his hands on his hips. "I'm staying here with Lucy."

Gerardo shook his head. "I'll stay here. You go."

Apparently, the effects of her *condition* still hadn't fully worn off. Would her pheromones ever let up? Frankie and Gerardo stood nose to nose, tall and proud, as they sized each other up. Hands on their hips, they narrowed their gazes in the stare-down of the century.

"Oh, come on, guys," Lucy muttered. "This is silly. It's just a drive to the stupid supply store. I'll be fine."

Kalli sighed. "I'm sorry. I didn't realize such a slight oversight could cause such tension."

Lucy gave her a reassuring gaze. "Don't be. Part of this is my fault. Some of my effects apparently haven't worn off yet."

Gerardo finally spoke. "Frankie can go. He saved your ass the other day. Now it's my turn."

Saved her ass? When?

Frankie arched a brow, clearly confused as her. "I did?"

"Mrs. Gunderson," Gerardo replied with a wink. "I think the words you used were, 'I saved Lucy's pretty little tush.'"

A slight blush crept to her cheeks. Did these guys forget her mother was setting right across from them? Although, having two blatantly gay men calling her tush pretty was a huge ego boost. Not that she needed any more of that right now.

Frankie rolled his eyes. "Oh please, you and I both know that's not the same thing."

"Oh yes it is!" Gerardo flung his arms across each other. "I've heard those feet are killer."

With a hiss, Frankie stomped an impatient foot. "I look beyond the feet."

Gerardo blinked. "Oh," he muttered through taut lips. Slumping his shoulders, he backed away from Frankie. He stuck up his chin. "I'm still staying with Lucy. I have reasons."

"What reasons?" Frankie prodded.

"Personal reasons." Gerardo crossed his arms. "That's all you need to know."

Her mom, who must have been an arbitrator in a previous life, cleared her throat. All four of them whipped around to face her. Victoria Gregory stood proud and authoritative, like a woman who knew how to take charge. That face used to have Lucy trembling in her moon boots as a child. Now there was the mother she remembered. "I'm sure Lucy's quite capable of performing such a menial task." She ran her fingers through her newly cut and colored hair and rolled her teeth over her lip. "Not that any of your work here is menial, you know."

Bemusement flooded everyone's faces. Gerardo and Frankie stood there in stark silence, while Kalli twisted a pink dreadlock around a finger. Her expression, however, leaned more toward amused than bemused. Lucy almost broke out into laughter. The stunned silence wasn't because of her comment about menial tasks. It was the fact that she'd finally stood up for her daughter.

"What?" she asked, gazing at each of them. She exhaled a deep sigh. "What I meant to say was... you know... the supply company is right next to Joshua Carlson's office."

So much for her mom's metamorphoses. She should've known her mom had an ulterior motive. So she still wanted her to schmooze with the snobs of Connolly Park? Not that Josh was a snob or anything, but still...

"Umm... he's getting married soon. Larissa Harding, remember?" Lucy snorted back a laugh. "I don't think it's good form for his ex-girlfriend to make social visits to his work." Could you say "awkward"? Especially after the pheromone overdose she gave him earlier this morning.

Mom shrugged and nibbled her lip. "They just don't seem to have that spark, you know?"

Lucy knew, all right. More than her mom realized. Joshua, bless his heart, wouldn't know what a spark was even if it bit him on the ass. But he was still a good person.

"I'll go," Kalli blurted. With a smile, she threw her mass of hair over her shoulder. How did she hold all that hair on her head?

Lucy pulled Kalli to the side. "Is it safe to leave me alone?" Rafe would be pissed if anything happened while he was gone. Not that she should care if he was mad or not, but for some reason she was. Stupid man.

Kalli grinned. "As I mentioned earlier, the shop is surrounded with Rafe's and my energy. You have nothing to worry about. And you don't have to worry about your newly budding fan club. You're protected all over."

Cool! Because she didn't stand a chance against a bunch of hormone-intoxicated men. "That's comforting."

Frankie's eyes flickered. "So you're a succubus, huh?"

"Afraid so." Flashing her pearly whites, she struck a pose. "Never would've guessed it, right?"

Gerardo rolled his eyes and a laugh rolled out. "Please, I knew it all along! You had *sexpot* written all over you." He reached across the front desk and pulled out his blasted portfolio. "Remember this?"

She should've known. Gerardo and that stupid photo. He just couldn't part with it. "Do you want me to sign my mug shot? It may increase the value." *Yeah right*.

Frankie arched a brow. "If it's *that* bad, we can use it as a before-and-after picture."

Lucy narrowed her eyes and arched her brow in befuddlement. Had the lunar eclipse done more than unleash demons into the world? These guys were talking like a bunch of silly willies. Scratch that; she was acting a little nutty, herself. Then again, she was entitled to, considering the circumstances.

Frankie, obviously mistaking her expression as look of intensity, gulped. "Not that the before picture is bad, but... you know... you're off the chart on the smokin' hot scale now..." Frankie's gaze darted around the room. "I think I'm gonna shut up now."

"I'm pretty sure that borders on false advertising, anyway," Lucy added with a chuckle. She could just see the advertisement.

Want to go from this to this? All you have to do is boink the life out of someone.

No way! "Then again, we could always add the line 'Results may vary.'" Taking in Gerardo's and Frankie's sidelong gazes and the excited grins on their faces, Lucy shook her head. "I'm joking. Don't get any ideas."

Both men blew out disappointed breaths—in unison! They could've been twins, save for Gerardo's swarthy skin and dark hair and Frankie's pale face and sandy blond hair. Then again, Gerardo wore feathers, and Frankie thought he looked like a giant flamingo. Besides being gay, the similarities pretty much ended there.

Gerardo puffed out his chest like the giant—albeit lovable—peacock that he was. "I'll stay here and protect Lucy." He jumped in the air and kicked. "Hi yah!"

Backing up, he bowed. "I've been dying to show you that move forever!"

Lucy's mouth gaped open. Gerardo knew karate? What else had the Latino been hiding? His ability to knit three sweaters in a single bound? "When did you learn karate?"

"I dated a karate instructor. He gave me private lessons." Gerardo winked and added, "And let me tell you, private lessons are much better than public ones."

Lucy didn't doubt it, but she didn't want to hear about it either.

Kalli coughed and sputtered. "Ahh... Frankie can go with me. Mr. TMI stays here with you."

For being a demon, or whatever she was, Kalli sure had the modern lingo down pat. Then again, she probably lived in this world before most of Lucy's ancestors. Maybe she should ask her how old she is, to sort of break the ice. The older-sister-type vibe rolled off her where Rafe was concerned. What a relief!

Smirking, Kalli leaned in and whispered, "Isn't it rude to ask a woman her age?" With a soft chuckle, she turned back to Frankie. "Let's go."

So she could read minds? Could Rafe too? Talk about awkward. Like she wanted the man she needed to boink knowing her every thought. Raking a hand through her hair and gritting her teeth, she tossed a surreptitious glance at Kalli. With an unconcerned shrug, she smirked. What else were these demons hiding from her?

Chapter 11

THE BLAST BACK TO LIMBO PROVED UNEVENTFUL AS always. Rafael had long grown used to the rush of icy winds barraging his face while he teleported. He glanced down at his companion. Squeaky, apparently, hadn't. Long arms wrapped around his chubby chimp body, he shivered. A sliver of ice dangled from his nose. Imps! Not developed enough to handle the transport between worlds.

But if what Kalli said was true, this wasn't any ordinary imp. This was Quetzalcoatl, long-lost god of the Aztecs. He must have done something horrible for the Fore-Demons to diminish him to an imp. Rafael shook his head. Not bloody likely.

One thing was certain; there was more to the chimp that met the eye.

"Let's not do that again," Squeaky shook crystals of ice from his fur.

The squeaks were too much. *Time to get this monster a muzzle.*

"Come," Rafael bit out. Yanking the pesky imp by his arm, he pulled Squeaky behind him. "The Fore-Demons await." The sooner he got this mess straightened out, the sooner he could join Nic in saving Coby.

Coby. How was Nic's rescue going? Remorse flooded inside. He should be the one rescuing her. They were bonded by blood. They were twins. Connected. He should be there, with the sweat, blood, and brimstone, fighting for his sister. Instead, the Fore-Demons sent him to Earth to get the blasted chest—the same chest that had put Coby at risk. The same chest that now held Lucy captive. He'd spit on the *Arca Inferorum* if he could. He, however, still valued his position as a Paladin. He hadn't even given one thought of Coby while on Earth. He'd been too busy with Lucy. Too busy becoming enchanted.

"Do you ever smile?"

I'll smile when I vanquish Belial back to the fires of Hell. He gripped the hilt of his sword. Perhaps if they realized he was ready to fight they'd reconsider his assignment.

"They won't change their minds." Squeaky hunched down on his arms and swayed back and forth. "Nice piece though." He reached out his bulbous hand. "May I?"

Rafael tightened his grip, the silver etching along the hilt digging into his palm. "Why?"

"I'm a connoisseur of fine swords. Especially seventeenth-century Ottoman sabers." Squeaky smiled. "Funny, I always pegged you for a Frenchie."

Rafael shrugged. "And I thought you were Aztec, not Italian."

"Oh, a wise guy, are ya." Lounging against the wall, Squeaky scratched his ape chin and chuckled. "There may be hope for you yet." He gazed at the sword, his tongue wagging.

With a deep breath, Rafael unsheathed the weapon. The silver glinted in the glow of the tapers hanging on the wall. Even though the sword had been his for over four centuries, he never stopped marveling at its beauty. Carved dragons and their intricate breaths of fire wrapped around the hilt and vined their way down the blade. Sapphires along with rubies dotted their eyes and emeralds sprinkled along their spines. Nothing matched its exquisiteness. Save for that seductive swirl of emerald and amber that flashed in Lucy's eyes.

Desire flooded his body. Rafael clenched his teeth. This obsession was unhealthy. He'd lost focus. He'd lost his edge. A loud grumble formed in his throat. He was going soft.

"Ahem!" Squeaky coughed out. "Earth to Rafe." He scratched his hairy chin. "Oh yeah. We aren't on Earth. Limbo to Rafe. Come in, Rafe."

Shaking his head, Rafael leaned against the hall's gilt wall. Too much gold for his taste.

With reluctance, he handed it to the imp. If it got the thing to shut up, he'd let it handle all his weapons.

"The sword was a gift from my Turkish trainer." Right before Nic and he traveled to Roanoke. The first strike. Thanks to Lamia and her bloodlust for children, his first assignment had been a failure. Nic had since proven himself. Rafael, however—the strikes were constantly against him.

The watch in his left pocket burned a hole in his jacket and singed his skin. Not literally, but it might as well have. He stiffened. Don't reflect on the second strike. *Not now.*

With a quick parry and thrust, Squeaky danced back and forth. Was that a flourish?

"*En garde!*" Squeaky lunged forward.

What the bloody hell? Rafael gazed down at his white shirt, now emblazoned with three slashes in the shape of a Z. Rafael grumbled. "My sister gave me this shirt."

"Your sister would tell you to remove the stick from your ass, Rafe."

Rafael jerked his head to lock gazes with Nic. Swiping a hand through his sandy blond hair, he shook his head.

"She'd do no such thing. We think alike."

Nic snorted. "How well you know your sister." His expression hardened. "I have news, by the way."

"Tell. Me. Now." From the sternness of his friend's gaze, it wasn't good. His stomach roiled and his head spun. The longer Nic waited, the more anxious he became.

Scratching his chin, Nic drew in a deep, calculated breath. He tugged on his ceremonial tunic, the red eagle emblazoned on his chest. "We know where they're keeping Coby." He clenched and unclenched his fists. "It doesn't look good."

"Why? Has she been thrown in the pit?" Rafael cringed at his question. If that were the case, all hope for his sister was lost. Icy shards raced through his blood.

Nic shook his head. "Quite the opposite, my friend." He paced the expansive marble. "I know how you prefer to stand to receive your news, so I won't beat around the bush." He rubbed at the stubble on his chin. "Your sister appears to be a welcome guest in Belial's palace."

Welcome guest? Coby had given in to that evil monster? He couldn't believe his ears. He gritted his teeth and his jaw locked. While he was strutting around Earth chasing a woman he couldn't have, his sister had been tortured so much that she'd turned to the dark. Beautiful Coby, the one who kept him balanced? Not bloody likely. He wouldn't give up hope. Not yet. Belial would pay.

After two haircuts and one capping, Lucy had time to relax. Taking a bite of her turkey club sandwich, she leaned back in her office chair and stretched her legs. The bland turkey and burnt bacon wasn't much, but it would do. Her tastes had matured.

A hot plate of Rafe, anyone?

Lucy shook her head. She wasn't sharing him with anyone.

Glancing at the computer clock, she sighed. *Five after two*. Where in the hell were Frankie and Kalli? They should've come back by now. Frankie's appointment was due to arrive any moment.

The doorbell chimed. *Like now?*

Just what she needed. An irate customer on top of her uncontrollable succubus powers. And no Kalli to teach her how to reign them in. Hopefully, this protection shield she and Rafe had put up was strong enough. Otherwise, she'd be S-O-L.

Gazing down at her half-eaten sandwich, she sucked in a breath. She just wanted a few minutes to herself to *think*. Her world was changing. She was changing. Energy she never knew existed ripped through her body. For the first time in five years, she was scared. Was her life a lie? Was she good or evil? She had so many questions. But only one truly plagued her.

If she was a sex demon, who was her father?

She shuddered. Obviously not Dr. Louis Gregory, orthopedic surgeon.

"Gerardo can handle one simple customer."

Pushing her sandwich away, she turned her attention back to the computer and clicked her mouse. What better way to pass the time away than an über-boring game of solitaire?

She aimed the mouse pointer at the ace of spades, letting it pop to the top right of the screen. *Yawn.* A seven of hearts here, a ten of clubs there. She moved a king of diamonds over and revealed another ace. *Yippee!* She prepared to click the card.

"Lucy!" Gerardo burst into the office, a wide, excited smile spread across his face. "There's this hunky guy up front looking for *you*!"

Gerardo's gaze floated to the ceiling and his breath hitched. Absolutely comical. Never a dull moment at Luscious Locks where Frankie and Gerardo were concerned. Now it was rubbing off on her. Case in point: Exploding shampoo bowls and demonic chests. *Yee haw!*

"Me?" Maybe Rafe's and Kalli's energy was wearing off. She hoped not! Why, oh why, couldn't Kalli have given her lessons before she went traipsing off with Frankie? She didn't like it one bit. Rafe wouldn't either. Something didn't add up.

"Yup!" He clapped his hands excitedly and jumped up and down like a giddy schoolgirl—sans the plaid skirt and stockings, thank goodness. "And he asked for you *by name*." He let out a dramatic sigh. "*Dios mío*, Lucy. You're one lucky *chica*."

Hardly. Being an overactive sex demon didn't necessarily exude luck—unless you were into that freaky shit. She flashed Gerardo a sidelong glance. Bedecked in a magenta feathered sleeveless shirt, he lounged against the doorjamb in his black leather skinny jeans. Now there was someone who got freaky with the best of them. Oh, the stories she could tell. Imagine that, a Mexican who couldn't hold his tequila.

"Men love me. What can I say?" Shrugging, she pulled herself from the desk. Not that she wanted the love. Not if it was as obsessive as it was earlier this morning. She saw how it affected Frankie and Gerardo. No, thank you! Being an object of one man's desires was good enough for her. She let out a long sigh of hope. *Hope?* Where'd that come from?

"Love is an understatement," Gerardo sauntered to the computer and flung himself into the chair. With a dramatic sashay, he swiveled around. "They *adore* you."

His dark brown eyes brightened and he waggled his brows. Not that expression! What now? "Spill it, Gerardo."

"Uhh..." He threw his hands up in exasperation. "*¡Dios!* I think he's with the modeling agency I sort of... sent your photo to."

Ugh! She knew he was up to no good, and now she had to run damage control. She blew out a long breath. "When will you learn?"

Gerardo shrugged. "I don't know. You'd be a great model, Lucy." He heaved a sigh, his gaze all of a sudden somber. "I told you that chest was bad."

"*Muy malvado*, right?" Maybe she was wrong. Sure there was a touch of evil in it, but she still sensed good. *Weird*.

Gerardo nodded and crossed his arms over his flamboyant sequins. "Too late now," he said with a click of a mouse. "You have more important things than being on the cover of *Vogue*. I'll let you give Mr. Bell the bad news."

"Thanks Ger. I *really* appreciate it."

Gerardo smiled, his white teeth sparkling. "Any time, *chica*."

She blew him a kiss and headed out of the office. One thing she appreciated about Gerardo—even when he was right, he never rubbed it in someone's face. If what Rafe and Kalli said was true, she had just unleashed a legion of demons on Earth. Not comforting at all. On the upside, if what the inscription said was true, she could control them too. Maybe it was as simple as just commanding them back in the box? Could it be that easy? She hoped so. Then again, nothing in life was ever simple.

There she went again, her inner pessimist—surgically implanted by her mom and her crazy family. It was time to show the Jennings family she was worthy of something. Saving the world was as good as anything.

She made her way down the hall, the strong scent of permanent solution wafting in the air. Stronger than usual, like someone dropped a ton of rotten eggs on the doorstep. Had Frankie and Kalli returned with some new industrial strength brand? Hopefully not! She wanted to keep customers, not drive them away.

There weren't any perms scheduled, though. The odor drifted away, and the cloying scent of cinnamon assailing her nose instead. She didn't know what was worse, the acidic burn of the solution or the overly heady aroma of spices.

Rubbing her nose, she headed into the shampoo area

and scanned the shop. Her gaze drifted toward the waiting area. At the front desk stood an angel. She'd never seen someone so golden. Wavy blond curls framed his tan face. A wide smile spread across his face, revealing pristine white teeth. He was everything Rafe wasn't. Bright and vibrant, where Rafe was dark and brooding. His amber eyes sparked bright and beckoning.

"You must be Lucia Gregory?" he asked, his voice smooth as melted butter. She couldn't place his accent, but it was sexy just the same. "You don't mind me visiting you at work, do you?"

She arched a brow. "Depends on the reason for the visit, Mr...."

"Bell. Jon Bell."

"I don't recognize your name, Mr. Bell." It was best to keep things formal. After all, it appeared to be a business call and she still wasn't sure of this man. Besides that, he was too hot for his own good. And in her experience, sometimes the hottest guys were the most trouble. She took cautious steps toward the golden god wannabe.

Mr. Bell smiled, stuck his hand in his designer suit, and flipped out a card. With a flourish, he handed it to her. Wow, he was smooth. Too smooth. "Here's my card."

Glancing down at the ornate script, she scratched her head. "Jonathan Bell, *River City Herald*." A newspaper reporter? "You want to write an article about us?"

Mr. Bell flashed that expert smile again. He was a man who got what he wanted. She had news for him. He never met Lucia Anne Gregory.

"I want to write a feature on local beauty spas and their offerings. Yours came *highly* recommended." He brushed his golden waves from his cheek. "I was in the area and decided to introduce myself." He drew out each of his words on a wispy breath and extended his hand to her.

He smiled, his paler than pale blue eyes swirling. Unnatural and creepy. Then her head buzzed. Tingles filled her body. She felt this way earlier. When Kalli demonstrated enrapturement. Alertness zinged inside. *Demon!*

Another demon? And from the creepy vibes he gave off, he wasn't one of the good guys. So much for protection. She should have gone to get the foils. So that's why Kalli wanted to go! She couldn't believe it!

Her brain kicked into overdrive. "So, Mr. Bell, would you like a tour? Perhaps a demonstration?" she took extra care to pronounce the word correctly. Couldn't have this fiend too cautious.

"Demonstration?"

She picked up the new silver sheers and twirled them in her fingers, a huge grin on her lips. "You know, a haircut?" She pointed to the plaque hanging at her station. "I'm a master stylist."

Mr. Bell scratched his hairless chin, his pale eyes intense. "I happen to like my hair, Lucy. You don't mind me calling you Lucy, do you?"

"Are you my friend, Mr. Bell?" He irritated her more as each minute ticked by. At the shake of his head, she snorted. "Then I mind."

He leaned in, his breath hot against her skin. The pungent spice mingling with rotten eggs wreaked havoc on her nose. Her stomach roiled. "I hoped we could become more than friends." A long fingertip scraped along her cheek. Her body shuddered, revulsion gurgling through her veins. Who in the hell did he think he was? She had to act—and fast!

Gripping the shiny new scissors behind her back, she raised her chin. "You've overstayed your *invitation*, Mr. Bell." *Hah! Beat that, demon boy!* Now he had to leave.

"Invitation?" The demon roared with laughter. "Those silly rules don't work with *true* demons, Lucia." The hiss of his words stung her ear. He yanked her against him, his pale blue eyes swirling into dark pools. His fingernails elongated, digging into her back. "Don't trust the Paladins. They're your enemy."

The demonic douche bag lashed out his forked tongue and traced it along her cheek as his clawed fingertips traced against her ass. Seduction wasn't his forte. Her stomach roiled and heaved.

"Let me go!" Still maintaining a tight grip on the shears, she wrenched her arm from his grasp. She raised her arm and arced down, slicing his chest. A circle of bright red marred his pristine shirt.

"We'll be so good together. You and I." He grabbed her wrist and squeezed, plucking the scissors from her entrapped hand. Examining the weapon, he clucked his tongue. "Silver. How very creative. You'll need a bigger pair of scissors to incapacitate me, my dear Lucy."

So this freak offered her a challenge? Lucy wasn't one to refuse. "There's more where that came from, a-hole." She probably wouldn't win points for snazzy comebacks with that one, but considering the circumstances it still was pretty good.

"Oh, really?"

"Yes really." She jumped high in the air, higher than humanly possible. *A-freaking-mazing.* Spinning in a complete three-sixty, she kicked her leg high and roundhoused the offending demon in the chest.

The force of the blow sent him staggering back. She grabbed the sharpened curling iron, gripping it like a wooden stake in a cheesy vampire movie. Alertness flooded her entire body.

In a flash, he righted himself and grabbed her hair, jerking her toward him. "Do not fight me, Lucy. I want to help you."

Help her? *Yeah right*. "What a nice way of helping," she said, curling iron at the ready.

Jon, if that was even his real name, snaked his arm tighter around her, his hot, moist breath creeping along her ear. If he thought he knew how to woo a woman, he was wrong.

"Put the curling iron down, Lucy." He fisted her hair, yanking her head up to meet his soulless gaze. Arrogant bastard. And here she thought Rafe was an asshole. He was an *angel* compared to this jackass.

He sneered, sharp fangs poking from his mouth. With a hiss, he angled her head to bare her neck. She had no choice but lower the curling iron. She loosened her grip, the iron hitting the floor with a loud clang.

"I wanted to help you, Lucy, but you've left me no choice." He inched his mouth down to her neck.

She shivered with utter revulsion. So this was where her life had taken her? She would die at the hands of a demon not twenty-four hours after learning she was a succubus? Not what she wanted in life. Then the proverbial anvil hit. She wanted to live. She wanted to prove herself. She wanted to save the world.

Making a quick upward thrust, her knee connected with the demon's groin. Howling in pain he doubled over, throwing her to the floor. With a loud crack, her head slammed against the tile. Stars danced in her eyes and the room floated around her. Fear and adrenaline warred inside her. One part of wanted to cower and hide, the other part wanted to fight. To live. The curling iron had to be nearby. With frenetic abandon, she grabbed for anything she could find.

Jon loomed over her, fully recovered from his ordeal. Peals of sick sardonic laughter boomed from his mouth. The heel of his designer shoe came crashing down on her fingers, grinding into her knuckles. Pain ripped through her fingers up into her wrist. She bit back the tears. She wouldn't show this bastard weakness.

"Looks like I've won, Lucy."

A gust of wind whipped through the salon, sending bells jangling.

"No, Belial. You've lost this time." The whiny voice she complained about only two days prior was now music to her ears.

An ax sailed through the air, thrown in an arc, with expert precision. A startled gasp gurgled in the demon's throat. He fell on top of Lucy and vanished in a poof of dust. Only the silver ax remained.

It had to be her imagination. Wrenching herself from the ground as she brushed demon dust from her sweater, she glanced up. There stood Mrs. Gunderson in the entrance with sword in hand.

Chapter 12

"Mrs. Gunderson?"

Lucy shook her head and rubbed her eyes. She had to be imagining the stout woman whose ankles put an elephant to shame standing there holding a sword like a knight preparing for battle. Her poised, confident stance would give a fencing champion a run for his money.

Mrs. Gunderson? Yeah right! Maybe the shock from having the wind knocked out of her had made her delirious.

The woman shrugged and sheathed her sword in the scabbard strapped to her back. "Only when I'm in your shop, my dear." Her voice, once high and whiney, morphed into deep and seductive tones. Damn these demons with their sexy sultry voices. Lucy might've been part demon, but her voice didn't hold a candle to Mrs. Gunderson's, or Kalli's for that matter.

"I suppose your name isn't Mrs. Gunderson, either?"

"Only when I'm in—"

"Yeah, yeah. You said that already." Wow, she wasn't that forthcoming with information? "What's your real name? Bathsheba? Jezebel? Salome?"

"Infernati's most wanted," Mrs. *Whatever* said. She snapped her fingers, her plump elderly muumuu-sporting body morphing into a tall, lithe, vivacious brunette. Her long wavy hair cascaded in rivulets down her back. Tight black leather leggings clad her too-perfect legs. Clunky brown orthopedic shoes were now red spiky stilettos. Adjusting the clingy bright red sweater that broadcast all her assets to the mortal world, she smiled. "Ahh, much better."

When your sole purpose was sex, you had to look the sexpot. There was no mistaking the succubus in her. "If you're into the whole 'come fuck me' look, I suppose." Duh! She probably was.

"Oh, you have your father's wit! Wonderful!"

Father? "You know my dad?"

Mrs. Sex-on-a-Platter gnawed on a perfectly manicured nail. "Hmm. I can't say too much, I'm afraid. Belial's lackeys may still be lingering." Concern sparked her golden eyes. "Where's your protector?"

"Protector?"

"The one who put up the enchantment." She kept raking her fingers through her luxurious mane. Didn't she know she already had the big sexy hair thing down pat? "If Belial weren't so strong, it might have worked."

How many demons would come out of the woodwork? Demons, demons, everywhere. And how did she know this woman was one of the good guys? After all, look at Kalli. She'd up and left just like that. Lucy couldn't trust anyone. Heck, she couldn't even trust herself.

She wasn't ready to spill secrets. "So what brings you here? Obviously not pedicures."

The brunette threw back her head in laughter. "You're a smart one too. Then again, I always knew that."

"Always?" Great, she had demonic stalkers too.

She grinned. "I wouldn't go that far. Oh, and call me Lilith."

"You all need to teach me that trick."

Lilith arched a brow. "What trick?"

"The whole mind-reading thing. Or at least tell me how to block it."

A frown creased her lips. "Only a few of us can do that, and even fewer Paladins. Tell me they didn't send her."

"Kalli?"

"Kalliope." She scrunched her nose. "How much has she told you about herself?"

"Not much." Lucy crossed her arms. "But if you're worried about her protecting me, there's no need to worry. She isn't the one they sent."

Lilith nodded. "Who did they send?"

"Me."

Rafe's voice teased her ears, her heart pounding. She loved that voice. She spun around to lock gazes. He stood tall, his hand resting on his waist. Was that a sword strapped to his side? "Where's your fuzzy little friend?"

"Squeaky is protecting the chest, at your house."

The demoness smirked. "Rafael Deleon, how lovely to see you."

"Lilith." His voice lacked emotion as he stalked next to Lucy. "What brings you here?"

She rolled her eyes. "Where were you while Belial attacked your ward? Lucky for you, I was in the area and came to Lucia's aid."

"She was in capable hands."

"Capable hands that have since wandered off," Lilith bit back with a huff. "Kalli? You know how she despises our race, yet you leave her to protect Lucia?"

"Kalli's changed." Rafe drew his mouth in a straight line. "She's proven herself many a time to the Paladin cause. She won't fail us." His eyes swirled in a look of determination. It drew her to him. It made him seem almost *human*. She wanted to wrap her arms around him... comfort him. What could cause such despair?

In a flash the glimmer of sadness morphed into his usual stony façade. "I'll ask once more, Lilith. What brings you here?"

Six degrees of demon separation? Or was it the six hundred and sixty-six degrees? Was there a demon that didn't know one another? "So I suppose they have succubus and Paladin mixers in Hell?"

Rafe blew out a disappointed breath and groaned.

"We live in Limbo, thank you very much." Lilith crossed her arms in front of her. "Lucifer and his princes, along with Belial's Infernati and the damned, reside in Hell."

Rafe nodded and popped a squat, never once taking his glare from Lilith. "Why is one of the Sexubis' most prominent figures protecting a common succubus?"

Common? Screw him. Even when she was still 100 percent human, she was anything but common. She balled her hands into tight fists. "What the hell am I? Chopped liver?"

"No Lucy, you aren't chopped liver." Rafe reached out and wrapped his arms around her waist and hauled her toward him. With gentle force, he sat her next to him.

Shocked, she could only gape at him.

"You're special, I can feel it." He ran a tender finger along her cheek. What the hell was happening? He angled his gaze toward Lilith, who stood there with mouth equally agape. "And since the High Priestess of the Succubi takes an interest in you, that only confirms my suspicions."

Lilith arched a perfectly manicured brow. "I'm not allowed to show an interest in one of my subjects? I'll have you know, I'm a real people-person."

Rafe smirked. "I suppose you want to take over her training?"

"She needs to learn the ways of a succubus. And since I'm one of the oldest, who better to instruct her?"

She wasn't lacking confidence. She stood there, all six feet of her, with her hands on her hips. Pride sparkled bright in her glittering amber eyes. Lucy liked her better as Mrs. Gunderson than this over-confident stack of steaming sexpot. "Kalli and Rafe will teach me all I need to know."

Lilith rolled her eyes, a sarcastic laugh rolling from her lips. "They aren't succubi. They can't train you."

"I know how to screw, fuck you very much."

Lilith huffed. "I made a promise to your father that I would protect and train you if you were to ever come into your powers."

Lucy attempted to bite her tongue, but she was too damn angry. She didn't care what this woman had to say. Louis Gregory was her father. This incubus was only a glorified sperm donor. Never mind. Nothing like that should be glorified—ever. "My father died ten years ago."

"How wrong you are." Lilith flashed a cryptic smile.

"Try me."

Rafe sucked in an uneasy breath. "Is all this animosity necessary?"

"It's the way of the Sexubi. We're very territorial by nature." Lilith sauntered toward where Lucy sat and crouched down to face her. Taking her hands in hers, she smiled. "I don't plan on infringing on your space. I've already got my own territory to *satisfy*."

Lucy controlled the snort that threatened. Satisfying? From what she'd read about succubi, there wasn't anything satisfying about it. Unless you enjoyed having the energy boinked out of you. "So, where's your domain?"

"Las Vegas."

She snorted out a laugh. "How appropriate. Sin City. I bet you make a *killing* there."

"I don't kill my victims. Only those who've joined the Infernati do." Lilith huffed. "I suppose I'll let your father explain everything to you. I'm making a mess of things."

"That'd be a good idea." Lucy narrowed her eyes. Hopefully her gaze threw daggers at the sexpot. "But my real father died ten years ago. I don't deal with demon sperm donors."

"Lilith, why not come back later, after Lucy's had time to deal with everything?" Rafe shot the sexpot a pleading gaze. He had that expression down pat.

Lilith nodded. "I see that you care for her, Rafael. I'll honor your request." Cared for? What the hell did she mean by that?

"I've been sworn to protect the chest, and with it... *her*."

Lucy's heart sank. Was he only doing this as a duty? At least Belial, even with the stench of rotten eggs and cloying spices, seemed genuine. Genuinely concerned with himself, her inner conscious challenged. Then again, he tried to kill her. "Oh."

"Good, Rafael. Just make sure she doesn't end up like all the other females in your life. I heard your sister has taken residence in Belial's palace?"

Rafe's eyes blazed, his jaw twitched. "You'll keep your mouth shut, succubus."

"Pardon me, I forgot your ineptitude of protecting the fairer sex was such a touchy subject."

Clenching his fists, Rafe rolled his tongue over his lips. He opened his mouth to retort, but the busy jangle of bells cut him off.

Kalli and Frankie burst in the room on a gust of air. Kalli scanned the room, her eyes narrowing on Lilith. "What is she doing here?"

"I'm here for Lucy. I've been watching over her."

With a sarcastic snicker, Kalli shrugged. "I'm glad they've put her in such capable hands." She scrounged around in her coat pocket. "I'd like to know why there are so many succubi in one single town. Two I can chalk up as a coincidence. But three? That kind of throws the coincidence theory out the window." She pulled out a photo and handed it to Lilith.

"Oh dear," Lucy's would-be mentor murmured. "Not good."

Rafe jumped to his feet. "What is it?"

"Nothing for you to concern yourself over, Rafael." Lilith handed the photo to Lucy. "Do you know this woman?"

Lucy blinked. Gerardo and Frankie hovered over each of her shoulders. Their gasps in unison lightened the tense situation, but only slightly. She looked again. There, her tightly wound blond hair in a severe bun, suited up in a dark blue Armani pantsuit that put Hillary Clinton to shame, stood Larissa Harding, Josh's fiancée—the one who'd *stolen* him from her. "But she's so boring!"

"An act, I'm certain." Kalli wrinkled her nose. "Why she chose to single you out is beyond me. You're only half succubus."

Sidling next to Lucy, Rafe snatched the photo from her hand. "There's more to Lucy than you all realize." He turned the photo over. His silvery eyes swirled, his breath caught. That look of despair and agony ripped through him again.

"Rafe, are you okay?" Lucy asked with concern. For some bizarre reason, she reached to take his hand. Strangely enough, he didn't pull away. He gripped tighter.

"This can't be." His voice cracked. "She's dead. I saw her die."

Kalli flung her dreadlocks behind her head. "I wish I had better news, Rafe."

"There has to be some mistake."

Lilith shrugged. "No mistake, I'm afraid."

"But she was innocent." Rafe's eyes clouded as he stared at the photograph.

"You know Larissa?" Lucy asked, her eyebrow arched in wonder. She wrapped her arm around Rafe's bulky shoulders.

Rafe jerked away and stalked to the far corner. "Her name was Amanda Newell and she died in my arms almost two hundred years ago."

Chapter 13

WHAT SORT OF TRICKERY WAS THIS?

Rafael's jaw twitched. Two hundred years of repressed memories threatened to rise to the surface. She'd died; he'd felt her soul leave her body.

"She's my ex-boyfriend's fiancée," he heard Lucy say through the myriad memories wreaking havoc in his mind. "Aren't succubi supposed to be... you know... sexy?"

Rafael spun around to face Lucy. "She is... was a beautiful woman."

Lucy gnawed her lower lip—a rather delightful quirk. He stiffened. How could he dwell on Lucy when the woman he thought he killed had come back to haunt him? Then again, maybe he deserved it, as punishment for his attraction to Lucy.

"Sorry, Rafe. I didn't mean she's not beautiful." Lucy balled her hands into tight fists and paced in front of her shiny shampoo bowls. "I mean, she's not the most outgoing of people. From what Josh says, she's not that adventurous, if you get my drift."

"Oh, she's an adventuress, that's for sure. At least she was." Lilith stretched out her long supple legs, stilettos scratching across tile. "Sorry to be the bearer of bad news, Rafe, but your prim and proper Regency miss wasn't that prim and proper."

Lunging at Lilith, Rafael leaned over her and grabbed her shoulders. "What do you mean?"

"She's one of Lamia's now." Lilith spoke the name as if it contained venom. "She's always been under that traitorous bitch's spell, even when she was a mortal."

Rafael turned to Kalli, who stood there with stony silence. "Am I as weak as the Fore-Demons seem to think?"

Kalli shook her head. "No, but remember why they sent you there in the first place."

"They believed it was an incubus attack."

Lilith nodded. "Miss Newell was bait."

"For me? Why? I'm nobody." Why did Lamia have to hold a grudge?

He angled his head toward Lucy, who winced and shook her head. "Oh, shut up. You are somebody."

"You weren't the prey originally." Lilith pulled at her sweater to readjust it. "You've improved your grip over the years." She lounged back and crossed a long leg over the other. "Now where was I? Oh, yeah. They were trying to trap my brother."

"King Lilu?"

Kalli nodded. "The one and only."

"Lamia?" Lucy blew out a deep sigh. "More demons for me to remember?"

"I suppose you didn't tell Lucy about her?" Kalli smirked. "And before you ask, yes, the Sexubis have an affinity for names starting with the letter L."

Lucy shrugged. "I didn't pick my name."

"But you aren't complaining either, are you?" Lilith punctuated her question with a chuckle.

"I was named after my father. Dr. Louis Gregory." She crossed her arms, a defiant spark in her hazel eyes. "So I'm very proud of it."

He allowed his lips to curve upward. She'd give Lilith a run for her money. Rafael hid his smirk. It was about time someone put Lilu's sister in her place. And from what he'd seen, Lucy would be more than happy to do it.

Sisters. How could he forget Coby? His own sister lay at the mercy of Belial's men. Belial was becoming stronger. He'd been able to journey to Earth. He'd seen Lucy. He'd be back. Rafael wouldn't put another death on his conscience.

She shook her head. Mrs. Sex-a-lot was the king's sister? Interesting. Then again, with the arrogance she possessed, she should've known better. Lucy steepled her fingers as devious thoughts of comeuppance raced through her mind. She would enjoy knocking the woman down a few notches.

She glanced up at Rafe. His grin had once again straightened and the sparks in his silver eyes faded. His hands balled at his side. What had she done now? Talk about hot and cold.

She had enough. "What the hell is your problem? Do I disgust you that much?" With as much force as she could muster—more than she realized she possessed—she grabbed Rafe's arms and wrenched him to face her. "Well?" Sure she wasn't as pretty as Larissa-slash-Amanda-slash-stupid bitch, but she sure as hell wasn't boring. Her dad always told her she was extraordinary. He even called her his little demon. Maybe he knew something no one else did. He was a smart one, her dad.

She heaved a huge sigh. All the pain came back threefold. Anger, despair, and worst of all, guilt. She always blamed herself for her father's death. And now to find out he might not even be her father? The pain gripped her heart and twisted. God, how she missed him. Especially in winter. Not because of the holidays, but the kick-ass snowball fights.

"Oh dad," she muttered under her breath. "I'm so sorry."

She picked a wonderful time to go all emotional. She refused to cry in front of everyone. Her tears had since dried up. Where'd all this emotion come from? Rafe?

"It's not your fault, Lucy." Rafe's tender voice soothed and comforted. His strong arms wrapped around and pulled her closer to his heated chest. Whoa! Here they went again on the wild roller coaster ride that was Rafe.

She rubbed her eyes. "I just want to get out of here for a while." She wanted to go somewhere she'd dreaded going for over ten years—her mom's. If this whole sex demon thing was true, then one thing was certain, her mom felt guilty too. Maybe that's why she was so overly enthused earlier?

Her decision made, Lucy raised her chin and stalked to the coat rack. With a determined yank, she pulled the coat off the hanger. "I'm going to my mom's. She needs me."

"How far is it?" Rafe grabbed her arm, sending shivers of heat racing through her. If he kept it up, she'd be taking him to the privacy of her own home instead.

"Three blocks from my house," she said, zipping her coat. Living in a small town, it was virtually impossible to avoid family completely. Yeah, she could've moved, but then she wouldn't have the salon, or Frankie,

Gerardo, and Serah to harass. She didn't want it any other way. Besides, her house had a key. She could always lock her mom out.

"You aren't going alone." Even though she just met Rafe, there was no mistaking his succinct tone. He wouldn't take no for an answer. "I'll go with you."

Time with Rafe? Yummy! Her internal naughty girl reared her now not-so ugly head. "Fine with me."

Lilith wrung her hands and gazed around the room. Another person—uhh—demon hiding something? Not surprising in the least. She paced the ceramic tiled floor, tracing a finger along a silver-plated flat iron. How she was supposed to slay a demon with that would remain a mystery to her.

Lilith shrugged then arched her lips in a knowing grin. "Sizzle and burn."

Did these women enjoy rubbing their demonic talents in her face? Would she ever learn hers? Did she even have any to boast of?

Lucy rolled her eyes. Just what she wanted, all these demons knowing her deep and dark fantasies. Heck, the way Kalli looked like she was ready to burst into chuckles, she already knew.

"Reading thoughts is overrated," Kalli said, flashing her apparent nemesis a sidelong glare. "I'd rather have the kung fu moves I heard you used on Belial any day."

"It's not that I'm jealous or anything." She bit a fingernail. "It kind of violates my privacy." Then again, *kind of* was a big understatement.

"It's easier to be instructed by someone who isn't afflicted. Someone like…" She scratched her head, a devious grin spreading across her face. "Rafe."

Yeah right! She angled a surreptitious gaze his way. He stood ramrod straight, with his lips taut. Any tighter, and he'd pull a muscle in his jaw. It looked like Rafe would rather undergo a root canal than spend any alone time with her.

Lilith blew out a breath. "How exactly are you planning to get there?" she asked, her eyes narrowing. "As I was patrolling the area, I noticed your friend drive off in your car."

Crap! In all the excitement, she forgot that she lent her car to Serah. Glancing at the clock on the far wall, she grumbled. From what she'd said earlier, it'd be a while.

Grabbing her cell phone from her pocket, Lucy punched Serah's speed dial. One… two… three… four… voice mail.

"Hello, you reached Serah SanGermano. Leave your message at the tone." Not even bothering to leave a message, Lucy hung up. Must've been an important meeting. Serah never missed her calls. That's what made her a great friend.

"Here, take mine," Gerardo said, stuffing his keys in her hand.

Lucy cringed, recalling the last time she borrowed Gerardo's car. Mounds of wrappers, cups, and plastic bags filled nearly every recess of his vehicle. It amazed her how he stayed as skinny as he did.

Noticing her cringe, he smiled. "Don't worry. I just had it detailed."

"Thanks, Ger. You're a lifesaver." She gave him a big ole bear hug. "Just so you know, I would've taken the car either way." She had to see her mom.

"Is it safe to be traveling in public, where any of

Belial's goons may be lingering?" Lilith ran a hand through her shiny brunette tresses.

"I'll judo chop them," Lucy said, posing like the boy from *The Karate Kid* movie—the old school version. "Rafe will be protected."

Lilith and Kalli broke out in simultaneous snickers. Catching their faux pas, they snorted—again in unison. With a huff, Kalli crossed her arms and tapped her toe.

Lilith, on the other hand, plopped back down on the seat, crossed her leg, and flipped her hair over her shoulder. Each avoided the other's gaze like she had the plague. What was the deal with those two?

Rafe pulled on his leather coat and zipped up. "I don't need no stinkin' protection."

Laughter filled the entire salon. Newsflash! Rafael Deleon, Paladin Demon, had finally found his sense of humor. Perhaps the time he'd spent with Squeaky did him some good.

Rafe shrugged, the muscles rippling against the leather of his jacket. He rolled his eyes. "I can be funny when I want to be."

"Better late than never, I guess," Kalli muttered. "I have no qualms with you taking Lucy to check on her mother. Sometimes in times of distress, having your family close by can be a blessing."

Groaning, Lilith shook her head. "I'm not so sure that's a good idea."

Heads turned to Lilith. Every band of heroes always had a naysayer. Leave it to Mrs. Sex-o-holic to be the one. Fancy that—Lucy imagined it would've been Rafe. Then again, he seemed to be rather supportive since he returned.

"She may be a target." Lilith rubbed her fingertips together. "A trap to set Lucy up."

Rafe turned to face Lilith, his jaw firm. "If it's a trap, then her mother is in danger. We are going." The finality in his tone was unmistakable.

It unnerved her, the way she could read this man. She never had such a connection with any man. And the way his gaze burned, she knew he felt it too.

"Guess it's three to one." She smiled and blew Lilith a kiss. "Sorry, toots."

Frankie giggled. "Hey, that's my line."

"It's a catchy line, you know?" She gave Frankie a hug and turned to Gerardo, who'd remained abnormally quiet. "What's up?"

Shrugging, Gerardo flipped his fingers through his hair. His gaze lowered to the floor; he let out a deep sigh. "I am responsible. I let that *thing* into the salon." He shook his head. "I should've known better."

Lucy sucked in a deep breath and took Gerardo into her arms. "It isn't your fault, Ger. From what I've been told about Belial, he's very strong."

"But *mi mamá* always warned me about evil. I should've known."

She swatted Gerardo on the arm. "Hey, he almost got me, so it's my fault too."

Lilith blew a deep breath out her nose. "It's true. Belial is one of Hell's strongest kings." She brushed her fingernails with the pad of her thumb. "He almost got me at one time."

Lucy arched a brow. Lilith didn't seem the type to broadcast such a failure.

Her lips arched into a sheepish grin. "I've been

around over two thousand years. I wasn't always so talented, you know."

"I heard about the whole flood incident. Fortunately for you, God took the blame," Kalli muttered. "It pays being the king's sister, doesn't it?"

Lilith bolted from the sofa and lunged at Kalli. Her nails extending into long claws, she wrapped her hands around Kalli's neck. "Get over it," she hissed out.

"No," Kalli seethed, squeezing her nails into Lilith's fingers as she pried them from her neck. With a deafening snap, she twisted Lilith's wrists and held firm. Her amethyst eyes flickered and sparked. Fangs poked from her mouth. Where'd she been hiding those?

As if Lucy had just turned on the nightly WWE program, the women sized each other up like two professional wrestlers. Thank goodness there wasn't any mud! If these women kept it up, she'd have another disaster to clean up in her salon. It wasn't time for a catfight.

Lucy puffed out her chest and stomped toward the two. Planting herself in between the two raging demonesses, she spread her arms, pushing them both apart. Lilith went hurtling against the wall, a large crack resounding throughout the room. Now that had to hurt.

In a just as loud clanking and clattering, Kalli flew into Gerardo's station. Combs, shears, and curling irons lay askew on the floor. Double the pain, double the destruction. Demolition was now her middle name.

"There's more where that came from," she said, hands on hips.

"*¡Madre de Dios!*" Gerardo flailed his hands. "My station's ruined."

"Nothing that can't be cleaned up, right Kalli?"

"I suppose." Kalli crossed their arm and huffed, angling a defiant glare at Lilith. *What the hell? Were these women reliving their grade school years?*

"Can't we all just get along?" Frankie asked. His thick southern accent wafted through the air like an angel's herald. Amen, Frankie.

Lilith threw up her arms and rolled her eyes. "Fine. For now."

Kalli's gaze darted around the room, then reluctantly focused on Lilith. "I suppose."

"Kiss and make up," Gerardo chimed in.

Rafe snorted. "You do realize the two spent time on a Greek island together."

Aha! From the way these women acted like two wild minotaurs, she knew which one. "Crete?"

"No." Rafe tugged at his luxurious locks.

She scratched her chin, channeling her high school geography class. Her teacher had been a huge ancient Greece fan. "Rhodes?"

"Rhode Island?" Frankie rolled his eyes. "I wasn't a geography major, but I do know that's not a real island."

Everyone burst into laughter, including Rafe. His silver eyes sparked with mirth. Absolutely amazing.

Frankie bit his lip. "What's so funny?"

"Duh," Gerardo said with a roll of his eyes. "There's a big different between the island of *Rhodes* and Rhode Island."

Frankie shrugged then allowed a small smile to curve his lip. "I hated geography class."

She ran out of islands to choose. There was only one left, and she didn't want to go there.

"Lesbos?"

Kalli arched her glare from Lilith to plant it on Lucy. "Just because I was one of Sappho's muses means nothing."

Lucy's head reeled from all this creepy reminiscing. Sappho's muse? Suddenly, nothing about this woman surprised her. She stifled the giggle that threatened to spill. "That's interesting."

"I'll have you know. I was Homer's muse too. So I'd quit that train of thought."

Okay, she'd had enough. She and Rafe were vacating—*now*. The sooner they were alone, the sooner she could learn how to block out the Misses-Pick-Your-Brains—both of them. She grabbed Rafe's arm and yanked him toward the door. "We'll be safe," she said as she pushed the door open, not leaving him any chance to refuse.

"Fine," Lilith said with a wave of her hand. "Don't worry about Kalli and me wreaking havoc in your salon. I'm leaving. You know how to reach me." She snapped her finger. In a swirl of fire and smoke, she spun into her more familiar form. Wild, violet, orchid-laden muumuu and tan orthopedic shoes adorned her now plump form. "See ya." The high-pitched whine she remembered so well filled the salon.

"Mrs. Gunderson?" Frankie gasped, swooning to the floor.

Good ol' Mrs. Henrietta Gunderson. She would miss that old broad.

Chapter 14

"WHICH CAR IS GERARDO'S?" RAFE ASKED AS THE door shut behind them. He stood tall, the crisp cold air whipping his hair behind him. He kept his jaw firm as he gazed down at her. Damn! He was tall! Even at five-eight, Lucy wasn't exactly short. But she was when she was with Rafe... massive... muscular... sexy. Her mind drifted back to earlier, to Rafe's mouth on hers. She could still taste the spicy sweetness of peppermint as his tongue rolled against hers. She had to do it again!

Muscles strained against leather as he led her across the street to the parking lot. Her breath caught. He was magnificent. She fidgeted with her new designer sunglasses and pushed a lock of hair behind her ear. Snow swirled around them like big fluffy puffs of cotton. Some clung to his hair, sparkling against the sun's rays. Once again, this man had rendered her speechless.

"Lucy!" His firm tone sent jolts of awareness racing through her.

"W-what?" she managed, glancing away sheepishly. Thank goodness, this man couldn't read minds, or he'd know how badly she wanted to jump his demonic bones.

He raked a hand through long locks. "I asked which car was Gerardo's."

"Oh." *Come on brain, don't fail me now.* "Umm, the purple PT Cruiser over there," she replied, pointing at

Gerardo's car. "So I suppose you can't poof in broad daylight?"

Rafe nodded, his gaze searching. Silvery mists circled their depths, like two giant oceans. Deep and mesmerizing, like someone who'd experienced life. "You figured correctly."

Blinking, she approached the car and laughed. "Funny, Gerardo," she said, perusing his new bumper sticker. In big blue letters, with a rainbow in the corner, it read "We Are Everywhere." *Doo-bee-doo-bee-doo*.

Rafe came to stand next to her, his body inches from her. She loved the heat that rolled off him. "Should I ask?"

"Probably not," she replied with a click of a button. Gerardo's car beeped in response as the alarm was disabled. "I promise I'll be gentler this time," she said, lacing her reply with innuendo. Lord knew her inner naughty girl had no gentle intentions.

Rafe snorted. "I hope so."

"Gerardo's car is roomier." She extended her arm. "After you."

Rafe swung the door open. "These modern inventions never cease to amaze me."

Did she amaze him? He certainly amazed her. With a smile, she opened the door, sending a pile of snow flying in her face.

With a shiver, she brushed off the cold flakes. What a wonderful way to make an impression on the Adonis.

"Cold?" Rafe asked as he stepped into the car. Was that a wink? Was she now an object for his amusement?

She shrugged. "Just a tad."

Taking a seat next to Rafe, she slipped on her seat belt and popped the key in the ignition. With a quick twist, the car hummed to life. The sooner they blew out of here, the better. She pressed her foot to the brake, turned to Rafe and smiled. "Hold on to your shorts." With a quick tug, she pulled the car into reverse and backed out.

The expression on Rafe's face would remain etched in her mind. Ramrod-tall, teeth clenched, and fingers firmly gripping the door handle. Like they were going to the moon, not her mom's.

She shook her head and rolled her eyes. "Have you ever ridden in a car before today?"

"The last car I've traveled in was a 1910 Model T." Rafe's lips curved into a wide grin.

Whoa! That long? "Wow, it's been a while, hasn't it?"

The silver in his eyes sparked. "About twenty years."

"Huh?"

With a tiny grin forming on his lips, Rafe raked a hand through his hair. "The Fore-Demons sent me to stop a small blood-demon attack at an antique car show. It was the only thing available."

"Did you get the bad guys?"

Jaw twitching, Rafe nodded. The bright silver of his eyes swirling and stormy. "Not without some casualties, but no humans died."

"That's awesome."

Shrugging, Rafe looked away, out the window at the passing scenery. "A small success."

"Small?" Lucy's eyes widened. This guy had a serious inferiority complex. And she thought she was bad. "You saved lives. There's nothing small in that."

"I suppose," he said on a sigh.

That was an improvement... of sorts. The bout of awkward silence announced the conversation was done. And they were making such progress, too. Taking a right onto Lover's Lane, she secretly wished she'd brought a safety helmet. There wasn't anything lovely about the road at all. Potholes, snow, and ice didn't mix. With a jerk and a jolt, she drove over a hole the size of Lake Michigan.

"There goes the alignment. Gerardo will be pissed." This time she swerved to avoid the Atlantic Ocean. Three things were certain when traveling Michigan roads in winter: ice, snow, and huge-ass potholes.

Rafe winced as his head bounced against the roof. "How much longer?"

Slowing down the car, she hung a left onto Stonebrook Road. "About five or ten minutes." She'd never felt so awkward in her life. Here this totally sexy man sat in her car, and she was at a complete loss of words. Small talk had never been her forte.

It was time to change that. "So how old are you?"

"Old enough." Rafe scrubbed a hand through his hair. Apparently he wasn't much of a conversationalist either.

"Look, Rafe, I know you have things you'd rather be doing," she said as she took another right. "But if we're going to work together, we need to you know… communicate."

"Four hundred and fifty-five."

Lucy arched a brow. "Huh?"

"I'm four hundred and fifty-five years old." Rafe shrugged. "I stopped keeping track in the late nineteenth century, so I needed some time to go back and count."

Talk about the fountain of youth. "Wow. You don't look a day over one hundred."

Rafe smirked. "Thank you, I think."

"You're welcome." She took the final turn onto Wellington Road—her mom's street.

"That's my mom's house right there." She pointed to the two-story canary-yellow Cape Cod. Wreaths bedecked each window. Santa and his reindeer stood guard in the front yard. Blow-up snowmen and polar bears bearing gifts sat proud. Strings of sparkling icicles and snowflakes dotted the eaves. Gaudy, yet pretty in a strange sort of way.

"Wellington, eh?"

Lucy shrugged. "The people here have a thing for historical names. I live on Waterloo Drive."

"I aided Wellington at Waterloo," Rafe replied, his gaze somber.

"Don't tell me Napoleon was a demon?"

He shook his head. "No, but he was plagued by them. Greed, power, and envy, mostly. It was one of our tougher assignments."

"Didn't the English win that battle?"

"Not without casualties," Rafe said, his voice nondescript.

Would he ever give himself some slack? "It's war. There's bound to be deaths. And since Napoleon was defeated, I'm guessing you sent some demons packing."

"I suppose." Rafe's jaw twitched.

Pulling into her mom's driveway, she craned her head to meet Rafe's gaze. Maybe she could soften him up another way.

With boldness she didn't know she possessed, she reached across the seat and traced her finger along his jaw—slowly, tenderly. Heat crackled between her finger and his skin, a heavy inferno racing between them.

He sucked in a breath. "Lucy…"

"Shh," she whispered, drawing her fingertips down further and lingering over the thrumming pulse at the base of his neck. "You *are* a hero."

The silver in his eyes swirled and sparked like sensuous waves of a turbulent sea. She didn't care much for waxing poetic, but it was worth a sonnet or two. With more brazen wanton, she leaned across the seat.

"What do I have to do?" she asked, her tone seductive, or what she hoped was seductive. She was new to all this sexpot stuff and didn't know what the hell she was doing. She fumbled with the zipper of his jacket, her mouth curving into a wry grin.

"For what?" Rafe asked on a choked breath.

She angled her gaze upward and brought her pinkie to her mouth. Nothing like a little teasing to lighten the mood. She reached back over and rubbed Rafe's shoulder.

"To block Kalli's and Lilith's mind breach, of course."

A frown curved his lips. The silver oceans of his eyes became placid ponds. "It's easier to instruct you in a more comfortable environment."

"How about a tiny clue?" she asked with a little pout.

"Close your eyes," he said, his tone firm yet gentle.

She obeyed him like an obedient puppy. A cute fluffy puppy, nonetheless. "And?"

"Hmm," he said, his tone thoughtful. "Turn your head to face me."

Without reservations, Lucy angled her head to face his. "Okay?"

"Stay still."

"I'm trying," she replied, her grin wide.

"Don't try to tempt me, Lucy." His breath, hot and

heavy, inched along her cheek and to her ear. Shivers of excitement jolted through her body. "You might not like what you get."

Like hell she wouldn't. Her breath hitched. The energy crackling through her body must've jumbled all thought and speech processes. "I doubt that," she managed with a squeak. Ugh, not that stupid squeak again.

"I love that squeak," Rafe said. "Especially when I first stepped into your shop." He shook his head, doubt clouding his eyes. "You've entranced me beyond words."

She couldn't control herself any longer. Without hesitation, she opened her eyes, wrapped her arms around Rafe's neck and laced her fingers through his hair. They were going to kiss again. Outside her mom's house, nonetheless. In broad daylight. She trained her gaze toward the garage. Her mom's snow-white, gas-guzzling Cadillac Escalade sat big and proud in the driveway, glinting in the afternoon sun.

Ooh! Mom was home! Talk about living dangerously. What would the neighbors think?

Screw the neighbors, her inner sexy self whispered. She was beginning to like this inner demon.

She grabbed on to his hair, her grip tight, and pulled his face to hers. "The feeling is mutual," she said, grinding her lips against his. Pure molten fire coursed through her veins, the energy erupting inside like a volcano. Swirling her tongue hungrily against his firm lips, she prodded them open.

She'd never felt such intensity with any man ever in her almost thirty years. Her heart hammered in her chest. And that taste! Peppermint and musky spices exploded in her mouth as his tongue swirled against hers.

"Mmm," she murmured against his lips. With wanton daring, she took his lower lip into her mouth and sucked. That wasn't enough. She wanted more. Nibbling gently, she crushed herself against him. Her nipples hard enough to bust through her bra, she rubbed her breasts against his leather clad chest. How she wished they were in her bedroom, in her bed, and of course naked.

Windows fogged up around us. Like *Titanic*. She was Rose and he was Jack. All that was missing was her handprint on the window. Oh, and they weren't in that Model T, either. Too bad she wasn't born twenty years earlier. She would've been all for doing Rafe in the back seat of an antique car.

Then again, maybe *Titanic* wasn't the best analogy. After all, didn't Jack die in the end?

Rafe jerked away from her and turned to gaze out the passenger side window. With the swipe of his hand, he straightened his hair. Wiping off the condensation from the window, he grumbled. "What in the bloody hell?"

"W-what is it?" she asked, still breathless. She swiped her palm across the window, clearing the evidence of their late-afternoon tryst, if it could even be called a tryst. A movement near the side of her mom's house caught her eye.

"Not *it* again," she mumbled.

Hovering above her mom's snow topped bushes, the hooded apparition from Macintosh's, black flowing robes, hood, and all, floated along the house. Despite the darkness of its façade, she didn't get that dark vibe from it at all. Then again, she didn't get that vibe from the *Arca Inferorum* either, and look where that led her. Hell on Earth.

Rafe's brow jutted upward. "You've seen him before?"

Nibbling her lip, Lucy nodded. "At the restaurant, when I was out to dinner with my mom."

"Then he was here before you opened the chest?"

This just kept getting weirder by the minute. "Yeah, I guess so," she replied, her voice cracking.

The hooded figure hovered above the snow-speckled bushes, snow sparkling and blowing through it. All of a sudden, it turned back toward the house and vanished inside.

Her heart leapt in her chest, her pulse instantly spiking. "That isn't good."

Look at what she'd done now. Her mom was in danger, and it was her fault.

Lucy clenched her fists. She wouldn't let an innocent person suffer for her mistake. Especially not her mom. Despite their differences, she was still her mother and only wanted what she *thought* was best for her. But enough introspect. She was ready to kick some creepy, cloaked demon ass.

"We better move," Rafe's voice cut into her thoughts.

She gulped. Nervousness crept in, scaring away any lingering lustful thoughts. *Think about your mom*, her new superhero ego burst out. *She needs you*.

But truth to the matter, it wasn't her mom who needed *her*. Lucy was the one who needed *her*. She just hoped it wasn't too late.

"I couldn't agree more." With that, she threw open the door to the car and flew out, ready to defend her family.

Chapter 15

WHAT IS IT ABOUT HER?

He should've been able to resist a succubus's charm, yet Lucy had him under her spell—completely. From the first moment they locked gazes he'd been caught. He could still smell the sweet scent of green tea that floated with her every step. Fresh, exotic, and absolutely intoxicating. Regardless of his lack of success as a Paladin, he still had almost five centuries of training beneath his belt. He should be able to resist. But the more he resisted, the more he wanted her.

He was a moth drawn to her flame. He'd never felt such passion from a simple kiss, even the kisses he'd shared with others over the centuries. Maybe the Fore-Demons had sent him to her as a test, a test he would fail horribly. "I'm doomed."

Once, he could shrug off as a fluke. But this had happened more than once. Twice they had kissed and twice, the reaction had been the same. Explosive passion. Lust and desire. If it hadn't been for those two inconvenient interruptions, they would've gone farther than just a kiss, and that disappointed him.

Bloody hell. "I'm losing my powers," he muttered beneath his breath.

It was the only explanation. Any time she came near, he couldn't help himself. Pure molten desire raced through him whenever they touched. He angled his gaze toward the driver's side window. Lucy stood in knee-deep snow, scanning the area. Hopefully she didn't have any questions about their unwelcome visitor. Because, frankly, he didn't have answers. At least not ones she wanted to hear.

The sooner he finished his mission, the better. The sooner he could concentrate on saving his sister. Maybe then he could forget about Lucia Anne Gregory and the almost obsessive hold she had on him. Had he known what he signed up for, he might never have accepted the mission. Then again, the Fore-Demons had made their choices. To go against them was to sign away your life as Paladin, forever wasting away in purgatory. What a bunch of good he'd do for Luc... Coby there.

"I'll contact the elder council later tonight."

Perhaps they could reassign him? Or maybe Nic would trade assignments with him. After all, Nic was more than capable of protecting Lucy, and he wouldn't falter. *Like I'm doing now.*

Not bloody likely, his inner self replied. Knowing of Nic's own private obsession, Rafael knew it would take a small act of God to get him to switch their missions. After all, this wasn't a small outbreak like they were used to.

"This is the dawning of the bloody Apocalypse, and I've been thrown right into it."

As a Paladin in training, he'd been warned of the impending crisis. Every Paladin's thorough training had prepared them for it. He'd always assumed he'd fight with Nic and Coby at his side. He would have to fight this battle alone. He craned his gaze back to Lucy, who trudged toward her mother's house, a string of expletives rumbling from her mouth.

She would not fight this battle. He wouldn't let her. Things were more complicated now than he ever imagined. It wasn't any normal apparition. It was a Sexubi. A rather powerful one at that. He hadn't gotten close enough to know whether it was a he or she or if it was one of Lamia's or not. Regardless, the situation was dangerous.

Lucy turned and tramped her way back toward the car. Knocking on the window, she threw him a piercing gaze. Bloody hell, he knew that look. Anger and frustration swirled in her eyes. To be honest, he couldn't blame her. He felt the same way about his sister.

Rubbing his jaw, he concentrated back to Coby. He could only hope that Nic was still pursuing her rescue. From their previous conversation, he hadn't seemed too hopeful. He clenched his fists. Some days he hated being a demon.

"Are you going to sit in the car all day? We need to vanquish a creepy demon *thing*." She crossed her arms and let out an exasperated sigh.

Rafael blinked. She was picking up the demon lingo rather well. Throwing open the door, Rafael nodded. "I was thinking."

"Thinking?" Incredulity laced her voice. "About what?"

"We should exercise caution."

She rolled her eyes. "No shit, but you, yourself, should know what I'm going through." Throwing up her hands, she harrumphed. "My mother is in danger!"

So someone told her about Coby? It didn't surprise him one bit. A gossiping lot Kalli and Lilith were. He didn't want to think about his sister, not now.

Stay strong. Don't let her see you weak.

"Maybe I do, maybe I don't." Rafael winced. He sounded like a spoiled little brat.

A deep growl rumbled from her as she pounded her gloved fist into her other palm. "Maybe you need me to kick your fine ass."

With as much fire as she possessed, she probably could. His jaw tightened and his heart raced. Her fire, strong, uncontrollable, dangerous… and he was almost falling into that fire—hard.

"Fine," she ground out. "I'll go by myself." With that she spun around and tromped toward her mother's snow-topped house.

With a sigh of resignation, Rafael swung the door open further and stepped out of the car. "Wait!" he yelled, plowing out of the car and into the snow. Glancing toward the western sky, his heart plummeted.

Dark billowing clouds swirled and churned in the distance. A black mist circled them, forming more menacing clouds. Winds whipped, growing stronger with each gust, sending white blasts of powder against his face.

"This isn't good," he muttered as he trudged up the driveway behind Lucy.

With cautious steps, Lucy shimmied toward the back of her mom's house, Rafe steady on her heels. Hopefully her mom still kept the key hidden in that blatantly obvious plastic rock. Only the person with an IQ of a rock would fall for that trick. Might as well just paint the word *KEYS* in big bright red letters on the front of it.

Tromping through a foot of snow, she swung open the gate as far as she could with a drift of snow piled behind it.

With a few muffled curses—some made up—she muddled through the snow. Nothing like climbing through knee-deep snow to burst her already-fraying nerves.

"I hate snow!" she grumbled.

As if sensing her displeasure, a whirlwind of the annoyingly cold fluff bombarded her face. "Damn!"

Tromping next to her, Rafe glanced up to the ominous gray clouds churning to the west. "Bloody hell."

"What is it?"

"Bad weather."

She rolled her eyes. "It's Michigan in December. Get used to it."

"Are your winter storm clouds usually that dark?"

"To be honest, I never paid much attention to the clouds." Squinting, she further inspected the dark masses. "The snow blowing in my face usually blocks my view."

"Those aren't normal storm clouds, Lucy." Rafe stuck his hand in his pocket and pulled out a black skullcap. Pulling the hat on, he turned to face her. "We need to move... *now!*"

Noting Rafe's patented stony intense glare, she fidgeted with her hat. "Okay. I'll go in through the back. You do your poof thing."

"I can't *poof* until you're inside. I need a person or place to visualize. I've never been inside your mother's house."

"You aren't missing much, unless hideous amounts of Christmas decorations are your thing."

"I suppose not." Rafe scratched his chin. "You go in through the back door, and I'll travel once you're inside."

"Sounds good to me," she said through blowing snow. "So what's the deal with the creepy floating guy?"

"I don't know," he replied, gazing up and away from her. Great, he was hiding something again. "I need to investigate."

"Fine," she said, her tone short. "See you inside." With as much pride as she could muster, she stood proud and stomped her way through the snow. The sooner she got to her mother the better.

Digging around in the snow, in bare hands nonetheless, she searched for the plastic stone. She craned her gaze to Rafe, who scratched his head, a puzzled expression etched across his face.

"I'm looking for the spare key," she said, sounding lame. "She keeps it hidden."

With the arch of a brow, Rafe nodded. "Just hurry."

"Yes master," she mumbled under her breath. Then again, being at Rafe's mercy did have some delicious merits. Her mind flitted off to him doing all sorts of deliciously naughty things to her. She knew she liked it kinky; she just didn't know she had that sort of kink in her. Her lips curved into a devilish grin. She so couldn't wait to get him alone to herself. If it was as good as his kisses... ooh-la-la. She bit her lip. The more time she spent with this man, the more daring she became. Alarmingly exciting.

Then her hand connected with cold plastic, breaking her from those ever rising lustful thoughts. "Found it!" She flailed the fake rock like it was a prize. Flipping it over, she pried the key from its hiding spot. Standing, she brushed the thick snow from her jeans and coat. It was time to take on Rafe's commanding tone. "Let's go!"

With steps as sure as she could take through the pile of snow, she tramped up the steps. Wasting no time, she inserted the key and unlocked the door. Without hesitation, she pushed open the door and stepped inside. She stomped her shoes and scraped them against the floor mat. Even in her urgency, she knew not to inflict the wrath of Mom. Wet, sloppy, snowy floors would trip her switch—big time.

Dashing through the breezeway, she stepped up the ledge and headed into her mom's kitchen. She'd gone all out this year. The scent of cinnamon and spice wafted through the air, tickling her nose. Piles of red and green sprinkled sugar cookies sat on the counter, beckoning her to steal one. If there was one thing her mom was good at, it was baking cookies. Santa and snowmen magnets plastered her refrigerator, while boughs of holly hung and mistletoe dangled from the doorways. Darn, where was Rafe when you really needed him?

As if answering her thoughts, in a misting swirl of ice and snow, Rafe materialized in front of her—right on top of her mom's snowman-bedecked table. Luckily for his head, he'd missed her crystal chandelier by a mere centimeter.

"Now isn't the time for a table dance."

Mumbling an apology, he climbed down from the table, leaving a pair of giant boot prints right on Frosty's face. Despite mom's wrath, she managed a chuckle. If he thought battling Belial would be bad, wait until he met her mom.

"Have you seen your mother yet?"

"No," she replied, loping into the living room. "Maybe she's in the basement doing laundry or—"

Her eyes bugged out of her head. Had her mom surrendered to Christmas fads? Apparently so. Even Lucy, a person who didn't spread the holiday spirit, couldn't believe it.

When she'd mentioned she was getting an upside-down Christmas tree, Lucy thought she was BS-ing. Seeing the bizarre thing there, hanging from her ceiling, Lucy let her mouth gape open. Tip pointing down, it twinkled and flashed, oblivious to the fact it was upside down.

"Something about that just isn't right," she mumbled to Rafe as he came to stand next to her. "Who in their right mind hangs a Christmas tree upside down?"

Mom, obviously! Then again, maybe she wasn't in her right mind.

"The Germans did in the Middle Ages," Rafe whispered, turning her toward the stairway. "We still need to search the upstairs and the basement."

"I'll take the upstairs, and you take the basement if you want," she said as she took the first step.

Eyes stony serious, Rafe grabbed her arm, sending bolts of sizzling energy through her. "No, we go together."

"Fine, follow me," she said, pushing up the steps. Turning the corner to take the last set of steps—

The muffled groan from upstairs rang in her ears, striking her speechless. Her heart plummeted into her stomach. "Oh God," she managed, her voice cracking. "We're too late."

Rafe grabbed her arm. Rough calloused pads brushed

against her soft skin. Heated friction sparked. *Not now*, her mind screamed.

"That doesn't mean anything," he whispered in her ear, the silky strands of his hair brushing against her cheek. With his thumb and index finger, he raised her chin so she could meet his gaze. His silver eyes swirled with unfathomable intensity. "Better late than never, Lucy."

Rafe's words of inspiration kicked her ass in gear. She straightened her back and raised her chin. With smooth steps, she swiveled around and took the remaining stairs two at a time. There were only four of them, after all.

Wrapping his fingers around her upper arm, Rafe turned her to face him. "Get behind me," he ground out, his gaze burning. "You're a woman. *I'm* supposed to protect you."

Oh hell no! He didn't just go there. But the stern glare said everything. Hadn't he heard of women's lib? "Look here buddy, it's the twenty-first century. You need to get with the times."

Another loud grunt and strangled groan drifted from the far room—her mom's bedroom. Off-limits since she was a kid. She'd make an exception this time.

Hello! This was her mother! She wanted to do the protecting. It was her fault her mother was in danger. *She* had to do something.

"Sorry, Rafe. I need to do this."

"What? You can't," he hissed, breaths of air teasing along her ear. "You have no training. You could die."

Shrugging, she ripped her arm from his grasp. "I survived Belial once. I can do it again."

"Lilith was there to protect you."

"Yeah, and you're here now." Throwing her hands on her waist, she threw him a defiant glare. "Consider yourself my backup."

The knowledge that this man wanted to put himself out there to defend her flattered her, but his gruffness infuriated her just as much, if not more. Her fists in tight balls, her nails dug into her palm. Didn't he realize she had an obligation to protect her mother? She'd never felt so driven in her life.

"I've failed too many people I…"

"You what?"

"I've been assigned to."

That's right. She was only an assignment. An inconvenience. If she had heard Lilith correctly, Belial's guards had kidnapped Rafe's sister. *And here he is, with little ol' me.*

Then to find out a woman he thought had died in his arms over two hundred years ago had joined forces with the big bad Infernati didn't help matters much either. She saw where he was coming from, though. He must've cared for Larissa—or whatever she called herself back then—a lot. Knowing she was now working for the bad demons must've been a total kick to the balls.

She chose her words carefully. "I know you've got a duty, Rafe. But I have a duty too. My mother needs me." She flashed him a pleading gaze. "Besides, you don't know what room is hers."

Rafe crossed his arms, his eyes thoughtful. "It isn't safe."

"I know!" She grabbed Rafe's shoulders and looked him directly in the eyes. "But the more we argue, the more unsafe it gets for my mom."

Drawing in a long breath of air, Rafe pulled her hands from his arms. "Lucy..."

She reached up and stroked a strand of hair from his chiseled cheek. "Come on, Rafe," she urged. "Besides, you'll be right behind me."

"Fine," Rafe growled. "Let's go."

"Thanks, hon." With a smile, she leaned in and kissed his cheek. Electricity crackled through her entire body. Just from one little friendly peck? She gazed up at him, mesmerized by the swirling of his silver eyes.

A loud moan echoed through the house, bringing thoughts back to her mom. Spinning around, she took off like an Olympian and sprinted down the hallway toward her mom's room.

"Lucy..."

She turned to face Rafe, his gaze stony serious.

"Rafe?"

He stuck his fists in his pockets, his jaw ticking. "Be careful." Yeah, his jaw may have been twitching, but the shimmer in his eyes was undeniable. It was like he actually trusted her.

She threw him a smile. "I will."

With that, she threw open the door to her mother's bedroom. And in a flash, she wished she hadn't. Her face drained of color, and as nausea set in, the saliva filled her mouth. Every child's nightmare had come true.

"*OMG! ICK!*" were the only two thoughts that she managed. She wanted to lose her lunch all over her mother's beige Berber rug.

The sight of her mother straddling a man other than her father in their bed would remain burned in her brain forever. Then again, so would the sight of Mom and Dad.

There she was, performing acrobatics Lucy didn't even know were possible at fifty-plus years. Mind-boggling. She probably had her beat too. She wouldn't know. Then again, maybe she didn't want to.

"Oh God!" She threw her head back in ecstasy. Thankfully, a blanket covered her naked body. "Oh, Lou!"

Lou?

Her mom was doing a man in the middle of the afternoon and she called him by her dead husband's name? Talk about messed up. Lucy needed to get out of there. She should've left already. Talk about train-wreck syndrome.

Maybe she could get out of there without them noticing. One could hope, right? She backed up slowly, not wanting to make one tiny sound. Stealthy wasn't a word that usually described her. Then again, maybe since she inducted herself into the realms of sex demons, that had changed.

Creak!

Her foot faltered on the loose floorboard. Then again, maybe not.

"Oh my gosh!" her mom's frantic voice rang in her ears.

There wasn't any way in hell Lucy was going to wait around and have a friendly heart-to-heart with dear old Mom. Not now. If her mom thought she was embarrassed, she was ten times more.

"Lucy, come back. It's not what you think."

"Yeah, whatever," she muttered, fleeing toward the bathroom. Instead, she came face-to-face with a brick wall. One of the most magnificent brick walls ever.

"Everything okay?" Rafe whispered as she reached for the bathroom door.

Her mom stood in the hallway, her robe wrapped tightly around her, the hair she'd done for her earlier a tousled mess. So that's why she needed a makeover? So she could get her freak on? *Thanks, Mom!*

"Lucy..." Rafe's tone took on a calming edge, and it worked for the most part. "You need to talk to your mother. It's important."

"It's all right," she murmured. After all, she was a woman. "She has needs, just like any other woman." Lucy just didn't care to know those needs. "Let's go. Looks like the hooded guy's gone anyway."

Rafe sucked in a breath. "No, he hasn't."

"Huh?" She narrowed her gaze. "I don't feel any negative energy."

"I'm still here, Lucy."

Now her ears were playing tricks on her. Either that, or her mom had pulled out the old home videos. Maybe this whole sex demon thing had taken its toll. It didn't surprise her at all.

"Lucy, look at your mother." There was no masking that authoritative tone. It always put her in place as a child.

She swiveled around to face her mother, her hair disheveled and cheeks rosy. Gripping her pink terry cloth robe tightly, she blew out a sigh of relief.

Behind her mother, tall and proud, stood the very image of Dr. Louis Gregory. The same way she remembered him, not a day older. Was this some sort of trick by the Infernati? Or was she the subject of some twisted practical joke? Whatever it was, she wanted to retch. In this case, she had a right to.

There's that expression "*You look as if you've seen a ghost.*" Lucy had, literally. She swiped a hand over her sweat-dampened forehead as her legs crumpled beneath her. Darkness took over.

Blessed darkness. At least for now.

Chapter 16

THE DARKNESS WAS SHORT-LIVED—THANKS TO HER mom. Lucy awoke to an ice-cold rag pressed against her forehead. Swatting the offending hand, she groaned.

"Get that thing off my head," she growled.

Her mom's attempt at a soothing voice came out like a squeaky hinge. "Lucy, dear, can't you keep it on for a little bit. I want to make sure you're okay."

"I'm fine!" She grabbed the compress and heaved it across the room. "Go away!"

Obviously her mom hadn't heard about the new sex-demon status. Maybe Lucy had tripped on something and cracked her skull before she walked in the room. Maybe she imagined her mom and dad doing the horizontal tango.

Her thoughts jumbled and her head spun. *That's it!* She had a concussion. Why didn't her head hurt?

She kept her eyes plastered shut, wanting to stay in the darkness a little longer.

"I should've locked my bedroom door," she heard her mother say. "I'm so embarrassed."

"Trust me, I'm more embarrassed than you." Lucy managed to peel her eyes open. With a swipe of her fingers, she rubbed her eyes. "I'm mentally scarred." And not because she'd walked in on mom and dad *in flagrante delicto*, either. It was because she walked in on her mom and her *dead* dad. Her stomach roiled.

"I'd like to talk about what you saw, Lucy."

Hell no.

"Let's not and say we did." If only she could have a lobotomy to remove that memory permanently from her brain. Alas, she wasn't so lucky. Where was a neurosurgeon when you needed one? Oh that's right—she broke it off. Not all neurosurgeons were as *dreamy* as the ones on TV. Dork with a capital D. He even had a T-shirt that read "Your Brain or Mine." Not someone she wanted operating on the most important organ in her body.

"I… umm… didn't see anything." It was her imagination. Come on, her dad died over ten years ago.

"Let me explain." Her mom's gaze pleaded with her, like an injured deer. Oh God, that look was worse than the puppy-dog gaze she used in the salon.

She had to get out of there. "Where's Rafe?" Obviously her mom was more than okay. She didn't need for her to dawdle around here. Squeaky probably wanted relief from chest-watching duties anyway.

"He had to make a phone call," her mom said, still wearing her robe.

"Where?"

Her mom blew out an exasperated breath of air. "He's in the living room…" Her expression grew serious. "…with your father."

"Father?" She wasn't imagining it? What the hell was happening with her mother? *Time to spread the sanity.* "Dad's dead."

Sitting down next to her on her old twin bed, Lucy's mom took her hand in a gentle grasp. "I know, I thought so too." Tears dotted her eyelids and trailed down her cheek.

Despite the weirdness, it tugged at Lucy's heart. And from all the crazy things that had happened since she opened that stupid chest, nothing surprised her anymore. *Dad's alive?*

Realization sunk in. Dad was alive—meaning he'd never died. For ten years, he still lived while Mom and she mourned.

"Why?" Anger and frustration swirled insider. Why in the hell did he do that to his family?

"Your father should explain." She brushed a wisp of hair from Lucy's cheek.

Controlling her snort, Lucy propped herself up on the pillows. "I'd love to hear why he abandoned us."

"Lucia Anne Gregory, is that any way to speak of your father?" Her expression stricken, her mother grasped her chest as if she'd slid a dagger through her heart and twisted it. "Your father has a good explanation."

She crossed her arms. "The old 'I'm a member of a secret government organization and had to go under deep cover for the last ten years' excuse won't cut it. Hollywood's overplayed that story line."

"That's not it," her mom ground out. She'd never seen her mother so angry. Even when she had dropped med school.

"The 'I witnessed a serious crime and had to go into witness protection' angle is washed up too." There wasn't any excuse that would appease her. Her dad had disappointed her—big time. Even getting grounded off the Nintendo for a week didn't compare. Sure, going a week without Super Mario Brothers was hell, but she probably deserved it. But they didn't deserve this.

It hurt more that he'd chosen to abandon them on her

big day—the day she became cosmetologist. The Coif Academy of Cosmetology took graduation very seriously. Being the top beauty school in the area, they had a right to. Lucy didn't like to brag, but she was the top student, as her instructors always pointed out. She was asked to give a speech. She hated speeches—still did. Just the mention of public speaking would send her running in terror. Dad promised to be there, to cheer her on.

He never showed. Lucy was devastated. It was the first time in her life her dad had promised and not delivered. Even her mom, as adamant as she was, came to the ceremony.

"Maybe he had to work late. He's a surgeon, you know," her mom had said, emphasizing the word surgeon. "Maybe something came up." As if her graduation weren't important. But that was the past, and she didn't want to dwell on it, at least not where her mother was concerned. They'd turned a new leaf.

Later that night, they received the call. Her dad was in an accident. He lost his control of his car and slid into a tree. According to the police report, he died instantly.

Lucy ground her teeth. *Instantly, my ass.*

A tear dripped from her mom's cheek and onto Lucy's pillow. It was too much. "Fine, I'll listen to whatever he has to say." She jutted her chin up, her gaze stern as she tried to channel Rafe. She failed miserably. "But I can't guarantee I'll be forgiving."

"Why are you always so stubborn?" her mom muttered, shaking her head.

Lucy shrugged then brushed a tear from her mom's cheek. She was just as much a victim as she was. "I learned from the best."

Her mom gathered her in her arms like she was that ten-year-old girl she used to love. Heck, she still loved her. "I warned him it would get him in trouble."

"Who says I was talking about Dad?" Lucy said kissed her mother's cheek. It was as if they were a family again. Anger boiled again. Had her father not left, they never would have stopped being a family.

Lucy tensed in her mom's arms, and she felt it. Moms were smart like that. "Lucy, please?"

"Like I said, I'll let him speak his piece." She withdrew from their embrace. "Aren't you at all upset?"

"I'm just thrilled to…" Her mom's cheeks grew rosy pink. "Spend time with him again."

I'll bet. However, despite the anger and frustration, seeing him again did give her joy. She wouldn't divulge that information to anyone—not until she found out what was going on.

"That makes sense," Lucy said, pulling herself up.

Her mom grabbed her shoulder. "Are you sure you're ready?"

You have no idea. "For the gazillionth time, I'm fine. The shock's worn off." No lie there. She was more than ready to talk to her Dad. And hopefully, Rafe remained near to keep her in check.

"Let me go with you." Her mom flashed that patented puppy-dog gaze, as a hopeful smile swept across her face. "Please?"

Thank goodness Lucy was immune to her pleading gazes. Bounding from the bed, she offered her mom a comforting pat on her shoulder. "I need to do this alone."

Her mom surprisingly relented. Not without a long emotional waterworks session, though. She was strong. She'd eventually understand and get over it. Lucy paced in front of the stairs, not wanting to make too dramatic an entrance. How lame!

Maybe she was just biding her time. Maybe she was scared. Regardless, she didn't look forward to standing face-to-face with the man who supposedly faked his death to do God knows what for ten years. Was it a coincidence that all of a sudden he was back *after* she opened the chest?

Maybe the angels up in heaven — she snorted — sent him back to protect her mother and her. Funny as that sounded, the creepy caped guy had literally vanished. Maybe her father had saved their lives.

"Why am I giving him the benefit of the doubt?" She shook her head in frustration.

"He's your father, that's why." Rafe glanced up from the steps, his silver eyes sparking. "And you love him."

"Ugh," Lucy blew out beneath her breath. "How'd you know I was here?"

Lips rolling against each other, Rafe sprinted up the steps and offered her his arm. "I... ahh... heard the door close."

Arching a brow, she took his proffered arm, feeling like a Hollywood starlet making her Oscar debut on the arm of a sexy model. All that was missing were those toe-breaking stilettos and a skimpy, wardrobe-malfunction-inducing dress.

Nah! That was more up Serah's alley... the shoes, at least. It was nice being escorted, nonetheless.

Wait one minute!

Why was she being escorted? She wasn't getting married, and she was too old for the senior prom. She wasn't a toddler. She knew how stairs worked. She might have fainted, but with her new super-sexy powers, she was fully recovered.

"Why so chivalrous?"

Arm flexing against hers, Rafe shrugged. "I'm almost five hundred years old, remember?"

"Should you be saying that out loud?" She angled her gaze toward the entrance to the living room. "Daddy's down there."

Rafe's gaze remained firm, sending heat crackling through her. Had she not just experienced the face-melting sight of her parents getting it on, she would've jumped him right then and there.

"Lucy. You need to talk to your father."

She nodded. His words, succinct and firm, left no room for refusal. "So is he a guardian angel or something?"

Shaking his head, he pulled her closer and led her down the stairs. "These questions are better left for your father."

Despite the gruffness of his words, his touch remained gentle. Even when she was an inconvenient duty. It warmed her... made her feel alive.

She turned to face him, almost falling into the silver pools of his gaze. "Thank you."

"You're welcome," he replied, his voice again emotionless and distant. He led her to her mom's paisley print sofa and patted the cushion. "You'll want to sit, Lucy."

She raised her chin. "No thanks. I prefer to stand." To meet her father eye-to-eye, of course.

"I'll sit instead." With an odd spark in his gaze, Rafe

tugged off his coat and slunk down into the khaki recliner next to the couch, the cushion caving beneath his muscled body. Stretching his legs out, he leaned back and blew out a long breath. Like he was relaxed.

What the heck? Maybe he'd knocked down a few brewskies with her dad. He'd always been a smooth talker.

"So my mom says he has a good reason for what he did." Pulling her sweater sleeves up to her elbows, she leaned against the arm of the couch. "Has he tried to schmooze you too?"

"I'd rather let him explain it." Rafe's gaze, even though intense, had a calming effect. "But it is very interesting."

Yep, her dad still had it. He'd managed to reel in the ever so stoic Rafael Deleon. What a feat. Her father could sweet talk a demon. A powerful one, at that.

Sweet talk a demon, her mind echoed. A lump filled her throat as the temperature in the room lowered by ten degrees. She refused to dwell on that explanation. She tugged at her sweater and shook her head.

She turned to face the cold draft of air. Standing before her was the apparition, swimming in a mass of gray cloak, the dark hood covering most of its face. It floated there, as if on its own invisible cloud. The familiar scent of musk and sandalwood wafted in the air. Where was Dad?

"So how can I help you, creepy cloaked guy?" she crossed her arms and raised her chin. "If you're trying to scare me, it's not working."

The cloaked figure raised its arms, its hands translucent. This thing took creepy to the extreme. She slid a gaze toward Rafe, who sat calm and still as a rock. Some bodyguard.

Pulling its hood down off its head, the apparition solidified in front of her. Sandy blond hair peeked from beneath the hood as greenish amber eyes sparked. His lips curved into a wide beaming smile, her father stood tall with arms opened wide to embrace her. *What in the hell?*

"Lucia, please. I missed you."

The floating caped figure was *her dad*? No way! Like she was on a soap opera adequately named *Demons of Our Lives*.

No! No! No!

With a shake of her hand, a deep chuckle rumbled from her mouth. "Wait just a minute. You're telling me that you're a demon?"

"Lucy," Rafe whispered, reaching for her arm.

She yanked it from his grasp. Pacing in front of the couch, she shook her head. She turned a sidelong glance toward Rafe. His jaw twitched and his silver eyes swirled gray. She'd noticed that expression before—when they talked about Larissa and her multiple personas. Frustration and hurt.

Ahh hell. Look what she'd done now.

"Sorry, but I don't understand," she mumbled, turning to face her dad. No longer translucent and now dressed in khaki chinos and his favorite blue check shirt, he stood there looking more regal than ever. "So you're the one who made me this way?"

A wry smile spread across his face. "Quite an accomplishment, don't you think?" His words, thickened by a deep Italian accent, danced in her ears. Accent? What else was he hiding?

"Fake accent, huh?"

Her dad blinked and his jaw clenched. He had the audacity to look affronted? "My accent is real."

Of course. But she'd promised that she would let him speak, and she wasn't one to renege on a promise. "That's some trick."

"I was born in Sumer but spent much of my life with the Etruscans. As the centuries change and humans evolved, so did my voice."

Whoa! Dad was old. She shook her head. Don't fall for his story, her mind screamed. "You're always full of good explanations, aren't ya?"

"Lucy…" Rafe's silvery gaze sparked in warning.

She threw her hands up in exasperation. "What? I don't have a right to be pissed?"

"You have every right, my dear." Her father came to stand next to her and took her hand in his. "I'd feel the same if I were in your position."

His touch was tender, just as it had been when she was a girl. His gaze pleaded, drawing her to him. She missed him so much, but now that he had returned under false pretenses, she didn't know what to do. She took a deep breath.

With smooth efficiency, she pulled her hand from his. "I told Mom I'd let you explain. So explain."

Her dad smiled. "Thank you, my little—"

Narrowing her eyes, she shook her head. "Don't even…" She didn't want to be called a little demon. Especially not now.

"Fair enough." He turned his gaze to the empty couch. "Will you have a seat now?"

She had no choice. She ambled to the couch and took her time getting comfortable. She gripped the arm tight to prevent her hand from doing something she would later regret. "Better?"

Rafe scratched his stubble as he scrutinized the father and daughter powwow. Why was he here? To hell with this protection baloney. Why was their family reunion any of his concern?

She turned to face Rafe. "No offense, but why are you here?"

Shrugging, Rafe sank further into the chair, his hands balled into tight fists. "It concerns me."

She gazed to father and demon and sighed. Both remained straight-faced and tight-lipped. Her words came out a little harsher than intended. "What the hell is going on?"

Her dad blew out a ragged breath and rubbed his temples. "I'm trying to find the right words."

"Say what? That you're a demon?" With bemused wonder, she scratched her head. "Easy as pie. 'Lucy, I'm a demon.' See?"

Her father let out a halfhearted chuckle. "I wish it was that simple."

"Don't tell me you're an Infernati warrior and you've come to bring me back to Belial."

Her dad's amber eyes sparked. Not at her, but at Rafe. Daddy wasn't the only one withholding information. "Belial?"

"Uh oh," Lucy whispered. Hopefully four hundred-plus years of demonic training would help him. But her dad's hard glare said it all. Worry for Rafe raced through her.

Clenching his fists into tight balls, Rafe squirmed in his chair. "I'm surprised Lilith didn't tell you."

Dad scratched his chin and paced back and forth. "I haven't summoned her yet."

Her eyes widened. Summoned? "Amazing."

"Pardon?" Her father's brow jutted upward.

"I'm amazed anyone could summon her. She seems pretty"—*bitchy*—"hardheaded."

Rafe coughed and shifted in the recliner. "That's putting it mildly."

Swiping a hand through his dark blond hair, her dad shrugged. "My sister wouldn't dare defy me."

"What are you?" she asked with a chuckle. "The Sexubi king?" And what did he mean by sister? She couldn't bring her mind to even wrap around the thought. Cringing in horror, she wrinkled her nose. "Tell me it isn't true."

Her dad narrowed his gaze. "To answer your question..." He paused, his eyes narrowing to increase the dramatic effect. "Yes, I am."

She didn't know what was more shocking, the fact that her dad was the king of kink or that the sex addict formerly known as Mrs. Gunderson was her aunt.

One thing remained certain: this time she wouldn't faint.

Chapter 17

HER HEAD REELED AS HER DAD RELAYED THE WHOLE sordid story. He'd come to Earth to "rejuvenate" himself. Sometimes sucking the energy from his subjects wasn't enough, apparently. He met Victoria Jennings right after she graduated college. He'd been up front and honest and said he originally planned on using some of her energy, but he'd fallen in love with her instead.

They even got married in a Catholic church! There went her spontaneous combustion theory right out the window. Then again weren't those who joined the Paladins blessed by angels?

Then came little Lucia in a baby carriage. What a shock that must have been, at least to her dad. Was she a miracle or an abomination? Hopefully neither. She wanted a normal life, not the life of a sex-starved succubus. Another reason to hate her dad.

"You were a blessing, my dear. I prayed that you never inherited my powers." He shook his head. "No one deserves to live like that." Could he read her mind too? Wouldn't be a surprise. Time to test the waters.

Supercalifragilisticexpialidocious. Shit on a shingle. Whittle me this. Whittle me that. Let's carve a big black bat.

Since her dad hadn't busted out in laughter, it was safe to assume he didn't have the skill she despised.

Instead of laughing, her dad's voice cracked as he

continued the story. "My sister informed me that Lamia and those who severed were planning to take over the kingdom." Taking a deep breath, he shook his head. "I had no choice."

"I guess a kingdom is more important than family or your daughter's graduation." Not that it was as grand an affair as med school, but it was important to her. He knew it, too.

Rafe reached across from his chair and took her hand in his. Leaning in, he whispered, "Let your father explain." His breath, hot against her ear, sent her pulse skyrocketing. In front of her undead dad, too? This man had her thoroughly enraptured. She didn't care what he said. Rafe had control over her in a completely dangerous and exciting way.

"I'm not stopping him," she mumbled. With a quick turn back to her dad, she crossed her arms. "Explain yourself."

Her dad's eyes grew wide and beseeching. Typical charmer. "If I stayed, the kingdom would've been thrown into chaos. That chaos would have spread to Earth."

He paced back and forth. "I always made sure you were protected. Your friend too."

"Serah? You never seemed to care for her when we were growing up."

"I wasn't able to tap into her." He sucked in a deep breath. "I have the power of suggestion. And nothing I suggested broke through."

"So she has a built-in anti-demon device, huh?"

"She is the anti-demon device," Rafe mumbled.

With a curious arch of her brow, she looked between the two men. "Umm, okay?"

"She had no marks and an innocent soul," her dad said, swiping a hand over his graying goatee. "She was harmless. She's taken care of you, Lucy. I'm very grateful."

"Cool. I'll let her know." And now the question of the hour, because *executioning* minds wanted to know. "Why'd you come back?"

"Lamia's prized minion showed her overly pretty face."

Rafe sucked in a ragged breath. His eyes swirled with turmoil. "Amanda."

Lucy reached over and took his hand in hers. Surprisingly enough, he didn't pull away.

"Leticia, Lily, Linda, and Laurel, to name a few more." Glancing over at Rafe and her, her dad shook his head.

With a quick jerk, they pulled their hands away. Rafe turned to the window, and she swiped a hunk of hair from her cheek. So much for consolation.

Dad cleared his throat. "She thought she'd be sneaky and use a different name this time, but Lilith was on the ball—as always."

Good ole Lilith. "Great disguise, by the way," she said with a snicker. "Gives new meaning to 'don't judge a book by its cover.'"

"My sister is a mistress of disguise."

"Among other talents, I'm sure." And why was the sex demon formerly known by five other names targeting her dad and her? It had to do with more than just Lamia. "What's so bad about Larissa taking Joshua off my hands?"

Her dad flashed a sidelong glance at Rafe. "Yes, Joshua Carlson wasn't the best man for you, but even so, to move in on another succubus's mate is against Sexubi code. Then again, Lamia makes her own code."

"Lamia sounds like a real winner." And hopefully she wouldn't have to meet her.

"I can handle Lamia." Rafe clenched his fist. "I have before."

Her dad crossed his arms. "Yet here she keeps coming back for more."

Maybe she was a masochist? Lucy turned the conversation back to Josh's fiancée. "So how does Larissa fit in?"

"Miss Newell, as she was known when I first lay with her, was one of Lamia's human servants. The enchanting aura of her sensuality enraptured me." Her father snorted. "I took her virginity."

Rafe sucked in a hard breath, teeth clenching as her dad revealed all the dirty details. "Go on."

"She told me she'd been with men. She lied. I might need sex to survive, but I swore as king to never take someone's innocence."

"She told me something completely different," Rafe mumbled.

"Amanda claimed to love me." Her father shook his head. "But it was a trap set up by Lamia. When her human form died, Lamia made her one of hers." Her father turned to lock gazes with Rafe. "I'm sorry you never knew, Deleon."

"People like keeping me in the dark. I'm sure it was done with good reason."

"She wanted to become one of Lamia's minions... completely." Her father's gaze grew apologetic. "She knew she wasn't supposed to touch you, yet she did anyway. She knew exactly what would happen."

"How comforting."

Rafe's voice, so hollow, tore at her heart. She wanted to wrap her arms around him and give him a hug. He needed to know someone cared and wanted to comfort him. Unfortunately, that time wasn't now. It was time to change the course of the conversation.

Thankfully, her dad went on to explain how he returned to Limbo, never wanting to step foot on Earth again. However, he grew weak and needy.

Then came her mother and those same turbulent emotions. As that clichéd line goes: *The rest is history*.

"So, the reason Larissa is here isn't Lamia, at all. It's all you. The woman was jealous of your mom and you. She wants to destroy you."

The joke was on her. Joshua Carlson and Lucy Gregory were doomed long before hot-legs Larissa Harding entered the picture. She couldn't help but smirk.

"Poor Larissa," she said with a pout.

Both her dad's and Rafe's brows jutted up with bemusement. "Huh?" Rafe asked.

"Josh and I were already on our way out. Her plan was for nothing."

"Perhaps." Her dad's gaze grew serious. "Perhaps not."

"What else does she want?"

"Your mother and you dead." Wow, Lucy couldn't have said it more succinctly.

Shaking his head, Rafe ground his teeth. "I can't believe it. Am I that foolish?"

"No, Deleon. You still have human emotions. I have been around for two millennia and still I was duped."

Her dad's eyes swirled like two fathomless amber pools. "I am more foolish than you."

"Fools or no fools," Lucy said, pulling herself from the couch. She placed her hands on her hips and glared like something reminiscent of a gunfight out of an old western movie. John Wayne had nothing on her—or so she hoped. "We have a demon infestation to stop."

Her dad's eyes sparked. "I love your pluck, but this won't be easy. No fun and games like you see in the movies. No stunt person to fall back on. It's real, and it'll be deadly."

She wasn't ignorant. She knew it wouldn't be all roses. After she locked fists with Belial and experienced the stench of brimstone and Atomic Fireballs, she'd learned that lesson. "I'm not a kid anymore. I can take care of myself. Rafe will help me."

She angled a beseeching gaze toward Rafe. "Right?"

"Your father is right." His gaze pleaded back, like two giant puppy dogs wading in silver pools. Ugh! For only just meeting her, he knew her too well.

"But you promised," she urged. "I'm the one who opened the chest, and I'm the one who needs to get us out of this mess. I feel responsible."

"I'm responsible," her dad interjected. "I should've brought you back to Limbo with me. I knew you had powers."

"The only powers I have are a good roundhouse kick and some serious kung fu knowledge."

Her dad raked a hand through his graying hair. "No, you have another ability."

"I do?" Her mind reeled as she thought long and hard. Then it hit like a ton of bricks. "Latin? Why Latin?"

"I spent time with the Etruscans and eventually the Romans. My language abilities passed to you."

"Gee thanks, Dad. So it's your fault the nuns at St. Mary's hated me."

"That and they may have sensed the demon in you. Holy people are attuned like that."

She put her foot down. "I'll stop Belial, with or without your help." She turned to Rafe. "Well?"

"It's up to your father."

Way to pass the buck, Rafe. "Dad? You know I won't take no for an answer."

He threw his hands up in defeat. "Fine." His gaze narrowed with seriousness as he stared out the window. "But be careful. A storm is brewing."

She looked in the same direction. Thick black clouds churned and roiled in the distance. Heavy gusts of winds sent snow drifts flying across the yard. Craning her gaze toward the driveway, she groaned. Gerardo's car, which was clean when they first arrived, already had at least six inches of snow piled on it. What in the hell?

Rafe rose from his perch. "They're preparing for the solstice." Pulling out his fancy pocket watch, he grumbled. "We have an hour."

"I don't like this, but I know my daughter." Her dad's lips curved into a wan smile. "Lucy won't give up until she gets what she wants."

She wouldn't argue that. She'd always been determined. Beauty school, Luscious Locks… saving the world. "Thanks, Dad." She turned to Rafe. "Ready to go?" Her eyes sparked as she loped to the door, leaving him no chance to refuse.

Chapter 18

JUSTIN TIMBERLAKE'S SERENADE POUNDED IN LUCY'S ears as soon as she plopped her ass down in the car seat. She made a quick mental note: *Change ringtone*.

Fumbling inside the abysmal handbag for the offending contraption, she groaned. "Stupid bag could swallow my whole…" she mumbled as she flipped up the receiver. "Hello."

"Hey girl," Serah's voice crinkled in her ear.

"What's up?"

"It's snowing like mad here," came through in bits of static. "Stay… work. Okay?"

"So you're staying at work?"

"Until… clears."

"Hold on a sec." Placing her hand over the receiver, she turned to Rafe. "Serah says it's too bad for her to drive here in the weather."

"I don't think that's such a good idea."

She took her hand away from the receiver. "Rafe says that's not safe."

"Driving back to your house isn't exactly safe either, is it?" Serah said in a moment of good reception.

"Good point. What if we sent Squeaky to protect her?"

"Squeaky?" Serah said with a bemused chuckle. "You want to send a chimpanzee to protect me?"

"Squeaky seems connected to her," Rafe mumbled. "He's a god after all."

"Cool, then it's settled." She turned her attention back to the phone. "Squeaky will be there in about an hour."

"You're serious?"

"There's more to Squeaky that meets the eye, Serah."

"Other than his three-foot furry body?"

"A lot more," she said, her voice firm. "He'll be there in an hour. Okay?"

"Umm, okay. I have some old gangster movies buried in here somewhere. No *Chimpfellas* though." Serah said then paused. "A customer just came in. Oh… a hottie too! Talk later." With that, the phone went dead.

Serah and her hottie clients, oh brother. With a smirk, she shoved the phone into her coat pocket. "Okay, let's go," she said as she put Gerardo's car into gear and pulled out the driveway.

Rafe looked surprisingly relaxed. His hand no longer gripped the door handle and his face wasn't scrunched in worry. Thank goodness he was getting used to riding in a car. At least it wasn't Serah driving!

She turned to Rafe, ready to make conversation as they crept at a steady fifteen miles an hour down the icy road. "So who's this Lamia I've heard so much about? Another ex?"

Rafe snorted. "I have more class than that. She takes the form of a snake and can change her appearance at will. After she joined the Infernati, she chose to nourish herself in a not-so-honorable way."

"How?"

"She feasts on the blood of children."

Her stomach roiled. "Disgusting! So I won't feel bad when I kick her ass, then?"

"In theory." Rafe scraped his fingers through his hair.

"That doesn't sound all that comforting," she said as she slid to a stop. A gust of wind blasted into the car, catapulting it sideways.

"Neither does that," Rafe said craning his head to glance out the frosty window. "Bloody storm demons. Step on it!"

She slammed her foot to the gas pedal, the car revolting by skidding and slipping on the icy snow-covered road. "Easier said than done."

When she had enough traction, the car lunged forward. Jerking the car to the left, she turned down the road and sped up as much as the weather would allow.

"Why would I feel guilty about battling a demon that bleeds children dry?"

"Remember, she takes many forms. An innocent baby, your prized family pet, a friend... a sister."

He'd said enough. Lamia had come to him as his sister. How terrible! As she prepared for another sliding stop, the car rumbling and groaning beneath them, she turned to him. "I'm sorry, Rafe."

Sucking in a breath, Rafe nodded. "No need. It's not your fault." His eyes flickered and flared with each word. "I'm glad the chest ended up in your friend's and your hands. Had it ended up elsewhere, we'd have an even more serious problem."

"But you yourself said I was inept."

Rafe winced.

"Okay, maybe not in such harsh terms, but you know."

"I apologize. I've just never seen any woman, demon or not—besides Jacoba—so determined to save the world."

"Jacoba?"

"My sister."

"Oh." Talk about an awkward moment.

The way too quiet pregnant pause was interrupted by the cell phone—*again!* Now she officially disliked Justin Timberlake.

"What now?" she muttered as she dug the cell phone from her pocket. Gazing down at the display, she arched an eyebrow. Home? What the hell?

"About time," came the squeak.

"Hey Squeaks," she said, her voice chipper. "What's up?"

Squeaky huffed, a sound that came out more like a strangled chipmunk. "Where the hell youse at?"

"We're almost there. It's a little slippery out here."

"Hurry up already. The Boss needs to eat."

"Boss? Eat?" *What the heck?*

"Fuggedaboutit," Squeaky growled. "As for eating, I still have to nourish the chimpanzee body I'm borrowing."

"There's food in the fridge."

"You call that food?" Squeaky giggled. "Frozen lasagna in a box ain't my idea of a meal. Don Corleone would be rolling in his grave."

Time to make this chimp her own offer he wouldn't be able to refuse. "So you want lasagna, eh?"

"Yes. Homemade lasagna, with fresh tomato, garlic, and basil." He harrumphed as if she wouldn't be able to honor said request. She had that ace up her sleeve.

"You're in luck, Don Squeakleone."

"How so?" His voice raised an octave in avid interest.

"When Rafe and I return, you're heading to Serah's work to guard her."

"How does this involve filling my chimp gut with lasagna?"

She rolled her eyes. "Serah's a caterer." She curved her lips into a wide smile. "An Italian caterer."

"Italian?" Squeaky asked in an inquisitive tone.

It was time to seal the deal. "Her lasagna is the best on this side of state. Even better than Vinnie's Ristorante."

"Tell me more."

Taking a deep breath, she recalled the first time she tasted Serah's signature dish. Heaven on a plate, yet still sinful. Her mouth watered just thinking about it.

"Homemade tomato sauce, oregano, and basil. Five cheesy layers, sausage, and beef. Mmm. Did I mention *real* ricotta cheese? No cottage cheese tainting her lasagna." That always hooked 'em.

"I'm drooling just thinking about it," he replied with giddy laughter. "So when youse gonna get here?"

"Five minutes, okay?"

"A'ight."

"Squeaky?"

"Yeah?"

"You need to lay off *The Sopranos*."

"Fuggedaboudit."

Oh well, she tried. "Bye," she said, snapping the phone shut.

Rafe blew out a deep breath. "All set?"

"Yep," she said, hanging a right onto her street. Home sweet home. "Squeaky thinks you don't like him."

Rafe snorted. "I was a little put off at first."

"He does have a unique vocal presence."

"Bloody annoying," Rafe said with a throaty chuckle. "But he's growing on me, voice and all."

"That's cool." Was she starting to grow on him too? From the way they locked lips, something grew. Every time they touched, whether just a simple brush or their *Titanic*-like kiss, one thing was certain. Electricity sparked in the air. Her heart raced. Dang, she was hopeless.

With a deep sigh, she took a left into the snow-piled driveway. Her tiny, yet completely functional, bungalow, despite the size, stood warm and welcoming. A trail of smoke blew from the chimney. Way to warm the house, Squeaky.

"We're back," she said as she chugged into the driveway and skated the car to a stop. Wind blew snow across the yard, and the maple tree swayed with each mighty gust. One way, then the other. Weird… strange… *unnatural*.

Branches snapped, falling into the cold fluff below. Completely reminiscent of a bad Stephen King made-for-TV movie. Now this was the storm of the twenty-first century—demons included.

Screams and howls rent the air. Thick cold breaths of snow sliced into her face as she trod up the walkway to the porch. A branch snapped and propelled into her chest.

Her breath left her body in a giant whoosh as she slammed backward. Strong arms wrapped around her waist, steadying her. The intoxicating scent of peppermint and exotic spices wafted to her nose.

Her body, despite the freezing cold, melted into him. Her head lolled back on his massive shoulder. "Thank you," she said in a breathy whisper. Allowing Rafe to loosen his hold, she pulled herself around to face him. She glanced up, absolutely amazed at his strong jaw, and the dark hair beneath his tight-fitting hat whipping as snow and ice blew. But most mesmerizing were those two silver eyes, sparking and churning with desire. She reached up, tracing a tender finger down his cheek. She was completely and utterly entranced. Not good when a bunch of storm demons were on the prowl.

Rafe's gaze grew stony as he hauled her into his chest. "What was that all about?"

The sinister chuckle sent her blood curdling. "Don't let me stop your torrid embrace." The voice, although haunting, sent shivers through her body.

Wrenching herself from Rafe's arms, she spun around. Red curls swirled around a porcelain face, full red lips pouting. Her ruby red eyes flickered menacingly. Red eyes? Photoshop obviously wouldn't help her photo. Not that Gerardo would want to take her picture anyway.

She clucked her forked tongue, sounding like a cross between Hannibal Lecter and Kaa from Disney's *Jungle Book*. "I'm not happy with you, Rafe."

She needed no introduction—the snake lady herself. "Lamia?" she asked in a hushed whisper.

Rafe offered a silent nod. "Leave her out of this, Lamia."

"Another woman for you to fail?" A shrill cackle erupted from her mouth, her eyes boring into Lucy. "Did he tell you he sent his sister to her death?"

Her body stiffened and she raised her chin. *Don't show her weakness*. "No, but we discussed how we would send you to yours."

"Oh my! A smart one, just like your father." Lamia's forked tongue darted in and out of her mouth. "That trait will get you killed, Lucia."

Rafe gripped Lucy's arm, his fingers like a giant vice.

"Don't let her get under your skin." Spoken like someone with experience.

"I never let anyone get under my skin." Not even Mrs. Carlson. She moved her hand to the inside of her jacket, where she stored the silver blade her dad gave her on the way out. Not moving one flutter, she rejoiced. Maybe she was stealthy after all. Gripping the hilt with newly discovered superhuman strength, she yanked the blade from its sheath.

"Don't," Rafe urged.

Yeah right. She wouldn't give into this bloodsucking bitch. No matter how hard Rafe tried to stop her, she wouldn't back down.

"Lucia, darling. Aren't you a little worried?" She slithered toward them, her green scaly tail swaying back and forth.

Who does she think she is? Lucy tightened the grip on her dagger. "Why should I be?"

"Your would-be protector." She ran long slender fingers through the corkscrew curls, a wry smile curving her lips. Two pointy fangs pressed into her lower lip.

"Protector?" she asked, feigning insult. She yanked Rafe's arms from her waist and pushed him away. "Do I look like I need protection?"

"Lucy," Rafe urged with a low growl, his silver eyes warning.

"Shh," she whispered. "I know what I'm doing."

"We can't risk—"

"Shut the hell up about risks for once, Rafael Deleon." She angled her gaze back to Lamia. "He's the one who needs protection. He's an insufferable boor. He needs his ass kicked."

Lamia snorted. "Doesn't surprise me one bit."

Rafe turned his head to Lucy and huffed, contempt rolling from him like a bad fog. "I'm full of surprises, unlike this woman. A real nag."

Her heart clenched and her body shivered. Why in the hell did it feel like her heart had just been ripped out of her chest?

Rafe turned back to the forked-tongued bitch. "So, where's your prized lackey? I thought for certain she'd come along."

"Anxious to rekindle your old flame, are you?" Lamia licked her lips. "I can summon her if you like."

"I find it hard to believe Larissa Harding, a woman who'd put a crowd to sleep, is a succubus." Then again, it took Lucy a bit to accept the fact that she was one too.

"You better believe it," Lamia said, lunging at her. "My best creation, and I owe it all to Rafe." She angled her gaze to Rafe, her long tail curling up his leg.

Bitch!

She gripped the dagger tighter. She should slam it into her overly-endowed chest. And here she thought Lilith was annoying. This woman made Lilith look like an angel.

With a low grumble, Rafe yanked his leg from Lamia's scaly grasp. "You won't succeed this time."

"We'll see, my darling." Her bright red eyes flickered with venom. "I've yet to fail where you're concerned." She clucked her tongue, the hissing grating in Lucy's ears. "So predictable."

"I'm not as naïve anymore." Rafe crossed his arms, his muscles flexing against his leather jacket.

"I have my ways." She drew her tail back and slithered away.

Lucy had enough. This woman would go down. "Hey bitch!" She raised her chin high, hand poised high with dagger glinting. "Don't walk away."

"I've come to deliver a message. Not to fight." She ran her fingers through her snaky curls. "No need to draw your weapon, Lucia."

"Deliver it," Rafe said through gritted teeth.

Shrugging, Lamia turned around, her serpent tail swishing. She angled her gaze over her shoulder. "Belial wanted to tell you what a gracious guest your sister is. A pity for you, isn't it?"

Ignoring the scaly bitch, Lucy gripped the dagger. "I have a message for Belial too," she said, her voice calm yet firm. With cautious steps, she sauntered toward Miss Hiss. She raised her chin and stared her right in the eyes.

"I suppose I can play messenger for a bit." Lamia grinned, her pointy teeth poking from her mouth. If only she could kick them out.

She bit her tongue, or she would've laid some not so pleasant words into this woman. Words she'd never dare speak in public. She'd put her family through hell. She angled a sidelong glance at the man who still stood strong and towering next to her. She'd put Rafe through hell. It was time to return the favor.

Rolling her eyes, she examined her blood red painted claws. They had manicurists in the bowels of hell. Fancy that. "Get on with it already. We don't have all day."

Lucy stood nose to nose with her, not even caring that her tail swished up her leg. "Oh yeah. Here's my message."

"Lucia..." Rafe cautioned.

Lucia? They were back to formalities again? No thanks to Lamia. She wouldn't regret this one bit. It was fine to fuck with her, but involving her friends and family was a whole different story.

"Spit it out." Lamia's eyes sparkled like two gaudy rubies.

Oh, she'd spit something out. Right in her smug face. With a quickness she was soon becoming acquainted with, Lucy yanked out the dagger and held it even with snake lady's heart—if the cold-blooded bitch even had one. She could simply slam the weapon in and send her wherever it was she came from. But now wasn't the time.

"I should kill you right now for everything you've done." She twisted the knife into Lamia's gauze-draped gown, her gaze blazing. "But you're a tool, doing Belial's dirty work."

"Belial doesn't control me!"

Lucy laughed. "Yet here you are, delivering his messages."

"I wanted to see my old friend." She whipped her tail from her leg and wrapped it around Rafe's waist, yanking him up against her lithe body. She was deliberately egging her on—and by the narrowing of Rafe's eyes, pissing him off. "I see why Amanda chose you. So strong and virile."

She yanked her gaze back to Lucy, the gauche gems of her eyes still flickering. Curving her lips into a self-satisfied smile, she inched her tail near his equipment. She was going down now.

Lucy poised her hand steady, ready to strike.

"Lucy, don't," she heard amongst her swirling

emotions. A female voice—her own voice. Her conscience. What a great time for her to make her presence known. Right when her dagger was ready to strike.

"Lucy, don't," Rafe echoed, taking her other hand in his. The heat and energy that radiated from him was no longer foreign, but welcome and comforting.

Lamia clapped her hands like a giddy schoolgirl. "Please tell me you haven't fallen again, Deleon. You're such a sap."

"No," Rafe replied. Despite the denial, he still gripped her hand in his. "I only care about my mission and protecting Lucia."

"I've seen that hunger in your eyes before." Lamia gazed down at the knife, still poised and ready. "When I sent my precious Amanda to you."

Now she knew what this bitch was trying to do. No way in hell would she let her manipulate Rafe. She'd injured him enough. Lucy saw it in his eyes. They swirled like two giant storms whenever Lamia said Larissa's real name. She also saw it when Lamia mentioned his sister. She had to stab this bitch right now.

And that's what Lamia wanted her to do. Maybe she'd play for a bit; make her think she'd won. But the rage building inside told Lucy something else. She played with fire. Lucy twisted the dagger into the gauzy gown. "If you're going to visit Michigan in December, try to fit in." Lucy withdrew the dagger and re-sheathed it. "Next time wear a coat."

Lamia threw her head back in laughter, the sound crackling in her ears. "The princess has a sense of humor. How divine."

Princess? She'd been trying to absorb the whole

day's worth of events and it finally caught up with her. Her father was king. She was a princess. Not a princess of anything she'd want to admit to in public, but still a princess.

Bow to me, Lucia, Princess of the Sex Demons.

She wrinkled her nose. Nope, not something she wanted broadcast over the eleven o'clock news. And she wasn't all that into the bowing thing, anyway. And now she was rambling again. Probably another of Lamia's tricks. *Evil bitch!*

"I have more than a sense of humor, but I'll save that for a different day." Stuffing the dagger back into her jacket, she backed away. "And here's my message to Belial: Fuck you."

Short and to the point. Lucy's sort of message. With that, she swiveled around and grabbed Rafe's arm. "Let's go. The stench here is making me want to yak up my lunch."

"You don't know who or what you're dealing with, Lucia Anne Gregory! You're making a grave mistake."

Shrugging, she led Rafe up the porch steps, not even giving the bitch a backward glance. She wouldn't let Lamia get under her skin.

Rafe leaned in, his breath teasing along her ear. "Very impressive. Even the strongest have failed against her charms."

"Thanks," she said as the snow barraged them. "But I wouldn't necessarily call them *charms*."

Rafe curved his lips into a reassuring smile. "Good point."

She liked the new Lucy—demon and all.

Chapter 19

As soon as the door slammed behind them, Rafael blew out a breath of relief. Not that Lamia didn't deserve a silver dagger slammed into her icy heart, but Lucia didn't deserve the guilt and anguish that went with performing such a cold-blooded act.

They called it a defense mechanism, to keep the Paladins from straying. In his opinion, it was no such thing. It was their conscience, the only thing human that remained. Sometimes he hated it. He tossed a sidelong glance at Lucy, her dark blonde hair peeking from beneath her knit cap. Today he welcomed it with open arms.

He opened his mouth to speak.

"It's about time." The squeak sliced into his eardrum.

The sooner he got Squeaky to Serah, the better. He just wanted to lay back, drink some wine, and just be himself for a while. Squeaky's talking did nothing to relax the mood. Not that he didn't like the little guy... umm... imp. He... erm... *it* had whittled its way in. But Squeaky wasn't the only one who had burrowed into the deep recesses of his heart. And that unnerved him even more.

Her scent, her taste, her... bloody hell... everything about her drove him to distraction. How could he protect her when he'd become as weak as a young puppy? The Fore-Demons were having a field day with this, no doubt.

Squeaky snapped his chubby chimp fingers. "Is everything okay, *compadre*?"

"Everything is fine," he said through gritted teeth. "Are you ready to go?"

"Fine," Squeaky huffed. "Eager to get rid of me, are you?"

He wouldn't let this chimp know he'd grown on him.

"You're needed at Serah's," Lucy interjected. With a yank of her hat, she shook her head, her stylishly choppy hair bouncing around her face. Breathtaking. "You don't want that lasagna to get cold."

"Since Mr. Deleon here controls me, I suppose I have no choice." Squeaky spread his chimp lips into a huge smile, revealing his big yellow teeth. "And two of my favorite things, Serah and lasagna. Now that's *amore*."

"Oh! Serah has an admirer." Lucy shuffled Squeaky toward the door. "Just be gentle with her."

Rafael blanked that thought from his mind. Some things were better left without visualization.

"It's only for this mythical lasagna I've heard so much about."

Time was of the essence. They'd socialized enough. "Ready?"

With a reluctant squeal, Squeaky nodded. "I prefer to drive, but since the storm demons have the whole town cluster-fucked, I have no choice. If I freeze one hair off my ass, I swear I'll whack you myself."

Rolling his eyes, Rafael groaned. "It's the only way to get you across town in less than five seconds."

Lucy arched an eyebrow, bemusement lighting up her hazel eyes. "Are you poofing him there?"

"Something like that," Rafael replied with a shrug.

"Oh, okay." With that delightful nibble of her lip, Lucy turned away and gazed out the window. She raked a hand through her tousled hair and heaved a sigh.

What is the matter with me? Curiosity was a common trait, amongst mortals and demons alike. It was only natural for her to wonder, and here he was acting like an utter cad. Times were tough. The Infernati were loose. He was insane with desire. Not a good mix at all.

"I'll handle the travel arrangements, Lucy. There are other things you need to learn, first."

Couldn't he say anything without sounding like a bloody bastard? He needed to worry about other things right now. Like protecting Lucy and the chest. The complexity of demon travel wasn't something he wanted to get into. Maybe later. Yes, definitely later. There so much he wanted to do with her. There his mind wandered again! He turned his gaze back to Squeaky. "Ready now?"

Zipping up a puffy black down jacket around his squatty chimp body, gold pinky ring sparkling, Squeaky nodded. "As ready as I'll *never* be."

"Good." Rafael closed his eyes and placed his hands on Squeaky's shoulders. "Go with the winds to the workplace of Serah SanGermano. Protect her."

With that, Squeaky nodded and lowered his head. In a burst of bright light and shards of ice, he vanished.

With mouth agape, Lucy stared at the pile of ice that had once been Squeaky. It was bad enough that was snowing enough outside to make an army of snowmen, but now

Rafe had to bring the ice and cold inside? Not to mention the fact he'd annihilated poor Squeaky. "What did you do to him?"

"He's fine. He'll just have a few icicles in some unmentionable places."

Poor Squeaky. "That doesn't sound fun at all."

"I just commanded him to Serah's business. He'll recover." Rafe pushed his way into the living room where the offending chest still sat, with the styling cape draped over it, oblivious to the fact that the chest it covered had once held a bunch of overzealous—or was it not-so-zealous—demons. Whatever the case, there was no way in hell she would open that chest again.

Ha! He was hiding something, and she just caught him. "I thought you couldn't poof where you haven't been."

"I've been to Serah's." Rafe grabbed a strange book off the coffee table and had a seat on the futon from hell. What a strange book. It was obviously old, with green binding, and it looked two times bigger than the Oxford dictionary. Rafe flipped open the book and took extra care with the pages as he turned them. "Ahh, Squeaky. You're much better than I thought."

It was about time he realized the little guy's potential. "What is it?" she asked, taking a seat next to him.

Turning the page, Rafe scanned the fancy script. "The *Liber Palatinorum*, the Paladin's manual."

"Please tell me I don't have to read the entire book." Not that there was anything wrong with reading, but most of her reading choices didn't exceed the seven-hundred-page limit. From the looks of this tome, it was well over a thousand.

"Only those parts deemed important enough by the

Fore-Demons." He pointed to some of the Old Latin script and set the heavy book on her lap, taking extra care not to drop it. "Can you read this?"

Squinting, she perused the ornate script. The crazy skill she had in high school came back to haunt her. Luckily, the nuns weren't there. "Uhh... yeah." She drew her finger over each word. "It says, 'To prevent another demon from invading your thoughts, close your eyes, surround yourself with warm white energy, and fill your heart with confidence.'"

"Close your eyes and try."

"Huh?" Didn't he say he couldn't read her thoughts?

Rafe's lips curved into a sly yet sexy grin. "Read this."

"'To catch a glimpse of someone's thoughts, concentrate on the subject you wish to explore, surround yourself with white light and meditate, freeing your mind of any negative energy.'"

Bloody hell, how many of her thoughts had he already read? "Gee, thanks for warning me."

"I can only catch a glimpse here or there, but if you allow me, I can read more."

Hell no, she didn't want him knowing how bad she lusted after him. That would scare him off. Then again, he didn't fight when she threw herself at him. "Uhh."

"Only for a minute or two, until you learn how to put up the block."

"Fine. Go ahead, but don't say I didn't warn you."

With a nod, Rafe closed his eyes and put his hands to his temples.

An incessant buzzing filled her brain, similar to the sensation when Kalli and Belial had tried to enrapture her. She shot out the strangest thought she could muster.

In a flash, she followed the book's instructions. And just as quickly, the buzz faded.

"What is a bologna pony?"

With a shrug, she slipped her hands into her jeans pockets and averted his gaze, her lips curving into her best attempt at a sheepish grin. This was easier than she thought. "Nothing, just some nonsense I thought up." Luckily he didn't hear the rest. "So that's it?"

Rafe nodded "I'm impressed." Admiration sparked in his gaze and he scooted closer. He flipped to another page. "How about this?" he asked in a whisper, his breath sending tingles against her skin.

"'To control your demonic powers, close your eyes, and take five deep and even breaths. Count to ten and surround yourself with cool blue energy.'" What the heck? Would she have to spin around while rubbing her belly and patting her head? Or was it patting her belly while rubbing her head? Whatever it was, it seemed hard. Too bad it didn't include illustrated instructions. Those damned demons. Couldn't make anything easy.

"Well?"

She gnashed her teeth. Her gaze remained on the book as she re-read the instructions. "You've got to be kidding me," she said, sounding like a whiney kid. "This can't be for real."

Leaning in, Rafe took her hand in his, electricity sparking between them. "Do you want to control your succubus charm or not? It isn't that hard."

Enough with these sparks. She wanted that inferno— bad. Too bad she had a ten-ton book on her lap. That and she had to learn how to control those overactive pheromones. Otherwise, she'd be dealing with more than just a legion of Infernati. Her mind wandered back to the events from earlier that morning. She didn't know what would be worse: fighting off a legion of Infernati or dealing with two sex-crazed Santa Clauses.

Recalling the jiggling ass full of jelly, she picked the latter. "Okay, I'll give it a try."

She closed her eyes. With slow, even breaths, she visualized herself submersed in a cool blue pool, swimming back and forth. It took all the willpower within her to resist the urge to imagine Rafe swimming with her. After a few minutes and confident with her visualization, she nodded.

"So how do I like test this out?" Shutting the book, she angled him a glance. His gaze smoldered, sending her hormones rushing. *Please God, don't let it work on him.* And how would she know for sure if it did work on mortals? Mortals? It was like she'd been injected into one of those cheesy vampire movies that looked like it'd been recorded on a college kid's camcorder.

"Do you feel anything?"

Bemusement flooded her face. "Huh?"

"I've heard from some of the Sexubi that it feels tingly, like tiny pin pricks on your cheeks."

"Guess it worked then."

Rubbing his jaw, Rafe frowned. *What the hell? Wasn't he proud of her?* "Wonderful," he mumbled as he turned his gaze to the window.

She wrinkled her nose. Snow whipped and blew, stronger than she'd ever seen, swirling like a freezing tornado outside her house, blocking the view of the neighbor's house across the street. Silently, she thanked Squeaky for the forethought to light a fire. At least it was warm and toasty inside. Her naughty side reared her not so quiet head. Mmm, Rafe and her beside the fire. *Yummy*.

So where was the section on getting one hot, hard, and sexy demon in bed? Enough with the hormones already! Her naughty self would have to wait. She had some training to do, much to Miss Naughty's chagrin.

Rafe's expression remained stark, his silver eyes swirling. Frustration, maybe? Was he angry? What on Earth had she done wrong now? "I thought you'd be happy for me."

"I am." He sucked in a deep breath, averting her gaze like she had the plague. What a great way to show excitement. Something wasn't right. And she'd be damned if she didn't do something about it.

With a shove, she sent the heavy book off her lap and onto the cushion beside her. Grabbing the collar of his leather jacket, she turned him to face her, their lips centimeters apart. His eyes swirled and glistened, beckoning her to fall into their mesmerizing depths. She sucked in a breath and composed her thoughts. "What is wrong?"

"It didn't work."

Huh? Her eyes narrowed as confusion flooded her body. Her grip remained steady. "What didn't work?"

"The block of your succubus charm."

With a scratch of her head, she sighed. "How do you know? I felt the tingles like you said I would."

Rafe's gaze burned, sending a flame of desire down her spine and into her toes. Her heart thudded and her mind buzzed. Her fingers brushed a path across a strand of hair and down his cheek.

"I still feel the same," he said, his breath catching.

"You've enraptured me. I'm doomed." Grabbing her wrist, he pulled her hand away.

"Maybe I'm the one who's enraptured." The exotic spices teased her senses, drawing her nearer, beckoning her to reach out and touch him. She wanted him... more than she had wanted any man in her life. Weird, yet strangely exhilarating. If he was doomed, she wasn't far behind. She had to touch him. "May I?" she asked, flashing him an attempt at a sultry gaze. She drew her finger millimeters from his skin. Better safe than sorry, right?

With a slow, reluctant nod, Rafe guided her hand to his cheek, stubbly beneath her soft fingers. Energy rippled between them, filling her with desire. Even though raging pheromones wafted in the air, he remained cool and completely composed.

The awkward silence was killing her. "So why are you so hard on yourself?" Despite her cravings, she knew he needed someone to talk to, to confide in. "From what I've seen, you're crazy brave. Braver than anyone else I know."

"My history isn't that glorious, Lucy."

That, of course, was a matter of opinion. And she didn't think much of his opinion on this matter. The man had managed to fascinate her, utterly and completely. A feat not often accomplished. She loved his drive, his intensity, and his devotion to his sister. "It's glorious to me."

Rafe's eyes sparked, the silver like two flashing daggers. "You don't understand. I am a Paladin. Failure isn't an option."

Perfection wasn't a virtue. "I know a hell of a lot more than you realize. Look at my shop. It's my baby, you know. There'll always be problems no matter how hard I try. Be it a shiitake perm or a bad waxing accident. Nobody's perfect."

"It's different for the Paladins."

Shaking her head, she rolled her eyes. "Perfect people, demons included, suck. The world would be boring without imperfections or failures." The only imperfections Lucy could see in this man were his stubbornness and self-doubt. Who knew those traits could go hand and hand?

"I've failed too many large missions," he said, crossing his arms. "The Fore-Demons will demote me. I have no other option."

Would she ever break through? "But you've had many small victories. Five small victories are better than one major one. Surely they understand that?"

"I appreciate your encouragement," Rafe said, taking her hand in his. "But I've dealt with this ever since Amanda died. It was horrible seeing her…" His breath caught and his eyes sparked.

"What happened wasn't your fault. You were an innocent bystander." Offering a tender stroke to his hand, she moved in closer. "And don't even think about taking responsibility for your sister. From what I've heard, she made her own decisions, whether you agreed to them or not."

"She's a stubborn woman." He flashed a halfhearted smile. "Just like you."

Stubborn? Me? What on Earth was he talking about? Who was she fooling? She could be as mulish as the best of them when it came to something important. "I guess that's a compliment."

"Yes, it was."

She breathed an inward sigh of relief. They were making progress. "Tell me about her."

"Coby?"

"Yes."

Scrubbing a hand through his hair, Rafe took a deep breath. "She's incredibly brave, has been her entire life."

"It must be genetic."

Rafe arched a brow. "Pardon?"

"You're pretty brave, too."

"Thank you. Sometimes I don't feel that way."

Lucy rolled her eyes. "Whatever."

Lowering his gaze, he turned his head. "As for my sister, she chose to protect the chest. Only the strongest and the bravest choose that.

"I begged and pleaded, as did Nic, our best friend." He shook his head. "She stood her ground and went behind our backs. She approached the Fore-Demon Council herself. They were all too happy to approve, even when they knew we didn't."

"Oh." *How bureaucratic!* "So democracy is out in Hell?"

"Limbo," Rafe muttered.

"Sorry. I'm still getting used to all this underworld shit."

"No apology necessary. Anyhow, Coby took her position, despite our pleadings." He let out a deep sigh. "She'd been doing an excellent job of it too. Damn Belial and his Infernati bastards."

Noticing his jaw twitching and his fists clenched, she took control of the conversation. "So how long did she protect the chest?"

"Sixty-five years." His grip loosened. "One of the longest held posts. She's extremely dedicated. I can't believe this happened."

He leaned back. "Even though I originally begged her not to join, I still take great pride in her achievements."

As he should. What a man, fiercely loyal to his Paladins and his family. She reached over and took his hand in hers. "She sounds fascinating. I can't wait to meet her."

"I appreciate your optimism, but Coby's chances are bleak." Rafe brushed a fingertip across her cheek, sending a stray strand of hair behind her ear and her senses roaring to life.

Not if she had anything to say about it. She'd be damned if she didn't do something to help him and his sister. She owed him, after all he'd done for her. "I'll find a way to help you rescue her. My father has connections, I'm sure." She turned to face him, gazing right in those beautiful swirling silver eyes. "If I have to storm the bowels of Hell myself, I will."

"No. It's too dangerous, Lucy. I won't risk your life."

"I have to do something. I care for you, damn it."

Had she just said that? Those words had a tendency to send men packing. Especially hotties built like Rafe. Heck, those words had sent her packing a few times. Case in point: the undreamy neurosurgeon. Then again, he'd said a few other words of affection that would make a greeting card writer vomit.

She was losing her cool. Rambling in her mind, catching her breath whenever he looked at her with that swirling silver gaze, almost swooning at his touch. Now she was certain. She had it bad for him.

Much to her delight, Rafe didn't run away. He only gripped her hand tighter in his. Waves of thick powerful energy radiated between them. Despite the heat, calmness surrounded them, drawing them closer. Was it so wrong to just to be wrapped in his arms, to wrap him in hers? She certainly didn't think so.

They should have been training, but the lure of his body, his scent... everything about him was too strong to resist. Sucking in a deep breath, Rafe sat ramrod straight. Yet he grasped her hand tighter. Despite the power in his grip, he clenched his teeth. Turmoil swirled deep within his silver eyes. What was he thinking? Did he want her? Did he hurt? She could only imagine.

His spicy scent wafted to her nose, filling her entire being. Intoxicating warmth spread from her head down to her toes, and some tender spots between. His hand gripping hers only intensified the effect as energy pulsed through their fingers. Every receptor in her body fired with need.

Damn him, he better act fast before I explode.

"Please, Rafe," she whispered. "Let me kiss you again."

With a daring she was now becoming accustomed with, she pressed her body closer, her cheek brushing the stubble along his chin. It sent delightful tingles racing through her body.

Taking a deep gulp of air, his body shivered against hers. His fingers poised to take her in his arms—or so she hoped. Yep, he wanted her. The pulse bobbing in his neck couldn't hide the fact.

"Oh bloody hell," he growled. Mmm. She loved that sound. Throwing that stubborn resolve of his out the window, he wrapped his arms around her and pulled her against the hardness of his chest. Pleasure spiked as energy flowed between them. Rafe's eyes glowed like two giant moons, full and bright. Good, he felt it too.

It filled them, sending heated jolts through their bodies. Strange as it seemed, they were connected. Not just in the physical sense either. It drove her mad with desire. Desire she never knew existed. There was no doubt now, he was the one who had the control over her—no matter how hard he tried to deny it.

Lifting her chin with his thumb and forefinger, he gazed down into her eyes, beckoning her to jump into the depths of the swirling silver pools. Yes, they shouldn't be doing this, but nothing seemed so right... so perfect.

Ahh... Perfect. She held back a chuckle. Rafe was wrong about one thing. Perfection did exist. And he was it. From his silky dark locks, every angle and curve of his ripped physique, and those eyes. Especially those eyes. Even now they sparked glints of silver. She could get lost in those eyes... Oops! She already had.

"Rafe?" she whispered, trailing her breath along his skin, aching to lure him deeper. Somewhere she desperately wanted him to go. Now she just needed to convince him.

"We're safe right now, you know." Tracing her finger along his cheek, she flashed her attempt at a sultry gaze. From his gulp, she guessed it worked. "You've warded the house, and Squeaky's now Serah's problem. We're finally alone."

"We still need to be careful," he whispered throatily.

"How bad can just one more kiss be?"

Without reservation, she brought her lips to his.

Should she close her eyes or keep them open? She'd never questioned herself before. More heat kindled between their skins. She kept them open. That way, she could enjoy the spark of his gaze.

Crushing her to him, he growled, a deep and guttural rumble that sent moist heat flooding deep into her core. She was done for.

"I can't control myself anymore." His gaze, full of longing, sent her heart rate skyrocketing. "You've enraptured me. And, for the first time ever, I don't bloody care."

Bonus! He wanted her. They would discuss this enrapturement later. Now, she had a demon to kiss. "So what do you care for, Rafe?"

"Right now?"

Trailing her finger down his cheek to his chin, she nodded. "Yes. Right now."

"All I care about is you, your body against mine, and…" he rolled his lip beneath his teeth.

"And?"

He blew out a deep breath, his silver eyes glinting. "Kissing you. There I said it. I want to kiss you."

"Sounds delightful," she murmured, toying with the zipper of his jacket. Leaning into his muscled body, she blew a warm breath of air along his earlobe.

The groan he made was music to her ears. She licked her lips, reveling in the ecstasy she was sure coursed through them both.

"That sound turns me on so much." Her lips feathered against his cheeks, down to his neck. All the while, her hands roamed across the mountains of his pecs and brushed across his black leather jacket. He didn't need that anymore.

"Why in the hell are you still wearing your jacket?" she asked, inching the zipper down. Allowing her fingers to linger along his arms, she pulled the coat down off his shoulders.

A slow smile curved his lips. "I have no idea," he murmured, tracing his tongue against the tender skin of her neck. Ahh, yes, he'd found her sweet spot. She melted into him, gasping as pleasure spiked.

With smooth efficiency, he whipped off the coat and flung it across the room. The tall lamp swayed back and forth as the coat sailed past. Ahh, accident averted. Then again, right then she wouldn't have cared if the house caught fire.

Curling her fingers in his hair, she pulled his mouth to hers. Whoa! It was great having such control over a man. Liberating. She trailed her hands up and down his chest, swirling her fingertips against each rigid plane.

Like the fire that roared in the fireplace across the room, an inferno raged inside her. She hadn't felt this way in... forever. No one—not even Josh in the five years they dated—gave her this spark, this insane desire. Only Rafe.

She needed him more than ever. The closer his body pressed into hers, the more her desire grew. Her heart thrummed an erratic beat and her breath caught. Now if he would only lower those gorgeous lips of his to hers...

"Rafe, kiss me. I know you want to. I see it in your eyes," she murmured, nuzzling her cheek against his. "Please?" Flashing him a pleading gaze, she swirled a fingertip against the hard steel of his pec. He sucked in a ragged breath as the pulse bobbed at his throat.

Sizzling energy cracked between them. She wouldn't back down now.

"Lucy," he murmured, fisting her hair and pulling her face to his. Ahh, it was about time. He took slow tentative nips at first, his lips grazing hers. Even the lightest of touch sent heat pulsing. They were connected… together as one.

Groaning, he pressed his lips firmer against hers, his tongue swirling between her acquiescent lips. Heck, more than her lips were acquiescent.

With care she'd never experienced from a lover, he edged closer, nudging her against the pancake-thin mattress. His hands teased and stroked, sending fire licking across her skin. Flames of need ripped through her veins, edging her on.

"Lucy," he whispered, tracing his tongue along her ear. "We shouldn't do this."

No way were they stopping now, not after they'd gotten this far. "Like hell we shouldn't."

Twisting her fingers in his shirt, she ripped it from his body and threw it to the floor. Her eyes widened. Hands of steel! Bonus!

"Oh, God, Lucy," he said with a ragged breath. He gazed down at the shredded shirt and back up at her. His eyes sparked, not in the gentleness she witnessed earlier, but something all the more primal. Her breath caught as liquid heat pooled in her loins. It was about time. For a brief second, he paused, confusion clouding his gaze.

"What are you waiting for?"

"I wanted to be gentle." Brushing his hands up her body to stroke the curves of her breasts, he lowered his mouth to her neck. Kisses became licks, then licks became nibbles as the energy grew, to consume them whole. Insane desire throbbed its way through her. If he remained so gentle, she'd burst into flames.

"I don't want gentle—not now." They could do gentle later, after they cooled down. And she knew she'd like gentle too. But now, she was too wound up, too hot and bothered.

Rafe pressed in closer, his silver eyes glinting with desire. From the size of the bulge nudging her, he was just as turned on.

She took matters into her own hands. With force she was now becoming accustomed to, she flung him back and straddled his hips. Leaning over him, she ground her pelvis against the bulge in his tight leather jeans. It felt so good.

A loud roar, deep and animalistic, burst from him. Sweeping his hands up her body, he pulled her sweater and T-shirt up. Her soft skin sizzled against his rough calloused fingertips.

"I can't control myself," he murmured, snaking his tongue along her ear.

"Me neither." This lack of control spurred her on and pulled her in deeper.

Hauling her against his body, he devoured her mouth like it was his last meal. Lips melded together while tongues clashed, feeding the friction. His hands, rough and strong, kneaded and massaged her sensitive skin as he edged the sweater up. If she thought she was exploding earlier...

"God, those hands," she murmured. Arching her back, she helped him pull the sweater off. The sooner they got naked, the better. If this was her inner sex demon, then she was more than willing to unleash it. She'd never felt this inferno before, and she didn't want it to stop.

"You're so beautiful," he murmured, tracing a fingertip along the underwire of her plain cotton bra. Ahh well, she knew she should've worn that lacy VS number. Now Rafe was stuck with Hanes instead.

"Sorry about the underwear. If I knew we'd be alone…"

He reached up and brushed a strand of her hair from her cheek. "I love it."

From the swirling of his silver eyes, he spoke the truth. This, of course, sent more rippling energy coursing through her body. Flashing a sultry smile, she threw her head back and ran her fingers through her hair. With a soft moan, she licked her lips.

Without hesitation, he wrapped his arms around her waist and moved his hands up her back, sending sizzles dancing across her bare skin. Any hotter and it would turn into the Fourth of July instead of Christmas.

"You amaze me. I've never been with such an assertive woman before," he said with a nibble to her ear. Fumbling with the bra hooks, he growled. "I see undergarments haven't changed much through the ages."

"Here, allow me." After all, assertiveness seemed to be a turn-on for him, and she wanted him turned on. With deftness she never knew she had, she slid one hook off, then the other. Slipping the straps off her shoulders, she allowed the cottony material to fall and expose the curves of her breasts. Who would've guessed she'd be doing a strip tease for a demon, or that she, herself, was a demon? So surreal yet so damned hot.

"So beautiful," he said on a broken breath. Tracing his

fingertips along the trim of her bra and the tender flesh of her skin, he tugged at the bra and freed her breasts from their cottony restraints. She hadn't bared herself to a man in so long, she thought she'd be afraid. After all, she was nearing thirty and her body wasn't near as young as it was five years ago. Strangely enough, with Rafe, she had nothing to fear.

Meeting his turbulent gaze, she took his hand in hers. Tension quivered between them as their hearts matched beat for beat. "What's the matter?"

"I don't want to hurt you, Lucy," he murmured as he brought her hand to his lips. Turning her wrist, he brushed them across her skin with petal soft kisses. "I haven't done this in over two hundred years."

Her breath caught and her heart hammered in her chest. "I already hurt."

His face fell, silver swirling into gray. "I knew we shouldn't."

Oh man, no way in hell were they stopping. She took his face in her hands and looked him right in those magnificent silver eyes. "No, Rafe. I hurt for your touch." She took his hand in hers. With a lick of her lips, she placed his hand on her bare breast. Tingles of heat radiated between them. She needed him, and he needed her too. "Touch me."

His movements excruciatingly controlled, he traced his fingertips along the undersides of each breast, the rough calluses of his fingers rubbing against her skin sent heated friction through the both of them. His eyes sparked, fueling her already raging desires. If he continued this teasing assault, she'd combust right there on the futon. Then again, was that a bad thing?

She pressed his hand closer. "I'm a big girl. I can take it."

"Are you certain?" he asked with a quirk of a brow.

Hell yeah, she was. "More than you know." She traced her fingertips down the planes of his chest to linger along the eight-pack that were his abs. The way those hard muscles tensed and flexed beneath her touch sent shivers of molten ecstasy ripping through her.

With a deep throaty groan, he traced his fingers across the ripened nubs of her nipples. They jutted up and pebbled in eager anticipation at his exploration. "So sexy," he murmured with a nibble to her neck. Zings of ecstasy erupted inside her.

The energy, hot and voracious, rolled from him, yet he still fought to remain gentle. Time to make his mind up for him. Her fingers darted lower, to trace along the buttons of his fly. Flicking them open, careful not catapult any across the room, she gazed up at him. "Please, Rafe?"

A loud groan burst from his mouth. "You're a temptress, Lucy."

"I learn from the best," she said, popping another button.

"Who's that?"

Sliding up his body, she smiled. With a sly grin, she lowered her mouth to his lips. "You," she breathed, her breath sizzling against his skin.

"I haven't had such a need in a long time."

"You said that already. And just so you know, I've never had this need before either." Her tongue darted from her mouth and traced slow circles along his lips. "So what in the hell are we waiting for?"

A low growl ripped from his mouth, sending her heart thrumming a crazy beat. In a blink, Rafe grabbed her and pulled her against him. His lips ground into hers, hard and demanding, sending her body aflame. Fingers laced in his hair, she closed her eyes and parted her lips. Her tongue lashed against his, quick and hungry. The cool peppermint lingered between their mouths, sizzling against the heat that burned inside.

Like smooth silk, Rafe's hands slipped down over her breasts to brush against her taut nipples. Taking one of the rosy nubs between his thumb and forefinger, he tugged and twisted. Liquid excitement swirled within her body. Fingernails grazing his chest, she returned the favor, swirling around one of his tender nubs. Taking it between her fingers, she pinched. Never had she been this forward with any man. Then again, none of her previous lovers held a candle to Rafe.

Rafe's breath of excitement spurred her on. "Oh God," he murmured as he swirled his tongue down her neck.

"Do you like that?" she asked, raking her fingernails lower down his steely abs.

His eyes clouded over, another moan escaping his lips. "Too much."

"There's no such thing as too much," she said, reaching for his waistband. Curling her fingers around the offending leather—offending mainly because he was still wearing them—she pulled his pants down further to expose the growth of hair that trailed down toward his secret treasure. And she wasn't one for secrets.

Neither was Rafe, much to her delight. His hands

moved with expert precision, swirling over her breasts down to her waist. Hands firmly gripping, he pushed her further into the cushions.

"Mmm," he murmured as he lowered his head, his breath inches from an aching nub. His tongue snaking around the sensitive peak, he took it into his mouth. Tugging the flesh between his teeth, he nibbled and sucked. Blazing energy ripped through her. Her fingers fumbled with his pants as a loud gasp rent the air.

And in a flash, Rafe ripped his mouth from her engorged nipple. Concern and regret flashed in his eyes. "Did I hurt you?"

Hurt her? What the hell was this man on? "No," she said through ragged breaths. "But if you don't do that again, you'll be the one hurting." With much gusto, she wrapped her arms around his neck and hauled his face down to her other breast.

His breath danced across her tender skin. With smooth practiced strokes, he swirled his tongue around the areola. Teeth grazing against the swollen nipple, he groaned. "I need you."

Those three words sent her over the edge. Not to mention, she felt the same exact way.

"Mutual," she said, her voice breathy. With a flurry of frenzy, she moved her hands back to his pants and scrambled to pull them down off his legs. Thick, corded muscles flexed beneath her fingertips, sending heat flickering between them.

"Do you have somewhere more…" He nipped the tip of a tender nub. "…comfortable?" He stretched his legs, as much as he could on the pancake-thin futon.

She drew circles around those massive quads,

reveling in the heat that radiated. With a lick of her lips, she smiled. "My bedroom."

With reluctance, she pulled her fingers from his ripped legs and pointed down the hallway. She'd only known this man two days, but it was as if their bodies were in tune, like they'd known each other much longer. And, now, here she was, about to bring him into her bedroom for some very private bonding. Not even boring Josh had that luxury in the five years they dated.

"Good," Rafe said, the hot breath along her ear broke her reprieve. Thank you, Rafe. No way she'd allow memories of Josh to ruin this moment.

Giving her no chance to change her mind, he hauled her up in his arms and bounded from the futon. With a kick of his leg, he sent his pants flying. Wrapping her arms around his neck and lacing her fingers in his silky hair, she allowed him to carry her.

Holding her tight in his ripped arms, he darted across the living room toward the hallway. Lips firmly pressed to his, she kissed him with a hunger she never possessed. Drinking in his minty essence, she traced her fingers across his chest.

Moaning against her mouth, Rafe returned the kiss as he stumbled over a blanket. With a sexy growl, he kicked it out of the way and took determined strides toward the bedroom.

Chapter 20

REGAINING HIS FOOTING, RAFAEL RUSHED DOWN THE hallway, Lucy clinging to his neck. Protocols be damned. He was too excited to think straight. There wasn't anything they could do now anyway, at least not until the storm demons let up. Soft curvy breasts crushed against his chest, she snaked her tongue along his lips.

"I love the way you taste," she murmured, her hands dancing along his shoulders to his chest. His heart hammered with each skilled caress. The erection of the century raged below. He would explode if he couldn't have her now.

Fumbling with the doorknob, he growled. Shifting Lucy in his arms, he kicked the door open and burst into the room. Soft greens and beiges greeted him as he stormed inside. Quite the opposite from what he expected. Returning his thoughts to the woman in his arms, he strode to the large bed in the middle of the room and deposited her there.

Gazing up at him with those disarming hazel eyes, she licked her lips. Then she frowned. His heart plummeted.

"What is it?"

She rolled her lip between her teeth. "I'm still wearing my jeans." Crawling toward him, she reached out to graze the tip of his erection. "And you're naked."

Her fingertips traced along his engorged length. Each

throb of his cock sent him closer to the breaking point. It took all his willpower to reach down and pull her hand away, but any more and he'd explode. And he wasn't quite ready to explode yet. Not until she was satisfied first.

Still holding her hand, he climbed on the bed next to her. With his free hand, he traced his fingers across her breasts and the rosy nubs. She sucked in a ragged breath, her hips arching. He wanted to drive her mad, like she had him. He wanted her hot and needy.

Molten energy radiated between them, like nothing he'd ever felt before. Energy cracked through the air, sizzling around them. Sweat dampened their bodies, glistening in the pale glow of the overhead lamp.

Fingers tracing down to her stomach, he swirled his index finger around her belly button. With slow methodical strokes, he inched further down. She wasn't the only one who hurt. He ached so much for her it drove him mad.

"Please, Rafe." Her eyes widened, the emerald and amber swirling like a tumultuous storm. "I can't take much more."

He groaned, deep from his chest. "Neither can I." He let go of her wrist, allowing her to reach up and pull him against her supple body. Tongues flicking and hands roaming, deep waves of torrid heat consumed them. With a wanton he never knew he possessed, he fumbled with the button of her jeans. Yanking the zipper down, he tugged at the denim clinging to her curves. How he wished he was clinging to her instead.

"I'm not used to modern clothes," he managed through deep breaths. With a final tug, he tossed her pants to the side. Moving to the undergarments shielding her feminine treasures, he traced his finger along the stretchy band of her white cotton bikini. With a devilish grin, he flicked the band.

A surprised gasp burst from her mouth, her body squirming beneath him. Twisting the fabric in his fist, he yanked them off her body. Yearning pounded its way through his veins. If he thought she was stunning with clothes, naked she was a goddess. A little of Diana's strength mixed with the passion of Venus. A combination that left him utterly breathless.

In that instance, all he could do was stare and soak up that beauty, take in every curve, every line. With silent appraisal, he let her now shredded panties fall to the floor.

"You're beautiful," he murmured, inching his body up along hers.

With slow teasing strokes, his fingertips traced along her thighs. Each swirl, each stroke fired more sizzling energy into every receptor of his body. If they didn't do something soon, he'd burst into flames. Her body, soft and supple, grinding and writhing against him didn't help matters much, either.

"Lucy," he murmured into her neck as he edged his way up along her body. Kissing down along her neck and collar bone, he allowed his hands to massage the swell of her breast. "I need you."

Fear clawed its way into his heart. Had he truly said those words? Was he weakening? But he didn't feel weaker. In fact he felt stronger than ever, like nothing could stop him. And it was all Lucy. Taking control of his thoughts, he pushed them to the far recesses of his mind. His only concern? To have Lucy. Now.

"I need you more," she growled, hips arching off the bed. With a forceful tug, she ripped her hand from his and yanked him against her body. Flicks of fire lashed out as skin met skin. Sweat sizzled on their flesh as the heat radiated between them. "Now, before I explode."

Member near bursting, he offered his own growl, deep and needy, from his chest. He knew he shouldn't but nothing felt so electrifying, so powerful... so right. Every thought of reason left his mind with each throb of his erection. "We shouldn't—" A hoarse moan ripped from his mouth.

Fingers wrapped fully around his hard length, she flashed a seductive smile, her hazel eyes sparking more desire. "Oh yes we should."

Any remaining blood flooded down to his cock. Never had he been with such an assertive woman, and it drove him to the brink of explosion. With slow, sweeping strokes, her hand slid up and down his throbbing erection, her smooth skin sizzling against the bulging veins. His body rigid with need, he squeezed his eyes shut and gulped down a strangled breath. He needed her. Now.

Unable to control the desires raging inside, he let out deep rumbling growl. "You're an enchantress," he said through a ragged breath. Pushing his body against hers, he took her lips with his. With deep savage strokes, his tongue lashed against hers.

Arching up and grinding her hips against his, she moaned against his lips. Her silky soft hand glided up and down his shaft, driving him over the edge... almost. With great restraint, he reached down and pulled her hand from his near-bursting erection.

"Don't you want me to touch you?" she whispered with a slow swipe of her tongue along his neck.

"No," he managed, his thoughts all jumbled.

Her eyelids slanted downward, lashes brushing cheeks. She threw her hands up in the air. "Damn it, Rafe!"

"I don't want your hands on me." He caught her wrists in a firm grip and held them above her head, gaze firm, ready, and wanting. Sliding his body up against hers, he traced his tongue across a nipple. "I want more." Cock poised, ready, and raging with eager excitement, he pressed against her.

"Yes, me too," she murmured, thrusting her hips upward against him. Her hazel eyes beckoned him, ensnared him. He had no other choice. Wrapping arms around her curvy waist, he pulled her to him and pushed inside.

Heaven. That was the only word he could describe her warmth surrounding him. Moist heat enveloped him as he slid in and out. Teeth clenched he fought the urge to bury himself deep inside as his release threatened to overcome him. Legs wrapped around his waist, she met each thrust with wild wanton. Her eyes sparked fire, as molten energy coursed through them, consuming them whole. And he loved every minute of it.

"Rafe," she said on a deep raspy moan, a sound that sent his body near the breaking point. Fingers digging into his back, she lunged upward. Scorching fire ripped through him as their bodies rocked against each other. Hot and hungry, his mouth devoured her lips. Nibbles, sucks, and licks matched time with each quickened thrust.

Gazing down at her with pleasure-clouded eyes, he let out a groan that sent the walls shaking. So very close. Picking up the pace he slammed into her harder, with vigorous strokes.

A moan to equal his burst from her mouth as he felt her body tighten around him. Good. She was close too. Teeth grinding into her lower lip, she threw her head back.

"So beautiful," he whispered, a long lick tracing her earlobe. Sizzles of pleasure erupted between his tongue and her skin. Reaching down to cup a breast, he swirled his fingertip along her tender nipple. With a quick squeeze to the rosy bud, he increased each thrust. He would burst at any moment.

Eyes squeezed shut and head thrown back, she writhed beneath him. Fingernails grazing a fiery path down his back, she managed a gasp, "Please. I've never…" Her words turned into a loud groan as he sank in deep.

As if connected, he knew what she needed. And he'd be a fool to deny this woman her pleasure. She needed it. He wanted her to have it. Completely. With a needy sigh, he withdrew from her.

Her hazel eyes flew open, frustration filling every curve of her face. "What are you doing?"

"Giving you what you need, Lucy." With that, he rolled off her and ended up on his back, his shaft rigid, ready and waiting. "I need you to take charge."

With the grace of a cat, she crawled up on top of him. "Are you sure?" she asked, her eyes wide. Slowly she let her fingertip trace along the tip of his erection. He quivered at her touch and his cock throbbed.

A strangled gasp burst from his mouth. All he could do was offer her a nod and hoped she'd hurry before he made a mess of things. "Please, before I—"

Then she inched herself down, slowly... with teasing torture. Rocking her body against his, she threw back her head and arched her back. Fingers digging into his thighs, she slammed to the hilt. Flickers and sparks of fire tingled as the friction built between them. He was close.

Instinctively, Rafael arched up and grabbed her waist, pulling her up and down with each thrust. Hands raking upward, to cup a breast, he traced the pad of his thumb over the hard nubs of her nipples. Angling upward, he took her mouth with his. Tongues swirling a savage dance, he groaned against her lips.

With wild abandon, she slid up and down harder and faster with each sweeping stroke. He would spill any moment.

Walls tightening around him, holding him in a pleasurable vice, she ground her hips into his. "Rafe," she growled out as she pulsed against him. Moist heat pooled as she tightened around him.

Unable to control himself, with one final lunge, he groaned. A sound so loud, it reverberated through the room. His cock shuddered against her tightening heat. With one savage sweep of his tongue in her mouth, he exploded inside her, spasming against the moist heat that melded them together. Not quite ready to withdraw, he hauled her curvaceous body against his. Tracing his tongue along her full lips, he wrapped his arms around her. He didn't want to let go.

Heart hammering and senses acute, he glanced up

at her. A wide, satisfied smile swept across her face as she traced lazy circles along his pectoral. A deep sigh of contentment blew out her mouth. A dreamy swirl clouded her hazel eyes.

"Damn," she breathed out, resting her head on his shoulder. "Who's the sex demon? I could stay like this forever." She nuzzled her cheek against his, the friction of her soft against his stubble sending more electricity rushing through him.

Odd. And here he was, full of energy. What in the name of the Paladins was going on? With a quick scratch to his head, he let the thoughts tumble through his mind. But one thing he knew. He hadn't been reduced to an imp. Strength filled his every pore, sending rockets of energy racing through him. Like nothing could stop him, not even a demon-induced snowstorm. With a quick scoop, he tossed Lucy on her back, molding himself to her every curve.

Letting his lips dance across her skin, he trailed them down her cheek, to her neck and allowed his tongue to graze along her collar bone. His member throbbed to life again. This wasn't natural, even for a demon.

"Rafe?" Lucy's voice sang in his ears, sweet like the richest honey. "Is that supposed to happen?"

A wicked smirk curved his lips. "This?" he asked, rubbing his erection along her supple thigh. "Not usually, but I'm not complaining."

Her gaze sharpened sending warnings streaming through him. "Not *that*." She propped her body up, angling her gaze to the cracked open door. "*That*."

Following the direction of her now pointed finger, Rafael narrowed his gaze. Intense bursts blinked and flashed, sending slivers of bright light poking through the cracked open door. His heart stilled and his stomach coiled into a knot.

"Bloody hell!" he bellowed, ripping himself from the comfort of Lucy's embrace. Maybe he would fail after all.

Chapter 21

RAFE FLUNG HIMSELF FROM THE BED AND RUSHED TO the door. With a forceful tug, he sent it flying open. With each flash, the light grew stronger, more intense. Like a beacon.

A beacon? Oh shit.

And it was all her fault. She was the one who egged him on. Her and her horny hormones. Lump in throat, she grabbed her robe from the floor and flung it on. Following Rafe, she raced down the hallway. Sitting in the middle of the living room was the chest, the purple styling cape twisted around it on the floor. How could she have been so stupid?

With a shake of his head and a deep breath of air, Rafe reached down and flung the fabric back over the dusty box. She hated that thing. She wanted to kick it and send it flying back to whence it came. Fingers balled into tight fists, she fought her rage. Rage directed at herself.

"This is all my fault," she muttered, fumbling with the ties to her robe. "I enraptured you. I'm sorry." Meandering her way to the futon, she slumped into its not-so-comfy recesses. Fingers scraping through strands of hair, she blew out a ragged sigh.

"You didn't enrapture me." Despite his firm tone, Rafe's gaze softened, comforting her. He took seat next to her and grabbed her hand. The heated sparks now replaced by tender warmth. "I would be passed out in bed, otherwise."

Entwining her fingers in his, she shook her head. Glancing out the window as the snow tapered to a steady fall, she sucked in a racking sigh. "We shouldn't have done that. I should've known better. Karma's a bitch."

"Everything happens for a reason." Despite the urgency of the situation, his voice remained calm, with clear surety.

"So how long do we have until the demons of Connolly Park come busting down my door?"

"I've got a protection charm in place, have you forgotten?"

She rolled her eyes. "That charm didn't stop Belial from waltzing into my shop earlier."

"True." Rafe scrubbed a hand across his chin. "But Lilith certainly weakened him. He won't be doing much *poofing* any time soon."

With a slow nod, she curled into Rafe's arms. "I hope you're right." Because she certainly didn't want to be the cause of another failed mission. She had a connection with him, stronger than any man she'd ever known—besides her father, of course. She sure as hell wouldn't let some post-coital mishap muck things up.

He lowered his lips to her cheek. "I've sworn to protect you, Lucy. That won't change."

"I appreciate that, more than you'll ever know." Teeth digging into her lower lip, she blew a long breath out her nose. "So how long do we have?"

Rafe swiped a defiant strand of hair from her cheek, the warmth still emanating from his fingertips. "You'll be safe. I'll protect you."

Despite his gentleness, a fire spurred inside her. Gentleness served its purpose, but she'd be damned if she just sat back while Rafe and his demon buddies did all the fighting. Especially if she was the reason all of them were fighting. She wouldn't take no for an answer.

"I don't need protection." Firm with resolve, her gaze met his. "I'm fighting, too."

Jaw ticking, he shook his head. "You're royalty. You can't."

"Royalty, schmoyalty. I'm good at judo, or did you forget?" With a quick bounce, she bounded up off the futon and flailed her fists. "Hi-yah!"

Rafe blew out a deep breath. "It isn't done."

With a tilt to her chin, she slammed her hands to her waist. "It is now. Besides, it's my fault you're in this mess."

"How so?"

Fists tight at her sides, she bit her lip. "I opened the chest."

"You didn't know any better."

"Yes I did. Why don't you just let me take the blame?"

"Belial is to blame." Rafe's mouth remained inches from hers. "Had he not attacked, the chest would still be in Limbo. You. Are. Not. To. Blame. Got it?"

With a silent nod, she unclenched her fists. "I'm still fighting."

"Your father won't approve."

"You'd be surprised."

"Daddy's little girl, are you?"

"Pretty much get what I want."

"Then why did your father threaten eternal damnation on me if any harm befalls you?"

"If." She waggled her brow. Sucking in a determined breath of air, she reached down and lugged the two-ton book of demon rules onto her lap and flipped it open. "So teach me how to protect myself."

"Lucy..." His voice firm, he narrowed his gaze. Why did she get the sneaky suspicion that he was hiding something?

Fine, be that way.

"Whatever, I'll do it myself." Finger tracing over ancient Latin, she perused the elegant script. Incantation after incantation and a string of spells and rituals filled the deep recesses of her mind. Invocations and potions were cool enough, but where was the section on kicking Infernati ass?

With a growl, she tore through the pages. "A little help?"

"Your father—"

"Knows better." Flipping a page, a huge smile curved her lips. In rich detail, emblazoned on the thick parchment, were all forms of weapons. Swords, daggers, crossbows, and modern defense mechanisms. Because nothing said, "Die, demon scum" better than a silver slug planted deep in their black hearts. Finally, she was getting somewhere—no thanks to Rafe. "So where can I get some of these?" She glanced over at the small dagger she so wanted to slice into Lamia's chest earlier. She needed another upgrade.

As if it were light as air, Rafe plucked the book from her lap and slammed it closed. "I won't send another woman to her death."

She reached over to grab the book back. "I'm not going to die."

Without missing a step, Rafe reached out and grabbed

her wrist. "No, you're not. I'm supposed to keep you safe, and I'm going to make damned sure of it."

"Have fun with that." Tugging her arm from his grip, she flashed a wry smile. Her finger traced a slow path down a rigid bicep. Warmth spiked to a blazing inferno. Too bad he'd put those stupid pants back on. She leaned in closer, her lips inches from his ear. "Where there's a will, there's a way. And I will find a way."

Eyes swirling and flashing, Rafe turned to meet her gaze. His jaw twitched and his fists clenched as a torrent of despair and frustration washed over his face. "My sister said something similar."

His words hit like a surprise jab to her stomach. She drew her lips into a straight line and clasped her hands together. He felt guilty about allowing his sister to join the guard. She should've known. Casting her glance down to her tightly laced fingers, she heaved a sigh. "I'm sorry, Rafe. Your sister—"

Crooking his finger, he lifted her chin to meet his gaze, warm and inviting. "Don't be." With tender care, he lowered his lips to hers.

Tingles and sparks danced across their lips. Throwing her arms around his neck, she laced her fingers in his hair and drew him closer. With teasing nips and nibbles, their mouths melted together. She never wanted it to end.

Nothing felt so perfect. Amazement, mixed with desire, flooded her veins. Warmth emanated from her every pore, every strand of hair, everywhere. A feeling she'd felt before, but never so intense.

What was going on?

Who was she kidding? She knew exactly what was happening. No matter how hard she tried to deny it.

His smile, although fleeting, sent her heart aflutter. His voice made her legs turn to mush and his kisses sent all sorts of energy coursing through her. And the sex, hot damn. Not only was it toe-curling, it was explosive and left her hungry for more. For five years, she'd been content without a man. But now, all she could think about was Rafe. She didn't ask for this. Not now, with so much at stake.

His lips lingered before he pulled away. With a long tender trace along her cheek, he gazed down at her. "What's on your mind, sweetheart?"

Sweetheart? Her heart thudded a wild beat. Gnawing her lip, she laced and unlaced her fingers. Should she tell him? What would he think? What would he say? She needed to show him she could be strong. She needed to show him she could fight.

"Nothing," she replied, her tone nonchalant.

"Very well." He punctuated his sentence with a kiss to her nose. Gaze swirling, His lip crooked up in a smile. "Your father warned me you wouldn't take no for an answer."

Her gaze remained indifferent as she crossed her arms. "Glad he hasn't forgotten me in ten years." She wouldn't deny it. She was thrilled that her dad was still alive. Him being the Sexubi king and faking his death—not so thrilling. Confusion and anger simmered inside. Like she could just forgive him.

"Your father loves you. He had to do it to keep you safe." His hand searched for hers, warmth guiding him like a beacon.

The fact that her dad, Lilu, whatever his name was, had shared more with Rafe didn't make matters any better. Then again, she hadn't been too receptive. A deep sigh pushed through her lips. "I know. I just need time."

Nodding, Rafe took her in his arms. With a brush of a stubborn lock of hair, he smiled. A breath of sheer contentment flowed from her mouth as she snuggled closer to him. Who would've known such a rock-solid behemoth of a man could be so gentle.

"I've come up with a compromise."

She glanced up at him with a bemused quirk. "A compromise for what?"

Hands gripping her shoulders, his gaze burned into hers. "You can fight."

"Really?"

"Yes…" He scratched his chin, thought clouding his eyes.

Here comes the "but."

"Spit it out." She tossed a rogue lock of hair from her cheek.

"You can fight only if you're in danger and your life depends on it." With that, he reached for the book and pulled it open. Pointing to a long katana, he smiled. "This will be a good weapon to match your martial arts skills."

Skills she didn't have to train to acquire. Granted it wasn't reading minds or poofing here and there, but coupled with the Latin, she couldn't have asked for any better talents. "Sounds good. So where do I get one?"

"I'll have Kalli get one for you." Rafe flipped the page. "Hopefully it can be prepared in time."

Her eyes widened. "Prepared?"

"Every weapon needs to be purified before we use

it." He flipped a few hundred pages. "Here. This is the ceremony."

Looking down at the beautiful illustration, she took in its beauty. Holding a sword up with both hands, an angel floated above a rose-bedecked altar. Flanking the altar, several other angels held their arms high, their white gossamer floating gowns flowing around them. "Do I need to be there?"

"No," he replied with a shake of his head. "The angels' power is strong enough. Besides, it isn't safe for you to travel to Limbo just yet."

She gave him an acquiescent nod. He did have a point. "How long will it take?"

With a shrug, Rafe whipped his gaze around the room. "Where's my jacket?"

"Over there," she said, pointing toward the corner where the light had teetered just hours before.

A sly smile curved his lips. "Glad your lamp is still intact." With that, he shuffled to the corner and grabbed the heap of leather off the floor. Rifling through the pockets, he pulled out the BlackBerry he'd used earlier.

"I still can't get over the fact that demons need cell phones." She stuck her hands in the pockets of her robe and lounged against the futon. "I would've thought you'd have more sophisticated communication methods."

"Very few Paladins have telepathic skills. And on Earth, those skills are somewhat diminished." He punched in a number and rested his thick body against the floor lamp, dwarfing it. With an irritated growl, he fumbled with the phone. "I don't care for modern inventions, but they're an unfortunate necessity."

"Where would the world be without BlackBerrys?"

Rafe snorted. "BlackBerry? Is that what it's called? There's nothing sweet nor juicy about it at all."

She snickered at Rafe's attempt at a joke. Not a very good one, but she still gave him props for effort. "Yeah, I never knew why they called it that."

After several attempts, Rafe blew a satisfied breath of air and put the phone to his ear. "Kalli. Have a katana sent here for Lucy." In a second, his lighthearted tone flip-flopped to his customary stick-up-his-ass one. At least it wasn't directed at her right now. Her heart skipped more than a few beats. She had it bad for him.

"We're fine. Her mother—and father—are safe."

Pacing the length of her living room, he shook his head. "We don't have time to explain, just have the weapon ready." As soon as the last word was out, he slammed his finger down on the end button. Stuffing the phone back into his jacket pocket, he gazed down at her. "You'll have your sword soon."

"Thanks, Rafe." She slinked toward him and wrapped her arms around his neck. Brushing her lips across his cheek, she laced her fingers through his hair.

Lifting her chin with his thumb and forefinger, he shook his head. "No. Thank you, Lucy." He brushed his lips against hers, taking slow tentative strokes. Sparks ignited between them, and she pressed closer. With a slow swirl, her tongue traced each spark. The mixture of their energy and the delicious peppermint spice sent her libido back into uncharted heights.

His hands roved across the silky lengths of her kimono to massage her ass. His hands moved with precision down her thighs. His desire, hard and heavy, pressed against his jeans as he ground his hips into hers. Her mind wandered back to the bedroom, where less than five minutes after they finished, he was up and ready to go again. This was all new to her, but undoubtedly welcome. The times she'd tried to initiate some post-coital coitus with Josh, he'd simply roll away and say he was too tired. Ugh! Talk about frustrating.

"Wow," she managed to breathe his lips. Allowing her fingertips to trace along each contour of his sculpted pecs, she latched onto his lip and nibbled. Her fingers wandered lower, not that they needed much prompting, and scratched a path down the hard lines of his abdomen. Time to take those pants off again.

Then her phone rang.

"Bloody hell," Rafe growled. "Your phone couldn't have rung at a more inopportune time." Raking a hand through his hair, he pulled himself from their embrace.

An irritated growl escaped her mouth. "I suppose I should get that. Demon infestation and all."

Rafe offered a slow nod. "It could be your friend."

Blowing out an exasperated breath, she jetted toward the gigantic purse of many colors and fished inside. Flipping open the receiver, she checked her missed calls. Serah it was. She hit the send button and listened as Lady Gaga crooned in her ear. Whoever invented ring-back tones should be shot. Then again, she wasn't any better, with her Justin Timberlake ringtone.

"Hello?" Serah's voice crackled on the other line. Stupid cell phone reception.

"Hey girl. You rang?"

"Yeah. Okay if Squeaky and I head on over? The storm's let up."

"Let me check with Rafe."

Serah's huff crackled through the phone. "What happened to the Lucy I used to know. The one who did stuff without asking?"

"Still here, goober. But I want you safe and not some crazy demon's dinner."

"Whatever, I have Squeaky here to protect me."

"Whatever, my ass. These demons are powerful. Look at the blizzard that just rolled through here. Something tells me they aren't done yet."

"Fine, go ask Rafe."

"Okay." Covering the phone, she turned to Rafe, who pulled his T-shirt back on. She held back a sigh. There was no more time for play. "So Serah wants to come back here."

Rafe shook his head. "It isn't safe. Even Kalli is keeping vigil in the shop with your employees."

"All right." She put the phone back to her ear. "He says it's still not safe."

Serah's long breath of air reverberated in her ear. "Fine, bye. Squeaky and I are going to watch *The Godfather* trilogy for the millionth time. Why can't he have a fetish for historical sagas instead?"

"Sorry, girl. I'll call you back when Rafe and I have more news."

"Rafe and you," she said, sarcasm dripping on each word.

She bit her lip to prevent herself from lashing out. It wasn't like she wasn't the only person who was stressed. Taking a deep breath, Lucy composed herself. "Look, I'm just as aggravated as you. I'm cooped up in this tiny house with *your* dusty box and only Rafe to keep me company."

Serah snorted "Try spending the evening with a

stupid primate and *The Godfather* movie marathon. At least you have a sexy man to keep you company. I have a fucking monkey!"

"But you love Squeaky. And, remember, he's a chimp, not a monkey."

"Kiss my ass."

Her eyes rolled to the ceiling. "Whatever. Just wait a few more hours. Rafe says that once the solstice has passed, the threat lowers."

"Fine. I suppose I can play *Donnie Brasco* or *Prizzi's Honor* instead. That'll keep him occupied for another three or four hours." There was no masking the sarcasm in her voice.

"Good."

"Are you sure I can't come over? There's something about Rafe I don't like."

Blowing out a breath, she adjusted the phone at her ear. "I know he comes off as standoffish, but he means well." She smiled. "He's very protective."

"That's what you think." Serah clucked her tongue. "He's hiding something. Has he done anything to you?"

Did she know they did it? Her mind reeled. She hoped not. "No. He's been all right."

"Only all right?" Her voice raised an octave. "I would've thought he'd be better than that." Was that a lip smack? Then again, it shouldn't surprise her. Besides shopping, Serah had one other weakness... the opposite sex.

"If anything happened between Rafe and me, you'd be the first to know."

"Good." The phone scratched a bit. "Squeaky! Stop. I'll call back later." The phone went dead.

Flipping the phone shut, she turned to Rafe. "That was weird."

"Your friend seems strange in general."

She shook her head. "Weirder than usual."

With silver eyes blazing, Rafe strode toward her. His expression still stern, he raised her chin to meet his gaze. "She just found out her best friend is a sex demon. Give her a break."

And just earlier, she'd said she didn't trust him? Yet Rafe had just defended her. "Yeah, I will."

Rafe smiled. "Good." He reached down and took her hand in his. Bringing it up to his mouth, he let his lips brush across her fingertips. Tingles and sizzles raced through each finger down to her toes. He had a way with... everything.

"Thanks, Rafe. I know this isn't how you planned on spending your winter solstice."

Rafe chuckled and pulled her closer. "We don't have seasons in Limbo." He gazed down at her, his silver eyes sparking. "Regardless of my initial displeasure, there isn't anywhere I'd rather be."

"What about your sister?"

"Shh." Rafe brought his fingers to her lips. "Her rescue is in capable hands. The Fore-Demons brought me here for a reason."

"Yeah, and they brought Squeaky here for a reason. I've yet to learn why. The little guy seems more attached to Serah than you."

He sucked in a deep breath. "I still don't fully understand how the Fore-Demons work. But over the centuries I've learned not to question them." A slow smile crept to his lips. "Enough chitchat. We need to clean up before Kalli arrives with the sword."

"I suppose we can't have her smelling us on each other," she said with a shrug. Truth be told, she enjoyed the spicy scent he left on her. She didn't want to wash it off at all.

A loud chuckle burst from his mouth, a sound that was becoming more frequent. "No, I just thought you would like to freshen up. Kalli's pretty astute. She'll know what we did, with or without showers."

"Yeah, she is. I'm sure reading people's minds helps somewhat." Thank goodness she'd learned how to keep inquiring minds out.

"A little too much, I'm certain." Rafe reached out and hauled her against him. The hardness of his chest against the soft roundness of her breasts caused her skin to sizzle. "One more kiss before you shower." He took her lips with his, savage hunger filling both of them as tongues tangled and swirled against each other. His hands moved up and down her back, strong, demanding, and protective. Heat flamed between them, hotter than Hell itself. She never wanted it to end.

A gust of ice cold air swirled around. What the hell? A ball of cool blue energy floated in the air. Growling, Rafe pulled himself from the embrace.

"W-what's going on?" she mumbled, pulling her flimsy robe to her body. It did little to protect her from the biting cold. There was only one explanation. Senses now fully acute, she charged toward the table, letting her robe fly behind her. Reaching out, she palmed the dagger and spun around, ready to slice.

Chapter 22

"Lucy! No." But it was too late. She spun around, eyes blazing as she gripped the dagger, ready to strike.

Materializing next to him, in a pile of ice shards and swirling fog, Dominic swiped icicles from his hair and shoulders. "Did I arrive at a bad time?"

"Turn and drop your weapons."

Lucy stood firm, her voice commanding. It took Rafael's breath away.

"I guess I did," Dominic muttered. "Why on earth do I feel compelled to obey? What in the hell is going on?"

With a slow swivel, Dominic turned around, his eyes widening. "Whoa! Is this your succubus?" he asked, flipping his coat back and extracting his ceremonial Paladin sword. He plunked it to the floor and pulled two daggers from his belt, letting them clang on top of the sword.

"Enough chitchat." Lucy kept her tone even. With a flourish of her dagger, she kept it trained on Dominic. "I sense another sword." At that, she gasped, her mouth forming a perfect *O*.

Her royal powers had grown stronger. No doubt. "You'd do best to obey her, Nic."

"Very well." Reaching behind his back, inside his long black leather trench coat, Dominic pulled out a magnificent jade-sheathed katana. Trimmed with gold and encrusted with rubies, it was a treasure worthy of a king. How had Nic come across such an exquisite weapon? Kneeling down, with gentle care, he placed the weapon on the beige carpeted floor.

"Wow, someone's watched one too many episodes of *The Highlander*." Still gripping her dagger, Lucy glanced down at the katana. "Nice piece though."

Rafael came to stand next to his friend and wrap his arm around his shoulder. "Lucy, it's okay. He's one of us. May I introduce Dominic Duvane, my commander?"

"Commander?" Dominic rolled his eyes. "I thought we were friends." He took cautious steps toward Lucy and extended his hand in greeting. "So you're the succubus?"

Lucy narrowed her eyes into a pensive gaze. "In the flesh, and you're the one who's supposed to rescue Rafe's sister?"

Rafael winced at her biting tone. Poor Dominic didn't know what he was getting into.

Dominic gulped. "Indeed, I am," replied, extending his hand further.

Drawing her robe closed, Lucy gazed down at the proffered hand and back up at Dominic. "And why aren't you out looking for her?"

"Oh, I do love your spark," Dominic said with a friendly smile. "But I have news for Rafe and a gift for you."

She narrowed her eyes and pursed her lips. "A gift?"

A sheepish smile curved Dominic's lips. "Kalli mentioned you needed a weapon and since I needed to speak with Rafe, I decided to deliver it myself." His gaze lowered to the katana.

"That? Is my sword?"

Ah, now it made sense. A weapon worthy of a

king—or a princess. There wasn't any better weapon for Lucy. It was perfect, just like her.

Dominic grinned. "Indeed, it is, blessed by the Angel Gabriel himself." He leaned closer to Rafael. "Even I have yet to have a weapon blessed by an archangel. We've more than just your sister to discuss."

"I suppose we do. But why not let Lucy try out her sword first."

Dominic nodded. "Very well." Reaching down he picked up the katana and handed it to Lucy. "Be careful, it's—"

With elegance and precision, Lucy pulled out the sword. Gripping the carved jade hilt, she swung the sword in a graceful arc, the silver blade sparking.

"—sharp." Dominic's eyebrows quirked up, shock and bewilderment clear on his face.

Lucy drew her finger across the blade, a small drop of crimson pooling then instantly fading away. "Yep, it is."

With a sly smile, she slid the blade back in. Setting the blade against the table, she pushed a strand of hair from her brow.

"Thank you, Rafe. For allowing me to fight."

Rafael nodded, casting his gaze down to the floor. He couldn't let Dominic see him like this. He wasn't weak. "You should thank Dominic."

"Of course!" She took Dominic's hand in his, a friendly smile sweeping across her lips. "Thank you, Mr. Duvane." Watching her fingers clasp his friend's, he rolled his tongue against his lips. Did Nic feel the same heat? His jaw twitched and his blood boiled. For his sanity, he hoped not.

Dominic eyes glowed a soft gold, not the molten

spark he'd seen when he was with Coby. Rafael breathed a sigh of relief. "Call me Nic; everyone else does."

Her gaze warm, she withdrew her hand. "Thank you, Nic. The katana is perfect. I need to take that shower now." Angling her gaze back to Rafael, her amber eyes sparked. The little temptress. The thought of Lucy naked in the shower sent all the blood in his body right down to his shaft.

Not in front of Nic.

With a shimmy of her hips, she turned around and sashayed down the hall, the silk robe dancing against her legs.

"I'll be back." The seductive tone floated to his ears. Blasted vixen knew what she was doing. "Have fun, boys." With that, the door snicked shut.

Dominic rubbed his hand along his jaw, his gaze narrowing. "Tell me everything."

"What of my sister?"

"Something tells me this might be a tad bit more important." With a flourish, Dominic whipped off his coat and flung himself onto the futon. His face scrunched into a wince. "Does your succubus enjoy a little torture too?"

"My succubus?"

His friend threw his head back in laughter. "Don't try and hide it. I saw the way you look at each other. That, and the scent of sex clings to the air."

He lifted his head and sniffed around the room. "Damn good sex, too."

Bloody hell. Nic and his over-sensitive nostrils. He could smell brimstone a mile away. An impressive skill to possess, when needed. And Rafael didn't need it now. "It was only sex."

"Whatever you want to tell yourself," Dominic said with a roll of his eyes. "So tell me why she's so powerful?"

Rubbing his temples, Rafael took a seat in Lucy's dilapidated easy chair. This time, he'd forego reclining. But he couldn't forego the truth. "Her father is a powerful incubus."

His friend's eyes narrowed, and his brow creased. "Just how powerful?"

Rafael couldn't beat around the bush with Dominic. "Her father is the king."

His friend's eyes widened. "Lilu?"

"Is there anyone else?"

His friend raked his fingers through his hair. "No wonder Lamia and her minion were lurking about." He blew out an aggravated breath. "I should've known there was a reason Kalli wasn't forthcoming."

"Kalli doesn't know. Yet." Rafael narrowed his gaze at his friend. "Spying, I see?"

"I prefer 'keeping tabs.'" The elder demon's lips curved into a wry smile. "For your protection, of course."

"I don't need protection."

Dominic clenched his fists. "I promised Coby that I'd keep you safe."

He winced at his friend's strangled words. "I know you have feelings for her."

Dominic sucked in a breath as he adjusted his large frame on Lucy's futon. "Is it that obvious?"

"As obvious as a bump on a log." Since they'd already broached the topic of his sister, Rafael was ready to hear more. "So what about my sister?"

Drumming his fingers on the wrought iron arm of the futon, Dominic nodded. "Coby's alive, in Belial's palace. She seems unharmed." An anguished breath wrenched from his mouth. "Too unharmed."

He leaned in, his eyes sparking. "I'll rescue her, if I have to storm the hellhole myself."

Rafael steepled his fingers and nodded. He'd known Dominic long enough. He spoke the truth. "Thank you, Nic. Coby and I are lucky to have you as a friend."

"And I you," he replied with a friendly pat on the back. His gaze shifted down the hall. "How long does it take your *princess* to shower?"

"I haven't any idea. How long do humans usually shower?"

"It depends on how *dirty* they are," his friend replied with a punch to his arm. "Doesn't she know demons don't need to shower?"

"There are many things she needs to learn." And he wanted to be the one who taught her. He owed it to her.

"And you plan to instruct her, don't you?"

"If it will benefit the mission, and the Fore-Demons allow it, yes."

Dominic nodded. "They have." He leaned in, lowering his voice a few notches. "I know you care for more than just the mission, but I won't hold that against you. She's quite a magnificent creature."

She was more than a creature. She was Lucia Gregory, sassy hairstylist that just happened to be a sex demon. She was fascinating and he wanted her more than ever.

Blast Nic for being so astute.

He ground his teeth into his lower lip. As insane as it seemed, he more than wanted her. He *needed* her. More than any other woman. Ever. The intensity should worry him, yet he felt comfortable. Alive. With a quick swipe of a wayward strand of hair, he turned his gaze to Dominic. Did he feel the same way for his sister? More than likely. Even though they both tried to deny it.

"So you're protective, aren't you?"

"I was given orders."

Chuckling, Dominic shook his head. "True, but your protection goes deeper, does it not? Like you'd do anything for her?"

"How would you know?"

His friend let out a long whoosh of air. "Because it's how I feel for your sister, you fool."

Curse him. Always making a valid point. A point he couldn't afford to agree with right now. Maybe later, after he skewered Belial and sent the chest back to Limbo.

Flicking her hair back, Lucy allowed the cascading water to lick and caress her skin, wishing it were Rafe instead. Unfortunately, the pleasure would have to wait, thanks to the other demon who had made an unexpected visit. Did these guys have to take lessons in looking sexy? Dominic, tall and ripped, had a cocky smile, wavy sandy brown hair, and a golden tan. Sexy in his own right, but he didn't hold a candle to Rafe. Maybe she could set him up with Serah. She had a thing for the Matthew McConaughey types.

With a resigned sigh, she cranked the faucet off, the pipes groaning in response. Thus ended the shortest shower ever recorded. Not that she was complaining. The faint scent of Rafe and all his sexiness still clung to her.

"*Mmm*," she said, bringing her arm to her nose. A

wide smile spread to her lips as the exotic spices wafted. But enough orgasms already. They had a mission. They needed to return the chest. And when that was done, she would help find Rafe's sister. She owed it to him. Dominic Duvane be damned. He didn't know Lucia Anne Gregory, succubus extraordinaire. Yeah, she may have only been a succubus for a few days, but she had a lifetime of powers at her disposal—and now a kick-ass katana.

She *would* kick some serious ass.

Shuffling out of the shower, she grabbed a towel and patted herself dry. What in the hell were those two talking about? Putting her ear to the wall didn't help. They must have soundproofed the room.

With a resigned sigh, she made her way through the door that adjoined the bedroom. Throwing on a pair of purple yoga pants and a sweatshirt, she swiveled to the bedroom mirror. Hair no longer wet, she gaped in silence. If she knew she'd have instant self-drying hair, she wouldn't have bought that fancy blow-dryer last weekend.

"Unbelievable," she breathed out, scraping a hand through her hair. To her delight, it flipped out around her face. Screw that. It was more than surreal. It was magnificent.

She twirled a lock of hair around her finger and made her way out of the bedroom. Tuning her ears, she strained to catch the two demons' conversation.

"So how do you plan to storm Belial's castle?" Rafe's voice, although muffled, carried down the hall.

Now that's what I'm talking about. She would storm right alongside them. A determined grin spread across her lips. She wouldn't take no for an answer.

With a flourish, she stole into the room. "Castle storming? Count me in."

"I think not," Rafe said, placing his hands on his hips. "You're lucky I'm letting you in on this mission."

After a quick roll of her eyes, she raised her chin defiantly. "Oh yeah. We'll see about that."

The friction in the room spiked and energy crackled. She loved their little spats. Rafe's silver eyes swirled and his jaw twitched. So predictable, but it was part of his charm.

"Oh my, did you feel that?" With a shake of his head, Dominic gazed down at his arm. "My arm hair is standing on end. That's some electricity between you two." He turned to face Lucy, his smile apologetic. "Storming Belial's castle is my mission and my mission alone. The Fore-Demons requested it."

"If the Fore-Demons told you to jump off a cliff, would you?"

Dominic shrugged. "We're immortal, you know."

Another demon with a strange sense of humor. It took a couple of seconds for those words to register. Immortal? Then again, Rafe, himself, was over four hundred and fifty years old. "Does that mean I am too?" She'd read enough vampire novels and spent enough time with Rafe to know that immortality wasn't all that great.

Noticing her nervousness, Rafe edged closer and raised her chin to meet his gaze. "We don't know. One thing's certain though."

She rolled her lip between her teeth. "What's that?"

"Your life energy is strong. If you're not immortal, you will still live a *very* long time." His gaze was warm and reassuring—as much as it could be in this situation.

With a nod, she flashed a bright smile. "Hopefully not long enough that I'll need to resort to identity theft."

"Identity theft?" Dominic threw back his head in a loud guffaw. "We're demons. We make our own identities."

"Wow, comforting," she mumbled. "But don't you think storming a castle all by your lonesome a suicide mission, even for an immortal?"

Dominic shrugged, his wavy sandy hair brushing against his brow. "It very well may be." He turned to his friend. "Everything appears okay. The Fore-Demons will be pleased."

"The Fore-Demons can kiss my ass." After all they'd put Rafe through over the centuries, they needed to do a lot of it.

Sidling next to her, Rafe wrapped his fingers around her arm in a steely grip. "Lucy, not now," he whispered.

"These Fore-Demons don't scare me." she stood proud. When this situation with the chest was settled, she would give that council a piece of her mind. "I don't like the way they make their decisions." Then again, if it wasn't for them sending him here, they would have never met.

"It's worked since the dawn of time, Lucy." Dominic's lips curved into a friendly smile. "May I call you Lucy?"

"Yes, it's what all my friends call me, and a friend of Rafe's is a friend of mine." She offered him her hand. "I suppose I'll give this elusive Fore-Demon Council the benefit of the doubt—for now."

Rafe's friend took her hand and gave it a hearty shake. "That's all I ask. It was a pleasure to meet you,

Lucy, daughter of Lilu." He turned to Rafe, his expression serious. "I'll let you know if I learn any more of your sister."

"Thanks, Nic." With a nod, Rafe and Dominic grabbed each other's elbows and squeezed. *Oh! A secret handshake!*

"Cool," she said, her brow arched. "I always wanted to join an organization with a special handshake."

Dominic chuckled. "In time, Lucy. The Fore-Demons may have good use of you."

Eyes flickering, Rafe drew his lips into a straight line. His nostrils flared. "Unfortunately, it'll be Lilu's decision on what his daughter does."

Her father's decision? Not this again. "Actually, it'll be my choice, thank you very much." And knowing her father, he always ended up seeing the light.

Arching a brow, Dominic let out a mirthful chuckle. "A familiar situation, is it not?"

"Too much," Rafe muttered. Scraping a hand through his hair, he blew out a frustrated breath and sidled a glance her way. "But I'll deal with it."

With a quick roll of her eyes, she shrugged.

Dominic glanced at Rafe and her, and then back to Rafe. "I'm sure you will." With that, he bent down and grabbed his weapons, attaching them to his person. Adjusting the lapels of his trench coat, he smirked. "I have a council to attend. I'll let you know if there are any new developments." He turned to her and bowed. "Lucy, it's been my pleasure."

Nodding, she offered him her hand in a not-so-secret handshake. She'd learn the secret one later. "Same here."

He took her hand in a firm shake. "Certainly. Well, I've tarried too long." Offering Rafe a quick nod, he pulled his jacket closer and tied the trench coat. With a snap of his fingers, he vanished, fog and ice shards swirling in his place.

"Great! More ice piles to clean up," she said with a low chuckle.

"One of the hazards of *poofing*."

"What's it really called?"

Rafe scratched his chin. "It's called *Peragrans*... Traveling."

"I should've known it'd be Latin."

"It's a very old language, spoken for hundreds of centuries."

"Still a well of information, aren't you." She reached down and grabbed the katana, pulling the sword from its sheath. Silver sparks flashed with each swipe of the blade. "So let's get back to this training."

"This is insane, but I did promise." Rafe flung open the closet. Procuring yet another magnificent sword, he turned to her. She could only gape in astonishment at the beautiful weapon he gripped. Was that a dragon carved down the blade? Emeralds, rubies, and sapphires flickered and flashed, sending a rainbow of light dancing on the wall.

Did all demons' weapons glow so bright?

"That you did. *En garde!*" Lunging forward, she thrust her blade and pointed it at Rafe, beckoning him in challenge.

Brow jutting upward, Rafe twisted his wrist, his blade circling in the air. "Nice stance."

"Why, thank you." With that she swung her sword,

careful to not to aim too high to mar his face and, of course, not too low, to avoid his other parts.

Lifting his lips in a teasing grin, he brandished his sword and blocked her move, the zing of silver against silver renting the air. She spun around and swept the katana up, slicing a thin strip of his T-shirt.

Rafe's eyes widened and his grin returned. "I let you have that move. Let's try again." He raised his sword, the silver glistening in challenge.

"If you can handle it," she teased. She resumed her stance, the katana ready to strike.

The jingle of Rafe's BlackBerry reverberated from across the room. Eyes alert, he lowered his sword and re-sheathed it. "That may be Kalli with news." Sensing her disappointment, he added, "Don't worry. You did well. Very impressive for a beginner."

"That's my daddy's fault."

"It probably is." With that, he swiped the phone from the coffee table and clicked the send button. "Kalli, what is it?"

Rafe paced back and forth in front of the table, scraping a hand through his hair. "The chest has been activated." With a low groan, he shook his head. "We didn't have time to tell you." Covering the mouthpiece of the phone, he pulled it away from his ear. "Damn Nic," he muttered under his breath.

"What is it?" she asked, her nerves prickling.

With a long drawn-out breath, he shook his head. "In a minute." He returned the phone to his ear. "I've got her house warded and she can now protect herself."

Rafe nodded. Fingers gripped tightly around his BlackBerry, he paced back and forth.

She wrung her hands. What was going on? Was it the shop? Were her friends okay? She hated being kept in the dark. She opened her mouth to speak.

"Where is Dominic?" He growled. "Bloody hell!"

And she promptly shut it. The call was about his sister. From the sound of it, it wasn't good. She simply plopped onto the futon and sat back, letting Rafe to his call.

"I can be there in five minutes, but I don't want to leave Lucy unattended for too long." Rafe drew out another long breath of air. "Thanks, Kalli." With that, he ended the call.

"What was that about?"

Rafe's gaze turned to stone. "Dominic tried breaching Belial's castle. He's MIA." Jaw clenched, he sucked in a ragged breath. "The Fore-Demons request my presence."

No, this didn't sound good at all. "How long will you be gone?"

"An hour at the most. Just long enough to receive an update."

"What about your sister."

Rafe's gaze grew cloudy. "I wish I could say it's good."

"How do you know it isn't?"

He rolled his teeth over his lip. "Meetings like this never are."

Taking long, confident strides toward Rafe, she grabbed him by the shoulders and narrowed her gaze. "Don't give up on her Rafe. She's your sister."

"I don't plan to." His expression softened. With a gentle finger, he swiped a few stray strands of hair from her face and placed a kiss on her cheek. "I'll be back as soon as possible."

"All right. You're sure I'll be safe?"

"I've placed a ward around your house and you have some training." He raked a hand through his hair. "Granted, it's not as much training as a normal Paladin has, but it should suffice. It's not completely dark out yet, anyway."

With a quick nod, she placed a kiss on his cheek. "I'll be fine. I'll stay right here." She plopped onto the rock-hard futon and stifled a grimace. Picking up the remote control, she turned on the TV. "I've got five hundred channels to keep me occupied."

"Sounds good." With a bittersweet smile, he closed his eyes. Ice shards and snow flurries swirling around him, Rafe vanished in a puff of frost and fog. Only another pile of ice remained.

She hated this traveling shit.

Chapter 23

NOT A THING ON ANY OF THOSE OVERPRICED CABLE stations, she grumbled, ready to fling the remote at the TV. Not even the Spanish soap operas seemed interesting. Then she landed on the medical channel. If that wasn't bad enough, it was a documentary showing a rhinoplasty, blood and broken cartilage included.

Shivers of horror raced down her spine. "Thanks, but no thanks," she muttered, mashing the power button.

Reaching for one of her many hairstyling magazines, she sighed. What was the deal? Rafe had only been gone for a half an hour and she already suffered from an extreme case of cabin fever.

"Bloody hell!"

Had she just said that? No way. Now she was talking like that sexy-as-sin demon. Just the thought of his hands brushing against her skin and his lips on hers sent her pulse into overdrive. Lucy was the one who was enraptured, not him.

With a swipe of her hand through her hair, she leaned back on the futon. Flipping through the pages, she perused the plethora of hairstyles, ranging from dull and boring to moderately tame to weird and wild. A little something for everyone, she supposed. Her interest in the latest in celebrity updos waned as thoughts of Rafe rushed forward.

"Bloody—"

Not again. Fisting tufts of hair in both hands, she threw her head back. No matter how hard she tried, her thoughts always strayed to Rafe. His dark shiny waves of hair and the muscles that bulged against every shirt he wore. Even when he wasn't with her she was horny. What was a girl to do?

Her question went unanswered. As if reading her mind, the cell phone announced its presence like a bad canker sore. She now officially hated Justin Timberlake.

Then again, he wasn't Rafe.

Bah! This wasn't healthy at all.

With an irritated growl, she pulled herself from the futon and stumbled across the room toward the phone. Lifting the receiver, she let out a deep whoosh of air. "Hello?"

"Lucia?" Serah's voice came through low and cautious.

She rolled her eyes. "No, it's the pope dressed in drag."

"Not funny," she said, her voice irritated. "Are you alone?"

A loud sigh burst from her lips. "For now, why?"

"We're coming over, that's why."

"No, you're not."

"Why not?"

She crossed her arms, even though Serah couldn't see her. "Why? Because Rafe said so, that's why."

"You're whipped."

"Am not," she replied with a loud huff meant to reverberate in her friend's ear.

Serah retaliated with her own, "Are too!"

She ambled toward the kitchen, needing a fresh pot of coffee. Coffee, sex, Captain and Coke, and Rafe. Her latest vices.

"I just want you and your *La Costra Nostra*–loving friend safe. Is that so wrong?"

"No. Not at all." There was a long pause. "But I'm afraid I have some bad news."

Oh man! What now? More demons? She clenched the phone tight to her ear, her heart thudding. "Bloody hell," she mumbled. "What now?"

"Bloody hell?" Serah's voice raised an octave or two, a questioning tone in her voice.

"Don't even ask."

"Very well. I won't."

Very well? That didn't sound like Serah at all. Then again Rafe told Lucy to give her the benefit of the doubt. Serah had been through just as much as she had. "So spill the news."

"Oh, yes, that. Unfortunately, we're already on our way over." Serah's singsong sweet tone rankled her nerves. Just like her to do her own thing. But she meant well.

She gritted her teeth, frustration pounding its way through her head. Would she ever get through to her? Probably not, but that's what made Serah—well—Serah.

"We told you to stay put. Why the hell couldn't you just stay there a few more hours?"

Serah smacked her lips a couple of times as the phone rustled. "I have to talk to you. It's important."

"You think everything you have to say is important." Ouch. That didn't come out right. "What I mean is you have a tendency to exaggerate."

"This time it *is* important. Trust me." She ended her sentence on a whisper. "Please?"

"Bloody hell." This time she didn't care if she used one of Rafe's favorite lines.

"I'm serious. We're almost there. Squeaky misses you too." The phone rustled a bit. "Right, Squeaky?"

"Yeah," she heard squeaked in the background.

A frustrated sigh burst out of her mouth. "Rafe won't like this."

"Like we give a fuck what Rafe likes or doesn't like."

Blinking, she pulled the phone from her ear. Now that was odd. "What the heck's going on? Isn't Squeaky Rafe's pet?"

"That's why we need to talk. We're almost there anyway. What's Rafe going to do, send us back across town?" She let out a deep chuckle. "Then again, he probably would."

What was up with Serah's sudden disgust with Rafe? What kind of line had Squeaky fed her? Yeah, he and Squeaky had started off on the wrong foot, but hadn't they worked out their differences? Maybe the freezing-cold poof had affected Squeaky's brain.

"Rafe's trying to protect you, can't you see?"

Serah blew a deep breath of air into the phone. "We don't need nor want his protection."

Lucy had enough. Serah would speak before she reached into the phone and beat some sense into her. Now that'd be a cool skill to possess. "What the hell's going on?"

"I'd rather talk in person."

"Tell. Me. *Now!*"

"We're right outside. Why not just let us in?" With that, the phone cut off.

"Whatever," she muttered, slamming the phone shut. Flinging it onto the black granite countertop, she sighed.

But like Serah said, what would Rafe do? Certainly not send them back.

The doorbell chimed, announcing the arrival of her unexpected guests. Not wanting to dawdle, she padded back through the living room and to the foyer. With a quick glance out the peephole, she spied the distorted image of what appeared to be Serah's impatient glare. She pulled up the sleeve of her pink marshmallow-esque jacket, looked down at the diamond-trimmed watch on her wrist, and sneered.

Arching a brow, she pulled the door open. Next to Serah stood Squeaky in a black wool overcoat, gold pinky ring blinging in the moonlight. He stomped his oversized chimp foot with clear impatience.

"Can we come in or what?" Eyes narrowed, Serah tilted her head, her brunette curls bouncing beneath her knit hat. "It's freezing out here."

Swinging the door wider, she nodded. What else could she do, let them stay out there in the bitter cold? She was a better friend than that. "Fine, come on in. Rafe will deal with it."

"I'm sure he will," Serah replied, ripping her hat off. With a quick scan of the living room, she rolled her lip between her teeth. "So where is he, anyway?"

Lucy flung herself into the easy chair and leaned back against its worn out splendor. "He had to go back to Limbo for a while."

"Perfect," she said with a breath of air.

Nodding in agreement, Squeaky bounded onto the futon and made himself at home. "Have we got news for you."

"Very big news," Serah added as she sauntered

toward her. With a quick swipe of a curl, she pursed her lips and tilted her head.

"So spill it already," Lucy ground out, her fingernails digging into her palms.

A loud huff burst from her lips. "Very well." Serah turned back toward Squeaky. "Should it be you or me?"

"One of you better say something before I scream."

Squeaky arched a furry brow. "Why don't you do it? My voice is annoying."

"Fine, I thought you were supposed to be a familiar." Serah crossed her arms and bit her lip.

"I'm not a familiar, remember."

Serah narrowed her eyes and kicked the chimp. "Enough."

"Not a familiar? Weren't you sent to help Rafe?" Bemusement laced her tone. "Someone better explain." Lucy reached for the cell phone. "Before I call Rafe."

Serah snagged the phone from her grasp. "No need," she replied, her voice stony. "Rafael Deleon is no longer a Paladin. That's why he was sent back. You're in danger."

She angled her gaze toward the imp. "That's the real reason they sent Squeaky. To bring Deleon back to Limbo."

"That's crazy." What? Rafe? Demoted? Why would the Fore-Demons send him here then change their minds? Then again, Rafe had said everything they did was for a reason. Now, she hated this Fore-Demon Council more than ever. Shaking her head, she clenched her fists. She would bust down the gates of Limbo and give these old crusty demons a piece of her mind.

"I'm afraid so." Serah scanned the room, searching

every corner. With a quick snort, she narrowed her eyes, yet said nothing. Clearly this whole sex demon thing had taken its toll on her. She turned her gaze back to Squeaky and nodded. "Let her read the letter."

Lucy arched another bemused brow. "What letter?"

A squeaky huff flew from the chimp's mouth. "This letter." Reaching into his coat pocket, he pulled out a rolled parchment. Leave it to those Fore-Demons to go all out with an antique and faded scroll.

"How very… umm… official." Unrolling the paper, she gazed down at the script. Latin, of course.

To all Paladins and the like:

It is hereby noted that the Paladin, Rafael Deleon, has severed ties with the Fore-Demons and his fellow Paladins. He and his sister, Jacoba, have been spotted consorting with the enemy, Belial, Prince of the Northern Regions of Hell. It is recommended if you come in contact with either that you exercise caution, as both are armed and extremely dangerous. The Fore-Demon Council offers a hefty reward for the capture of these two Infernati—dead or alive.

Infernati. Seeing that word used to describe Rafe sent aching chills through her body. The dead-or-alive bit only intensified the ache. "Wow. That's harsh."

Serah grabbed her shoulders, her sapphire eyes sparking. "He's working for Belial!"

"Belial?" She still couldn't wrap her head around it. "But his sister!"

Squeaky snorted. "His sister is not a prisoner. Trust me."

"You need to get out of here. It isn't safe. You need to trust us." Fingers digging into her skin, Serah pulled her toward the door. Cold chills raced from her arm, through her body. This wasn't right. Never had her friend's touch been so icy.

Stomach clenched in knots, she let the cold realization sink in. This may have been Serah's body, but it wasn't Serah. How could she have been so stupid? Even after Rafe's previous warning.

"*She takes many forms. An innocent baby, your prized family pet, a friend... a sister.*"

Lucy didn't care how convincing she was; she should've known better. She was taught better than that. Fucking bitch!

So Lamia was taking the BFF costume for a test spin? Maybe it was Lucy's turn for a test spin—one of the silver katana variety. She managed to control her anger earlier when Lamia fondled Rafe. Something told Lucy she wouldn't have much control this time.

Now what was she going to do? Then again, didn't a demon have to leave when they were no longer welcome? She wrenched her arm from Lamia's grasp. "I can take care of myself. You both need to leave."

Try and get out of that one, bitch!

Lamia scratched Serah's chin, her blue eyes swirling and stormy. "No."

Huh? What the hell? Then again, she was working with the Infernati, and from what Lucy could tell, the Infernati didn't follow rules. Just her luck.

"You aren't safe here. Rafael is dangerous," Squeaky

squeaked out, a wince of irritation sweeping across his furry face. Every time he spoke, a similar look of constipation clouded his expression, as if his own voice annoyed him. One of Lamia's cronies, obviously.

"So where did the elusive Rafael Deleon wander off to?" Lamia twirled a curl around a fingertip.

Reaching down, she grabbed the blade and lunged over the table. The sound of metal against metal rent the air as she pulled the katana from its sheath. Her eyes narrowed into tiny slits, she held the blade to Lamia's neck—far enough away as to not mar her friend's skin.

"Cut the crap, bitch. I know who you are." With a quick swivel, Lucy turned to face Squeaky's body. *Larissa*! "And here I thought you were such a nice woman."

Larissa opened Squeaky's mouth to speak.

A gust of chilling air swirled throughout the room, filling her with icy dread. Her heart plummeted as her breath caught. Her fingers damp with sweat, the blade slipped from her grasp.

The icy air intensified and swirled, stronger and stronger by the second.

"I'll be taking that," Lamia said, extending a scaly arm, swiping the katana from her grip.

With a loud cackle, she swung her other snake-like arm out, sending Lucy crashing against the wall. Body crumpling against the hard surface, Lucy sent a quick thanks to the gods and goddesses for her newly acquired high pain threshold.

"Larissa! Now!" Lamia screeched.

However, those thanks were short-lived. A flash of silver caught her eye as searing pain ground inside her stomach, radiating through her entire body. Squeaky's not-so-innocent chimp face stood over her, twisting a dagger. With a maniacal gleam in his eye, he pulled the dagger out and wiped it on his expensive overcoat.

What have I done?

"I wanted to do that for the longest time." Larissa punctuated her sentence with a swift kick from Squeaky's foot, Lucy's head slamming against drywall in a giant thud that reverberated throughout her entire body. What kind of silver was this bitch using?

"Enough," Lamia hissed. "Belial wants her unharmed."

Unharmed? He who attacked her in her shop? Then again she did draw the first move. Her jumbled thoughts moved back to Rafe. She had to protect him. She didn't want him hurt because of her stupidity. She didn't want to be the reason his mission would fail.

Pain still lacing through her body, Lucy reached for Squeaky's foot. Her head in a fog, she dug her nails into his furry toe. Slamming his heel down on her hand, Squeaky let out a loud cackle that almost burst her eardrum. "Give it up, you stupid bitch."

Rafe's body formed from the ice and mists. Flinging the shards from his body, he stepped forward.

Serah stepped from the shadows, the new katana in her hand. Red eyes flashing predatory gleams, she gripped the sword tightly. She turned her gaze to Lucy briefly, a maniacal grin spread across her face.

Lucy needed to act fast.

Rafe's silver eyes focused on her, his face draining of color. "Oh my God… Lucy!"

"Rafe!" she managed to gasp. "Behind you!"

"Too late, Deleon." Serah's double clucked her

tongue. "This makes up for Monday night." With that, she thrust the sword into Rafe's back.

Rafe spun to face Serah, blood pouring from his wound. Wielding his own sword, he flailed it in the air, missing Serah's neck by a mere centimeter. Serah countered his attack, by spinning around and slicing a long gouge into his stomach. Slumping to the ground, he grabbed his middle, a river of dark crimson pooling around him. Never had she seen blood so dark.

Blood. Her mind spun. Rafe's blood. Her stomach twisted and her head spun, spots flashing in front of her eyes. Bile rose into her throat and her breath caught. Tears, thick and salty, dripped down her cheeks as despair clawed its way into her chest.

"Oh, Rafe. I'm so sorry." Hands and knees of mush, she scrambled her way across the floor. She had to save him.

"Lucy," he gurgled out, coughing out a thin trail of blood. "I'm the one who's sorry... never... should have... left you alone." His eyes flickered, the silver fading. He let out a ragged gasp.

"Sorry is, as sorry does," Squeaky said, his voice laced with sarcasm. With a quick kick and stomp to Rafe's lifeless body, he grinned. Another flash of silver flickered as he raised his hand in the air. Gripping her prized silver candlestick high in the air, he brought it crashing into her skull. A bright flash of pain followed by empty darkness. She had failed Rafe. She had failed the world.

Chapter 24

BAM! SLAM! BUMP!

"Ouch," Lucy muttered, struggling to open her eyes. Reaching up to rub her achy head, her hands smacked against cold glass. Leave to those two demonic wenches to handcuff her. Silver too, no doubt. Legs folded in ways that would make a contortionist jealous, she lugged herself up.

Cramped in the back of her own car like a sardine, she wriggled herself around. Head careening against the back door, she let out a muffled *oof*. Were these bitches deliberately looking for every pothole in the blasted state? And where were they taking her anyway? To Hell, probably. It sure felt like it.

"Thank the Dark Master I can finally be rid of that disguise," Larissa—who had since discarded her chimp suit—said, rustling her fingers through her always immaculate golden tresses. "The stench was horrible. I can still smell him on me."

There's the Larissa she remembered. Always immaculate, always perfect. How wrong she was. Lounging the seat back, not caring that it was crushing Lucy's knees, Larissa heaved a sigh. "How much longer?"

"Quit with your incessant chatter, woman. We'll get there when we get there." Lamia, hands on her steering wheel, threw back her blood-red curls.

Blood. Rafe. Oh God. Was he... dead?

And it was all her fault. With a frustrated grunt, Lucy fidgeted with the cuffs binding her wrists. These bitches would pay. Adrenaline pumping in her system, she lunged toward the front seat. A slicing pain laced its way from her stomach to her brain. A deep growl of agony wrenched from her mouth. What had they done?

"Where's Rafe?" she managed to growl.

Lamia adjusted her rearview mirror to gaze at her reflection. "Oh, look. The princess hath woken. Your fuck buddy isn't dead. Belial isn't quite done with him. Unfortunately, we had to leave him for now. So hard to clean upholstery, you know."

"Oh, so kind of you." She clenched her fists and the cuffs jangled. "I'm going to love kicking your ass. Upholstery stains and all."

"Should I put her back to sleep?" Larissa asked, her singsong sweet voice grating on Lucy's eardrum.

"No, let her stay awake for this." Lamia turned to face her directly, the red rims of her obsidian eyes glimmering. "Comfortable?"

She could only manage a slight roll of her eyes. "Like you care."

"Oh, I care, all right. Belial is paying me rather well for your safe capture." She snaked her hand out, allowing a scaly finger to creep along Lucy's cheek. Clenching her teeth, Lucy fought the nausea that churned within. She should've stabbed the bitch when she had the chance.

"Yeah, right. You care." The only thing the bitch cared about was sucking the blood from innocent children. Lucy's stomach lurched. Lamia needed to be sent back to Hell, and, given the chance, she wouldn't hesitate to do it. But that time wouldn't come now. The danged silver handcuffs made sure of that.

Tugging at the handcuffs, she prayed she could channel some superhuman powers to free her wrists.

"Won't work. You haven't been accepted as a Paladin." Larissa smirked from cheek to cheek. "And after tonight, you won't ever."

With that, the car bounced over a huge pothole, sending Lucy's head crashing into the ceiling. Rubbing her head, she growled.

"Where are you taking me?"

"To Hell, of course."

"Hell? I wasn't a geography major, but isn't Hell a little further south?"

Lamia threw out a low chuckle. "Unfortunately, we don't have the power to make that journey."

"I'm confused. You just said we were going to Hell. And now we're not. Make up your mind, lady."

Larissa turned her über-gorgeous head and smirked. "Oh, we're going to Hell, all right. Hell, Michigan."

Hell, Michigan? Oh please. These bitches would be unpleasantly surprised when they got there.

Lucy flashed a secret smile. "I hate to break it to you... umm... ladies, but the only thing Hell, Michigan, and your Hell have in common is the name." Unless ice cream parlors with cheesy lounge singers were demonic. Then again she, herself, was demonic and didn't know it.

"So you've been there?" Lamia's eyes sparked demonically.

Time to play with these bloodsucking bitches.

"Yeah. But be careful. You sneeze and you'll end up in Heaven instead."

Larissa reached across the seat and slapped Lucy's face, sending her flying backward. "Not funny. You forget. I've been there too. And we've confirmed it's the perfect place for the ceremony."

Lamia grabbed Larissa's hand, her grip firm, dimpling into her servant's skin. "You've said enough." She loosened her hold and traced her finger against Larissa's lips. "Ahh, silence. If only I could do the same to you."

"And why can't you?"

"Cocky little bitch. That'll get you killed, you know."

"Whatever. So what's this ceremony Belial is putting together? Has he decided to have his *bris*?" If only they could be that fortunate. She heard it hurt like hell. "I'd be more than happy to do the honors. I'm pretty good with a scalpel."

"If your skills are as sharp as your tongue, I don't doubt that one bit."

With a shrug, Lucy craned her neck to check the highway mile marker. Ugh. Still another hour to go. Lansing's lights whirled by as she sucked in a deep breath. This wasn't a dream. It was real. She needed Rafe. Even though they just met, they had a connection. Aw heck, it was more than a connection. She loved him. And now he was lying on her floor in a pool of blood and she couldn't do anything to help him. Teeth clenched and hands fisted, she struggled to remain calm. Tongue between teeth, lips pursed, she let the gnawing pain combat the anger that boiled and flamed inside.

"And to answer your question, it's a wedding ceremony."

Glancing up at the star speckled sky, she shook her head. "Wow, that's surprising."

"Most women, human and demon alike, would jump at the chance to become Belial's wife. He's one of Hell's strongest princes."

With a wrinkle of her nose, she recalled her one run-in with the wannabe prince of darkness. "If they can get over the stench of cinnamon and rotten eggs. It smells like someone cut a huge one and tried covering it with cheap air freshener."

A steaming hiss erupted from Lamia's mouth. "I should've known."

Boo yeah! She found a kink in their plans. She mentally steepled her fingers with devilish delight. "That your boss smells like a rotten cinnamon roll?"

"Very funny. He's spent most his life in the bowels of Hell. When I say bowels, I mean bowels. If you can smell him, you've been blessed. Damn Lilu!"

"Gotta love Dad." Lucy smiled triumphantly.

Lamia turned her head, her sneer burning. "Just a *minor* setback, my dear. So stop gloating."

She chose to ignore. "I'm blessed! I'm blessed. Lord help me, I'm blessed." Maybe if she annoyed the witch long enough she would kick her to the curb and leave her on side the road in some boondock town.

"What has been blessed can be unblessed." Lamia's mouth curved into a snide smirk. "We'll need just a few more items."

With that, she pulled out a red-and-black striped iPhone and punched a button. The red matched the rims of her eyes way too perfectly. Holy cow, these Infernati and their minions went all out where communication was concerned. An annoying beep emitted from her phone. "Blast it. The battery's going dead."

"Even demons are slaves to technology, eh?"

"Whatever," Lamia muttered, fidgeting with the charging cord. "Another minor setback. And I can make calls and charge at the same time."

With a triumphant, in your face smile, she mashed her finger to the phone. "Ooh, it's ringing."

"Yippee!" Lucy twisted her arms behind her back. Surely there had to be a way break free from these stupid cuffs. She was the princess of the Sexubi, after all. There had to be more than just kung fu and Latin translation. Not that those were bad skills to possess.

"Would you like me to put the speakerphone on?"

"Nah, it's cool," Lucy said, leaning back into the stiff seat. "Belial and I started out on the wrong foot." And they would stay on that wrong foot too.

Lamia's mouth slithered into a creepy smile. Lucy cringed inwardly.

"It's not customary for the bride to talk to the groom before the wedding, anyway." She brushed her finger over her lips, shushing Lucy with a soft hiss. "Yes, I have her…"

Yeah, Lucy should've figured she was the bride. It made perfect sense. After all, these demons were pretty backward as it was. So she was supposed to be Belial's meek little wife, barefoot and pregnant in his hellish kitchen? She had news for him.

"Actually, the rules state a groom can't see his bride before the wedding. No rules about talking to her." Lucy made her best attempt at a friendly smile.

"So what happens when Belial and I say 'I do'?" If it was anything like Hollywood theatrics, the Earth would split, emitting flames and bursts of lava into the air. "Do I get a T-shirt that says 'I married Belial and all I got was this lousy T-shirt'?"

Lamia ripped the phone from her ear. "Silly girl. Your banter will get you nowhere. If you must know, Belial takes ownership of everything in your possession."

Sucked to be Belial, since the chest was actually Serah's. "I've got bad news for you, girl."

"Oh?" she asked, her lips quirking up with delight. "About the chest belonging to your friend? It was easy to convince her to gift it to you. It's yours now, darling."

Her heart plummeted. They hurt Serah. They would die. "What the hell did you do to her?"

"A little torture never hurt anyone. She was stronger than I expected."

Lucy gritted her teeth. "What. Did. You. Do?"

"Nothing that can't be reversed... with a little surgery."

Cuffs clanking as she struggled with her hands, Lucy growled—deep and guttural. "Bitch."

"One of Belial's hired assassins kidnapped her and the chimp, and delivered them to me." Her jaw clenched and her red eyes flickered. "Your friend put up a good fight. The assassin, however, did not."

"Good for Serah."

"Larissa took care of the assassin, not Serah. I can't have too many people knowing our plans."

"She's your tool."

Lamia shrugged. "She enjoys it, though. See." She craned Larissa's head around to face Lucy. A calm, almost sweet smile, crept across her face. Such a masochist.

Hell, next right, emblazoned in reflective tape, caught Lucy's eye.

With that, Lamia cracked her head up. "Oh goody. We're almost there."

"I hate to tell you, but you still have at least another hour to go until you reach Hell." Yes, it was the exit, but Lamia failed to realize that the road to Hell—pun absolutely intended—was a bunch of backwoods county roads and highways. If she was lucky, Lamia would take a wrong turn and end up in Climax—Michigan, that is—instead. One could only hope.

Grinding her finger into her phone, she punched buttons. " Lovely! I enjoy a scenic trip every so often."

"Hope your suspension doesn't mind."

"Pardon me?"

"Michigan... country roads... Winter. Do the math." And, as if to illustrate her point, the car rumbled over an icy chunk of asphalt, sending her head into the ceiling—*again*!

Her only satisfaction was watching Lamia's head crash against the ceiling too. "Devil's balls! How much further until we reach Hell?"

"As I said earlier, another hour or so," Lucy replied with a nonchalant shrug. "You'll be disappointed. Hell is a hole."

"Belial is quite confident it'll work for our purposes." The red flashed around the irises of her eyes. "Try all you want to dissuade me, my dear. It won't work. I'm almost as powerful as your father."

"But not quite."

"Belial has promised me more power." A sinister smirk crept across her lips. "And then I'll take over your father's kingdom."

"You're such a tool."

"A tool? Me? I think not."

Lucy shrugged. "Whatever, lady. Belial is only concerned with Belial. I could tell just from looking at him."

"We'll see."

Yep, she knew one thing. Larissa was an extension of Lamia, the biggest tool of them all.

Chapter 25

PAIN, GRINDING AND THROBBING, SHOT THROUGH HIS entire body. Eyes squeezed shut, he groaned. But nothing was as painful as the sight of Lamia and that bitch Larissa manhandling Lucy's body. If only he had just an ounce of strength. He could've saved her. Immortality came with some drawbacks. Instead of death, pain plagued your body until your wounds healed.

The metallic tang of blood curled along his tongue. These wounds cut deep, just barely missing his heart. It would take at least a day for him to properly heal without treatment.

Treatment. *Kalli*, his mind screamed.

Digging into his pocket, he fished for the phone. Blood pooled around him, thick and crimson. It was a miracle he remained conscious.

Fingers slipping on buttons, he pushed the button to dial Kalli. Another miracle. She was the last person he called.

"Hello?"

"Kalli," he sputtered out.

"Rafe? What's wrong?"

"Lamia... has... Lucy."

A loud breath of air rumbled in his ear. "I'm on my way."

Dragging his bloodied body across the floor, he reached for the dilapidated chair—Lucy's favorite—and pulled himself up. There was no way in any part of the afterlife that he would cower in fear. The Fore-Demons chose him for a reason. He—*they*—Lucy and he—wouldn't fail. He owed it to her. Sucking in a ragged breath, he shook his head. There wasn't any need to fool himself any longer. He wouldn't save her because he owed her. He would save her because he *loved* her.

A sudden swirl of adrenaline pounded through his system. Blood pumping in his chest, he hoisted himself up and stood tall. Rays of heated energy radiated through his veins, warming him, comforting him... *healing* him. Even as the freezing swirls of Kalli's arrival flew around him, the energy pulsed through his body, sizzling against the icy crystals.

"How is this possible?" he muttered, gazing down at the jagged gash in his abdomen as it faded and blended into his skin. All that remained was a thin pink line.

Bursting out of the wall of ice, Kalli allowed her gaze to rove around the room. "Rafe, where—" Gaze locked with his, she arched a brow. "I thought you were hurt."

With an irritated huff, she crossed her arms across the magenta lace of her bodice. "We don't have time for jokes, Deleon." Pacing back and forth in her ripped fishnets and tall army boots, she scrubbed her fingers through her rainbow mat of hair. Still perplexed by her strange choice of garb, he shrugged. He'd seen images of her through history, had seen her beauty. Not that she wasn't beautiful now...

"Stop reflecting on my life and tell me what's going on? I don't like leaving Lucy's friends unattended."

"I healed myself."

Kalli blinked. "You what?"

He blew out a frustrated breath of air. "Exactly what I said."

"That's impossible. Even I can't heal myself." Kalli shook her head. "Would totally rock if I could though." Scanning the room, she blinked. Dark crimson blood trickled and coated the floor. No denying that fact.

"Good God! Is that *your* blood?"

"Yes. I'm telling you the truth. Look." Ripping up his T-shirt he traced the thin line that remained of his scar. "See."

Leaning in for a better view, Kalli traced a finger over the faded pink jags. "Definitely a fresh heal." She narrowed her eyes and pursed her lips. "You lost a lot of blood. Even I can't heal someone that fast."

"What's happening?"

"Duh," Kalli said, planting her leather-clad ass on the futon, the only piece of furniture not coated in blood. "I don't know. I'm a healer, not a miracle worker."

"What's that supposed to mean?"

Kalli angled a serious gaze his way. "What do I mean? No demon has ever healed himself. It isn't supposed to be possible."

"Well, it is."

Kalli grumbled. "We need to talk to the Fore-Demons. Do you remember anything at all before you healed? Anything you said? Thought? Anything?"

Lucy. He'd thought about Lucy. Saving her. *Loving her.* "Lucy."

"You were thinking about Lucy?" Bemusement and amusement both swirled in her gaze.

"I need to save her."

Kalli's lips quirked up into a knowing grin. "That's it?"

"She needs our help. They're taking her to Belial. I owe it to her. I..." he cut himself off. No way was he ready to admit to Kalli he'd fallen for Lucy.

Kalli's brow jutted upward. "You what?"

"Nothing. I just want her safe. She's Lilu's daughter."

With a shrug, Kalli crossed one leg over the other. "There has to be more. Maybe the Paladin manual will say something." Angling her gaze down to the large bulky tome next to her, she smiled. "Still as massive as ever." She lugged the book to her lap and flipped it open. "Don't just stand there looking dumb. Help me read it."

"Section 24-6-A." He'd spent hours poring over that book during his early years as a Paladin trainee. There wasn't any sentence or word he didn't know. The section in question pertained to the healing skills... skills he shouldn't have... skills reserved for certain Paladins only.

Swiping the mop of hair from her face, she scrunched her brows. "You need to get out more often, Rafe." Glancing down at the book, she drew her finger across the ancient text. Narrowing her gaze, she let out a deep grumble. "There's nothing here about self-healing. Where's an index when you really need one?"

Rafael recited the words, as if he'd just read them yesterday. "To heal yourself, gather your internal energy and focus on that part of you which needs healing."

"Where in the heck did you read that?" Kalli thumbed through several pages, scanning each line. "There isn't anything like that in this entire section." With a frustrated grumble she flung the book at him.

Flipping the pages, Rafael scanned through the text,

his gaze flying over word after familiar word. He knew he read it somewhere, but where? Bloody hell! He knew he wasn't going insane, but he certainly would be if he didn't get to Lucy in time.

"I swear to all that is the Paladins I read it." He turned the page to where he'd seen it. "It's missing a page." He turned the page back and forth, frustration and anger creasing his brow. Jaw ticking, he slammed his fist down on the book.

Kalli perused the book. First she pointed at page 792 then to 793. "Does this look as if it's missing a page?"

Shaking his head, Rafael clenched his fists. "There *was* another page when I read it."

"Sure. Maybe you dreamt you read it. Maybe the Fore-Demons know more about you than you know about yourself."

"What do you mean?"

"I mean this: you're more powerful than you realize. Maybe it isn't Jacoba who's the Chosen Paladin."

"Bullshit," Rafael ground out. "Jacoba is the only logical choice. She hasn't failed any of her missions." *Like I have*.

With an exasperated breath of air, she shook her head. Turning to face him, she grabbed his shoulders, her gaze stony serious. "You're too hard on yourself, Rafe."

"I have reason to be. I've failed the only two women I... I've had to protect." He'd almost said loved. Curse him. He couldn't have Kalli knowing of his weakened state.

She arched her brow in that annoyingly inquisitive fashion. "I'd suggest visiting the Fore-Demons, but we don't have time. Do you remember anything at all?"

Rubbing his temples, he closed his eyes. Reluctant to relive the painful memory of Lamia and Larissa's abuse of Lucy's lifeless body, Rafael sucked in a ragged breath of air. They could kick him any time, any place. Seeing them slapping and kicking defenseless Lucy sent a pain shooting right to his heart. The fact that he couldn't do anything to stop them still chilled him to the bone. What had happened to the woman he had cared about two hundred years prior? His stomach roiled and churned in disgust. How could he have missed it?

"Anything?" Kalli asked, breaking him from his thoughts.

He shook his head, struggling to remember the words that floated around him in a foggy shroud. Lamia and Larissa were arguing about Hell and which way would be the fastest. They were going to Hell. But how? He hadn't even shown Lucy how to journey to Limbo. A journey to Hell would take much more energy.

"Bloody hell," he growled.

Kalli's head jerked up, her gaze alert. "What?"

"They've gone to Hell."

"Hell?" Kalli rolled her pierced tongue between her teeth. "That's impossible."

Rafael shuffled his feet across the carpeted floor. "I heard them talking as I drifted in and out of consciousness. They're going to Hell."

"Hell? That's highly unlikely." Kalli yanked at her magenta bodice and stretched her legs. "They haven't enough energy, and we've warded the portals to Hell. They aren't going anywhere."

"They were arguing about who would drive," he mumbled, rubbing his temples. *Drive?* Demons didn't drive to Hell. With a disappointed groan, he shook his head. He'd imagined the whole bloody thing.

Kalli tapped her fingers on her fishnet clad thigh and shrugged. "That's odd." The annoying tone of Kalli's phone pierced the air, silencing her. With a drawn-out huff, she pushed a device wedged in her ear. Bluetooth, if he remembered correctly.

"Hello? Is the shop secure?" She adjusted the earpiece. "I'm with Rafe. He says they're taking Lucy to Hell." She shook her head. "No... there's no way they can get there. Rafe says they were driving there though." Kalli's brow tightened. "Oh? I'll call you right back." With that she flipped her phone shut. "Driving you say?"

"I imagined it."

"What if you didn't?"

"Driving to Hell is impossible."

"What if Hell is on Earth?"

Clenching his fists, Rafael gritted his teeth. "I haven't the time nor the patience for your cryptic banter, Kalli."

"Maybe you're right about them driving to Hell."

"How so?"

With a roll of her eyes, Kalli flounced up from the futon and padded to the desk in the far corner. With a push of a button, Lucy's computer fired to life. Punching some keys on the keyboard, she clicked the mouse.

"Come here."

"What is it?" he asked, moving next to Kalli. Leaning down, he scanned the screen.

"It's called a computer."

Rafael growled deep and low. "I know what a computer is. I'm not that uneducated in human technology." Placing a hand on the back of her chair, he leaned over to look at the monitor. "What do you want to show me on Lucy's *computer?*"

"This!"

Rafael blinked as he read the screen. A blog post about a woman's recent trip to Hell... Michigan. This had to be a joke. "Who in their right mind names a town Hell? This can't be real."

"Gerardo says it is." Kalli clicked something within the text and another site loaded. "Yum. Ice cream," she said with a click to the picture. A larger picture of an ice cream parlor appeared. She punched more keys and clicked enter. The colorful website that looked like a pamphlet for Halloween gone bad vanished, a map taking its place.

"Zip code, 48169." Pointing at the map emblazoned on the screen, Kalli shifted in the chair and snorted. "And here I was expecting to see 666 in there somewhere. Nope! All they get is a little 69."

Rafael blew out a deep breath. Leave it to Kalli to crack a joke when times were dire. "Bloody hell! This isn't the time for jokes." With an irritated growl, he clenched his fists. He struggled to fight the urge to pound his fist into the first inanimate object he came across. "I need to save Lucy—*now*!"

Kalli rolled her tongue ring between her teeth and spun the chair to face him. "I want to save Lucy too, but we can't just up and travel there. First, we've never been there. We could get lost in the portal. Also, it's too far, even if you're able to focus on Lucy. On top of that, Belial's probably blocked the area from any traveling." She blew out a frustrated breath of air. "Bastard."

Rafael drew his lips together. Excellent points. "How far is Hell?"

Kalli punched some more keys and hit enter. Scanning the website, she scratched at her rainbow mop of hair. "A couple hours by car."

Computers, Rafael mused. Was there anything you couldn't find or do nowadays? "Impressive. Time to throw away that atlas."

"You need to get out more."

"What am I doing now?" Crossing his arms, he narrowed his gaze. "So I guess we're driving."

"There's one itsy-bitsy problem." Kalli played with her tongue ring, the metal clanging against her teeth.

Bloody hell. Clinging to every last bit of control, he took a deep breath. "What is it?"

Kalli scraped a red lock of hair from her face and lowered an embarrassed gaze to the floor. "I don't know how to drive."

"You've been here for how many years and never learned?"

"You never learned either!" Kalli crossed her arms. "I distinctly remember an accident with a Model T I was sent to clean up."

Now wasn't the time to bring up the past. "I wanted to keep myself separated from Earth."

He refused to dwell on Miss Amanda Newell, all the pain and heartbreak she'd caused him. His jaw twitched. At one time he would've cried, but now he just felt anger. Not at Amanda or Lamia, but himself. He wouldn't let them get the best of him again. He would rescue Lucy, and he knew what to do.

Ripping his cell phone from his pocket, he punched in some numbers.

"Who you calling?"

Rafael, despite the direness of the situation, let a smile spread across his face. "We have friends who can drive."

Kalli arched both of her brows, bemusement swirling in her gaze. "Friends?"

"Gerardo and Frankie!" he boomed, excitement lacing his tone.

Eyes widening, Kalli chuckled. "Why didn't I think of them?"

"Gerardo?" Rafael cupped the receiver to his ear.

"*Sí*," the Latino responded in his native language. "Who's there?"

"Rafael."

"Rafe?" The man's effeminate Latino accent echoed in his ear. "Where's Lucy? Kalli said something happened. What's going on? Is everyone all right?" The words flew out in a jumbled rush.

"Lucy was kidnapped by a couple of Belial's minions. They're taking her to Hell. We need your help."

"*¡Ay, Dios mío!*" A string of other words Rafael didn't recognize rang in his ear. Frankie's frantic voice muffled in the background. "Lucy's been kidnapped."

There was no mistaking Frankie's gasp in the background. "What happened?"

"*Un momento*," Gerardo rattled off.

The scraping sounds of the phone shuffling scratched in his ear. In the background, Gerardo quickly relayed a brief and completely paraphrased explanation. "See! We have to go. Right?"

In truth, he didn't like bringing humans into a demon's battle, but he had no choice—not if he wanted to save Lucy.

"Yes, Lucy's life depends on it."

On the other end of the line, more hushed arguments followed by more scuffling. Now wasn't the time to argue over a phone.

"What do we have to do?" Frankie's usually soft southern lilt screamed urgency.

"We need you to take us to Hell, Michigan."

"Hell? You're joking. It's way out in the boonies. There's nothing there."

How wrong Frankie was. "There is now, and we haven't much time. Kalli and I are on our way. Be ready in—" He reached in his pocket and pulled out his old timepiece, the one he'd cherished for so long—the one given to him by the enemy. He flung it against the wall, metal, glass, and gears flying and skittering across the floor. "Five minutes." With that, he clicked the button to disconnect the call.

Kalli stood there, arms crossed, twirling her lip ring with her tongue. "That's an antique, you know."

"It's worth naught but a bitter reminder of a love that never was. I'd rather let go of the past and move on to the future."

"Fair enough." Kalli slinked over to the broken bits and scooped them up. "Always cleaning up after you, aren't I?"

"Whatever, Kalli. We need to go. *Now*."

"Certainly." Bowing her head, she raised her arms and shot her hands toward the ceiling. In a swirl of ice, snow, and frost, she vanished.

Summoning the portals, Rafael allowed the frigid wind, ice, and freezing snow to surround him and pull him through the portal. The sooner he slipped through, the better.

Winds, bitter and cold, lapped at his skin. Sleet licked at his face. Ice twined its way through his hair. The tunnel, which normally transferred him in seconds, seemed to be taking minutes... no, *hours*. Had traveling always taken this long? Bloody hell. *Time doesn't fly when the woman you love is in danger.*

Allowing the winds to spin around him and reanimate his human form, he closed his eyes. It was about bloody time. Swiping the ice chunks and frost from his hair and face, he opened his eyes. Kalli, twirling a coil of ratty hair, propped herself against one of the shiny silver-trimmed shampoo bowls. A scowl etched her face.

"We've got bigger problems."

Shaking the rest of the ice from his clothing, Rafael groaned. This didn't sound good. Should he ask? "What is it?"

"Serah and Squeaky are missing."

Chapter 26

"Are we there yet?" Lucy asked for the third time, using the same annoying voice a child would use while on their way to an amusement park. But they weren't going to an amusement park. They were going to a town in the middle of nowhere that just happened to be named Hell. Poor Belial and Lamia. They would be disappointed.

Lamia turned to glare at her and clucked her forked tongue. "Try as you may to annoy me, my dear Lucia. It won't work."

She arched a brow. "Are you going to silence me like you did your tool?"

"Unfortunately, no." A wide smile crept across her face, making her look almost pretty. "Belial needs your voice intact, so you can speak your vows."

"The only vow I'm giving him is the one where I promise to kick him back to the netherworld... preferably in his nether region." Lucy flashed her own sweet smile. "After sending you there first, of course."

Too bad they still had her cuffed. Her fingers curled and clenched. She kicked at the back of the driver's seat, the silver chains clanging in a rhythmic tone that taunted her, driving her to the breaking point.

The bitch was going down. Lucy angled a glance toward the passenger seat, where Larissa slept, a peaceful expression sweeping across her *angelic* face. *And her little friend too*. When she woke up, of course. Lucy wanted her to remember the beatdown she deserved. For the hell she'd put her friends through, but especially for the torment and agony she'd inflicted on Rafe. And that was truly unforgivable.

"Strong, aren't they?" Lamia threw her head back, her cackle reverberating in Lucy's ears. "Forged in the pits of Hell. Amazing, huh?"

Poor demon that had to make these things. It probably killed them. "Yeah, amazing, considering demons are *allergic* to silver."

"Only on Earth, my dear. When we are in our natural habitat, we can touch silver all day long, if we choose."

Lucy rolled her eyes. "Lucky you!" With as much strength as she could, she lugged her shackled legs up onto the seat. If only she and Rafe had had more time. She could've gone to see those Fore-Demons and accept the Paladin way. Then these cuffs would be history and she'd be kicking some snake-lady ass. If only her dad would've been more honest with her mom and her. Now wasn't the time for blame, though.

Now was the time to kick Lamia's scaly ass. With a determined smirk, Lucy pulled her legs up. Luckily for her, Larissa had inadvertently left just enough slack for her to be deadly. And here she used to think the pretty little blonde was smart. Who knew clichés could be so true.

"So, are we there yet?"

Lamia straightened in her seat, her hands gripping the steering wheel like two giant vices.

Lucy's grin spread wider. She almost had Lamia where she wanted her. "Well?"

One.

"Well?"

Two.

"Are we? Huh? Are we?"

Three.

"Well, are—"

"*Shut up you insolent bitch!*" Lamia whipped around to face her, her red eyes swirling. *Perfect!*

Wrenching her legs apart, she pulled herself around. Hopefully she could channel some of those ninja moves she discovered earlier. She arched her back and bent her knees, lightly grazing against the back of Lamia's seat.

"Why the hell are you squirming? Is the princess scared?" Lamia eyes blazed bright, further fueling Lucy's ire.

She had two choices: Either sit still in the backseat like a weak-minded fool while Lamia drove her to certain death. Oh, Lamia could try and sugarcoat the whole marriage thing, but knowing Belial, he had no intentions of providing his new bride a life of wedded bliss.

The second option? Surprising Lamia with a swift kick to her head. With a quick shake of her shackled ankles, she hid her smile in the darkness.

Either way, death was imminent. And Lucy would rather go down now, before Belial could do whatever it was he needed to do with the *Arca Inferorum*. She twisted her wrists behind her and cracked her knuckles.

"I'm not scared, but you should be," she muttered beneath her breath. She heaved her legs up further and did something she hadn't done in a long time. She prayed.

She prayed like she'd never prayed before. She

prayed for the strength her father had to leave her mother and her. She prayed for Rafe's courage. She prayed that she could channel even an inch of his resolve. She only hoped whoever was listening hadn't completely given up on her.

"What was that?" Lamia barked.

Now or never. With a quick jerk, she launched her legs higher in the air. Tumbling against the hard backseat cushion, she kicked her feet out. Neck kinked to the left, she swung her legs across the top of the driver's seat.

Crack!

The heel of her tennis shoe slammed against Lamia's ear, sending her head flinging to the side. Another loud crunch echoed as her head smashed against the window. Wrenching her neck around, Lamia growled, loud and primal. Clawed fingers reached out and snaked around Lucy's leg, hurling her body to the floor.

Struggling to maintain her balance, Lucy wrestled with the handcuffs that bound her wrists. Lamia, her body snaking and slithering, hovered over her, spittle and blood dripping from her scaly lips onto Lucy's already bloodied sweater. The car swayed and swerved with each movement. This wouldn't be good at all.

"What would Belial say?"

A loud hiss ground from Lamia's lips. "Belial is a fool, but he needs you."

"The tool calling Belial a fool. Ha-ha! Very funny."

"Don't make me slap you."

"Maybe I'm into that kinky shit."

Her scaly hand lashed out and snaked around Lucy's

neck, pulling her eye-to-eye with her crimson one. Eyes flashing, Lamia's fingers coiled around her neck, tightening their slithering grip.

A niggling deep within Lucy's brain poked and prodded, even as she choked and gasped for fleeting air. How the hell was Lamia still driving?

"You…" Lamia squeezed her neck tighter. "are…" She shook Lucy's head like she was James Bond's favorite martini. "…a bloody fool." With that, Lamia's slithering fingers loosened, sending her crashing to the floor.

The car careened and swerved, sending her head sailing against the back door. "What the heck?" she muttered, wishing desperately that her hands were free to massage her aching skull.

Another swerve sent the car jerking to the left. Lucy's head banged against the passenger side door and her back cracked against hard floor.

"Shit!" Lamia's shrill exclamation shredded Lucy's eardrums.

Tires squealing, the car veered to the right. A horn honked. Like an overused rag doll, Lucy's body crumpled, slamming against the other side. Her head swam, her back ached, and her fists clenched.

Plastic and metal ripped and twisted in an agonizing cacophony, the impact pulsing in her ears. Lamia's body catapulted forward, then back, her loud hiss reverberating throughout the tiny confines of the car. Or was that the radiator?

"Bloody fool!" Lamia, in her true form, hovered over her, slithering like a snake being charmed from a basket.

One thing was different. Lucy certainly wasn't the

one doing the charming. Hauling herself up, she stared her in her slitted eyes. "I did that on purpose."

"Oh, I'm sure you did." Lamia's forked tongue darted out and whipped Lucy's nose. "Belial won't like this."

Lucy's eyebrow quirked up. "I thought you didn't give a shit about Belial."

Lamia's scaly tail lashed out and wrapped around her neck, pulling her closer, the grip tightening. "If it weren't for the treasures he was offering, I'd kill you right now."

She opened her mouth to offer her usual bit of sarcasm, but only managed an intelligible gasp. Wow. Lamia finally found a way to shut her up. Score one for Lamia, much to Lucy's chagrin.

Lamia's tail loosened its grip and slithered away, returning to her slightly improved, human form. Crimson curls cascading down her head, she spread her lips into a wide smirk. "That got you to shut up, didn't it?"

"Yes, mistress," she coughed out.

Her red-black eyes flickered as a snarl revealed two very long pointed fangs—fangs she'd used to suck the souls from innocent children. She'd show her where to stick those fangs.

Up Larissa's pert little ass.

As if knowing Lucy was thinking about her and that body that would make a model jealous, Larissa shifted in the passenger seat, a soft sigh escaping her too-plump lips. Why did the evil ones have to be so damned cutesy sounding?

"And, so you know, my dear Lucia." A wry smile curved Lamia's lips, her arm stretching and snaking around her. With absolutely no effort, she hauled Lucy up and flung her against the backseat. "Nothing you say or attempt to do will stop us. The Infernati will prevail."

"We'll see about that."

"Oh, yes we will." Her greenish-gray tail slinked and slithered across Lucy's cheek, the cool smooth skin sending shivers of revulsion coursing through her. Lucy fought with every fiber of her being to keep the bile from rising to her throat.

The trilling of a cell phone broke the silence. With an aggravated huff, Lamia pulled her appendage away from Lucy's face and snatched up the phone, her body slithering back into its human form.

She clicked the button and jerked the phone to her ear. "Speak." A mortified gasp blew from her mouth. "My apologies. I didn't realize it was you." She flashed a warning glare.

Tool, indeed.

Lamia continued her conversation. "There's a slight delay."

Slight delay, my ass.

Peering over the car seat and out the cracked windshield, Lucy attempted to survey the damage. Steam rolled from beneath the hood as the car creaked, clanked, and shuddered. The passenger side door dangled precariously, allowing cold gusts of air to hit her face. Shock had clearly hit.

"Your *bride* managed to get us in an accident." Lamia scraped her clawed fingers through her blood red curls. "Is this worth it, my prince?"

Lucy chuckled to herself. Lamia, for as much as she claimed to be all for her own glory, she had herself firmly wrapped around Belial's golden finger.

"I'm sorry, Prince. It shall not happen again." She pushed open the door and lumbered out of the car. "I'd rather discuss this with you in private. *She's* a handful." With that, she slammed the door shut, the mangled hunk of metal moaning in response.

Lucy craned her head to watch Lamia pace next to the car, her claws clenching the phone. Any tighter and they'd be digging inside. She shook her head, mouthing a few unnamed curse words. With a sharp twist, she turned back toward the car, her glowing red glare boring into her. Lucy returned her glare with one of her own. Nope. She wasn't shaking in her boots. There was too much at stake.

Cramming her phone into the pocket of the black skinny jeans that clung to her every snakelike curve, she flung the door open. "Get out, bitch. We're going to Hell after all."

"I'm sure *you* are." Lucy flashed a toothy grin. "And I'm going to enjoy sending you there."

"Ha-ha. Very funny." With that, Lamia grabbed her by the collar of her coat and yanked her from the car. "Have you ever traveled?"

Lucy shrugged, a tiny smirk spreading across her face. "Nope. I never learned. I'm afraid you're out of luck."

"Oh, I have plenty of luck, Lucy." Crimson lips spread into a wide smirk, she snapped her fingers.

With a soft gasp, Larissa jerked her head up. Scratching her head, she squinted. "Wha... What happened?"

"Stupid bitch got us in a car accident." She narrowed her gaze and gave Lucy a searing hiss. "We have to travel now."

Rubbing her eyes, Larissa let out a long drawn out yawn. "How'd that happen?"

"Never mind that," Lamia barked. "Get the hell out of the car."

With a quick jolt, Larissa reached for the door handle and pulled. Yanking and jerking the handle, she grumbled beneath her breath. "Bloody hell. The door's stuck." Pushing and pulling, she fought the crumpled scrap of metal.

"Incompetent!" Lamia growled. "Can't you do anything right?"

With a soft yelp, Larissa flinched, her rosy red lips forming a tiny pout. "Yes," she mumbled, exhaustion and frustration creasing her brow. If she hadn't been such a bitch, Lucy might have felt sorry for her.

But beneath that beauty and grace lay a monster. A vicious heartless monster who'd hurt someone she loved. A wound she'd let fester for over two hundred years. If it weren't for the cuffs, she'd give her three hundred years of wounds. Unfortunately, even that wouldn't be enough to make up for the abuse she'd put Rafe through.

With a groan, Larissa heaved herself over the gearshift and plopped down into the driver's seat. Swinging to the side, she pushed herself out of the car. "Are we close enough?"

"At this point, I don't fucking care." Lamia growled out. Her talons gripping into Lucy's shoulder blades, she yanked her to her. Her forked tongue lashing out, she hissed. "Either way, she dies." She leaned in close, her cold, lifeless breath crawling against her skin. "Yes, you'll die, and it'll bring me much pleasure."

Adrenaline pounded through Lucy. "What did I ever do to you?"

Lamia jerked her head to meet her red-rimmed glare. "You were born."

"Don't blame me for that."

"If you weren't born I'd be the Sexubi Queen." Larissa sauntered to stand next to her mistress, her true self shining through. Pristine pale skin swirled and molded into green scales. Spiked tale whipping back and forth, her pupils narrowed to tiny slits.

"Instead, you're the Lizard Queen. Sucks to be you, huh?"

Lamia grumbled, her other hand literally snaking out to stroke Larissa's scaly cheek. "Now, now. You remember our plan, my dear."

Larissa's gaze shifted to the ground. "Yes, mistress. I remember."

Lamia's lips slithered into a sly smile. "Good."

"So what was your plan?" Lucy asked, cocking her head to the side.

Lamia's tail slithered and twined around her leg. "We were going to kill your father so I could take over the kingdom."

"But daddy fell in love and ruined all your little plans." She let out a low chuckle. "Score one for love."

Larissa snorted, shaking her green scaly head. "Love doesn't exist, right, mistress?"

"That's the human in her." Her other snakelike hand traced through Lucy's hair and down her cheek. Anger and revulsion reared their ugly head. She bit her tongue.

"Oh yes it does," she managed. "And it's love that'll kick your asses."

"We'll see, my dear." With that, Lamia curled her tail around her, pulling her closer to her slithering body.

"Hurry!" Larissa punctuated her screech with a point of a clawed finger.

Lamia turned her head, a low growl forming deep in her belly. "Bloody hell."

Curiosity wriggling its way through her, Lucy joined in. Light reflecting against the snow, a car barreled its way down the road. At least 80 miles an hour, easy. Her spirits lifted. Deep in her heart, she knew that car was on its way for her. Rafe was nearby, getting closer by the second.

"I told you love would kick your—"

Deep bone-wracking cold permeated her entire body, freezing her in place. Arctic air swirled and blew around her, slicing into her face. Ice crystals formed in her hair and her lashes. Any colder and her eyes would freeze shut. Thank goodness she didn't have a runny nose. Talk about snotcicles!

Frost darted across her cheeks and over her face, the ice glazing over her eyes. Headlights dancing and reflecting against the thick sheen. She sucked in a cold, bitter breath. *Almost here*. Lamia's iced-over tail still kept her tight in its grasp. Tires squealing and moaning, the car slid to a stop.

"Lucy!" Rafe's shout echoed through the bitter cold night and throughout her mind.

Lamia's deep chuckle reverberated through her ears. "Too late!" she shouted as the car doors swung open.

With that, the ice cracked and shattered, the sound screeching in her ears. As if she were swept up in a giant tornado, her body twisted and pulled as the winds sucked her in. A loud pop reverberated, bursting in both her ears. Her eardrums pounded and throbbed as the blood rushed to her head. She used to think flying in an airplane was bad, but this was ten times worse. Spiraling and whooshing through the portal, she had no choice but to let snake-lady tighten her hold.

With a violent gust of air, the portal slammed her forward. Face freezing as wind licked at her cheeks, she kept her eyes closed. This would, no doubt, be messy. Insides squeezing and constricting, she struggled for a breath of air. Her head pounded and her stomach heaved. Would traveling be like this every time? If she managed to survive, she hoped not. Hopefully, if she was lucky, the journey would kill her, and all of Belial's plans would backfire.

The familiar, gut-wrenching odor of cinnamon intermingling with rotten eggs wafted through the air and straight up her nostrils. Her stomach roiled and bile rose. Saliva, thick and heavy, coated her tongue. Belial, golden mane swirling around his head, stood tall, his beady amber eyes glowing in the darkness. A large, sinister smirk crept across his face.

"Ahh. My bride has arrived."

Nope, luck wasn't on her side.

Chapter 27

Rafael raced toward the icy swirls, Lamia's cackle echoing in his ears. The remaining winds churned and swirled around him—mocking him. The cold snow pelted his face, feeding his despair. With an eerie pop, the portal closed. Lucy was gone.

"*¡Mierda!*" Gerardo flew from the car and came to stand next to him. With a shake of his head, he let out a defeated sigh. "I tried to warn her."

Rafael blinked. Warn her? He turned to face the Latino, his glare steady. "When?"

"Hmm." Eyes glazing in thought, Gerardo twirled a bright red feather around his finger. Were there any shirts in this man's wardrobe that didn't involve some sort of plumage?

"Before you arrived at the shop," he finished, his mouth spread in a wide toothy grin. "The day I tried to touch your hair."

What in all that is holy? "You remember?" Rafael gritted his teeth. Humans never remembered enrapturement. They only remembered the suggestions left. And Rafael had only left Gerardo one. Never touch a demon.

"Oh yes, I remember everything. Including the rather intriguing conversation with Mrs. Carlson. Absolutely fascinating, I may add." With that, he reached out and patted Rafael's back. "Mighty impressive Deleon."

Rafael reached up, grabbed Gerardo's wrist, and yanked him to face him. "What are you?"

All of a sudden, Gerardo reached out with his other hand and grabbed Rafael's other wrist. Gaze narrowed, he drew his lips into a straight line. "Not Infernati, so don't worry about that." What was it about this town? Never in his four hundred-plus years had he never encountered such a concentration of magical beings. This wasn't natural.

"Just someone who cares about Lucy."

Rafael's grip grew tighter. "This isn't the time or the place for cryptic banter. Lucy is in danger and I'll be damned if I let anything happen to her."

"We are in agreement." Gerardo's smile spread from cheek to cheek. He loosened the hold on Rafael's wrist and raked his fingers through his hair. He smoothed the feathers on his shirt and turned his back to Rafael. "This is what I am."

Throwing his hands up to the sky, he bowed his head. Bright bursts of energy poured down, showering Gerardo in radiant light. Bloody hell, Rafael had seen that light before. And usually, it meant things were worse than the Paladins knew.

Feathers, as white as the snow spiraling around them, crept from Gerardo's back, spreading farther and farther across, each plume as thick and fluffy as the last. With a flick of his new grown wings, Gerardo turned to face him. "I can't show up in public like this, you know."

Gerardo was an angel? And if he could keep his disguise around demons, he wasn't just any angel. "Who are you?" Rafael demanded.

"Gerardo Martinez." His grin spread wider. "I'm Lucy's guardian angel."

"It certainly explains the affinity for feathered shirts but doesn't explain how you managed to become a guardian angel for a succubus."

"Without feathers, I feel naked." Gerardo plucked a feather from his shirt and tossed it into the wind. "And Lucy's only *part* succubus. She's also human, you know. Upon discovering this, I decided she needed more guarding. I wasn't exactly sure what she was, but the way Lilith, in her Mrs. Gunderson getup, kept lingering around the shop, I had my suspicions."

Rafael rubbed his jaw, the stubble scratching his fingertips. He had no choice but to trust Gerardo. After all, he'd taken care of Lucy. "Very well. Speaking of Lilith, where is she?"

"With Lilu protecting Lucy's mom."

Bloody hell. In his urgency, he'd forgotten Lucy's mother. With a silent breath of relief, he nodded. "A very awkward family reunion, I suppose."

Gerardo snorted out a chuckle. "Amazing. You've grown a sense of humor."

"I've always had one," Rafael interjected. "I just seldom show it."

The sounds of heels clacking against pavement broke their conversation. With a quick shuffle, Kalli came to stand next to him. "I've tried opening a portal. The bastard Belial has blocked the entire—" Her eyes widened in shock as she registered Gerardo's appearance. "What the hell! The Fore-Demons sent an angel?"

Frankie, who lumbered behind, stopped in his tracks as he gazed Gerardo from head to toe. "Where in the hell have you been hiding those things?" Brows arched and eyes wide, he tilted his head to the left.

"They've always been here," Gerardo drawled with a flick of his snow-white wings. "I just chose to keep them hidden... for obvious reasons."

Frankie arched a manicured brow. "Why?"

"I couldn't do that to Lucy. Either they would stay away in fear, or come in droves and gawk like the salon was some sort of sideshow exhibit." He blew out a breath of air. "If you thought the small crowd that followed Lucy was big, it'd be ten times worse."

Frankie pursed his lips. "I'm still trying to figure this all out. But if you're a guardian angel, why in tarnation did you allow Belial into the shop?"

"I have a good answer." Gerardo grinned. "How is it that Lilith arrived at that precise time? I sought her out and told her Belial was near."

"And why in the name of all that is holy did you do nothing to protect her?" Rafael balled his fists in an attempt to tamp down the sudden desire to throttle the would-be guardian angel. Fingernails digging into palms, he threw Gerardo a dagger-like glare.

"Believe me, I would have if I could, but to show oneself to one's ward when the time isn't right goes against angel protocol." Gerardo's gaze grew pleading. "She was in capable hands."

"Whose capable hands? Belial's or Lilith's?" Yes, Lilith might have been Lucy's aunt, but he'd heard stories of her exploits in Las Vegas. She'd done more than drain her victims' energy. She'd sucked their life force, as well.

"Neither."

Rafael furrowed his brow. "Whose?"

"Yours." Gerardo's lips swept into a wide grin.

He blinked. His? "I don't understand."

"Of course you wouldn't. But there's no time to explain. You will learn soon enough" He spread his wings, urgency creasing his face. "We need to go. Now."

"What about him?" Kalli asked, nudging Frankie on the shoulder.

Frankie stood tall, his chin jutting out in determination. "You ain't leaving me. I may be human, but that don't mean I can't fight."

Everyone's gazes turned to Frankie. He gripped his hips and stood tall, his face as serious as stone. "Well?"

He'd be damned if he let one of Lucy's friends get hurt. "If you come with us, you will freeze to death." Rafael flexed his arms across his chest. "If you think the winter here is cold, the portal is much worse."

Kalli nodded in agreement. "The human body isn't made for traveling. You could, quite literally, freeze an appendage off." She lowered her gaze to his groin.

With a startled gasp, Frankie grabbed himself. "Really?"

Rafael only offered a static nod. Unfortunately, Kalli spoke the truth. There wasn't any easy way to sugarcoat it. "And that's not the worst of it."

Frankie's eyes sparked. "I don't care. I need to help Lucy. If that means losing Frankie Jr., then so be it."

"I won't put one of Lucy's friends in danger."

Frankie stomped his foot, sending snow flying. "It's not fair. I *have* to do something!"

"It isn't safe," Kalli flipped a knotty lock from her face. "We can't—"

Gerardo flicked his wings. "I can take him. We *angels* aren't as restricted as demons." Of course, demons were essentially evil creatures. Only those who proved their willingness to repent were chosen for the Paladin, but still there were boundaries even the Paladin couldn't break. Transporting humans, for one.

Flapping his wings, Gerardo bound into the air. With a quick flick downward, he descended and motioned to Frankie to join him. "Hop on."

"You gotta be joking," Frankie squeaked. "Honey, I like you... but not *that* much."

Fists clenched, Gerardo drew his lip straight. "This isn't a joke. Do you want to help Lucy or not?"

"When you put it that way, how can I refuse?" With a quick jog, he bounded toward Gerardo and grabbed a bunch of feathers from his shirt. Flinging a leg over Gerardo's back, he climbed on. "I'll just imagine I'm Perseus riding Pegasus in *Clash of the Titans*."

"Whatever floats your boat. Now hold on tight, it'll be a wild ride." Without a further utterance, Gerardo flapped his wings and burst up toward the heavens, a streak of dust following in his wake.

"Ooooh-weeeeee!" Frankie's voice echoed in the distance.

Now came the bigger task. Breaking through Belial's block. He turned his gaze to Kalli, who paced the snow-blanketed road, her footprints converging on one another. Fists clenched, she grumbled. "Fuck it. I'm calling in the Fore-Demons."

"No, you're not," Rafael growled, grabbing her by the lapels of her trench coat. His gaze blazed. To call in the elders signified defeat. He hadn't failed Lucy yet.

Scratch that. He *would not* fail her. "I'll call in Dominic. The three of us should be able to break through the block." The flame firmly burning beneath his ass, he closed his eyes. "Dominic Duvane!"

"Whoa, buddy," Kalli said, waving him off with her hands. "Take it easy."

Rafael unlaced his fingers from leather, smoothing out the wrinkles along the lapel. "Sorry. I just—"

"Love her?" Kalli's lips swept into a devious smile.

He kept his emotions as tamped down as possible. "I'm supposed to protect her."

"You keep telling yourself that, Rafe."

A fierce burst of wind rushed in, sending a knotty strand of Kalli's hair in a violent barrage against her face. Ice-cold crystals sliced through the air as the winds continued their wanton spinning. Dominic, gaze narrowed, swiped a few snowflakes from his leather-clad arm. Clutching the sword at his side, he scanned the area. "Need help, huh?"

Rafael wasted no words. Time was near extinction. "Belial's blocked the area. We need your help."

"If we concentrate, we can push through the block. All three of us are strong enough. Rafe especially, more than he realizes."

Dominic raised an eyebrow in bemusement. "Oh, is that so?"

"Kalli thinks I'm the chosen." Rafael snorted. Him? Chosen? But it was supposed to be Coby. He balled his fists. And it still would be. Rafael had never been so sure of anything in his life. He didn't want to be chosen. He wanted to be loved… by Lucy.

Lucy. Who knew in a matter of a few days he could

grow so attached. Who knew a saucy minx of a beautician could wrap him around her finger and then some. Who knew he'd fall in love again. He certainly didn't.

He'd tried to blame his initial attraction on the untapped sexual energy she radiated. But it wasn't that at all. This attraction went deeper, under his skin, to his loins... and straight to his heart. Blast it all. He had to save her. His sanity depended on it.

"What are we waiting for?" he barked. "Let's do this."

Belial, in his swirl of cinnamon and brimstone, hovered over her, the sickening smirk still wide across his face. Had she not been cuffed in silver, she would've gladly rearranged that annoying smile.

His long clawed finger traced a lock of hair from her face, sending shivers of revulsion worming their way through every receptor in her body. "I feel your tremors. Excited, are you?"

"Oh, don't you wish."

His eyes sparked gold and he clucked his tongue. Lamia stood to his right, arms snaked around each other, annoyance etched firmly into her face. Another countenance she wouldn't mind reshaping.

"Is that any way to talk to your betrothed, m'dear?" His words, intended to be smooth as honey, scraped like a Brillo pad.

"I'd rather marry lump of steaming horseshit than you." Lucy jutted her chin out. "Smells better, too."

Belial shrugged, grabbed her around the waist and hauled her up to face him. His gaze burned like two giant amber flames. A look that would normally send people trembling in their boots only filled her with anger. She clenched her fists, silently cursing the silver cuffs that still bound her wrists.

"So you're truly part succubus?" His fingertip traced down her cheek and slithered down her neck. Her skin crawled. He threw his head back and chortled, the sound slicing into her eardrums.

Fuck him. It was him and his stupid Infernati that had put her in this mess. She would give this man—demon, rather—a piece of her mind, and, hopefully, more. "What's it to you, cinna-stank-licious?"

"Everything!" His voice boomed, echoing through the clearing. The tiny pink-trimmed chapel shook in protest. Lucy blinked. Hell had a chapel?

Rubbing her eyes, she scanned the area, surprisingly bright so late at night. Where was all that light coming from?

She spun around. Tall wooden totems with hideously painted faces stood surrounding a rock-lined fire pit. Sitting right in the middle of that pit was that damned—and she meant it in the most literal of ways—chest. She was more than ready to send it back from whence it came. If it weren't for that chest, the scene would've been funny. Like a deleted scene from *The Brady Bunch*'s Hawaii vacation. Bad juju for sure.

"How'd you get that thing here?"

Lamia shook her head, the cackle bursting from her lips. "Does it matter? All that matters is that it's here now."

"Whatever." She was probably better off not knowing, anyway.

Lamia rolled her eyes. "If you must know, I sent it to Belial while you were unconscious. Traveling isn't just for demons you know."

"You should start your own company."

Lamia narrowed her eyes. "What the fuck are you talking about?"

She shrugged. "You could make yourself a fortune as a delivery company. Call yourself 'In-Ex.'"

"In-Ex?" Larissa scratched her chin. "We don't understand."

"Infernati Express? Or maybe DPS–Demon Parcel Service."

"We don't want our secrets exposed... until we have the world under our control."

She should've known these evil demons wouldn't have a sense of humor. They never did. And there went her chance to stall them.

"Enough lollygagging! We need to start the ceremony as soon as possible!" Belial grabbed her by her bound wrists and dragged her toward the chest.

"Hey," she ground through her teeth as she struggled away from his grip. "Is that any way to handle your future wife?"

"Ahh, my dear Lucia. It's about time you embraced your new destiny." His lips curved into a menacing grin. "Shall I ring your father? You need someone to give you away, do you not?"

"My father doesn't give a shit about me or my mother. He only cares about all the sex fiends he controls." The lie that flowed effortlessly from her lips still sent aching pain to her chest. Yes, he left, but now she knew why. He loved her mother and her and didn't want them harmed by evil. Little did he know, though, evil always found a way. It was her duty to stop it. For the world, for her family. For Rafe.

"Sucks to be you, doesn't it?" Swiping a strand of blonde hair from her cheek, Larissa sauntered next to her. The tight black leather clung to her legs with each step. "Serves you and your mother right. Lilu belongs with me."

Yep. It was confirmed. Larissa was dumb. She truly believed she'd end up with Lilu and become queen? Had she not heard a word of what her partner in crime uttered? Or was she completely under Lamia's control? Of course, she was.

Time to test the waters. "What will you do when Lamia kills Lilu?"

"She's not going to kill him," Larissa replied, her ice-blue eyes sparking.

"But he won't be king anymore, and you'll be nothing."

Larissa growled, her nostrils wide and flaring. "Bullshit!"

Lucy scratched her chin. "That's what she said when you were looped out in the car."

"Enough!" Lamia bellowed. "Don't listen to her. She's trying to turn you against me."

Larissa narrowed her eyes and turned her glare to Lamia, to Lucy, and back to Lamia again. "What will happen when you take over the Sexubis?"

"Nothing! Lilu will still be king of those not willing to join me."

"Oh," Larissa said, her brow scrunching. "I see."

Something told Lucy she didn't, but she wasn't going to argue that point. The first step was to get the cuffs off.

"So when can I get these things off?" she asked, with a clank of silver.

Belial stomped over to the pit and looked inside the chest. "Are you ready, my subjects?"

The shouts and wails erupted in the air. Moans and groans echoed in wretched agony. "Not quite ready."

Oh hell no. If this bastard wanted to marry her, he'd have to do it without restraints. "Would you rather have a willing or unwilling bride?"

Belial scratched the golden growth of hair on his chin, his amber eyes sparking. "I suppose I can make some sort of arrangement for your release." He motioned to Lamia. "Unlock her."

What? That's all she needed to do? Ask? She should've just laid the honey on Lamia earlier. Then again, never mind. The bitch didn't even deserve a layer of lye.

"Is it wise, my liege?" Lamia asked, her head bowed to the ground. Now if that wasn't a sight. The woman—erm—thing was a tool after all.

"Very wise. Now do as I say and stop questioning me!"

"Yes, my lord Belial." She turned to Larissa. "The key?"

Wow. The Infernati worked on a pyramid scheme. If these demons were businessmen, Belial would be a billionaire and those below him wouldn't know what hit them. How utterly ironic! But she wasn't complaining. It would get her out of these cuffs after all. Then she could show these assholes her new kick-ass kung-fu moves.

With a nod, Larissa reached into her shirt and produced the key. Her face contorted into a contemptuous sneer, she brushed past Lucy. "Here, master." Kneeling before Belial, she kept her face toward the snow-packed ground, her hand outstretched.

What the hell kind of nightmare did she end up in? A bondage peep show? What was next? Whips and chains? "If you expect me to get on my knees and kiss your stinky feet, you got another thing coming."

"Oh, my dear betrothed, I do enjoy your sharp tongue. Such a welcome breath of fresh air."

Fresh air, my ass. "Just what you need."

Belial reached down, snatched the key and kicked Larissa out of his way. "Go."

With a small squeak, Larissa stumbled and scurried off, on all fours, toward the ice cream parlor.

"Lamia, when are you going to get some *real* help?" Belial swept a golden curl from his cheek, a frustrated breath of air escaping his lips.

"She's one of my best succubi." Lamia's gaze remained fixed to the earth below. "And my most loyal."

"Devil help you then." Belial dismissed Lamia with a flick of his wrist and dangled the key in front of Lucy's nose, like a fisherman tempts a fish. With each swing of the key, he clucked his tongue. "Will you behave, my dear?"

Depends on what he meant by behave? Consorting with evil demons certainly didn't constitute behaving in her book. "Oh, I'll behave. You have my word."

"How can I be certain, my dear Lucia?" His smile crept upward, taunting her. Keys jangling in the cold wind, he swung his hand back and forth. "After all, you're blessed."

"I'm an honest woman. Either you believe me or you

don't." She gave her hair a nonchalant toss. "It makes no difference to me. I'll get these cuffs off one way or the other."

"What if I had something... or someone... you care about? Would you behave then?"

Her heart plummeted. Her stomach coiled into knots. "Oh God," she whispered beneath her breath.

"What was that? I didn't quite hear you." His eyes sparked and menacing dimples formed in his cheeks.

Who did he have? Frankie? Gerardo? Her Mom? Rafe? *Oh please don't let it be Rafe.* Shivers slinked up her spine. Despite the fear coursing through her, she raised her chin. She wouldn't show this asshole weakness. "You might as well get it over with, Belial. I'm not one for surprises."

"Fine. Either you behave or your precious friend dies." He flicked his cape and spun around, the wind whipping it around his feet. Throwing the cape open, he threw back his head and chortled, the sound grating on her eardrums. In one hand, the glint of a ruby jeweled dagger sparkled in the glow of the stupid chest. But it was what was in his other arm that caused her skin to crawl.

Chapter 28

HER BEST FRIEND, BODY LIMP AND EYES CLOSED, FLUNG over his shoulder, like a worn-out Raggedy-Ann doll. With a nonchalant shrug, Belial hoisted her off his shoulder and tossed her to the ground.

Bastard.

Serah moaned, her head lolling to the side. "My head."

Kneeling next to her friend, Belial grabbed her neck and angled her head to meet Lucy's gaze. His dagger at her neck, he arched his eyebrow quizzically. "Do we have a deal?"

"I will behave," Lucy said through gritted teeth.

"Good. I'm glad we're in agreement. We'll make a splendid couple." Sheathing his dagger, he dropped Serah to the ground. "Oops."

"If you hurt her, I'll be more than happy to send for her bodyguard." Belial didn't need to know this bodyguard was pint-sized with a voice that could break glass.

"Oh, do you mean him?" Belial snapped his fingers. A violent gust of wind sailed past her, an agonizing wail carrying in the air. A very high-pitched wail. The ball of ice slammed against a tree, silver chains snaking around Squeaky's frozen form.

She needed to think—before she ran out of time. If she made the slightest misstep, her friends would die. She couldn't fail. She had too much at stake. Besides,

Rafe and Kalli couldn't be far behind. Perhaps she could just go along with this charade for a little while.

"Do we have an agreement, Lucy?"

She raised her head to meet the embers of Belial's gaze. If only she could extinguish those embers. "Yes—"

"No Lucy. You can't." Serah, slinking and crawling on the ground, gazed up at her, her eyes pleading. "Don't let this monster—"

"Enough already," he said with a deep gravelly growl. A cryptic smile contorted his lips as his wing tip loafers connected with Serah's gut.

Serah groaned and curled into a ball. "Please..."

"Spare us the soap opera melodrama," Lamia said, joining Belial. Reaching down, she grabbed Serah by the collar of her blood-speckled coat and dragged her across the snow-veiled earth.

"So do we have a deal?"

"My friends go unharmed."

"Very well. Lamia, back away from the prisoner."

With an irritated growl, she slithered away from Serah, her snake arms disengaging from her friend's limp body. "She won't stay like this forever, you know."

"Who's in charge here? You or me?" Belial, his eyes sparking, lashed out his hand. In a burst of bright light, a ring of fire erupted around Lamia's scaly legs. Shaking his head, he chuckled, the sound, despite its quietness, came out low and menacing.

"You, my prince." With that, Lamia slid away to join her partner in crime.

With an irritated breath, Belial spun the keychain around his finger, the clanging of metal taunting her. He took slow meticulous steps around her, his hands roving up and down her body. Her skin crawled and her stomach roiled. His toxic stench hung heavy in the air, growing thicker with each caress.

"You'll make a perfect wife." He leaned in, his breath crawling across her skin. Grabbing her wrists, he shoved the key into the lock, the click music to her ears. His grip tightened on her wrist as he slid the first cuff off.

She sucked in a breath, fighting the pent-up rage. "Indeed, I will." She'd be a perfect wife... for Rafe.

"Nothing will stop me, you know that?" Belial traced a saliva trail down her neck, his fingers working the lock of the other cuff.

"Ooh wee!" echoed in the distance. What was going on? Did he have Frankie now too? She'd have a nice long chat with Kalli after this ordeal was over. Fat lot of help she was guarding her friends.

"What in all that is unholy?" Belial growled. Wrapping his arms around her waist, he yanked her to him. "You didn't behave, Lucy. Now your friends will die."

Panic flooded her body. Twisting and yanking herself in the vice of his arms, Lucy looked up. High in the gray cloud-cover sky, a flutter of white wings flapped. Wings attached to a pink feather shirt clad body. Gerardo. But who was that gripping on for dear life?

"*Oooooooooooooh weeeeeeeeeeeeeeeeeeeee!*" the figure on Gerardo's back shouted louder, the southern twang singing through the air.

It had to be her imagination. "Holy shit," she breathed, her heart thudding a wild beat. Gerardo? Wings? Flying? Her eyelids fluttered.

Belial's grip grew stronger. Grabbing a handful of

hair he yanked her head back. "You don't truly expect me to believe you knew nothing?"

"I don't expect you to believe anything," she said, straightening her back and raising her chin.

Lucy's gaze wandered about Belial's makeshift encampment. Squeaky, still firmly chained to the tree, struggled against his bonds. Larissa, that evil bitch, growled and sent her fist sailing into the poor chimp's cheek. Squeaky moaned, his head lolling to the side.

"Bitch!"

Serah scrambled to her feet and lunged at Larissa. Arms wrapped around ankles, Serah and Succu-bitch went sprawling. Snow flew, fists flailed, and legs kicked. Larissa took a bunch of Serah's curly hair in her fist and slammed her face into the snow. Fingers digging into snow and frozen earth, Serah coughed and sputtered.

Gerardo swooped in. Frankie gripped onto feathers for dear life, his legs whipping back and forth with each of Gerardo's turns. With a fling to the left, Frankie gritted his teeth, his skin growing three shades lighter. Gerardo banked to right, throwing his hand out. A white ball of energy flung from his fingers, toward where Belial and Lucy stood.

Vibrant white light erupted around them, encircling them in its bright intensity. Lucy embraced it, welcoming the warmth that filled her. She angled a gaze at Belial.

With a deep angry growl, he lost his grip on the dagger and covered his eyes. "Lamia!" he bellowed. "Do something!"

Watching the ruby-studded dagger plummet into the

pile of snow beneath their feet, Lucy allowed adrenaline to take over. With a sharp twist, she yanked herself from his grip and dove for the weapon. The sooner she sliced this demonic asshole to bits, the better. Fumbling in the cold fluff, she sought out her quarry.

Strong hands gripped around her waist, claws digging into her sweater and skin. Scratching through the snow and earth, she continued her frantic search.

Belial hovered above her, sardonic laughter rolling from his mouth. His fingertips crawled across her cheek. "Give it up, Lucia. You—and the chest—will be mine. All of Earth will be mine."

"Like hell I will. There's only one man I'll let have me." She punctuated her sentence by spitting in his face. And *they*—Rafe and she—would send the chest back to Limbo.

"Too bad he's too late," Belial whispered, his tongue trailing along her ear. "And I have a special surprise for your Rafe. You'll see where his true devotion lies."

"What are you going to do to him?"

Belial, fingers tightening around her wrist, smiled. "I guarantee you'll enjoy the show." He allowed a fingertip to trace down her neck and circle a breast. Bolts of disgust raged through her as she wrenched herself away. "Rafael, on the other hand... he probably won't."

"Where is he?" Rolling over, she glimpsed a flash of silver. It was within reaching distance. If she could just inch a little closer.

Belial simply shrugged, his mouth curved in a sinister smirk. "Don't you worry about that, my dear."

"What the tarnation, Ger!"

Heart racing, she scanned the area. Lamia and Larissa

stalked and slithered around Gerardo and Frankie. Both man and angel stood tall and alert. Did angels have weaknesses? She hoped not.

Eyes sparking, Lamia slithered around Frankie, her tail snaking up his leg. Lucy managed a grin. If the bitch aimed for seduction, she would fail miserably. Frankie, unfazed by the slithering tail, kicked out his leg. Lamia lunged at him, claws drawn and fangs bared. Frankie sidestepped to the left and spun around, grabbing her tail and pitching her upward. Whoa!

Lamia growled, loud and guttural as she sailed through the air. "You'll pay for that!"

Gerardo, reaching behind his back, pulled out a long sliver-tipped spear. Wings fluttering to keep him afloat, He sent the spear sailing through the air, just grazing her scaly green tail. With a resonant crack, the spear connected with the tree, right above Squeaky's furry head, which bobbled up and down from the impact.

Eyes bugging from their sockets, Squeaky looked up and gulped.

The battle had begun... Yet still no sign of Rafe.

Rafael growled. The longer they dawdled, the longer it would take to rescue Lucy. It no longer was a *mission* that spurred him into action, but pure rampant need. He wouldn't lose Lucy. He loved her too much.

"How much longer?" he asked through gritted teeth.

Dominic slammed the Paladin manual shut and jerked his head up. With an irritated glare, he hauled the tome across the car hood. It skittered against metal and came to rest next to where Kalli sat.

"Jeez, Duvane, have a care." With a dramatic sigh, Kalli turned over onto her stomach, opened the book, and scanned the pages.

Dominic turned to face him, his obsidian eyes stony serious. "You aren't the only one who's got something at stake, you know." Jaw ticking, he lowered his gaze to the snowy ground.

"Coby," Rafael whispered. How could he forget? Only a few times had his thoughts drifted to his sister. What would she think? He sucked in a ragged breath. He'd be damned if he'd lose two women he cared for. "I've abandoned her."

"You haven't abandoned anyone." Eyes flickering with intensity, Dominic came to stand next to him. In a completely slow, cautious, yet strangely casual movement, his friend wrapped his arm around Rafael's back. "The Fore-Demons gave you a mission. That mission was elsewhere. Coby understands where our duties lie."

With a slow nod, Rafael pulled from their friendly embrace to look his friend in the face. Dominic was right. Coby knew about duty. She was always the one who put duty over desire. Her dedication to the Paladin cause was legendary.

"And, keep in mind, Coby has a good rescuer. Not that I'm bragging or anything." Dominic swiped a hand through his neatly shorn dark blond hair, a sheepish smile curving his lips.

"I still feel guilty."

"Coby will understand. She's always wanted you to be happy, you know. Ever since the situation with..." Dominic let his words trail off. "She'll love Lucy. She's the perfect woman for you."

So this was what it was like to wear your heart on your sleeve? Fancy that, he didn't even know he was doing it. "I'm merely completing a mission."

The moment the lie slipped from his lips, his heart plummeted and his blood ran cold. He fully expected a lightning bolt to shoot from the sky and smite him right where he stood. He'd deserve it, too. "I admit I've come to care for her." Not a complete lie, but it still left him empty.

"Better than nothing, I suppose, right Kalli?"

Kalli scratched her head, her gaze thoughtful. "Certainly the breakthrough of the century." She rolled over and winked at Nic, a hint of secrecy in both their glances.

Rafael never was much a fan of secrets. He crossed his arms. "Am I an object for your amusement?"

"Only when you act stubborn." Dominic gave him a hearty slap on the back. "Don't worry. We forgive you."

"Stubble it." He had to rescue Lucy. Their witty banter and secretive stares would have to wait. Deep down he knew they meant well. Right now he was too wound-up to care. He loved Lucy. He'd be damned if he let anything happen to her.

"Touchy, are you?" Kalli sighed and went back to reading the tome. The moment her eyes met the page, she jerked her head up and jumped from the car. "I got it!" she exclaimed with glee.

Rafael and Dominic turned in unison. Dominic's gaze was alert, intense. "What have you got, Kalli?"

"Come here!" she said, waving them there with her hand. "I found a way to break the Infernati ward!"

Rafael rushed to where Kalli sat perched on the hood,

her head buried deep in the tome. Leaning over her, he scanned the page she read.

"Right here," Kalli said, her finger tracing over a line of text.

Rafael bent down to read the passage.

Only those who are true to themselves and their emotions can lift an Infernati ward.

Leave it to the Fore-Demons to incorporate self-awareness lessons into an instruction manual. "What sort of tripe is that?"

"It's not tripe," Dominic growled. "It's the Paladin way. Admit your feelings."

"Why don't you admit yours?"

"The more the merrier," Kalli said in a singsong voice. "But the more you two argue, the less time we have to save Lucy."

Lucy. This was about Lucy. It always had been about her. From the moment he stepped in her shop. He was ensnared. Everything happened for a reason, or so they say. That reason was Lucy.

"It's just that..."

Remember the last time you bared your soul? His internal naysayer boomed. Amanda, her beautiful blonde hair. Her gentle smile. The innocence that seemed to radiate from her. Her reaching to touch him. Him turning away, not wanting to shatter that innocence.

It was all a lie.

Why didn't he see it? That spark, that energy. Nothing Amanda ever did electrified him as much as Lucy. No one, not even in his mortal days, affected him in such a way. He was thoroughly and madly in love with Lucy. He'd gladly shout it from the top of

Mt. Everest if it would save her life. He'd shout it from the deep dark recesses of Hell if it brought her to him.

Was it that simple to unlock a ward with those three simple words?

"Rafe? It's just that, what?"

"I'll do anything for Lucy," he said, raising his chin and standing tall. His voice boomed, despite the turmoil raging inside him. "I love her."

But did she love him? Yes there was attraction, but she was a sex demoness. What's not to say it wasn't her succubus urges that drew her to him. Hope turned to dread. Was he setting himself up for another disaster?

At this point, he didn't care. He only cared about Lucy. He needed her now more than ever. His internal naysayer would just have to stubble it. It was about time.

His initial dread evaporated, replaced with pure adrenaline and energy. He was through doubting himself. He was Rafael Deleon. He was a Paladin, and, damn it, he was in love. Right now, that was all that mattered.

"Rafael?" Kalli's concerned voice broke him from his thoughts.

"Yeah?"

"You okay?"

Rafael nodded. He was more than okay. He'd kick Belial back to the underworld. "I'm fine."

"From the spark in your eyes, my friend, you're more than fine." Smiling, Dominic slapped Rafael on the back. "You're ready, aren't you?"

"More than ready."

"That's what I like to hear. Let's do this." He turned to Kalli. "Well?"

Kalli smacked her forehead and rolled her eyes. "I'm waiting for you two!"

"Good." Rafael needed to teleport. Now. "So how do we do it?"

"I'm still reading." Kalli returned to the tome, scanning each page. "Nothing too difficult, it seems."

He'd gladly spin on his head while riding a unicycle if it brought him closer to Lucy.

"Here it is!" Kalli narrowed her gaze. "It says to break the ward, you must state that which your heart desires most. Hmm, already did that." She flipped a page. "Then you join hands with those close to you and close your eyes. Then one of the archangels will crack the ward." A frustrated sigh escaped her lips, her brow furrowing. "Bloody hell. More angels?"

"If it means saving Lucy, I'd deal with an entire host of angels."

Kalli nodded. "Fair enough. Dominic?"

Dominic glanced up. "This will bring us that much closer to Coby. I'm in."

"Okay!" Kalli hopped from the car hood. "We are so going to kick some Infernati ass."

She flung open the car door and heaved the book inside. Engaging the lock, she stuffed the keys into her pocket. "Sorry, we can't bring the book along."

"Fine by me," Dominic said. "Now get over here. We haven't much time."

That was the understatement of the century. Rafael reached into his coat pocket and grabbed his BlackBerry. He hated electronics, but since he'd relinquished his broken timepiece to Kalli, it was all he had. Glancing down at the digital display, he grumbled.

Eleven-fifty. Only ten minutes left.

In one fluid motion, he reached out and clasped Dominic's hand. He extended the other toward Kalli. "Here. Now."

"Sure, big guy," she replied with a shrug. With quick, lithe steps, she stood arm to arm with him and laced her fingers with his. "It's now or never."

With that, they all closed their eyes. Gusts of winds swirled and spun in a subzero vortex that sent him reeling. Arctic blasts of snow pelted his face and shards of ice nicked his face. Icicles dangled from his hair and his face iced over. He wouldn't have been able to open his eyes if he tried. If the Paladin's portals were cold, this was a bloody glacier. And he didn't care. He'd let them freeze off all his appendages if it meant saving Lucy.

"Now, now. How would Lucia like that?" an ethereal voice boomed. A voice he recognized well. The one who'd sealed him to the fate of Paladin. The angel who blessed him.

An archangel? He'd been blessed by an archangel. His mind reeled and his heart stopped. What the bloody hell was going on?

"In time, Deleon. All shall be revealed soon."

To hell with soon. He wanted answers now. "Who are you?"

The angel blew out a long breath of air. "Always the impatient one, Deleon." He paused. "Very well. You may open your eyes."

Rafael flicked open his lids. Opening his mouth to speak, he promptly shut it. Shock and surprise swirled within. The angel smiled, long pale golden hair sweeping across his pristine white wings. Bedecked in a golden breastplate and flowing red robes, he stepped forward, the gold of the matching greaves adorning his shins glinting in the snow. Even without the sword and shield, there was no mistaking who stood before them.

Michael. The warrior. The one who sent Satan to hell. And, apparently, the angel—no, make that *archangel*—who blessed him.

Dominic and Kalli opened their eyes and gaped, just as shocked as him.

"Shocking, isn't it?" Michael smiled, handing Rafael a shiny crossbow and silver gilt quiver and arrows.

Rafael went down on one knee and lowered his head.

Dominic coughed and Kalli snickered. What the bloody hell now?

After a brief lapse of awkward silence, Michael spoke.

"Stand, Rafael Deleon. There's no need to bow. You're the one we've been waiting for."

"What do you mean?"

"You're the Chosen Paladin. Rise, or I'll be forced to join you on one knee."

His mind spun. But he'd been certain Coby was the one. She was the most dutiful. The most dedicated. She'd never failed a mission. His head snapped up. He refused to hear it. "You're mistaken."

"Not a good idea, Rafe," Dominic warned.

Kalli cleared her throat. "Don't ever doubt the words of an archangel. Haven't you learned anything in your four hundred plus years as a Paladin?"

With cautious steps, Rafael stood. "But what about Coby? She's never failed a mission."

"Your sister, although brave, still has her own struggles. She'll have her time. Just not now. Now is your time, Rafael Deleon. Do you accept your fate?" Michael held out the crossbow, a stern gaze etched into his stoic face.

"I will accept any fate, as long as it saves Lucy." Rafael reached out to take the offered weapon. Even though saddened that it was him and not his sister, a sense of pride still welled in his heart. Poor Coby. She deserved to stand here. His heart fluttered. Coby. What would happen to her? He glanced over to Dominic, who stood in stark silence. What was he thinking?

"What about…" He feared the worst.

"Your sister's soul is tarnished. But even beneath the thickest coat of dirt, silver still glistens."

Michael and Dominic exchanged scrutinizing glares.

"As I said, she will have her time."

Dominic wrenched around and stalked away.

"Don't forget. Everything happens for a reason."

Adjusting the quiver and crossbow to his back, Rafael nodded. "I understand."

"I was speaking to your friend."

Dominic grunted and nodded. "I understand."

"Good. I'll unlock the portal now." He raised him hands high and threw his head back. In a blinding flash, energy shot from his palms up toward the heavens. "May the lord bless and keep Rafael Deleon and his friends safe and allow them access to the portals to lead them wherever they so choose."

With a loud whoosh, the clouds split open. Vibrant rays of light came pouring down from the heavens. Bright violets, greens, and blues bathed him and his friends, warming him amongst the cold bursts of wind. He fully expected to hear angelic choruses echoing through the night. Alas, the only things he heard were the beating of his heart and the winds spiraling upward.

Michael, ice and snow circulating around him, unsheathed his sword and held it high. Brilliant rays of light bounced and reflected from the ornately etched blade, sparkling around them. Like giant flakes of glitter, the light danced through the air.

"Portals open for Rafael Deleon and his friends, Dominic Duvane and Kalliope of Lesbos."

Dominic arched a brow.

Kalli growled. "Don't even go there."

"Fine," Dominic muttered.

"Enough chitchat." With a stern glare, Michael thrust his sword in the air. Sparks flew. Lightning flashed, brightening the dark cloudy sky. Thunder rolled and clapped. In one silent instance, it all stopped. The snow, the wind, the lightning. Everything went still. In a sudden burst of energy, a flickering ring of fire and sparks formed a tunnel. The tunnel that would lead him to Lucy. A tunnel that would help him meet his destiny.

Michael lowered his sword and bowed his head. "'Tis finished. Go, my friends. Rescue Lucy. Send Belial back to Hell. Together, you will save the world."

Rafael held his head tall. "I will. And I'll enjoy every minute of it." He turned to his friends, beckoning them to join him. "Shall we?"

With determined steps, he marched toward the portal. Without a glance back, he stepped in and headed to his fate. No, not his fate. To Lucy—his destiny.

Chapter 29

"SEE HOW MUCH YOUR PRECIOUS RAFE CARES FOR YOU?" Belial dragged her toward the chapel, taking two steps at a time. "He isn't here to save you, is he?"

"He'll be here soon."

He threw back his head and a loud rumble of laughter burst from his mouth. "You keep telling yourself that. He can't possibly make it here in time. I've planned everything so perfectly. This will be the wedding of the millennium."

"Considering we're only about ten years into the millennium, that isn't saying much, is it."

Belial snarled then allowed his lips to curve into a creepy smile. "You know, at first your sarcastic wit grated on my nerves. Now it's growing on me." He ran his fingers down her back to trace along the curve of her ass. "Yes, you'll make a fine wife. Just a little molding, that's all."

"The only thing that will need molding is your face after Rafe rearranges it."

With a naysaying shake of his head, Belial clucked his tongue. "But he isn't here yet, is he? Speaking of Rafe, it's time for you to meet someone."

Meet someone? What had he done? Who else was left to meet? Her heart plummeted. Coby. His sister. Leave it to the wannabe prince of darkness to hold the ace in his hand. "If you've harmed Rafe's sister, I swear I'll personally kick your ass."

"Rafael's sister?" Belial's incredulous tone rankled her nerves. His sardonic chuckle drove her further over the edge. "I merely want you to meet my priestess. The one who will officiate our *little* ceremony."

"Fuck your priestess."

"Already have… many times." Belial smirked. "A fine lay, but I'm sure my little succubus bride will be better."

Her stomach roiled at the thought of Belial and his naked cinnamon and sulfur-scented body anywhere near her. Shivers of revulsion coursed through her body. "I just threw up in my mouth."

"Very funny. Now move," he said with a not-so-gentle push inside the chapel door.

Tall, dripping candles lined the walls, casting pale shadows throughout the chapel. At the front of the chapel stood the priestess, cloaked in billowing dark capes. She stood there in stark silence, darkness shrouding her face. The air thickened with a heaviness she couldn't distinguish. A hard lump filled her throat and her heart constricted. Remorse.

"Priestess, show yourself to my bride-to-be."

With a slow, submissive nod, she stepped away from the podium and made her way toward her. With the agility of a cat, she weaved through the array of metal folding chairs that were scattered about. And here she was expecting something more demonic.

"I am the priestess." Her voice, although beautiful, held no life. Like a robot. "I shall perform your wedding rituals."

"She doesn't seem too thrilled, *sweetie*." More waves of revulsion rolled through her. Had she actually said sweetie? She bit her tongue. There was only one man she wanted to call sweetie.

"She's thrilled, aren't you dear?"

The priestess nodded. "Indeed, I am."

"See?" Belial grinned. "Now let's head back outside. It's time for us to marry."

"We aren't marrying in here?"

"No. This silly chapel has been blessed. The people of Hell are more religious than I realized."

"Sucks to be you, doesn't it?"

"On the contrary, my dear. I believe it sucks to be Rafe." With that, he gave her a violent shove out of the chapel.

What was this fixation with Rafe? Belial was a prince of Hell, and Rafe was a mere centurion in the Paladin forces. She could easily pawn it off on jealousy, but something deep inside kept nagging her. Yes, it was Rafe's mission to recover the chest, but she couldn't help but wonder if there was something more.

"Definitely won't be getting any husband-of-the-year awards," she said, catching her balance on the doorjamb. "And what's with your obsession with Rafael Deleon? You can't stop talking about him. Are you sure you don't want a bro-mance instead?"

Belial's eyes sparked like two demonic ambers, hot and angry. He reached out, wrapped his fingers around her neck, and yanked her to him, sucking the breath from her body. "I've never met the man. But as soon as his slow vehicle arrives, we'll become *very* acquainted."

"Could've fooled me." She stood tall. Proud. "And then you'll get his sloppy seconds."

The winds picked up swirling around them. Warm

and humid winds. Steam and vapor sizzled around her. Snow melted. Ice dripped from the trees. Maybe Gerardo had sent for reinforcements. He was smart like that.

"What?" came a screech from the melee of demons, humans and angels. With claws bared, Larissa lunged at her. "How dare you?"

"How dare I? You're the one to talk. You made no qualms about snatching Josh from me. Sucks that we were already on the outs, though, huh?"

Lizard tongue flicking, Larissa hissed, her scaly palm connecting with Lucy's face. "I saw the admiration in your eyes. I saw how you still cared for him."

The winds built, like a giant vortex of hot and steamy air, whipping around them with eager flicks. For some reason, it spurred her on, gave her life. *Rafe*. Her heart thumped in excitement.

"I care for Josh as a friend. There's a big difference, you know." Lucy threw back her head and chuckled. "Oh never mind, you probably don't."

She fully prepared herself for the physical lash that would soon follow. She welcomed it. She wanted Larissa angry. Instead, Larissa threw back her head and cackled, the sound cracking in her ears. "But I know this, Lucia. Rafael Deleon loved me first."

Those words sliced into her, filling her with anger. With a deep growl, she lunged at Larissa and wrapped her fingers around her slender throat. Boiling rage bubbled inside her as she tightened her grip. The bitch had put Rafe through so much. She deserved to suffer.

"Yes," she gasped out, her smile remaining. Of course she'd be into that kinky shit. "Anger, mmm. Yes, Rafael loved me first."

The humid winds swirled and spun, creating a cocoon of intense warmth and energy. Calming, relaxing. The familiar scent of peppermint and spice wafted to her nose.

"You're mistaken," Rafe's voice boomed through the mists. "I cannot love a monster."

The steam fizzled away as Rafe, flanked by Kalli and Nic, burst into action. Reaching into his black leather coat, Nic pulled out a dagger, ready to strike. Rafael grabbed his shoulder, his silver eyes stormy.

"She's mine." Even through the snow, Lucy caught the spark in his silver eyes.

Shaking his head, Dominic extracted his arm from Rafe's hand.

Larissa grinned. "I'm still his," she hissed in her ear. "I'll always be his."

Her attempts to make her jealous only further fueled the anger. Anger she desperately needed to control. If there was one thing she remembered from the book, it was never let emotions, especially anger, rule your decisions. She made one decision. She wanted to join Rafael. She wanted to help him and his cause. She wanted to become a Paladin.

"I, unfortunately, don't have such high hopes."

She spun around to lock gazes with Kalli. Dreadlocks flying about, she growled, deep and animalistic. Like a mother bear protecting her cub. The air crackled. In that instant, Larissa flung Lucy to the side and lunged for Kalli, pulling at her hair, thus confirming suspicions. Kalli's dreads were real.

Kalli flung Larissa from her hair and lunged with her sword. Larissa sidestepped her and drew her own weapon. Lucy blinked. Kalli's weapon was reminiscent of what Lucy had seen in her short-lived fencing class, and Larissa sported Jack Sparrow's sword of choice, a long cutlass.

She shrugged. Whatever floated their boats.

The clashing of metal against metal rent the air and reverberated in her ears. Kalli lunged forward and swiped her blade across Larissa's chest. A trickle of dark blood pooled onto white gossamer.

"Bitch," Larissa growled, swiping blood from her cheek. She pounced on Kalli, both women sprawling into the white fluff below.

Craning her neck, she spotted Frankie, Gerardo, and Squeaky pummeling the snake out of Lamia. She hissed, flailing her olive-green tail in a futile attempt to smack the boys around. Squeaky, with a grace no normal chimp would have, dodged the tail and sent an uppercut to Lamia's chin.

"There's more where that came from," Squeaky said, jumping up and down on Lamia's chest.

Screeching, she dove for Squeaky, wrapped her claws around his chubby ankles and sent him sprawling. Gerardo, each flap of his wings more urgent than the next, flew into the air and dive-bombed Lamia. She sailed backward, dark blood spurting from her floppy tail. With a resounding snap, she hit the same tree Squeaky was chained to earlier. She moaned as her slithering body slid down the tree.

Spinning around, Lucy locked gazes with Rafe. He stood there, tall, dark, and foreboding, holding an ornately carved crossbow over his shoulder. Steamy fog swirled around him as his silver eyes sparked. Despite the roiling of her stomach, she breathed a sigh of relief. Rafe was here. He was safe.

"Lucy!" Rafe rushed to her. Strong arms enclosed around her, cocooning her in his warmth. "We haven't much time."

His whispered breath against her ear sent energy racing through her body. Not sexual energy, but another energy altogether. And it was ten times stronger. It filled her with warmth, made her strong and determined. What in the heck was going on?

"I wouldn't if I were you, Rafael Deleon." Belial's sinister voice boomed, freezing her in place. Anger and frustration swirled and boiled inside Lucy. She was raring and ready. She wasn't a runaway bride. She was a rampaging bride. She would destroy him. After all, she couldn't destroy Larissa. She sidled a gaze toward Kalli, who sliced her blade through Larissa's flowing gown. Her gaze stony and determined with each thrust and parry, she growled. Then again, Kalli was already going commando on Lamia's pawn. A pity—*not!*—for Larissa.

She turned to glance at Rafe. Gripping the crossbow tightly, he aimed it at Belial, ready to pull the trigger. But he remained staunch and stony, the only glimpse of emotion was the storm brewing in his silver eyes. Hatred and anger rolled from him, yet he remained still. Absolutely amazing.

The words she read in the Paladin manual came blaring at her. *Do not allow anger to rule your actions.* It sounded so much more interesting in Latin but still packed a punch in English.

"Why shouldn't I?" Rafe said, keeping his bow trained on the demon.

Smirking, Belial snapped his finger. In a biting cold gust of air, his priestess shimmered and materialized, her gaze still firmly planted toward the ground. "You've yet to meet my priestess."

Nic, stoic as ever, stood next to Rafe, his head held high. "I pity the priestess that serves you."

"I beg to differ." Belial tugged the cloaked woman closer, his chuckle echoing through the bitter cold. With an evil flash of his golden eyes, he yanked the hood of her robe down. Strands of hair as silver as the moonlight cascaded and swirled, as if it tangoed with the wind. She kept her gaze planted to the ground in shame.

Rafe let out a sharp breath of air, his arm tightening around Lucy, protection mixed with anger. She turned her head to glance up. His silver eyes churned like a giant storm and his jaw tightened.

Slowly she raised her head, the familiar spark of silver flashing in her eyes. Lucy's blood ran cold. This was Coby—Rafe's sister.

The sound of steel scraping filled the air. "Bastard."

Rafe and Lucy snapped their gazes toward Nic. He stood with sword drawn, ready to strike.

Belial, obviously pleased with his unveiling, threw back his head as thick, grating laughter erupted from him. "Lovely, two distraught Paladins for the price of one."

"Let her go," Nic demanded, gripping his sword, his knuckles turning white.

Belial's lips curved upward. He traced his finger down Coby's cheek. "Perhaps she doesn't want me to let her go. Right, Jacoba?" With that, he pulled Coby to him and lowered his mouth to hers. His lips enveloped hers, like he would suck out her soul.

With a muffled murmur, Coby wrapped her arms around Belial's neck and pressed closer. The bile rose in Lucy's throat. He'd already sucked out her soul. *What about Rafe? What will he do?*

But Rafe stood in place, steely and confident. The only movement was his dark hair flicking with the wind. His reserve kept Lucy balanced. Her own six-foot-four bottle of Prozac. The strangest thing ever. Even as demons, angels, and humans collided, she remained still. Confident. Complete.

Alas, not all of them were so lucky. "You'll pay for this!" Nostrils flaring, Nic bared his teeth. With a crazed gleam in his eyes, he swung his sword like a wild Norse berserker.

"Nic, no," Rafe breathed, reaching for his friend.

With an angry growl, Nic wrenched his wrist from Rafe's grasp and charged toward Belial. "Don't you care for your sister?"

Rafe reached out to hold Nic back. "Of course I do."

"Prove it. Destroy Belial."

"Anger isn't the way."

"You coward." Nic sneered and lunged toward Belial.

Both Rafe and Lucy dove for Nic. Without a backward glance, he kicked them away.

Belial shrugged and turned toward Rafe's sister. "Jacoba, darling. Protect me."

"Yes, my master," her voice, haunting yet anguished, burned in Lucy's ears. Palming a long jewel-hilted dagger, she spun toward Nic. A brief flicker of recognition flashed in her eyes, only to be replaced by stony indifference. She kept the weapon trained on him.

Nic stopped dead in his tracks. "Coby, no."

"Do it," Belial ordered, his voice commanding. "Show them who you serve."

With that, the dagger sailed through the air, faster than she'd ever seen any weapon thrown before. Nic's gasp cracked through bitter cold and shattered the air into a million pieces. Glancing down at the dagger now firmly implanted in his chest, he stumbled backward, confusion and sadness etching his face. "Why?" he managed with a soft groan. With that he fell to the ground and vanished into a puff of ice and smoke.

"I had to do it." Her words, although succinct, held a cryptic edge. She locked gazes with Rafe. "If you don't give Belial what he wants, you'll be next." With that, she turned away.

Belial smirked. "Do we have an agreement?"

"She's truly lost." Rafe's voice, although a muffled whisper, packed a punch that sent her senses reeling. He grabbed Lucy's hand, his grip tight. "Now I understand."

Was he giving up on his sister? If he gave up so easily on her, what would he do with her? Grabbing the collar of his jacket, she pulled him to face her. He couldn't give up. "She sent him back to Limbo. Big deal. She didn't kill him. You can't give up. Not now. Your sister needs you."

"You need me more. The only way to defeat Belial is for me to let her go."

"But she's your blood."

With his thumb and forefinger, Rafe lifted her chin. "Michael said Coby would have her time. I'm not so sure of that anymore."

He couldn't give up on his family, not after he helped her get hers back. "But there has to be a way."

Rafe's gaze flickered. Reaching out, he traced a finger down her cheek. "She's been under Belial's control for too long. She needs to be destroyed."

She reached down and grabbed a discarded dagger from the frozen ground, the cold metal biting her skin. "You'd let him take your own sister?"

"She won't ever be the same. She's lost her position as a Paladin." His fists tightened as the silver oceans of his eyes churned. "Trust me, it's what Coby would want."

"Sorry, I don't agree with adult euthanasia."

Belial coughed, pulling them from their conversation. "I asked if we had an agreement."

Rafe's despair urged her on. Belial was going down. If he was supposed to put his sister out of her misery, she wouldn't be denied giving Belial the same pleasure. "I think we can only agree to disagree, you demonic dickhead."

With that, she scooped up Nic's sword from the snowy ground. Somersaulting through the air, she lunged for Belial. He needed to go down—*now*.

Chapter 30

"LUCY! NO!"

Rafe's plea, although loud, echoed faintly in Lucy's ears. If he didn't think he could save his sister, maybe she could. She had to.

"I have to stop him," she ground out. With a quick thrust, she lunged for Belial.

Like a quick gust of wind, he spun away, the blade barely scraping his arm. He reached out and snaked his arms around her, yanking her against him. His chuckle, low and sinister, chilled her to the core. He plucked the sword from her hand and dropped it to the ground, his fingers steaming. Blowing a cold breath against his palm, he shook his head. "Let's face it, Lucia. You'll be my wife whether you want to or not."

With a deep growl, Lucy struggled in his hold. Now she understood. She went after Belial in anger. Because she let her anger take over, she was back where she started.

"Like hell she will." Rafe's voice boomed, reverberating against the buildings.

Lucy snapped her head up to meet his gaze. Rafe's gaze churned like two giant oceans, anger brewing on the surface. He stood with crossbow trained at Belial, aimed and ready to strike.

She threw him a pleading gaze. *Please, remain in control.*

There were three emotions stronger than anger. Determination for one, courage for another. And, of course, love. And she had plenty of them all, especially love. She allowed each emotion to pound their way through her body. She had to survive. She needed to send the *Arca Inferorum* back to Limbo. She slid a gaze to Rafe's sister. She needed to save Coby. Saving her would save Rafe.

"Hmm." Her angelic voice lifted through the air. Coby scratched her chin. She turned to glance at her brother, her gaze empty. Rafe jerked his gaze away.

"See how he denies you, Jacoba?"

Lucy bit down hard into his wrist. "Don't listen to him!"

"So who are you going to save, Rafael Deleon?" Belial threw back his head and chuckled. "Your flesh-and-blood sister?" He flung Lucy forward, his claws deep in her arms. "Or the succubus you've been fucking?"

"Bastard," she breathed under her breath.

"Yes, I am." He hauled her against him, the hard planes of his body jabbing into her. The stench of brimstone and cinnamon engulfed her... swallowed her. Were those his lips? Sloppy, wet, and fetid.

Rafe roared, the sound echoing in the air. The eerie snap of the crossbow followed. Belial gasped, the arrow wedged deep in his shoulder. Lucy jerked herself from his grasp and tripped across the snowy ground. Hopefully Rafe could load another arrow as quick as he had that one.

With a sardonic chuckle, Belial ripped the arrow from his shoulder, the almost-black blood dripping steadily down his arm. In all the excitement, she'd failed to notice that blood no longer scared her. Maybe it was because he deserved to bleed.

"Jacoba, dear. Kill him."

Lucy's heart stopped and her stomach lurched. Screw the blood. He deserved more. He deserved to go back to Hell.

Jacoba reached behind her back and grabbed her dagger, aimed at her brother and ready to strike.

Rafe stood there, grief creased his face. His jaw locked. He clenched the crossbow tight, any tighter and the thing would split in half. "Coby, it's me. Rafael." Despite the thick tension in the air, his voice remained calm and clear. "Your brother."

Jacoba narrowed her gaze, her nose scrunched. Silvery strands of hair whipped with the wind. Dagger poised and ready to fly, she took a long breath of air. "Some brother," she muttered. With sheer fluidity, she traced her finger along the blade, like she was admiring its shiny surface.

That walking sack of demon excrement had pulled a number on her. Lucy had to act quickly or Coby would do something she'd regret. She took cautious steps forward, holding her hand out like she was approaching an injured doe. "Your brother loves you. He's done nothing but support you."

"Support me? Where was his support when I sat in the dungeons of Hell?" She clenched the hilt of the dagger, her gaze slicing.

"The Fore-Demons sent him here instead. Believe me, he would've rather been there rescuing you had he the choice." She inched closer to Rafe, ready to defend.

Belial growled, his claws digging into Lucy's arm. "Kill him now, Jacoba."

Lucy pleaded through her pain, "Your brother loves you. He's told me all about you. Don't do it. You're his sister, his flesh and blood. That's got to mean something."

A flicker of remorse flashed in her eyes. She bit her lip as a glisten of a tear formed in the corner of her eye. "Rafe," she murmured. The dagger dropped to the ground, the snow enveloping it in a frozen cocoon. Lucy breathed a sigh of relief. There was hope for Coby after all.

"Lucy! Coby! Watch out!" Rafe's voice, full of urgency, reeled her back in.

She swiveled around.

With a loud, garbled roar, Belial ripped out a long, serrated blade, the tips sparking against the ice and snow. "You worthless bitch! You failed me. Now you die."

"So be it," Coby mumbled.

In a literal flash, the blade sailed through the air. Lucy's breath caught in her throat. She just stood in place, her head hanging low, ready to accept her fate.

Fortunately for Coby, Lucy wasn't ready to accept that fate. And she had news for Coby: neither was Rafe. She sailed in the air, toward Rafe's sister.

"Lucy! No!"

Rafe's new phrase of choice. Regardless, she wouldn't turn back now. There was too much at stake. She did this for him. She loved him. She couldn't let Belial take his sister away from him.

Wind whizzing through her hair as she flipped through the air, Lucy smiled. She wouldn't fail. With a not-so-graceful somersault, she dove for Coby. In a flutter of her heavy priestess robes, they tumbled to the ground, snow and ice flying.

"Aren't you big and brave," Belial seethed. Armed with a long, simple dagger, he flew at them. His golden eyes sparked like violent flames. Long gnarly horns ripped from his head. Anger and rage contorted his face, his tawny mane whipping around his head. A roar, deep and primal, ripped from his mouth as he continued his grotesque metamorphosis.

She could add shape-shifting to Belial's long list of demonic feats. And it was only appropriate he'd shift into a lion. Then again, lions didn't usually have horns.

In the distance, a bell tolled. Belial stopped in his tracks. Did someone invite Hemingway to this little foray? For her fear of old men and seas, she hoped not.

"Belial! You're too late." Rafe stood tall, the crossbow poised and ready.

"Your silly arrows won't keep me detained more than a few weeks at the most."

"How about an archangel's arrow?" he asked, his finger poised on the trigger.

An archangel had blessed Rafe's weapon? Lucy's heart soared. She scanned his expression, stony and severe. Not a lick of emotion spread on his face. Perhaps it was only a bluff. Even if he were bluffing, she knew he could do it.

"As if an archangel would bless any of your weapons. I've seen your record." Letting out a loud guffaw, Belial lunged for him.

With one fluid motion, Rafe pulled the trigger, the snap of the crossbow a welcome echo in her ear. The silver tip of the arrow sparked as it sailed through the air.

With a loud pop, the arrow hit Belial's chest.

Dark blood pooling from his chest, Belial let out a gurgling gasp. Blood trickled from his mouth and nose as he clutched the sliver arrow wedged deep into his black heart. His once-vibrant gold eyes faded to black. He stumbled forward and threw his hands out, ready to grab Rafe and bring him where ever he was going.

"Rafe! Look out!"

With a quick leap, Rafe sidestepped Belial's grasp. Belial, with a gurgled groan, fell forward and landed in the puffy snow, blood tainting the pristine whiteness as he withered away, a coating of gray ash and dust the only thing remaining. With a biting cold blast of air, the ash blew away in a violent whip of wind.

"Rafe!" Full of relief, she flung herself into his arms and pressed her lips to his. Wrapping her arms around his neck and latching onto his silky hair, she pulled in closer. She never wanted to let go. Her lips roamed and prodded his as her tongue swirled and pushed its way inside. Zings of warm energy rushed through every vein in her body. Not as hot as before, but still as intense. Reluctantly, she pulled her lips from his and nestled her head on his shoulder. "You did it," she breathed.

"We aren't finished yet," he stated with a quick peck to her cheek. He turned her to face the *Arca Inferorum*, still glowing like a giant demon beacon. Sparks and shadows swirled around it. Smoke and fog danced in eerie accompaniment.

"The demons are loosed and ready for your control." Rafe's sister padded toward them, her head still cast down. "I am your humble servant."

Rafe sucked in a deep breath and reached for his

sister's hand, his eyes swirling with warmth. "Coby, you're free."

Coby jerked her hand from his grasp and turned away. "Free? You call this free? How can I possibly be free now?" Silver eyes flashing, she snorted. "If you know what's right, you'll just let me be, *Rafael*." With an annoyed huff, she spun away and stalked toward the road.

The scathing use of his given name sent cringes racing through Lucy's system. Fists clenched at her side, her blood boiled. This was the thanks she gave her brother—her own flesh and blood—for saving her life? "Now wait just a minute," she ground out. "Your brother risked his life to save your ass. Be a sister, damn it."

Coby shrugged, a cryptic smile spread across her face. "No, he risked his ass to save *yours*. But it was worth it." She disregarded Lucy with a toss of her spun-silver hair and turned away.

"Hey there, aren't you mine to command?" Lucy asked, doing her best to sound authoritative. She stood tall, her arms crossed.

Coby strode off, her hair swaying with each move of her hips. "You already have," she called over her shoulder as she faded into the mists.

Turning to Rafe, she brushed a lock of stray hair from his brow. "I didn't tell her to do that, did I?"

Rafe shook his head. "No. It's common for the Infernati to twist someone's words."

Her stomach knotted. "She's Infernati?"

"Not completely, but enough to remain a threat."

"But she refused to kill you. You're just going to let her walk away?"

"Coby does what she wants and doesn't let anyone

stop her." A small half-smile curved his lips. "At least that part of her is still intact."

"Then there's still hope? Someone has to go to her."

"That, unfortunately, isn't my mission." Rafe gazed down at her, a bittersweet mixture of silver and gray swirling in his eyes. "You—not Coby—not even the *Arca Inferorum*—are my mission."

"What?"

"When Michael presented himself to me, I finally understood. He also said Coby will have her time. All isn't completely lost."

"What about Nic? How can she get over that? She killed him."

"Nic isn't dead." His gaze flashed a hint of somberness. "At least not his body. He loved her, you know."

"Oh Rafe, I'm so sorry." she pressed close to him, allowing her warmth to mingle with his. She traced a finger through his hair, just wanting to give him comfort—to show she cared. Heck, she wanted to show him she loved him too.

"The Fore-Demons knew the only way I could defeat Belial was if I stepped from my sister's shadow. I've kept myself secluded too long. It took one saucy succubus to cure me."

"I cured you?"

"More than you realize."

"And I didn't even need a degree in medicine to do it." She nudged Rafe toward the circle of rocks, ready to finish the mission—together.

She scanned the area to check on her friends. Squeaky, wearing a ragged suit coat and crumpled fedora, flexed his chimp muscles for Serah. With a snort,

Serah laughed then doubled over, wincing with pain. Squeaky, ever-attentive familiar that he was, turned Dr. Ross on her and examined every bone in her body.

Kalli, arms crossed, leaned against the side of the chapel, dreadlocks mangled and fishnets gaping with even larger holes. Cigarette poised between her lips, she took a long drag, spirals of smoke puffing into the air. With a brief flicker of amethyst eyes, she offered a cursory nod Lucy's way and turned to stare off at the cloudy gray sky.

She'd leave Kalli to her thoughts. She knew most of Lucy's as it was.

Frankie and Gerardo, on the other hand, fought and bickered. Gerardo flicked a snowy white, slightly mangled wing while Frankie ripped off the sleeve of his sweater into perfect strips. Despite the minor injuries, everyone was okay.

"Everyone's safe, honey," she whispered in Rafe's ear. "Let's send this baby back to Limbo." She laced her fingers with his and led him toward the damned chest. The sooner they sent it back, the sooner she could start her life—with Rafe.

Kneeling in the snow, she peered inside. The chest's energy washed over her, its tentacles of warmth crawling over her skin. If this was their idea of ecstasy, they never spent a night in bed with Rafael Deleon.

Rafe's grip tightened on her shoulder. "Be careful. Its energy is very intoxicating."

She soaked in the minty scent that wafted from him as he knelt beside her. Placing her hand on his chest, she smiled. "Not as much as you."

His heart thudded against her fingers and he drew

in a deep breath of air. Inky black hair blowing against snowy white flakes, he brushed a snowflake from her cheek. Despite the biting cold wind, tender warmth swirled between them. She needed to concentrate, or she'd end up a pile of mush in the snow. Reining in her hormones, she took in a deep breath.

"So what do we do?"

"It's all you, Lucy. I'm just here for moral support."

"And here I thought it was because you loved me."

Wow, way to drop the L word, Lucy.

A slow smile widened his lips. "That too."

Her eyes widened. "Really?"

"Yes, Lucy." He grabbed her by the shoulders and pulled her to him, the heat of his chiseled chest pulsing from him and filling her with sizzling energy. His silver eyes bored into her with a fervor she never knew. "I love you."

He didn't wait for her response. Instead, he lowered his mouth to hers and kissed her. His lips, firm and protective, crushed against hers. Coaxing her mouth open, his tongue swept inside, melting her against him. As quickly as the kiss started, he pulled away.

"Why'd you stop?"

Rafe brushed a fingertip over her kiss-swollen lips. "The *Arca Inferorum*, remember? We'll continue the kiss later."

Nodding, she threw a dagger-like glare at the chest. She wanted to send that chest back to Limbo now... more than ever. She had purpose. She'd save the world. She'd save her friends and family. She would save her shop. She'd continue that kiss with Rafe. That, itself, made it all worthwhile. "I look forward to it." She stood on strangely steady legs. With a wide smile, she offered Rafe a hand. Not that he needed her help, but she just needed his skin against hers. She knew she had to be the one who wrangled the demons back in the chest, but having him with her made all the difference. He was her man, and she'd definitely stand by him.

"Thank you darling." Rafe brushed snow from his jeans and placed a gentle kiss on her cheek. "Now let's get your minions collected."

"*My* minions?" Even though she went through enough weirdness in the past couple of days to last a lifetime, it still was surreal. She could control a whole legion of demons. That was a lot of power. She shivered as the pulsing and flashing energy from the *Arca Inferorum* tried to weave its spell. She didn't want that power.

"Don't let it seduce you."

"Only one person can do that. And it certainly isn't some dusty old box."

With that, Lucy spun around and glared down at the chest. The one thing that had turned her life upside down, sideways and inside out. The only good thing that came from it was Rafe. That's what made this whole ordeal worthwhile.

Lucy took a deep breath. Did she have to say anything special? It couldn't be as easy as just saying "Get back in." She closed her eyes. Soaking in the energy around her, she allowed it to spur her on.

She opened her mouth to speak, the Latin flowing from her tongue like butter. "All my loosed minions, I command you return to the *Arca Inferorum*."

Angry screeches intermingling with tormented moans rent the air. A bitter cold blast of air whipped around them. The chest glowed brighter, a beacon for the lost souls. Violent gusts of air spiraled, sending their hair flying in every direction. Even as the icy winds flicked at their faces, they stood proud and remained calm. The wind intensified, spinning and whirling from the center of the chest. She snapped her head up. The eerie gray vortex flung itself around, the echo of the winds hissing in her ears. Screeches and groans, squeals and moans cried out in a terrifying cacophony as the greenish gray clouds rotated and intensified, sucking in her demonic minions with each brutal twist. But she and Rafe stood tall. She could do anything, as long as he was by her side.

Reaching out through the tornadic wind, she took Rafe's hand in hers. His grip, strong and sure, sent waves of determination coursing through her. Hands still clasped, they stood together as the chest sucked the remaining Infernati back to whence they came.

"Please!" a haunting voice whined. Fingers, thin and long, clawed at her legs, latching on. "Don't send us back." The demoness's claws dug into her jean-clad legs, her icy grip weakening with each cyclonic gust.

It was a test. No matter how sweet and innocent the woman sounded, she'd been put in the *Arca Inferorum* for a reason. And it wasn't because she won the Nobel Peace Prize. Despite the evil that she eradicated, Lucy still felt a little guilty. She closed her eyes, her heart constricting in her chest. She pursed her lips together and bit back the tears. A trickle traced down her cheek and over her lip, the odor of iron wafting to her nose. Blood. These weren't her tears.

"I'm sorry. It's the only way." Lucy shook her leg

and the demoness's claws loosened. The blood tears faded and her sorrow lifted, only to be replaced with anger and rage. *Bloody Infernati*. With a swift kick, she sent the demoness flying backward, her screech fading into the violent spin of the wind. The cyclone fizzled and the glowing energy faded away.

She took a deep breath and slammed the lid of the chest down, the loud snap of the lock reverberating against the buildings. Reclaiming Rafe's hand, she let him draw her close and envelop her in his warmth. There was no other place she wanted to be. Maybe one other place… her bedroom.

With a quick review of the area, she saw her friends, all together, smiles and cheers bursting from their lips. Squeaky's chimp form jumped down with enthusiasm as he clapped and hollered. Kalli offered a sly smile yet remained strangely aloof. Frankie and Gerardo hugged and high-fived each other like they'd just watched their favorite football team win the Super Bowl. Weird. But right now, she didn't care. They just saved the world.

"You did it," Rafe's breath teased along her ear, sending delightful shivers racing through her body.

She snuggled closer. "No, *we* did it."

"Indeed." He wrapped his arm tighter around her. She never wanted him to let go. Relief washed over her as his heart thrummed in her ear. She smiled. Rafe couldn't call himself a failure anymore. He'd helped rid the world of a legion of demons. His mission was a success.

Lucy turned to him, longing to say those words that had tickled her tongue for so long. "I love you, Rafe. Ever since the day you walked into my shop. I've never felt so strongly for anyone. It's fiercely hot yet warm and tender." Great. She was on the verge of turning into a Shakespearean sonnet. "I know this sounds cliché, but it's magical."

Rafe chuckled, deep and throaty. "It's not magic, it's love, and it's how I felt when I first met you."

He pulled her close and brushed a strand of hair from her cheek. "I would do anything for you. I can't say it enough, I love you."

Lucy wrapped her arms around his neck and pressed her lips against his, warmth and love filling her every pore. "Magical indeed."

Rafe traced a finger across her lips. "I wouldn't have it any other way."

Lucy placed tender kisses along his fingertips. Neither would she.

Acknowledgments

I'd like to thank the many people who have read bits and pieces of this manuscript, either for feedback or critique. Especially Tanya, Peggy, Kim, Susan, and Juli. HUGE thanks to Bobbi Smith and Judi McCoy. If it weren't for Bobbi's awesome writing workshop and Judi's awesome Post-it notes plotting workshop at the 2008 Romantic Times Convention, this book wouldn't exist. Also thanks to Judi Fennell, CJ Redwine, and Kerri Nelson for assisting me with perfecting the dreaded query letter. You all rock!

About the Author

Sidney Ayers loves infusing her stories with humor. What would the world be without a little bit of laughter? She writes in a wide variety of genres, ranging from historical to paranormal to contemporary. A native of Michigan, Sidney still lives in the same town she grew up in. No matter how hard she tries, she just can't seem to get away. Michigan is in her blood. Scary thought, huh?

For more from Sidney Ayers

Read on for an excerpt from

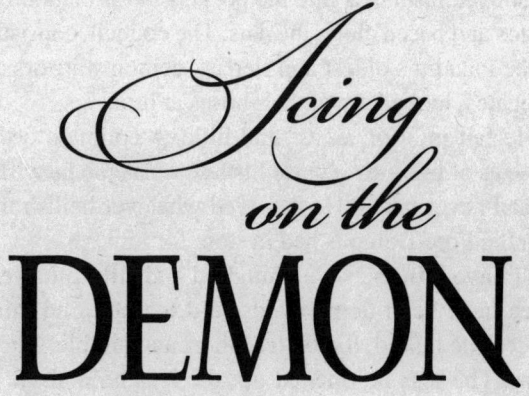

Icing on the **DEMON**

Available December 2011

From Sourcebooks Casablanca

Prologue

"So, you've finally decided to join us?"

The loud voice boomed in Matthias Ambrose's ears. He shoved his hands into the pockets of his camouflage cargos and paced along the dais. The council, consisting of the Paladin's oldest and fiercest demon warriors and delegates, looked down their noses at him.

He felt inferior, weak, and little. A common occurrence as of late—ever since his last job. A job he wished he had never taken. He deserved whatever hellish mission the Fore-Demons had in store for him.

"I have." In the seven hundred and fifty plus years since he'd been demonized, he'd learned one thing: the less he talked, the better. Short and simple. End of story. The less he opened up, the less he'd show his weakness. And that was the last thing he wanted at this moment.

"Very well, Ambrose, step forward." The high-demon stood and clapped his hands. "I need to summon your handler."

Matthias rolled his eyes. Leave it to the Fore-Demons to run their operation the way the CIA ran their spies. "Summon away, my lord."

"Do I sense sarcasm in your tone, Ambrose?" The demon clucked his tongue. "I can always reassign you to another mission. How does Siberia sound?"

Knowing the Fore-Demons and their non-existent

sense of humor, they weren't kidding. Might as well play along. "Cold."

"Ahh, still as witty as ever." The elder demon scraped a withered hand through his white beard. "Unfortunately, now is not the time for jokes. We have serious problems on Earth and we need all the help we can get—even yours." There was no mistaking the contempt in his voice.

He controlled the snort that threatened. As if he was the truly evil one. If they only knew the truth. Maybe then the almighty Fore-Demons Council and their ever-so-virtuous Paladin wouldn't be so quick to make assumptions.

What in Hades had he gotten himself into? He had never felt the need to prove his worth to anyone before. Now it was the only thing that drove him. He wanted to belong. He wanted to help. It unnerved him.

And it was all *her* fault. How could one simple job cause him to doubt his own existence?

He was a paid mercenary. He'd never chosen a side. Now he was ready to jump on the Paladin bandwagon. Why now?

The answer was simple. Serah SanGermano.

The moment his eyes met hers, his world spun out of control. And when he saw the mark on her hand, he knew exactly why the Infernati wanted Serah SanGermano. The two dots separated by a long slash showed him all he needed to know. She was a Pure Blood. Despite his fear at the discovery, other emotions roared inside him. The scar only accentuated her beauty. Because of her, he'd almost failed on his last mission. The only comfort was that when it was all over and done, he'd made certain Miss SanGermano wouldn't remember a thing.

The curse of his demonic existence was the ability to remove all memories and thoughts. He could swoop in, do his business, and no one, not even one of those blasted slayers, would remember a thing. Part of his heart constricted at the thought. Why would he want her to remember him? He'd nearly sent her to her death.

She was a spitfire for sure. He'd been lucky to make it out alive from the fight she and that chimp of an imp had put him through. That sort of fight would only get her in trouble—especially in Belial's clutches.

Belial. That name would forever leave a bad taste in his mouth. That bastard deserved the vanquishing Serah's friends had given him. If only he could've joined in the fight... but Belial had the last laugh. He took advantage of him. He found a weakness.

Never again. He'd not let his guard down. But then there was Serah. Her curly brown hair that framed her face. Bright eyes that sparkled like the most vibrant sapphires left him entranced. Steamy sexuality rolled from her every move, yet still an aura of purity surrounded her. Confusing and intoxicating. Dangerous.

He had to stay away from her, yet she needed protection. A pint-sized imp of a chimp would not do—not with the battle he could feel brewing. Then again, with Rafael Deleon and the bevy of demons in Connolly Park, Serah would be well protected.

Why couldn't he stop thinking about her? He hadn't thought about a woman in that way since that fateful day over eight hundred years ago. He drew his lips tight. Now was definitely not the time to draw up the past. He wanted to concentrate on his future. A future where he could fight evil... preferably on his own. Alone.

"Are you done brooding, Ambrose?" The dark, rich tone prickled in his ear.

Matthias's head snapped up. He ground his teeth and clenched his fists tighter. If *he* was here it could mean only one thing. "What the hell are you doing here?"

"Ambrose, you will respect your fellow Paladins if you wish to join us," the only female of the Fore-Demon council admonished. To iterate her point, she threw back her arm and launched a warning fireball whizzing just past his shoulder.

Rafael Deleon shrugged and leaned against the marble dais. "No worries, Councilwoman Astra. He has his reasons, I'm sure." He turned back to Matthias. "As for your question, Ambrose, I could ask you the same thing."

Taking in Rafael's countenance, Matthias blinked. Was this the same man? Where he had once been brutally formal and uptight, his aura now remained peaceful and serene. He could try to mask it behind all his pomp and arrogance, but Matthias knew better. The rumors were true. He'd fallen in love with the half-succubus he'd been sent to protect. Blasted odd—he'd always thought love a weakness in demons. Yet here stood Rafael Deleon, as proud and strong as ever.

Matthias raised his chin. "I don't need to answer to you, Deleon."

Rafael snorted. "I beg to differ."

"Are you a member of the Fore-Demon council now?"

"No."

"I only answer to them or who they choose for my handler."

Raking a hand through dark hair, Rafael turned to the council. "So you haven't told him yet."

"We were just about to, Deleon," Astra said with a flick of her barbed wings.

Rafael nodded. "I might as well do the honors." With a devilish smirk he turned back to Matthias. "Ambrose, you will answer to me because I—much to my chagrin, I assure you—am your handler."

Handler? Deleon? Why? This couldn't be. He needed a mission somewhere far away from Connolly Park and Serah SanGermano. With her best friend's demon lover as his handler, all his hopes of escape slipped away. "I cannot agree to this."

"Why ever not?" asked the elder demon. "Deleon is one of the finest Paladin and he needs your help."

"My reasons have nothing to do with Deleon and are personal in nature."

"If you let your personal grievances sway your decisions, then you will never make it as a Paladin. If you want to prove yourself to the cause, then you will accept Deleon as your handler."

Exactly what mission was he signing up for? What was so urgent that the great Paladin Rafael Deleon needed his help? After all, wasn't he the one that was prophesied? "Fine. I accept Rafael Deleon as my handler." As soon as he muttered the words, he was certain he'd regret it.

As if reading his mind—which he was certain they were—the Paladin council stood and nodded to him. A cryptic smile crept across Astra's lips. "Very wise decision, Ambrose. Now it is time to hear your mission. Deleon, do the honors."

Rafael nodded in return. "Thank you, my lieges." With stony silver eyes he glared at Matthias. "Your mission is this: You will guard my fiancée's best friend: Serah SanGermano."

The frozen tundra of Siberia sounded better, after all.

Demons are a Girl's Best Friend
by Linda Wisdom

A bewitching woman on a mission...

Feisty witch Maggie enjoys her work as a paranormal law enforcement officer—that is, until she's assigned to protect a teenager with major attitude and plenty of Mayan enemies. Maggie's never going to survive this assignment without the help of a half-fire demon who makes her smolder...

Praise for Linda Wisdom

"Hot talent Wisdom does a truly wonderful job mixing passion, danger and outrageous antics into a tasty blend that's sure to satisfy."
—RT Book Reviews

"Entertaining and sexy... Ms. Wisdom's stories have something for everyone." —Night Owl

"Wickedly captivating... wildly entertaining... full of magical zest and unrivaled witty prose."
—Suite 101

978-1-4022-5439-0 • $7.99 U.S./£4.99 UK

Hex in High Heels

BY LINDA WISDOM

Can a Witch and a Were find happiness?

Feisty witch Blair Fitzpatrick has had a crush on hunky carpenter Jake Harrison forever—he's one hot shapeshifter. But Jake's nasty mother and brother are after him to return to his pack, and Blair is trying hard not to unleash the ultimate revenge spell. When Jake's enemies try to force him away from her, Blair is pushed over the edge. No one messes with her boyfriend-to-be, even if he does shed on the furniture!

Praise for Linda Wisdom's Hex series:

"Fan-fave Wisdom… continues to delight."
—*Romantic Times*

"Highly entertaining, sexy, and imaginative."
—*Star Crossed Romance*

"It's a five star, feel-good ride!" —*Crave More Romance*

"Something fresh and new."
—*Paranormal Romance Review*

978-1-4022-1819-4 •$6.99 U.S. / $8.99 CAN

by Linda Wisdom

"**Do not miss this wickedly entertaining treat.**"

—Annette Blair,
Sex and the Psychic Witch

Stasi Romanov uses a little witch magic in her lingerie shop, running a brisk side business in love charms. A disgruntled customer threatening to sue over a failed spell brings wizard attorney Trevor Barnes to town—and witches and wizards make a volatile combination. The sparks fly, almost everyone's getting singed, and the whole town seems on the verge of a witch hunt.

Can the feisty witch and the gorgeous wizard overcome their objections and settle out of court—and in the bedroom?

978-1-4022-1773-9 • $6.99 U.S. / $7.99 CAN

Strange Neighbors

BY ASHLYN CHASE

HE'S LOOKING FOR PEACE, QUIET, AND A MAYBE LITTLE ROMANCE...

Hunky all-star pitcher and shapeshifter Jason Falco invests in an old Boston brownstone apartment building full of supernatural creatures, and there's never a dull moment. But when Merry McKenzie moves into the ground floor apartment, the playboy pitcher decides he might just be done playing the field...

What readers say about Ashlyn Chase

"Entertaining and humorous—a winner!"

"The humor and romance kept me entertained— a definite page turner!"

"Sexy, funny stories!"

978-1-4022-3661-7 • $6.99 U.S./$8.99 CAN/£3.99 UK

The Werewolf Upstairs

by Ashlyn Chase

She should know better...

Attorney Roz Wells is bored. She used to have such a knack for attracting the weird and unexpected, but ever since she took a job as a Boston Public defender the quirky quotient in her life has taken a serious hit. Until her sexy werewolf neighbor starts coming around...

Roz knows she should stay away from this sexy bad boy, but she can't help it that she's putty in his hands...

What readers say about Ashlyn Chase

"Entertaining and humorous—a winner!"

*"The humor and romance kept me entertained—
a definite page turner!"*

"Sexy, funny stories!"

IN OVER HER HEAD

by Judi Fennell

"Holy mackerel! *In Over Her Head* is a fantastically fun romantic catch!"

—Michelle Rowen, author of *Bitten & Smitten*

○ ○ ○ ○ ○ HE LIVES UNDER THE SEA ○ ○ ○ ○ ○

Reel Tritone is the rebellious royal second son of the ruler of a vast undersea kingdom. A Merman, born with legs instead of a tail, he's always been fascinated by humans, especially one young woman he once saw swimming near his family's reef...

○ ○ ○ ○ ○ SHE'S TERRIFIED OF THE OCEAN ○ ○ ○ ○ ○

Ever since the day she swam out too far and heard voices in the water, marina owner Erica Peck won't go swimming for anything—until she's forced into the water by a shady ex-boyfriend searching for stolen diamonds, and is nearly eaten by a shark. Luckily Reel is nearby to save her, and discovers she's the woman he's been searching for...

978-1-4022-2001-2 • $6.99 U.S. / $7.99 CAN

WILD BLUE UNDER

by Judi Fennell

"Bubbly fun in a sparkling 'under the sea' tale."
—Virginia Kantra, *USA Today* bestselling author

THE UNDERWATER KINGDOM IS HIS...
AS SOON AS HE CLAIMS HIS QUEEN

Rod Tritone is gorgeous and irresistible—he could snag any queen he wants for his Mer kingdom, but unfortunately, it's not up to him. As fate would have it, the one woman destined to rule with him lives in land-locked Kansas and has no idea she's a princess. Somehow Rod has to prove to Valerie Dumere who she really is. But when she learns the truth, will she ever forgive him?

PRAISE FOR *IN OVER HER HEAD*:

"A delightful, quirky blend of humor, adventure, and passion." —*Star-Crossed Romance*

"A wondrous undersea adventure—molten moments, waves of sensuality, ripples of emotion, and depths of fun. Not to be missed!"—L.A. Banks, *The Vampire Huntress Legends Series*

"A witty, funny, fabulous story." —*Passion for the Page*

978-1-4022-2427-0• $6.99 U.S. / $8.99 CAN

CATCH OF A LIFETIME

by Judi Fennell

"Judi Fennell has one heck of an imagination!"
—Michelle Rowen, author of *Bitten & Smitten*

WHEN HE DISCOVERS WHAT SHE REALLY IS,
○ ○ ○ ○ **THEY'RE BOTH IN MORTAL DANGER...** ○ ○ ○ ○

Mermaid Angel Tritone has been researching humans from afar, and when she jumps into a boat to escape a shark attack, it's her chance to pursue her mission to save the planet from disaster—but she must keep her identity a secret. For Logan Hardington, finding a beautiful woman on his boat is surely not a problem—until he realizes his life is on the line...

○ ○ ○ ○ **PRAISE FOR *IN OVER HER HEAD*:** ○ ○ ○ ○

"A charming modern day fairy tale with a twist. Fennel is a bright star on the horizon of romance." —Judi McCoy, author of *Hounding the Pavement*

"Fennell's under-the-sea suspense will enchant you with its wit, humor, and sexiness." —Caridad Pineiro, *NYT* and *USA Today* Bestseller, *South Beach Chicas Catch Their Man*

978-1-4022-2428-7 • $6.99 U.S. / $8.99 CAN

Praise for Judi Fennell:

"I don't know what is more amazing: that Judi Fennell started with such a stunning debut or that she's followed up with so many excellent books. She is definitely an author to watch."

—Diana Holquist, author of *How to Tame a Modern Rogue*

I Dream of Genies
Judi Fennell

He needs to change his luck, and fast!

Matt Ewing would gladly hunt down a fortune in lucky pennies if he thought it would help save his business. But for all his hoping, Matt's clueless when his long-awaited lucky charm falls in his lap in the form of a beguiling genie. He just can't believe that this beautiful woman could be the answer to his prayers...

She's been bottled up for far too long!

Spending 2,000 years in a bottle would make any woman a little stir-crazy. So when Matt releases Eden from her luxurious captivity, she's thrilled to repay him by giving him the magical boost he needs...

But for all her good intentions, Eden's magical prowess is a little rusty and her magical mistakes become more than embarrassing. And though Eden knows falling in love will end her magic and immortality, she can't help but be drawn to the one man who wants her just for herself...

"Filled with laughs, action, and an absolutely magical romance, this book is one for the keeper shelf."
—Kate Douglas, bestselling author of *Wolf Tales* and the Demonslayers series

978-1-4022-4189-5 • $7.99 U.S./$9.99 CAN/£4.99 UK

OUTCAST

BY CHERYL BROOKS

Sold into slavery in a harem, Lynx is a favorite because his feline gene gives him remarkable sexual powers. But after ten years, Lynx is exhausted and is thrown out of the harem without a penny. Then he meets Bonnie, who's determined not to let such a beautiful and sensual young man go to waste...

"Leaves the reader eager for the next story featuring these captivating aliens." —*Romantic Times*

"One of the sweetest love stories...one of the hottest heroes ever conceived and...one of the most exciting and adventurous quests that I have ever had the pleasure of reading." —*Single Titles*

"One of the most sensually imaginative books that I've ever read... A magical story of hope, love and devotion" —*Yankee Romance Reviews*

978-1-4022-1896-5 •$6.99 U.S. / $7.99 CAN

ROGUE

BY CHERYL BROOKS

Tychar crawled toward me on his hands and knees like a tiger stalking his prey. "I, for one, am glad you came," he purred. "And I promise you, Kyra, you will never want to leave Darconia."

"Cheryl Brooks knows how to keep the heat on and the reader turning pages!"
—Sydney Croft, author of *Seduced by the Storm*

PRAISE FOR THE CAT STAR CHRONICLES:

"Wow. Just…wow. The romantic chemistry is as close to perfect as you'll find." —*BookFetish.org*

"Will make you purr with delight. Cheryl Brooks has a great talent as a storyteller." —*Cheryl's Book Nook*

978-1-4022-1762-3 • $7.99 U.S. / $9.99 CAN